The Road To Alright

To Susan
Best wishes
Jimmie Van
[signature]
Dec 2019
X

The
Road
To
Alright

Yvonne Van Lankveld

iUniverse®

THE ROAD TO ALRIGHT

iUniverse books may be ordered through booksellers or by contacting:

iUniverse
1663 Liberty Drive
Bloomington, IN 47403
www.iuniverse.com
1-800-Authors (1-800-288-4677)

*Because of the dynamic nature of the Internet, any web addresses or links contained in
this book may have changed since publication and may no longer be valid. The views
expressed in this work are solely those of the author and do not necessarily reflect the
views of the publisher, and the publisher hereby disclaims any responsibility for them.*

*Any people depicted in stock imagery provided by Getty Images are models,
and such images are being used for illustrative purposes only.
Certain stock imagery © Getty Images.*

ISBN: 978-1-5320-6527-9 (sc)
ISBN: 978-1-5320-6528-6 (e)

Library of Congress Control Number: 2018914910

Print information available on the last page.

iUniverse rev. date: 06/18/2019

Traveling through the journey of life,
you always strive for everything to be perfect.
And on that long road, you come to realize that
maybe it won't be, and you eventually have to
settle for 'alright'.

This book is dedicated to John who
by default let loose my creative spirit, and to my greatest
accomplishments, Lee and Craig, and Melanie for being the wonderful
people that they are. It is a gift it to be able to love, laugh and write.

All of the characters, and names in this novel are
a work of fiction. Any perceived link to any real person,
including the author, is purely coincidental.

March 15th

It was the second worst day of my life. A Thursday in March. Probably a common day for employers to fire, or lay off their employees. I was in my twentieth year of employment at the Toronto site of Bernard Steel Works. I had hoped to retire at fifty five, then work part-time at a job where I could think less and move more. Something that kept me busy on days when I didn't feel much like doing anything. Maybe I'd work at a flower shop, where I'd have the pleasure of interacting with a good many content customers, as giving flowers was often seen as a gesture of kindness. Of course, flowers are sometimes sent by people trying to abscond from feelings of guilt about something they should, or should not have done. In any case, I'd find a less stressful job then the chaotic position I held as a benefits administrator in the company's Human Resources department. That didn't happen.

The first worst day of my life was the day my husband Blair was diagnosed with lung cancer. It was even worse than the day he died, because his diagnosis changed our lives forever. He smoked for thirty years, and said he enjoyed every cigarette. My persistent nagging accomplished only one thing. He stopped smoking for two consecutive years, just long enough to be approved for a life insurance policy through my company.

That was to be my nest egg, or secretly my vindication when his life ended early, just as I'd predicted.

We had been married twenty eight years, and met when I was sixteen. As a carpenter, Blair took great pride in his work. With what energy remained after long work days, he puttered around at home. A project was always in the works, using discarded material he pilfered from a construction site. I rarely complained because it upgraded our house value. Our combined income barely covered the bills and supported our daughter Tess, who was in university.

Blair was diagnosed with metastatic lung cancer just after Christmas. From January 4th until he died on March 1st was exactly eight weeks. I worked until two weeks before his death. He refused chemotherapy, stating the cancer was his burden, and not ours. Furious as I was with him, I had no choice other than to accept this as his destiny.

My only sibling, Sophie, accompanied me to the funeral home after his death. I numbly nodded as we processed the arrangements. Our small family supported each other during the visitation and service at the funeral home chapel. Those who attended represented distinctly different groups. Sophie's daughter and only child Mallory clung to my tall and willowy Tess. Her friends approached in timid clusters, meekly shuffled past me offering inaudible condolences until the real sobs erupted when they saw her. I found solace in my close friends, calmed by the small white pill Sophie fed me earlier. Blair's friends and co-workers, who were as uncomfortable as I was, came last. We barely knew each other, and their awkwardness fueled the stale discomfort in the room.

On the morning of Blair's funeral, I spent a long time looking in the bathroom mirror. Here I was, not quite fifty years old. On most days, my ordinary body felt youthful and healthy, but today I looked and felt like a haggard old widow. I pulled my dark hair back into a messy bun, and mascaraed my brown eyes, knowing it would be gone before anyone noticed. Assembling myself into my one good suit and adorned with my mother's pearls, I was as ready as I was ever going to be. Sophie and Mallory drove Tess and I, bundled up in winter boots and coats.

We buried Blair on a frigid winter morning. The snow captured our misery by blowing circles around our small gathering. The wind rearranged the red roses on his casket as it was lowered into the ground. Tess and I shivered, holding each other for warmth and comfort. Our lives, forever changed, faced a new uncertainty.

On yet another stormy Thursday morning in March, two weeks after Blair died, I returned to work at Bernard Steel Works. Looking forward to familiar surroundings, I noticed the flag in the front of the building was positioned at half mast. Typically lowered to honour the passing of a past or present employee, I wondered who had died. Before returning I had only spoken with Paul, my boss and HR manager, who encouraged me to take the time I needed. My colleagues who attended Blair's visitation avoided any conversation about work.

Entering the main hallway of the plant, I inhaled the familiar, musty smell of the factory. I glanced at the bulletin board in the hallway, where a nondescript two-paragraph posting, separate from the other notices, caught my eye. I read it three times before it sunk in.

MEDIA RELEASE

Due to the progressive softening of the North American automotive market and its inability to remain viable in a highly competitive global industry, the Toronto location of Bernard Steel Works, Stamping Division, has ceased operations effective immediately. Existing contracts with current customers have been transferred to Mexico, where some operations of Bernard Steel Works, a quality automotive product supplier, will continue.

Bernard Steel Works was established at its Toronto location in 1949 and at its peak employed 5,000 employees. It has been well known as a reputable employer and philanthropic supporter of the community. The closure of this facility has resulted in the immediate loss of 500 jobs. Employee and retiree inquiries will be addressed by the Human Resources department until April 30th, and via the company website thereafter.

Blood drained from my pounding head and pooled in my feet. I had ignored messages on my home phone and let unread newspapers accumulate. If Tess knew anything, she said nothing in the two weeks she was home with me.

I didn't know whether to run out the door or go to my desk, when Paul pushed the door from the HR department open. Startled, he me approached cautiously, with a look of despair. His usually crisp, oxford cloth shirt was crumpled and looser since my four week absence. He hugged me tensely, and I saw the sadness in his eyes. He needed more sympathy than me.

"Gracie, you shouldn't have found out this way. I called you three times, but your messages were full and you weren't picking up."

"I know. I shut down from everything."

My purse and lunch tote felt heavy as I shuffled through the HR door, and faced the space I had occupied for years. My desk was a merger of two work stations and counters, which I inherited when the department downsized. Amidst papers and unopened mail stood a bouquet of fresh daffodils. Facing my desk, I felt a new pang of anxiety, realizing this was not the familiar environment I left. When Paul's hand gently touched my shoulder from behind, I jumped.

"We're all on edge here. Come into my office and I'll update you." I shrank into my coat and followed him nervously. I sunk into the chair across from his desk, clutching my purse and lunch. "We haven't had time to breathe since the announcement." He coughed nervously. "Grace, we really missed you. You've never been away this long. I didn't bloody realize how much we needed you. How are you and Tess holding up?"

"Okay. She kept me grounded. She has wonderful friends, and at least one of them came every day. She went back to university yesterday."

Paul handed me a copy of the plant closure media release. His voice was strained as he updated me.

"We found out only three weeks ago. We're still in shock, and I can't imagine how you feel, especially after losing Blair." My mind went numb, absorbing only bits of his conversation, which sounded like it was buried in a tunnel. "We met with every active employee to formally advise them of the closure....all inactive employees and retirees were mailed a notice which you'll also receive....officially stopped production and shipped finished parts to a warehouse....corporate shut the plants down when the closure was announced to avoid sabotage....machines dismantled, shipped and re-assembled in Mexico....all hourly employees have their severance package details....thirty salaried employees are left, and most will be gone by the middle of April." I shivered, zoned back in and tried to focus. "The HR department will remain open until all the separation slips, references and benefit statements are mailed. The four remaining HR staff, including you and I, will stay until the door officially closes April 30th." *April 30th. Wow.* My head spun again as he kept talking.

"We have some flexibility, so you can work full time until then, or adjust your hours as the workload declines. Your six-month severance package, including health benefits and four weeks remaining vacation time, will start May 1st. I hope you stay, but I won't stop you if you leave before April 30th. You've been invaluable to us, and your reference letter will reflect that. I've said this dozens of times in the last week, but it's much harder to face you with the bad news than the others. You are my best employee, and I will miss you." He slouched in his chair and ran his fingers through his thinning dark hair. Within my own grief, I felt compassion for this very tired man who was not liked by virtue of his job and recent responsibilities. I didn't particularly like him, and was glad our personal lives remained private.

Feeling somewhat reassured that I had an income for seven months, I returned to my desk. It was so very quiet. The hum of the plant operations, which previously provided ambient noise, was now silent. There were no radios playing in distant offices, or bursts of laughter in the hallway.

I scrolled through endless e-mails without opening them. I looked at the unopened heaps of mail on my desk, then to the counter above it to see my name written on a small envelope tucked in the vase of daffodils. The card, dated yesterday, was written by a new retiree.

Gracie, thanks for all your help and for setting up my pension cheques. Retirement is great!

I pitched the card in the garbage and stared again at my desk. The day crawled at a snail's pace, unproductive and endless.

March 22nd

It took forever to catch up at work. I took sympathy cards home to read so that I could appreciate them, and not cry at my desk. I was humbled that so many people cared.

Being alone at home felt different than I had imagined. I wasn't lonely, but curious that the plant closure upset me more than Blair's death. Wandering around the house, I wanted to finish Blair's abandoned projects. It seemed when he was motivated, we had no money. Sometimes paint cans sat parked in a corner for months, warranting trips back to the paint shop to re-shake them. I realized I could paint without Blair criticizing me. Maybe if I budgeted wisely and found a new job quickly, I could tackle the manageable projects and contract someone to do the rest.

Blair made more excuses to leave the house, and the lawn care and garbage duties shifted to me long before he became ill. He began drowning himself with beer. He became tired and depressed, and no amount of nagging, as he described it, would persuade him to see his doctor.

I wondered if his prognosis would be different if he had sought help sooner. He coughed for years, especially at night. When I complained, he moved to the spare room, which was the same time we stopped having sex. He balked at my suggestion of counseling. He resented me when Tess came home from school, and pretended our life was wonderful. I don't think that we stayed together solely for Tess's sake, but rather that neither of us had the energy to leave. We were stuck in an uncomfortable, emotionless existence. I think a higher being chose his fate for him, because he was not happy on earth. If heaven and hell exist, and God is the arbitrator, I was grateful he took Blair, and left me to carry on.

March 23rd

I marked off the remaining work day on the Bernard Steel Works calendar, the months illustrated with pictures of industrial machinery. It was issued to all employees as a disincentive to hang pornographic calendars. My desk phone rang. I answered it, and spoke with an employee who wanted pension information. When I directed him to the website, he said he didn't know how to use a computer. I suggested that he take advantage of the company-funded courses and learn. He swore at me and hung up, typical lately of many resentful employees.

I selected an envelope from my mail basket, addressed specifically to me and marked *PERSONAL AND CONFIDENTIAL*. The letter, date-stamped the day before I returned to work, was from the life insurance company acknowledging their receipt of Blair's notice of death. Susan, one of the remaining HR staff, submitted the application and Blair's obituary to spare me the grief of doing it myself. The form letter was authored by a customer service representative, advising me that should my claim be approved, a cheque would be mailed under separate cover. I had seen similar letters, and wondered what I'd do first with the money.

A second letter arrived by courier the following week. Unexpectedly, it was written by a manager, rather than the person who usually sent it. A nice touch, which I assumed was out of respect. I was dead wrong.

March 12

Re: The Estate of Blair Sheehan, Loss of Life Claim
Plan Sponsor: Bernard Steel Works

Dear Mrs. Sheehan:

On behalf of the staff of The Protective Financial and Insurance Company of Canada, please accept our condolences for the loss of your loved one. We acknowledge receipt of the Notice of Death Application and obituary for Mr. Blair Sheehan submitted on your behalf by your Human Resources department.

In accordance with the terms and conditions of the Bernard Steel Works plan, the Loss of Life benefit is payable contingent upon acknowledgement and confirmation of our information on file. Our current records indicate Mr. Sheehan completed a Non-Smoking Declaration. Your signature as his spouse on this document also declared this information was accurate and true, however the application submitted by your Human Resources department indicated Mr. Sheehan _was_ a smoker.

We are requesting you confirm this status by forwarding copies of this correspondence to any and all health care providers that treated Mr. Sheehan in the last two years. This includes the providers of Mr. Sheehan's dental care. We are requesting copies of the following information:

- Any and all clinical notes, consultation reports, diagnostic test results for a period of two years preceding the day of Mr. Sheehan's death
- The autopsy report, if same was warranted and/or performed

Please be advised that should the requested information determine that Mr. Sheehan was a smoker, I regret to inform you that inaccurate information may invalidate this claim.

It is important that Mr. Sheehan's health care providers, and not yourself, forward the requested information directly to the undersigned to ensure that all documents are received in their entirety. Any inquiries regarding this letter should be addressed to the undersigned.

Yvonne Van Lankveld

Sincerely,

Holly Hill
Manager, Loss of Life Claims

I had never seen a letter like this before. Susan must have made an error by acknowledging Blair was a smoker. I was, however, impressed that the insurance company audited applications to ensure that accurate information was submitted. I made a list of the people Blair had seen, relieved that his health care providers would submit the requested information directly to the insurance company. The last time I accompanied Blair to his doctor was the day Blair decided to refuse chemotherapy. He wanted to die with all of his hair, as well as his dignity. There was no compromise. I had no say in the matter. To Blair, death was imminent. It was a done deal. And when narcotics didn't settle his rapidly failing body, the alcohol did.

Blair's dentist didn't know about his death because I was invoiced by mail for his missed appointment. I forwarded the insurance letters to the dentist and Blair's doctors. I wasn't interested in reading the medical documents, and worrying wasn't helpful, so I waited patiently for the cheque.

March 29ᵗʰ

The final insurance letter arrived two weeks later. I reviewed it many times in disbelief. Shock wrapped its fingers around my throat and squeezed my chest. It was not a mistake because insurance policy decisions were based on objective facts and policies, neither of which I could influence.

March 27ᵗʰ

Re: The Estate of Blair Sheehan, Loss of Life Claim

Dear Mrs. Sheehan:

This letter acknowledges receipt of all the requested documents from Mr. Sheehan's health care providers. In accordance with the terms and conditions of the Bernard Steel Works, a Loss of Life benefit is payable contingent upon acknowledgement and confirmation of our information on file. Our most recent records indicate Mr. Sheehan's status was that of a non-smoker, as per his Non-Smoking Declaration, however the application submitted by your Human Resources department and Mr. Sheehan's health care providers confirm Mr. Sheehan was a smoker.

To clarify Mr. Sheehan's status, three documents were received by The Protective Financial and Insurance Company of Canada from Mr. Sheehan's health care providers. History and clinical notes received from Mr. Sheehan's dental hygienist, and validated by his dentist, indicate Mr. Sheehan reported smoking two cigarettes per day. At his initial oncology assessment, Mr. Sheehan also divulged that he smoked three to four cigarettes per day. Pathology reports, which are regarded as objective clinical evidence, confirm that Mr. Sheehan was a recent smoker. In addition to being assessed by our adjudication services, this information was also carefully reviewed by our regional medical adviser.

Unfortunately, these findings do not support the terms and conditions of this claim, and we regret to inform you that your application for loss of life benefits has been denied. You have the right to appeal this decision, providing you submit new and previously unreviewed documentation within three months. Should no new information be received, this decision will be deemed final. On behalf of The Protective Financial and Insurance Company of Canada, please again accept our condolences for your loss, and we regret this decision could not be more favourable.

Sincerely,

Holly Hill
Manager, Loss of Life Claims

I yelled out loud. "You bastard!"

I had lost Blair, his income, my job and now my $100,000 safety net. The final blow. How could he do this? Anger maintained its grip, stifling another scream rising from deep inside. I wanted to keep screaming, just like he used to when our arguments heated up to a level beyond reason.

I was gutted. Done. I felt hopeless and lost. There was not a soul at work to console me, hear my desperation, or whisper to others that I was going crazy.

How could he do this to Tess, let alone me? Blair lied to me and to Tess, who criticized his smoking more than I did. He blamed the tobacco smell from his clothes on his co-workers. His breath smelled like mint and caffeine. Maybe that's why he avoided me. Was I that naïve?

My anger shifted to humiliation. Did my insurance contacts, which I had a great working relationship with, think I fraudulently submitted this claim? How could I communicate with them in the remaining weeks I had left?

I was jumping to conclusions. My head felt too heavy for my neck to support. I cradled it helplessly in my hands, feeling utterly alone. I couldn't think. I didn't know what to do next.

The shrill ring of a phone pierced the quiet office, then fell silent. I took the letter, hovered it over the shredder, and fed it in. The paper crinkled and immediately became stuck. The old machine rumbled from years of digesting too many staples. I instantly regretted what I did and yanked it out, tearing a bottom corner but miraculously preserving the script and letterhead.

My desktop screen saver flashed a picture of Tess standing on a cliff during a camping trip last summer with her friends. Their smiling faces beamed over a large length of white paper towel they held. Written on it, in red was: **'Love U Moms + Dads'.** How would I tell her what her father had done? How could I tell her that I didn't know how to salvage the remnants of our lives?

My heart was racing and I needed to leave. I taped a hand written note to the counter that said: 'BACK ON MONDAY'. It was 11:45 a.m. On Thursday. Yes, another Thursday with more bad news. Paul was out of the office. There was no one to notify, but what did it matter? I couldn't be fired from a job I'd already lost.

I walked out of the building into the quiet of the softly falling snow. I looked for my car in the parking lot. By now, they were all snow white. I stood alone, unable to think until Eddie, the cheerful senior security guard, came out of his kiosk. I remembered him greeting me on my first day of work twenty years ago. His sympathetic eyes met mine. He protectively wrapped his arm through mine, like I remember my father doing when he was alive, and led me to my car. His voice was soft and kind.

"Bad day, Gracie? They're all bad days here. Heading out for an early lunch?"

"No. I'm not feeling well and I'm going home."

"Sure thing, dear. Feel better soon." He closed my car door and shuffled through the snow back to his little shelter.

The snow was calming and peaceful, a stark contrast to the storm in my head. I started the car and turned the window defroster on. The windshield was covered with an inch of fluffy snowflakes, however from the inside, I saw something shiny and red tucked under my windshield wiper. I opened my car door and lifted the wiper, unsticking the small object from the windshield. I blew the snow off of a miniature Toblerone chocolate bar. There was no clue as to who had left it. I drove to the security gate, shuddering as I rolled down my window.

"Eddie, was anyone one near my car? The sparkle in his tired blue eyes hinted he knew something.

"Sorry, Gracie. We're security guards. Which means we guard secrets. You need something sweet to brighten your day."

"Thank you."

"Oh, it wasn't me. But he's harmless."

"That's not very helpful." He chuckled.

"Can you get yourself home safely?"

"I'll be fine."

"Then you best go straight home before it snows more, and make yourself a nice cup of tea. Maybe with a little shot of Bailey's."

It was the best advice I received all day, and I did exactly that.

April 1st

It didn't take long to realize that my financial status was beyond dismal. Blair's income evaporated when he was diagnosed. Our paltry savings paid for the funeral. With no life insurance as my cushion, I was petrified about my future and supporting Tess through school. My father had previously insisted that we have a financial planner, and when I called him, he apologized repeatedly for not knowing Blair had passed away. It was humiliating to tell him Blair's life insurance claim was denied. Until we settled all of Blair's legal affairs, he discouraged me from withdrawing what minimal investments we had.

Restless and home on my day off, I paced inside the garage, which had been Blair's domain. I wanted to throw out everything in it. Much of it was useless, outdated, redundant or ugly. Other than Blair's tools, it was full of what I classified as junk but Blair claimed was valuable. Unused or broken stuff was mixed with bitterness, dust and hidden beer bottles. Junk he brought home from wherever. Gadgets and tools he'd never opened or used. A new set of speakers sat tucked behind paint cans, which I vaguely remember Blair mentioning the was storing for a friend. That was ten years ago.

The blank sides of the faded real estate signs from our house sale became useful when I was struck an impulsive thought. I wrote 'GARAGE SALE SATURDAY' with a thick, black marker, slid the refurbished signs into their original steel frame, and hammered it into the front lawn. Fueled with coffee and ambition, I posted ads on-line and at the grocery store. I called Blair's old friend Simon for advice on selling Blair's tools and supplies, who suggested we combine a garage and tool sale. Having no idea of their purpose or worth, I accepted his offer to help at the sale. I stuck price labels on everything except the tools. I fell into bed that night, exhausted yet excited for the first time since Blair died.

Saturday morning was cool and sunny. Simon came early to price Blair's tools. I'd met him only once at Blair's funeral. Rugged and handsome, he was easy going and very helpful. He didn't smoke, so I couldn't fault him for that.

We dragged what we could onto the driveway and set up makeshift displays. Our customers arrived early, clogging up the street and disrupting our quiet neighbourhood. Curious pickers mingled with serious bargain hunters. The speakers sold first, and if Blair was storing stolen merchandise, I was relieved it was gone. I bravely negotiated many deals, with Simon's wisdom and good advice.

The sale was over by late afternoon. I was physically drained but refreshed in spirit, and I regained a garage! Simon lingered, casually sifting through the remains.

"Gracie, there's still some good stuff here. You shouldn't throw it out."

"I just want it gone."

"I'll come back and help you sort it out tomorrow." He shook my hand awkwardly, followed by a reassuring rub on my shoulder. Both of us knew I couldn't have managed without him.

Simon returned with a friend on Sunday to clean up. I escaped to buy groceries, pizza and beer. When I returned, both men were dust-laden, leaning on brooms at the garage entrance. As if on cue in a parade, they separated and marched to either side of the open door. Mimicking flagmen, I giggled as they helped me navigate my car on its maiden trip into the garage. The dust was still swirling as I got out. It was bittersweet. Except for a few garden tools, the lawn mower and garbage cans, the garage was spotless.

Simon beamed as we ate pizza and drank craft beer, perched three in a row on his tailgate. It was all they would accept for their effort. Simon reached back and handed me a large, heavy paper coffee cup sealed with duct tape. The container was cold and his hands were warm against mine. His voice softened as he cleared his throat.

"Gracie, Blair was proud of you. He always complained that the Bernard Steel guys made better money than we did. But we wouldn't trade our jobs for all the wood in Canada." Simon shuffled one work boot against the other. He moved closer to me.

"The guys took up a collection. It's not a lot, but it will help." Deeply touched, I hugged them both. The scent from Simon's sweaty clothes comforted me as he held me. I struggled to remain composed as I eased out of his embrace. They left quietly in Simon's truck, his warmth still with me as they drove away.

I unpacked the groceries as I eyed the heavy coffee cup. I peeled the duct tape off the lid, which was full of coins and bills, a few wood shavings, and a tiny bent nail. Things I emptied for years from Blair's pockets before washing his jeans. The cup held nine hundred dollars. Combined with the garage sale proceeds, I held fifteen hundred dollars in my hands. For just a moment, I felt a little less poor.

Midweek after the garage sale, I came home from another depressing workday. From my mail box, I retrieved a soiled, sealed envelope with my first name etched on it. I tore it open. A paper clip attached five crisp hundred dollar bills to a note penciled on the back of a blank lumber yard estimate sheet. It read:

"Hi Gracie.
We had a "yard sale" at the construction site
and sold the rest of your stuff.

Blair's Buddies

In awe of their generosity, I tried to remember these men from Blair's funeral, but couldn't. Only Simon's presence remained clear and distinct. He'd worn a tailored suit and tie, contrasting my vague image of the others, dressed in clothes that fit them better years ago. When I scooped the rest of the mail out of the box, I found another miniature Toblerone chocolate bar, like the first one left on my windshield at work. There was no note, other than the envelope from Blair's buddies. Although Eddie, the security guard from work would keep his secret, he would also report the sender if he felt I was at risk. I popped the chocolate in my mouth, a small comfort to follow the generous donation in my hand.

The garage sale earnings would cushion me for a few months, however with the uncertainty of my future, I had to sell the house, and the sooner, the better. Having a mortgage with no job, and the competition of five hundred terminated Bernard Steel Works employees in the same predicament, hastened my decision. I needed money for Tess to finish university. I called her, and after a tearful conversation, she understood. She had landed a full time summer job at school, which helped. Her life at home was in flux, and she wanted little to do with it.

April 6th

My hope was to sell the house by summer's end. The real estate agent was impressed with the upgrades, but cautioned me about similar houses on the market. He scheduled six showings the day after the house was listed. It sold in a bidding war for more than the asking price within two days, with only one condition. I had to move in two weeks. Fourteen days! I had barely adjusted to listing the house, and now I had to leave, with nowhere to go. I was totally overwhelmed. Again.

Logical and predictable activities, like getting coffee from the same place and having a glass of wine after work, became my coping mechanisms. Simon unexpectedly stopped by the house as I packed furiously, but not efficiently. He congratulated me with a hug. When I told him the closing date, he whistled loudly.

"Holy shit. We've got a lot of work to do!" *We?*

"Good thing the garage is clean. I'll round up some guys to help." *He's serious. Again.*

I knew I couldn't manage alone, and accepted his offer to help, but on moving day. I had no idea where my furniture would go, let alone myself.

Simon was divorced. Where our marriage shifted between turmoil and complacency, Simon had abandoned two wives, three live-in companions

19

that I knew of, and an assortment of 'friends with benefits'. I understood why women were drawn to him. He had a standard wardrobe of denim or flannel plaid shirts, jeans, grey wool socks with red trim and construction boots. He was prematurely grey, with green eyes and clear skin. Starting a relationship was the farthest thing from my mind, but there was something about Simon that made him easy to be near.

I alternated packing with searching for somewhere to live, and arranged to view some rentals on Monday after work.

April 9th

At work on Monday, I updated Paul. He listened intently, then offered a suggestion. Both he and his neighbour, named Olivia Bless, owned golden retrievers. Olivia, who he called Livy, traveled often as a buyer of imported furniture. Livy had a dog sitter, but when she was unavailable, Paul or his wife dog-sat. Like me, Paul also had an unpredictable future. Paul suggested Livy get a dog-loving house mate, and I was the perfect solution. When I said I wasn't interested, he eyed me over his reading glasses and told me not to kick a gift horse in the mouth. He insisted I meet Livy after work. Today.

Reluctant about living near him, or with a stranger and a big dog, I succumbed to pressure and agreed, but kept the other rental viewing appointments. I was certain, given the affluent and historic neighbourhood, that the rent was unaffordable. I followed him home after work in my car to a street named Chestnut Boulevard. Paul turned onto a side street and into his driveway. His home was a traditional two-story with colourful gardens. I parked in front, and approached him to say that I was wasting everybody's time.

"Beautiful place, but I can't afford this."

"Relax, Grace. I can't predict what Livy will say, but she knows we're both in the same boat with the plant closure."

"And that's a big boat."

"Right. She agreed to meet you because I've been pitching this idea to her for a while. She's new to this, too."

"But I don't want to see what I can't have. I'm regretting that I came."

"Look, you're here, so you might as well see it. You've got nothing to lose."

"I've lost almost everything else..." He ignored me.

"We just passed her house. She's not home yet, so I'll get her key." He disappeared into his back yard.

I slowly took in my view. Each house was unique and charming. Large, velvety lawns were surrounded by spectacular gardens. I reminisced about old dreams of white picket fences in suburbs like this. At this stage of my life, it would never happen. Paul came around the corner and we walked back the in same direction we drove from.

"Livy's house is back on Chestnut Boulevard," Paul said.

I sighed softly when Paul pointed to a majestic two story stucco home, which shared a corner with his back yard. It was beautiful and stately. The butterflies rising in my belly became still.

"I'm not going in."

"Don't be silly. Livy said come in and get comfortable. I already told her you're boring, but reliable and very trustworthy." I laughed, feeling defeated. He was right. I was as exciting as an eggshell.

We paused to admire the lush gardens, ornamented with shrubs and dense clusters of spring flowers. Two large leaded windows were centered in gables, embedded in a pitched slate roof. A wide flagstone sidewalk was drenched in sun and worn with age. Moss-covered stone steps were framed with oversized urns, brimming with pansies and tulips. A large stucco pillar supported the roof, which extended over the front entrance to protect the verandah. Rattan chairs and tables welcomed visitors. The massive oak front door anchored an ornate leaded window. Paul inserted an old key into the door latch which opened to a large vestibule floor, covered with small, honeycomb black and white tiles. A black border of tiles on the floor framed the word 'CHESTNUT'.

"Mmmmm.. Was Chestnut the original owner? You said Livy's last name was Bless."

"It is. Chestnut was the surname of the people, somehow related to Livy, who this home was built for. Livy's been here as long as we have, which is two years. Our dogs met before we did."

"How old is her dog?"

"I'm not sure. Wilson came with the house. When old Mr. Chestnut died, Livy bought him to keep Mrs. Chestnut company. Then she got sick and couldn't care for herself or Wilson. When she moved to a nursing home, Livy came to look after the dog and eventually moved in. It was fine when she was home every night, but now she's away more than she's home. She didn't have the heart to give the dog away when Mrs. Chestnut died. You could say they rescued each other."

"Any other family?"

"I don't think so. Livy's an only child, and adopted. Her parents are either dead or estranged. Whatever the case, she never mentions them."

"Interesting. And how old is Livy?"

"Forty something."

"I guess that makes us more compatible than if she was thirty something."

Paul unlocked the security code, and opened a second vestibule door. The sun's reflection illuminated the foyer floor. A pink leather jacket rested on a newel post. My gaze followed a carpet runner up the wooden stairs to meet the inquisitive black eyes of a golden retriever. The colour of French vanilla ice cream, Wilson's head rested on his massive front paws, hanging over the top riser.

"Wilson, come!" Paul called, and the dog bounded down the stairs, his shiny fur gliding back and forth across his torso. I knew nothing about dogs, other than they ate, barked, and pooped.

"Why didn't he bark when we came in?"

"He's used to people coming and going." Wilson circled me curiously, then poked his nose into my groin. A car pulled into the driveway. My heart thumped. *Why am I so nervous?*

"Livy's home." Paul squatted down and rubbed his ears. Wilson leaned against him, relishing the attention.

Olivia Bless matched her name. She was a stunning blond who did not look 'forty something'. I watched her tall, slender frame reach into her white Volvo crossover and pull out a matching leather satchel and purse. Dressed in a tailored pant suit, she appeared dynamic and successful. I instinctively looked at my very predictable navy slacks, designed to camouflage my gut and minimize my expanding hindquarters. My cream cotton sweater reflected my complacent wardrobe. *I desperately need new clothes.*

Paul opened the front door. She pecked him on the cheek and Wilson barked excitedly, dropping his shoulders and front legs to the floor and wagging his tail vigorously against my unsuspecting thigh. Livy affectionately shook the dog's ears and hugged him as Paul introduced us. We exchanged pleasantries.

"Ladies, Wilson needs to tend to his business. We'll be back in half an hour." Both of them bolted out the front door.

Livy welcomed me again with a warm, firm handshake. Her eyes were as blue as her scarf, and her smile reflected the 'after' picture of quality orthodontic work.

"I've got to get these off – too much effort to look good," she laughed as she wrestled her leather boots off. Predictably, they matched her purse, and landed in a small pile of high end footwear, strewn carelessly behind the door.

"So you're the Gracie that Paul speaks so highly of. You know that he adores you?" I flushed.

"Adores me?"

"Yup. He says you're the back bone of his department."

"I'm not so sure about that. He's had an unsettling couple of weeks. Everybody thinks he's part of a conspiracy, even though he had nothing to do with the plant closing."

"He ages every time I see him. I hope he survives this mess." Livy stretched her arms high above her head and yawned. "Enough about Paul. Let's talk about you, Gracie. Lovely name. You've had a tough month, too. And my condolences to you for losing your husband."

"Thank you."

"Paul said you sold your house in two days. The market's hot."

"Much quicker than I expected, Olivia."

"I prefer Livy. Only my great aunt, who lived here, called me Olivia, whether she was mad at me or not."

"Your house is a show piece, Livy. It's gorgeous."

"Isn't it grand? I just love it. Did you see the place yet? Paul told you that I travel a lot with my job. I love it here, but Wilson is not happy being alone all the time," Livy said. She didn't waste any time with the house tour. "Follow, me."

She started with the parlour, located off the foyer, which held a pair of overstuffed leather sofas facing each other, separated by an old blanket box. Wooden floors framed a thick, paisley rug. A large walnut fireplace was trimmed with wood carved into a twisted rope. An enormous, gilded mirror over the mantle reflected light from the stained glass windows, giving the room a comfortable elegance. Getting ahead of myself, I imagined reading a good novel in pajamas in this room.

"Livy, I already love the house and Wilson, but we should talk first. I'm not sure what you expect of me, but I don't want to waste your time. Can we chat about the rent first...." I took a deep breath, re-organized my thoughts, and carried on. "I just sold my house to free up my debt, and the plant is closing and..." Livy interrupted me with her index finger.

"You are absolutely right. We need to discuss this. Trust me, because I'm as anxious as you are. I don't know all the answers because this is new to me, too. First, we need to breathe, and have a drink. I've got to get out of this superwoman suit. Can you find some wine in the kitchen? I'll have red." Livy scooted up the stairs before I could answer. Within five minutes, a handshake had progressed to wine.

The centre hall ended in a beautiful black and white kitchen. My heart fluttered, then sank in this culinary paradise. Classic white cupboards reflected against shiny black granite counters. White California shuttered double doors separated the back yard. I found wine glasses and an open bottle of white wine in the fridge. I poured Livy's merlot from a new bottle on the counter.

I set Livy's glass down in the parlor and savoured the first sip of mine. The couch was comfortable and deep, its soothing butternut leather blending into the matching walls. Livy returned, dressed in faded jeans and a black turtleneck sweater, her blonde hair held up with with an oriental clasp. Easing into the couch, she rested her bare feet on the blanket box and raised her glass. "There. Much better. To Mondays."

"Cheers." I raised my glass and toasted the thoughts floating in my head, which I'm sure were different than hers.

"Gracie, you look like you're in church. Sit back and relax." I balanced my wine glass nervously while tucking my feet under a tapestry cushion. After some small talk about her flight and the traffic, Livy took a long swallow from her glass.

"Okay, so down to business, but first the backstory. I've lived here for three years. My great Uncle Ethan was admitted into a nursing home and my great Aunt Madeleine insisted that she stay here. She was fiercely independent, but equally forgetful. Kind of like me on some days. Anyhow, about four years ago she forgot a pot cooking on the stove, which started a fire that destroyed the kitchen and took three months to restore. I spent as much time as I could here, mediating between her and the contractor. By the time it was finished, she couldn't remember how to boil an egg. I was petrified she would burn whole house down, so the new stove remained unplugged. The kettle shut off automatically and the microwave had a sensor. I arranged for hot meals to be delivered daily." Livy finished her wine with a gulp, and continued.

"Anyhow, I gave Wilson to Aunt Maddy for Christmas to keep her company. To give her a purpose, and to worry about someone other than me. She and my uncle owned dogs before, so I knew she would love Wilson. We took obedience classes for seniors with dogs. Did you know they train dogs to sense danger? Wilson was great with my aunt."

"He didn't bark until you came home."

"He's a fantastic dog. I hate leaving him when I go away."

"What happened to your aunt?" Livy's eyes drooped.

"She missed a step, and broke her hip. She was hospitalized, and things went downhill from there. I told my great uncle why she couldn't visit, and I'm sure he died of loneliness. Aunt Maddy died three months later. It was so sad because they really loved each other, and this house. Not sure what to do, I just stayed here with Wilson. He needed me as much as I needed him."

"What about your family?"

"Well, that's a messy question. I'm adopted, but biologically related to my great aunt. My real mother, who was my great aunt's niece, gave me up at birth. I'm sure I'm the product of a one-nighter, because no one knows my real father. Rumour has it that her bedroom had many visitors. My adoptive parents literally bought me. They put my mom up at a shelter until I was born. They paid for her clothes, room, health care, everything. After she had me, she returned to Toronto for a while. My parents gave her money here and there, but she never quite got her act together, and eventually disappeared. Probably ended up on the street."

"Where is she now?"

"No idea. She could be dead. We lost contact twenty years ago. My adoptive parents weren't much better. They were high society drunks – always shipping me away to school and summer camps. I spent very little time with them. I felt abandoned long before I was old enough to make sense of it, and I'm sure that once the novelty of adopting me wore off, they regretted their decision. My adoptive father was violent and distant. He was running around creating new families, while my mother drank to cope with what thread of a marriage held them together."

"Tough childhood."

"I'm not sure tough is the right word, because I certainly led the life of privilege. It's the classic poor little rich girl story, but I sure was lonely. I would make up any excuse to stay here, or a friend's house. Anywhere that had two parents, a roof over their head, and a pack of kids running around. It actually was to my benefit to be as far away from them as I legally could, without calling it abandonment. If not for this place, and my great aunt and uncle, I'd be on the street like my mom."

For whatever unknown reason, I defended her parents. "People make mistakes, sometimes serious ones because they don't know what they're doing. Maybe their parents struggled, too."

Livy looked at me and smirked. "They weren't much better."

"Many people become wonderful, compassionate human beings because of the nasty things that happened to them. I see that in you." Livy sighed. "Where are your parents now?"

"Gone. Killed in a car accident. My dad was drunk and hit a tree. It was no surprise. In fact, I expected it. They died instantly. I was twenty-two and had just finished university." She tucked her knees up and wrapped her arms around them, pausing for a minute. "I've spent my life having other people look after me. They are still looking after me, like the people who manage this estate. Except now they have no biological connection to me."

"I'm sorry." Livy shrugged her shoulders.

"Don't be. Ultimately it took me to a better place, because I now realize that no one builds my life but myself." Both our glasses were empty. I hadn't anticipated being here long enough to finish it. Livy kept opening up.

"My great aunt and uncle saved me. I spent Christmas holidays here or with my friends' families, because my parents partied to avoid dealing with me. Who needs a kid around when you're naked on a yacht in the middle of the Caribbean?" Livy ran her hands up and down her thighs, as if she was rubbing creases out of her life. Restless, she picked up the empty glasses. "That was a long time ago, and we definitely need more wine." She stood up, both wine glasses in one hand and waving her other one. "Enough bad memories, right?"

"Right." She was back with full glasses while I was still envisioning naked sunbathers on a yacht. She spoke again.

"Okay. I'm ready to talk house business. Here are the bare essentials. Fact number one: I don't own this house. Fact number two: a law firm oversees its upkeep. The estate evolved because a number of childless relatives died off, with no philanthropic commitments. Fact number three: I have one very distant, remaining relative, my uncle Norman, who I have sporadic contact with. The law firm, here in Toronto, manages this estate which somehow Uncle Norman remains connected to. He lives in a little village in Niagara. I saw more of him as a kid, but now I see him once a year around Christmas. I go to New Pelham one year, and he comes here the next. He's a bit of a recluse, and sometimes I feel guilty because I should see him more often than I have to. I do write him the odd note, when I am away on business. The lawyers periodically send people here to make sure I haven't trashed the place." I shifted the conversation, hoping for answers.

"So if the estate manages this place, I assume you pay rent?'"

"Yes and no. There's no mortgage, but I pay the hydro, gas, phone bills. The estate pays the taxes, insurance and maintains the property. Last year the roof was replaced. This year the sun room was restored. It's a pretty sweet deal. When my parents died, I inherited their house. The mortgage was slightly less than its value. I sold it to clear their debts and cover their funeral expenses. Bottom line, I was left with some nice furniture, which is here or at Uncle Norman's. And some really gaudy jewelry."

Livy laughed, fingering an eternity ring on her right ring finger which wasn't gaudy at all. Clearly visible square diamonds in a channel setting. "Seriously though, I am very, very grateful to be here. I'm comfortable and secure here, as if my great aunt and uncle are still watching over me. Some day the bubble will burst, but right now it's all good."

I looked at my watch. My first appointment to see an apartment was in fifteen minutes. I forged on.

"I hate to rush things, but what are you expecting of me?"

"Right. That's where I was heading. Yes, I am serious about a house mate. I've got to keep Wilson and Paul happy." She sat down, shifted a few times in her seat, then stood up. "Can we chat a little more before I make any decisions?" I gave up on seeing the first apartment.

"Sure."

"You haven't told me anything about yourself. Please tell me what your expectations are. I'm going to re-fill these glasses." Livy returned balancing the wine with an exquisite tray of cheeses and crackers which someone had prepared beforehand. I didn't realize how hungry I was until I took the tray and set it down. I had many questions, hours of packing to do, and was wagering opportunity against precious time.

"So what exactly does a benefits, ah, person do?"

Explaining that I administered employee health, disability and death claims, she laughed heartily when I said some employees changed beneficiaries like seasons. Feeling more comfortable with the influence of good wine, I talked about Blair with as much emotion as discussing the weather, that we led a comfortable existence until he died, and his life insurance claim was denied. I told her I was most upset with Blair deceiving me. Livy rolled her eyes.

"That's a kick in the chops."

"Right now, I want nothing to do with men."

"Yeah, I've been there too." I became curious.

"You must have a very understanding boyfriend with your travel schedule."

"I'm single, and haven't been in a real relationship with anyone for at least two years, not since Taylor left. I go on the odd date here and there, but nothing serious. It is tough to plan things when I'm unsure where I'll be next week."

The front door opened, and Paul let himself in, unleashing the dog and leaning against the doorway. His cheeks were red from the crisp April air. Wilson ran to the kitchen, where the sloppy lapping of water was followed by a loud bang. Livy shook her head, popping a cracker in her mouth. "That's my Wilson. He picks up and drops his bowl to tell me he's ready for supper. Sometimes he'll bring it all the way here. Okay, okay, I'm coming!" Livy groaned, easing herself off the couch and heading for the kitchen. Paul remained in the doorway, shoving his red hands deep into his pockets.

"How's it going?"

"Good." I whispered. "She's perfect. The house is perfect. Everything's perfect. But we haven't talked rent fees. I think she's scrutinizing me."

"That's smart on her part. You'll be fine, Gracie. I'm sure you'll work out something fair." Paul zipped up his jacket and yelled into the kitchen. "Livy, I gotta run. The kids are home from school." Livy came back, balancing the refilled wine glasses and two more crackers between her lips. Well, I thought, at least she eats.

"Thanks, Paul. I'm home tomorrow and gone again on Wednesday. Carly will walk Wilson all this week." Paul raised both thumbs up, and left.

"So where were we?"

"Distracted by men. Livy, I don't want to be pushy, but I've booked a couple of rental appointments to see tonight. I'd re-schedule them if I wasn't so pressed for time." I deliberately looked at my watch. She nodded, finishing her snack. *Was she purposely stalling me?*

"Right, right." I suddenly felt self conscious about what I was wearing when she looked me over top to bottom. *I should have worn something nicer.* Livy smiled warmly, and I hoped she trusted me. "It would be nice to have someone else here. Paul has good judgement, otherwise, he wouldn't recommend you. He said this was a win-win situation for both of us. So why don't we give it a try?" *Just like that.*

I felt like the final candidate for a really good job, without knowing the duties, salary or benefits.

"I'd love to live here." I sighed, waiting for the financial bomb to drop.

"It's really just a house, and if you're willing to accept the arrangement, this can work for both of us."

"I'm listening." My palms were wet.

"Okay, so here's the deal. My expenses are essentially as I explained earlier. The hydro, gas, water, internet and cable invoices are the housing expenses I pay on an equal monthly billing plan. All combined, it totals about a thousand dollars a month. So, would it reasonable to split this?"

I quickly calculated how much rent I could afford on top of that.

"I can handle that, depending on what the rent would be."

"That would be the rent. No, let me rephrase that. Your rent would be walking Wilson on the days I can't."

I must have missed something, because it didn't make financial sense. "Let me understand this. You expect my total living cost to be about five hundred dollars a month? To live here, and walk the dog? Is that with everything included?"

"Yes. Is that reasonable? Too much? I want to be fair. In reality, you would physically be here more than I would. I pay that now for the dog sitter." I still couldn't believe it, and Livy patiently explained it again. Cautiously she said, 'If we can get along and be civil, it's a perfect arrangement for both of us."

"It's better than perfect." Livy smiled warmly.

"Right now, I'm only home a total of two weeks a month, so Wilson is your primary responsibility when I'm not here. Paul, or Carly, the dog sitter, would take over if you can't. You would be responsible for paying Carly. I'll cover any incidental house expenses not covered by the estate."

I felt light headed, and unable to speak. *I can't believe something good is happening.*

"Oh, I almost forgot. Gracie, there are two hitches to this," she raised her right index finger as my throat tightened, and I braced for disappointment.

"The first thing is for the benefit of both of us, and that is for you to sign a contract that confirms what we just agreed to, for an initial period of three months. If all goes well for both of us, we will renew the contract for a longer term. The second part is a little more complicated. Because the Chestnut estate manages this house, there is a clause in the agreement which says that the estate must approve of anyone living here, and can therefore override the contract. The law firm which does this has been very reasonable, so I don't expect any problems. If you're fine with this, I'll ask them tomorrow to draft an agreement for you to sign. I am in town tomorrow, which is Tuesday, but am gone for a week or more after that. I'll tell lawyers when I'll be back. Today is what, April 9? When does your house close?"

"April 20th."

"Wow. Less than two weeks."

"I know. Short notice, but I didn't want to risk not selling the house. To say the last few months have been a blur is an understatement. More like crazy. I move on the 20th. My last day of work is April 30th. My head is spinning just thinking about it, but having a place to live is a huge relief."

Her smile broadened. "It'll be fine."

"Thank you so much, Livy. I feel like I'm dreaming, and you're my fairy godmother." She laughed heartily and retrieved a business card of the law firm from her purse. I shook her hand, preferring to have hugged her instead.

"I'll call you tomorrow, or as soon as I hear something. The lawyers will ask you for a couple of references. You should use Paul, since we both know him, plus another name."

"I really, really appreciate this." Suddenly, I thought about Tess. "Wait, Livy. I forgot to tell you about my daughter. Tess. She's twenty years old and away at university. She's living on campus this summer, and resuming school in the fall. Would you have any objection if she stays over some weekends? She would love Wilson."

"No, no. Not at all. I'd love to meet her."

"I'm embarrassed I forgot about her."

"No worries. You've got a lot going on."

"I need to recover from selling my house and this job loss stuff, maybe coast for a few weeks."

"You'll be fine, Gracie. I'll also let the lawyers know about Tess." I looked up at the ceiling.

"I feel like there's someone up there who decided something good should balance the bad. I have something exciting to look forward to. Thank you, Livy. Thank you very, very much. And I must thank Paul tomorrow. Now, I've really must leave. I have decades worth of stuff to pack." I extended my hand again to Livy, but got a warm hug instead. It was what I needed most.

"Gracie, things will work out. For both of us. I'll call you as soon as I hear something."

I literally skipped out the door and down the slate walkway, feeling like I just won a lottery. The sweet scent of hyacinths aroused my senses. It wasn't until I unlocked the car that I realized I hadn't seen the rest of the house. I turned around and looked at the house again. It really didn't matter. Based on what I had seen, it could only be better that I imagined.

I emailed my references to the law firm Livy gave me and waited. Tuesday came and went. I had no reason to doubt her offer was sincere, and Paul re-assured me repeatedly. I picked up packing boxes from the movers. Most of my furniture would go into storage because my room at Livy's house was furnished. I packed Tess's things, except her furniture. In a corner of the living room, I set aside the few things that would go to Livy's house. By Wednesday I felt sick because Livy, nor her lawyer had called.

April 12th

I slept poorly, convinced that the agreement had fallen apart. I was desperately scanning through short term rental listings to tide me over for a few weeks when the law firm called, advising me that the rental agreement was prepared and ready for me to sign.

I showered and dressed quickly, fearful that if I didn't get there soon enough, they, whoever they were, would change their minds. The office was buried in a tower of granite and glass in downtown Toronto. I rode up the elevator, regretting that I had not dressed better. An impeccably outfitted lawyer named Kristen Castle reviewed the contract in a monotonous, waning English accent. The contract mirrored our verbal agreement, except that the moving date was delayed from April 20th to May 1st. Ms. Castle wanted Livy to be present when I moved in, and since she was away until April 30th, I couldn't move in until May 1st. This would also allow her some time to check my references.

Accepting the short delay, I signed the three-month agreement, which was subject to renewal provided that all parties were happy with the arrangement. I had to store my furniture offsite, which Ms. Castle explained, was because in a similar but unrelated situation, antique furniture was destroyed by carpenter ants. Pleasantly but firmly, she emphasized that the house contents were very high quality and must be preserved. I smiled pleasantly and was dismissed after her lecture. I was happy, but homeless for ten days. I picked up some roasted chicken and salad and drove home, weighing the cost of a renting a cheap hotel room against the cost of tolerating Sophie for ten days. The hotel cost was worth the peace and quiet.

Simon's truck was in my driveway when I got home. Dressed in work clothes, he came out carrying a six pack of beer and some fast food. Empty boxes were stacked in the bed of his truck. He tipped his baseball cap as he chirped, "Simon the helper, at your service." I was genuinely happy to see him. As I unlocked my door, he stood close behind me, the scent of his clothes warm and familiar. He skirted around some packed boxes, and followed me to the kitchen. The newspaper I was using to pack dishes doubled as a tablecloth as we shared our dinners.

It had been a month since Blair passed away, and Simon mentioned it first.

"I figured you could use some company." He was right. We talked about Blair for most of the evening. I told Simon I was angry that he had let Tess and I down. I occasionally missed his presence, but I didn't miss him. A newspaper article on the table, now stained with fast food grease, published the results of a recent survey about widows. The subtitle stated than ten percent of widows were happier after their husbands died. I told Simon I fell into that category. Simon looked out the window, then back to me.

"Regardless of what you think, Gracie, he needed you. He was proud of the things you did for your family that he couldn't do."

"Like what?"

"Like helping Tess make smart choices."

"I had to, because he wouldn't support me. It was frustrating." Simon nodded as he sifted through the uneaten fries before finishing the salad.

With nothing left to eat or say, Simon asked for things to do. He went upstairs and dismantled Tess's bed while I emptied my fridge into a cooler for him to take home. Tess would take the non-perishable food when she came home for Easter. I heard Simon whistle loudly. I barreled up the stairs to find him in my bedroom.

"Nice bed, Gracie. So this is where you two did the nasty." The room was a disaster. My bed was unmade, with clothes worn once on the dresser and a pile of unfolded clean underwear on the chair. "What do you want me do in here?" He grinned, relishing my humiliation.

"Leave it. I wasn't expecting you to come in here." The last man in this room, other than Blair, was the carpet installer two years ago. Picking aimlessly at the mess, I felt a nervous stirring, and had trouble assembling my words.

"Simon, I'm not there."

"Where?" Simon stood, legs astride, with his left hand on his hip and a screwdriver in his right hand.

"Where? Here. Right in here. Packing up this room."

"Hey, I was only trying to help."

"My sister will help." Strong and charismatic, Simon laughed, knowing I was blocking him from seeing my frumpy underwear. I was done, drained both emotionally and physically. I melted, embarrassed, with tears spilling down my face. I fell apart, not from losing a husband, not for all I had to do, but because this man was in my room, making me feel vulnerable, strange and standing in the core of my personal space. Simon stepped close, hesitated, then took me in his arms. My tears spilled onto his denim shirt. His touch shouldn't have, but comforted me in a way Blair hadn't for years.

"It's okay, Gracie. I'm messing with you. Cry as much as you want." He pushed my hair from my face. His eyes were calm and his breath was warm on my cheek. I wept harder, more now than all the previous weeks combined. He took my face in his rugged hands and smiled. "My, my, my. You're gonna need a little makeup to fix this face up in the morning." I couldn't help but laugh. He gave me another warm hug. "Let's go downstairs. I've done enough damage to you and your house for one night." I separated from him slowly, now feeling silly. He followed me down the stairs as I whimpered and wiped my eyes.

"There's so much going on. I barely manage one crisis and the next one comes along."

"It's not that bad."

"At least the house is sold."

"That's good news."

"And I have a place to live."

"More good news. Where?"

"This mansion on Chestnut Boulevard. At least it is to me. And instead of paying rent, I'm dog-sitting."

"Wow. That's very good news. Sounds like a great job." I pointed to the boxes, and the furniture.

"This stuff will all go into storage."

"Why?"

"It's only a three-month deal, subject to renewal, providing we all get along."

"When do you move in?"

"May 1st." My hands instinctively rubbed my forehead.

"What's wrong, Grace?"

"I move out of this house April 20th."

"So where are you staying in between?"

"I'm still deciding. My sister is so overbearing, and I won't impose on my friends. Probably a hotel." I was exhausted.

"That's expensive."

"It's an option. I literally found out three hours ago about the ten day gap. I'll think it though when I catch my breath. I can easily book a hotel."

"A hotel is a waste of money. Stay at my house." *What? His house?*

"Your house? Are you nuts? I can't do that."

"Why not?"

"That's not right. Be realistic. Blair's been gone one month. What would people think?"

"Which people? The ones you don't work with anymore? Your girlfriends that you just said you don't want to be around right now?" His shoulders were huge as he lifted his hands in the air to emphasize his point. "They'd be jealous if they knew. It's just a few days, Gracie. Well, maybe ten. It won't cost you a thing, and I won't even make you do my laundry," he chuckled mockingly. *I can't believe we're having this conversation.*

"Simon, I don't even know you. Well, I barely know you. I can't stay at your house."

"You're taking this much too seriously. Look at the bright side. It's an act of kindness. A nice change for both of us. I won't jump you, I promise." I stepped back from him.

"You're crazy. I must be crazy."

"No you're not. You're just under pressure." He stepped closer and rested his hand on my shoulder. "You're smart. You can't be spending money on hotel rooms. You'll need it for other things." *He's right.* "Remember, Blair was my friend, too. Pretend it's a little holiday." My face burned and my eyes hurt.

"I appreciate the offer, Simon. I can't think clearly right now, but I'm sure it's not going to happen."

"Look, you just said you can't think any more. So don't. I just live around the corner, so it's not a major inconvenience. I won't tell the guys at work, if it makes you feel better. Just think about it." He was generous, but persistent.

"Okay. I'll think about it and let you know by the weekend."

"Great. It'll give me an incentive to clean up the place. It's been a while since someone of the female persuasion stayed overnight."

"Don't get your dust cloth out yet. That's my last week at work, so it will be very emotional."

"No better reason than to have support, you know. Like a shoulder to lean on and all that soft stuff."

"Thanks, Simon." Simon looked in my eyes and became serious.

"Gracie, I miss Blair. I spent long days with that guy, some days more hours than you did. It will do us both good." He took a few steps back, his broad shoulders drooping. He put his hand on my front door. "The offer is serious, and I promise I'll leave you alone, if that's what you want. No strings attached." He appeared sincere. *Too much to handle right now.*

"Thanks. I'll let you know in a few days." I held the door. Awkwardly silent, his eyes met mine. He kissed my forehead, pressed his phone number in my palm, and curled it closed with his massive hand. I smiled weakly.

"Simon?"

"Yes?"

"Do you like Toblerone chocolate?"

"Tobler what?"

"Nothing. It's a type of chocolate." He frowned, scratched his temple, and skipped down my front steps.

The scent of Simon lingered in the house, in my hair, distracting me. The beer mellowed me as I tried to rationalize his invitation. What was his agenda? Maybe he really just wanted to help. Blair's death was further distanced by Simon's visit. *Could I spend ten days with a man I'd just a few times? Was I crazy?* I walked from room to room on the main floor, then upstairs. Simon had arranged the boxes and bed frame in Tess's room neatly along one wall. Memories of chicken pox, her first love and a card from a broken-hearted boy tugged at me. I shuffled on to our room. My room now, with clean underwear on the chair. Simon surely figured out by the white cotton briefs and full-support bras that our sex life was less than glorious. There was no black lace and fancy lingerie. Crawling into the bed I last made at least a week ago, I fumbled with the TV remote. The phone rang. It was Simon, not giving me a chance to speak.

"I've made the bed for you."

"Simon, I haven't even…."

"It's in the spare room."

"Simon…"

"Fresh sheets. They smell like lavender. I heard it helps you sleep."

"What makes you so sure I'll come?"

"I know you've already decided. And bring all that fancy underwear I saw on the chair." I felt bold.

"Have you got an agenda?"

"No agenda. Just helping a widow in need. Good night, Gracie." The phone clicked before I could object. I drifted off to sleep repeating Simon's words while watching a Seinfeld rerun.

I woke up nine hours later, still dressed from last night with Simon's scent on my shirt. I'd be late for work, but no one was at work anyway. I showered, picked up a bagel and coffee, and drove a calmer route to the office.

The atmosphere at work was dismal and each day dragged on. Occasionally an employee came in to complain about something I had no authority to change. I cleaned out the rest of cabinets that were deserted by my predecessors. I shook the crumbs out of the tablecloth we used for birthday celebrations. A women's shelter was the beneficiary of the reusable office supplies and furniture. Employee files were forwarded to the corporate office to become someone else's responsibility.

April 15th

My last Easter at the house began on a solemn note. Tess and I toasted both good and bad memories. My foot circled the notch in kitchen floor where I dropped the toaster years ago. The living room corner where the Christmas tree stood. The dogwood tree Tess gave me for Mother's day. The colour of the downstairs bathroom I hated. The hours of arguing in our room.

My sister Sophie and her daughter Mallory shared our last Sunday with us. Sophie was a rational person, but took needless risks. We were as opposite as sisters can be, but I loved her just the same.

Dinner was a medley of our favourite foods. Sophie and I reminisced while the girls crammed their adult bodies into the tiny tree house at the back of the house and ate Easter chocolates. For ambience, I lit the candles last used during a power failure. Sophie brought champagne, and with plastic glasses we toasted our futures. Sophie followed me to the kitchen, where I casually mentioned Simon's offer.

"What does he look like?"

"A nice-looking guy, but it doesn't matter. He was Blair's best friend."

"The grey-haired guy with in the good suit? Yes, I remember him from the funeral. I'd be jumping at the chance to look at that dude for a week. Where does he live?"

"Haven't got a clue. It could be in a tent." Sophie mocked me.

"He wouldn't be offering if he wasn't sincere."

"I know. His house has at least two bedrooms, and it's ten minutes from my office. Sophie, it's only six weeks since Blair's died, and regardless, I should not be staying at his best friend's house."

"So what? I doubt he intends to seduce his best friend's widow. Besides, sleeping there is different than sleeping with him."

"If I stay there, you and I have to keep this quiet." Sophie scoffed.

"Grace, when were you last really happy? How many years has it been since your fire was lit? Life looked pretty boring the last time I was here and Blair was well…"

"Stop jumping to conclusions. Regardless, I feel guilty about this."

"About what? Accepting a generous offer from someone who wants some company for a week? What if it came from a female?"

"That would be very different."

"Try to look at it another way. No responsibilities for a week. No bills to pay. Maybe a few dishes. Just bank your money and sit tight. Enjoy a fantasy vacation with your own cabana man."

"Yeah, right."

"Where's the house you're moving to?" Now that excited me.

"Want to see it? It's a twenty minute drive from here."

"Sure." I invited the girls but they were more interested in staying in the tree house.

As we drove to Chestnut Boulevard, Sophie argued the merits of staying with Simon. I knew she'd expect daily updates as payment for supporting me. The closer we got to Livy's house, the larger and more majestic the properties were. Sophie whistled when we arrived at the house. Petals from a blooming magnolia tree spiraled gently down across the front lawn. Stately and reserved, the house was a dramatic contrast to my current home. I took a deep breath and admired my surroundings.

"I'll need a to buy new car just to visit you," she chattered.

"Look at the gardens. They are gorgeous."

"Gracie, you deserve this." Rare as it was for Sophie to say this, I knew she meant it.

"I'll never live anywhere like this again."

"What's the inside like? It looks like no one's home. Let's pull in."

"No. My boss lives around the corner. He'll think I'm spying."

"No he won't. Just pull in the driveway," she commanded. As usual, I gave in and drove onto the two rows of concrete embedded in the grass, butterflies fluttering in my stomach.

"I've only been here once, and saw just the main floor. Sophie, it's right out of Architectural Digest."

"Let's see the back yard."

"We're trespassing. No."

"Yes. We're here already, so we might as well have a peek." She jumped out of the car. "Are you coming, or am I going back there alone?" Chiding her for breaking the law, I followed, cautiously checking for surveillance cameras. A tall black wrought iron gate separated the side of the house from the back yard. The heavy latch was unlocked as we followed the curved sidewalk around the back to face a magnificent glass domed solarium. Our sighs were simultaneous. The double shuttered doors in the kitchen opened up to this tropical escape. Cushions patterned with fuchsia orchids and soft pink geraniums nested in white wrought iron furniture. Large ornamental trees, with pink flowers, furnished the corners of this sunny room.

A loud bark behind me made both of us jump. It was Paul and Wilson, who was letting us know he was in charge. I rubbed his ears and made introductions.

"I thought I recognized your car."

"Sophie wanted to see the house and the back yard."

"Livy's away. It's a great place, and the neighbours will be happy you're here. Did you see the whole house, Grace?"

"No. But I'd love too." Paul tied Wilson's leash to the wrought iron newel post at the back of the house. He led us through the back portico entrance into a mud room. Small navy and white octagonal tiles were set within a border of the same colours. A soiled yellow towel with Wilson's name embroidered on it hung above a matching dog cushion.

"This is Wilson's room. On wet days he stays here until he's clean and dry. Paul pointed to two navy milk cans.

"Kibble and snacks." Wilson offered his paw until Paul passed him a dog treat. An armoire held Wilson's neatly folded towels and canned dog food. A bottom drawer was filled with more dog stuff. "The dog walker grooms him in here. Sophie looked out the window to where Wilson sat, pre-occupied with squirrels and chirping birds.

"I'd trade places with him in a heartbeat."

Paul laughed. "Me too." We entered the kitchen. Sophie whistled again.

"Wow."

"I told you it was gorgeous," I said.

"Who lives here?" Sophie asked Paul as she circled the room.

"A nice woman. When Grace told me she sold her house, I knew this arrangement would work for both Livy and Grace. Everyone, including Wilson, will be much happier." He let Wilson back in, who came right to me, shoving his nose in my crotch again. An awkward silence.

"I agree." I tilted the dog's head to face me and rubbed his ears.

Paul grinned. "Wilson thinks he's a person. In fact, the estate names him as an occupant."

"Really?"

"When the owners passed on, they didn't want him in a kennel."

"Lucky dog."

Paul looked at his watch. "Okay, ladies. You've got five minutes to check out the place before I'm due back home." Sophie kicked off her shoes before I could object.

"We'll be done in four," she said.

Sophie grabbed my hand, darting from room to room, alternating whistles with gasps. I chased her up the steps, curious to know which bedroom would be mine. At the top of the stairs, we faced three closed doors, and three open ones. One large bedroom was decorated in soft florals with two matching four-poster beds. Another room was a warm and welcoming den, with overstuffed couches and one of Wilson's yellow towels that designated his spot. The wooden hallway railing was curved, and ended at a large guest room that faced the street. Varying shades of cream and robin's egg blue created an atmosphere of distinguished serenity. A king-sized four-poster bed faced a walnut fireplace. Sophie plopped herself on the bed, with her feet remaining on the floor.

"Ah, paradise!"

"Get off the bed!" I hissed, fighting to smooth the bedspread as she ignored me and rolled over.

"I can't believe you're moving here!" She stood up and I quickly fixed the linen.

"Hurry up – Paul's waiting for us."

"Let's see the other rooms," Sophie whispered as she scurried around the railing and towards the fourth room, which also faced the street.

"No!" I followed her past a large antique black and white bathroom, complete with a huge, white, claw-footed bathtub in the centre.

"She'll never know."

"It's still not right!"

"It's unlocked."

"Sophie, I'm sure there's a hidden camera…" We both stopped, awestruck. Floor to ceiling, furniture to fabric, Livy's room was a sea of creamy white on white. The exception, and the focal presence of this room, was a life-sized portrait of a nude woman above the bed, centered in an ornate, gilded frame. She was reclining against a white sheepskin rug which laid on a black velvet chaise lounge. Long, thick blond curls lay carelessly on her and the back of the chaise. A strikingly beautiful face smiled at us proudly, with her fit body free of scars and imperfections. Her right hand rested over her well-endowed left breast, fingers parted slightly to reveal an erect nipple. Her left hand lay casually near her blonde pubic hair. Sophie squinted to read the gold, handwritten inscription at the bottom of the portrait.

"It says, 'Happy 40th. All my love, Taylor'. Who's Taylor?" she whispered.

"Until now, I thought it was her ex. As in husband."

"She looks more like a wife to me."

"Shut up."

"Will this change things?"

"No. I don't think so. It's, it's just…not…what I expected. I'm surprised Paul never said…"

"If I looked like that, I'd have my portrait done like this too," Sophie said, gazing closely at the image.

"And hang it where? In your living room?"

"Sure. Right where the mailman could see it," Sophie cackled.

Paul forced a cough at the bottom of the stairs. I worked hard to remain composed as we came down.

"Did you figure out who's sleeping where?"

"Sure did," Sophie piped in, poking me in the back. Sophie asked Paul if he'd ever seen the upstairs.

"No, but I'm sure it's laid out as nicely as it is down here."

"Sure is," Sophie chirped, as we followed Paul out. I gave Wilson a hug. He was happy, and for five hundred dollars a month, I was very happy too. That said, I needed to clarify any other expectations Livy had, and preferably sooner than later.

As I drove home, Sophie chattered about the portrait, suggesting the benefits of this arrangement.

"She won't steal your boyfriends."

"It will be a while before I have a boyfriend."

"Then maybe you can share clothes."

"She's taller and leaner, and in a very different fashion category. We won't be sharing anything."

"You never know."

"Shut up," I sneered, as we returned to my plain and simple house, and until recently, my plain and simple life.

Tess and Mallory were restless and anxious to return to school. The girls, less than a year apart, were often mistaken for sisters. Following a final round of tears and goodbyes, they left with Sophie, who delivered Tess to her place.

I accepted Simon's invitation when he called again that evening. He sounded enthusiastic and reassured me that I'd be fine. I finished packing, and struggled with my conscience for telling Tess before she left that I was staying with a friend.

April 20th

I woke up much too early on Friday morning to the sound of a soft rain. I slipped into Blair's plaid flannel housecoat, came downstairs, and settled into one of the tired Adirondack chairs on the front porch with a steaming cup of coffee. I hoped the new owners would appreciate these chairs, which were left for us by the previous owners. The signs of spring were coming alive and would welcome the new occupants in just a few hours. Looking at the clouds, I thought of Blair. I drew his soft but hoarse voice from somewhere in my thoughts. I drained my coffee cup, sorting through memories of being together. Some were good, but mostly they made me sad. It was my turn to make peace with him. Harbouring anger and resentment had no lasting value, and in order to move forward, I needed to put the past behind me. A small rabbit, nibbling on blades of grass for breakfast, paused to look at me, as if to encourage me to move on. I buried myself in Blair's housecoat, and inhaled the last faint traces of his existence. I breathed in deeply until I felt I had let him go. The rabbit vanished into the hedge as I stood up to face my final serene moment here.

I shed Blair's housecoat and added it to the charity donation box in our room with the last of his clothes. An agency was scheduled to pick it up later today from the front porch. Heading for the shower, I caught a glimpse of my naked frame in the mirror. While I was grateful to inherit my mother's youthful skin, the rest of my body was succumbing to gravity. Not quite hopeless, but another man would need to accept me with my thickening middle and thighs. I showered quickly, and chose a crisp white shirt and jeans. The movers arrived on time, and quietly but expertly emptied the house within a few hours. I splurged on a cleaning service which arrived shortly after the movers finished. Simon and his friend arrived in separate pickup trucks, and parked on the street. Simon greeted me with a broad smile.

"Good morning! We're here to help, but it looks like we're too late." He folded his muscular arms across his chest and turned to his friend. You'll make it to your golf game early." Simon's friend tipped his baseball hat, wished me well, and disappeared as quickly as he came. The movers sealed the back doors of their rig and headed off to the storage facility. We silently watched until only the the smell of diesel fuel fumes remained. Simon put his arm around my shoulders, squeezed me closer to him and I inhaled the fresh scent of his clean skin in the air. "How're you feeling, Gracie?"

"A little lost. Most of my life's possessions are in the back of that truck. And what's left is in my car."

"Anything else left in the house?"

"A few plants, but I'll get them later."

"I'll put them in the truck right now. What else?"

"Just the lawyer's office and a few errands."

"You're on your own with the lawyers." He pulled out a set of keys and an address on a receipt from his pocket. "I'll meet you there in a few hours. Are you okay to close the house up?"

"Yes. I need to do that on my own." He loaded the plants into his truck within minutes. "Thanks again for all your help, Simon." He pointed to the plants.

"Maybe you should see what the plants look like when they arrive before you thank me." He secured the pots with bungie cords, opened his truck door, and smiled again.

"I'm looking forward to the company." He waved and left. The cleaning crew left the house scrubbed and smelling of strong antiseptic. There was nothing left to do. I took one last tour of the house and the yard. The grass was wet from rain, and smelled fresh and clean. Tears flowed freely as I recalled the memories our small family created here. I left a welcome card in a potted hydrangea shrub on the porch for the new owners. I locked the doors and said a final goodbye to the house, and to Blair. I was moving on.

The law office was quiet, and the silver haired lawyer, who had handled our affairs since Blair and I had married, was kind and sympathetic. I signed over the house, and handed him a copy of my rental agreement for safekeeping. He was genuinely pleased for me.

"I live near Chestnut Boulevard, so if you have any legal concerns, please call." We exchanged farewells and I left.

In my car mirror, I checked my appearance. My tears washed away what little makeup I had applied earlier. I did my banking, picked up tea, coffee, wine and salad ingredients. I studied Simon's address. I hadn't even driven by his place. Maybe it's a dump. *Don't be stupid, Grace. Blair would have mentioned it. Or not...*

I navigated my overloaded car to a small street in an older subdivision. The address was a small stucco bungalow with white shutters and a red front door that matched Simon's red truck. I parked beside his vehicle, in front of a two car garage. A small backyard was protected by a tall wooden fence with decorative hearts carved into the wood at equal intervals. Tidy and uncluttered, it was a pleasant surprise. I opened my trunk and caught Simon's expression as he approached from the back of the house. He pointed to my swollen eyes and smiled.

"Better than I expected. Women have looked like that leaving my house, but never arriving. You're early."

"I had nowhere to go, and my brain is drained." We grabbed boxes and I followed him through the back door and up four stairs, each with a pair of shoes neatly parked on the right side. The scent of furniture polish and cleaning products impressed me. I entered a spotless, recently renovated kitchen, which led to a tiny hallway where four doors led to two bedrooms, a bathroom and a sparsely furnished living room, where my plants already filled the empty corners. A well-stocked entertainment unit, coffee tables, black leather couch and chair were the staples, and the room was probably accessorized by his last bedmate. I wondered why she left, and how long she stayed. It didn't matter. I had ten days here.

Simon pointed to a cheerful room facing the back yard. My room. A celery green carpet matched the farm animal wallpaper and duvet cover. Simon answered before I asked.

"No, I don't have kids. But some of my guests did." *I wonder how many 'guests' slept here?*

"It's perfect. If I can't sleep, I can count sheep." Simon put my suitcases next to the bed and retrieved two worn navy blue towels from his room. *I'll buy towels as a thank you gift.*

"I don't have a linen cupboard, so if you need more towels, they're in my closet. The place is yours, so get comfortable. I'll be out for a few hours, but if you haven't made dinner plans, I can throw a few burgers on the grill."

"Sounds great. I brought some salad stuff."

"Perfect. I'll leave you to unpack. Need anything else while I'm out?"

"No thanks."

Simon went to the bathroom and closed the door. The stream of urine splashing in the toilet was followed by the sound of the toilet seat hitting the porcelain rim, then the water running from the sink. Simon opened the door, wiping his hands in a towel.

"Not unpacked yet?" I laughed nervously.

"Not quite."

"Okay. See you soon." Simon shut the back door as I sat down gently, then lay back carefully on the bed. *So far so good. This might be a pleasant hiatus after all.*

Simon was polite, clean, put the toilet seat down, washed his hands, and made me feel welcome. Today he also looked handsome. I unpacked and called Tess. She knew the house sale closed today. I asked her enough questions to reassure myself that she was both physically and emotionally fine. I inspected the bathroom. Very clean. The toilet seat was definitely down. I glanced into Simon's room, where the light grey carpet, recently vacuumed, blended with the darker walls. Crisp white bed linens with black piping and black accent pillows must have been chosen by a female. I knew about Simon's many partners, but never why those relationships ended.

Deciding to explore the neighbourhood, I changed into a hooded sweatshirt, pulled out my sneakers and grabbed a bottle of water from the dozen I had just put in the fridge. Simon had put the salad ingredients away. Judging by the fridge contents, he could cook. And he had a pet. Two empty dishes labeled 'GEORGE' sat on a mat in front of the dishwasher. I filled one with water. The search for George led me to a partially finished basement. My gut churned when I recognized some of Blair's things from our garage. An open area hosted a washer and dryer, where drying work jeans hung on hooks suspended from ceiling beams. There was no response from whoever George was when I called his name. I opened the back door and inhaled the crisp spring air. New shrubs were spreading their shoots in the back yard. Three empty clay pots waited to be filled, perhaps with red geraniums or begonias. I walked briskly through the subdivision, similar to the one I just left. Neglected homes and gardens were seeing new life with the ambitious efforts of young families. Their lives were progressing, leaving me to feel somewhat alone. *Why did seeing Blair's things in the basement bother me when I had insisted that Simon take them?*

The landline phone in the kitchen rang as I entered the back door. Instinctively, I answered it. A raspy female voiced asked who I was. I identified myself as one of his friend's wives.

"You're the poor old widow he's helping out." *Old widow?*

"Can I leave him a message?"

"No, I'll catch up with him later." The phone display said 'Private Name, Private Number'. I shouldn't have, and won't answer that phone again.

I put the kettle on to make tea. Gentle, warm pressure against the back of my lower legs gave me goosebumps. An enormous black cat with emerald eyes meowed loudly, and sauntered over to his empty food bowls.

"Well, well. You must be George," I whispered. He nuzzled into my hand as I scratched his neck. I picked him up, groaning with the resistance of his weight. He responded with a deep purr, arching his neck and kneading my chest. When the back door squeaked open, George jumped out of my arms to greet his master.

"I see you've met the boss," Simon said as the cat weaved repeatedly through his legs.

"I've never seen such a big cat."

"He's a mane coon. They usually weigh about twenty pounds, but are rarely black. That's Midnight, my security guard."

"Midnight? I thought his name was George."

"George was a crazy Jack Russell terrier," Simon said as he unpacked bottles of wine, strawberries and miniature Toblerone bars. "George moved out a few years ago." When I pointed to the chocolate bars, he offered no explanation. "His bowls were in the dishwasher when he moved out, and no one came back to get them. Midnight doesn't care what they say, as long as they're full." He picked the cat up. Midnight sat contently in Simon's arms, inspecting me while I inspected the Toblerone bars again. Still no explanation.

"You've had a few guests here." He shrugged his shoulders.

"They stay, and then they leave. Maybe it's Midnight. I know it's not my cooking." Simon checked the kitchen clock. "I'm starving. I'll prepare the barbecue if you make the salad." Midnight was back at his dish by the time Simon went to light the grill.

Our dinner conversation carried us through the first bottle of wine. Simon banned me from the kitchen and cleaned up. I settled in the living room, finding my space in a corner of the couch. Midnight jumped onto the back couch, curled his paws under his girth and fell asleep. Simon filled our glasses with more wine, bringing strawberries and chocolates. He sat down on the opposite end of the couch, resting his feet on the coffee table and opened the conversation to his past.

Simon told me the house rules for his past girlfriends. They all paid rent, so legally, they were not common law partners. I wasn't sure why he told me, knowing it had no bearing on me. He was married twice, and would never marry again. Fishing excursions with his friends trumped any other plans. Nobody drove his truck, and he controlled the remote when he was home. I wondered why we were having this conversation.

"I'm easy to live with, but I need my space. I've been hurt before, so no woman will ever mess with my head, or my heart, again. My heart has retired."

"Retired?" I chuckled into my glass, my feet tucked under me.

"Yup." The wine eased my spirit.

"The right heart will unlock yours again. Love is about timing, and learning from past mistakes. The last time wasn't right. She'll arrive when you least expect it."

"No way. Never again." He took a sip of wine. "Blair was lucky. You never complained when we went out."

"I didn't know he went out. I thought he just worked a lot."

"If our job finished early, we went out for a few pops."

"But that only happened once a month."

"Oh, it was more like….." He stopped.

"Like what, Simon?" Simon lifted his hands.

"Gracie, I don't want to create conflict. I do my best to avoid it. You had a great marriage, and a guy who worshipped you and Tess. Let's leave it at that." He transferred his long legs to the couch, brushing his feet against my knees, parking a warm foot close enough for me to feel it.

"Wrong, Simon. It wasn't a great marriage. It was a boring existence between two people who were too passive to create conflict. Neither of us had the energy to challenge the other. But every time I got the courage to consider a new life, I knew I couldn't manage financially on my own. Blair's gone, and I should be a grieving widow, but I'm not. Here I sit, at his best friend's house, with a little nest egg, and no job. But I am looking forward to starting over."

"There's nothing wrong with that."

"And what's also very clear to me is that no matter what happens now, I'm not spending the next thirty years of my life like I spent the last fifteen. I want something better." Simon frowned.

"Did I hit a nerve?"

"Yes, you did. I cried more today than the day he died. In seven weeks, I've lost a spouse, his income, his life insurance, my job and because of these, sold my house. And here I sit, physically and mentally spent."

"Then aren't you glad you came here instead of a hotel?" I didn't expect to hear that. I answered, well under the influence of the wine.

"Yes. I am."

"Mmmm, that's interesting. Tell my why." Simon poured more wine. I took a gulp, sinking deeper into the couch. His socked feet connected with my knees and neither of us moved. The socks were very white.

"If I stayed with friends, they'd be tip-toeing around me, and I would have to pretend to feel sorry for myself. Instead I'm schmoozing with Prince Charming who's getting me drunk while keeping secrets about my dead husband from me. Then I get to stay the night, and even sleep in tomorrow. Is that a good enough explanation?"

"Mmmm. I like the Prince Charming part. And yes, you should sleep in."

"Thanks. And now I've got to get off this couch..."

"This prince turns into a frog at midnight."

"Lucky me. And I know you'll stay on your own lily pad tonight." I struggled to stand, grateful not to have to think or drive tonight. Midnight followed me and meowed outside the bathroom door. Coming out, I saw Simon had taken over the couch and the TV was on. It was dark outside. Unable to concentrate, I headed to bed.

"Good night, Prince Charming."

"Good night. Oh wait, Cinderella, Midnight will want to sleep with you tonight, so leave your door open a little, because he won't stop howling until you do."

I shut the bedroom door and changed into a camisole and my favourite oversized flannel pajamas, the least provocative set I owned. And just as Simon said, Midnight meowed loudly until I opened my door. I left it slightly ajar, and slid under the crisp sheets. Simon turned the volume down. The wine, coupled with the scent of lavender, put me to sleep within minutes.

April 21ˢᵗ

I woke up with Midnight's nose inches from mine. The coffee maker was sputtering and dishes rattled in the kitchen. In the bathroom, Simon's wet towel added to the dampness of the small room. I washed my face, ran a comb through my hair and clipped it up. In the kitchen, Simon's naked back hovered over the sink as he filled two mugs with water and heated them in the microwave.

"Good morning."

"Morning, Cinderella." I wasn't used to complements. Simon dumped the steaming water out. He glanced at my baggy, wrinkled pajamas and grinned, then poured coffee into each mug and turned around. An even growth of graying hair covered his sculpted chest. Loose jeans hung low on his hips and exposed a line of dark hair below his navel. He was barefoot.

"You microwave your cups?"

"I like my coffee hot. I bought cream. Low fat, right?"

"How did you know?"

"I just do."

"I don't believe you."

"You used to text Blair to buy cream, and he drank his coffee black."

"That I believe." The first sip was perfect.

The Toblerone chocolates were back on the counter.

"Why did you buy that chocolate? I mean, why that brand?"

"You said you liked it."

"Aahh, right."

"Chocolate keeps women happy."

I followed him into the living room, choosing the chair this time. Midnight followed Simon, and both made themselves comfortable at the opposite ends of the couch. "Mmmm. Last night, we shared the couch, but this morning you pick the chair. We're moving backwards, and I've already showered."

"I haven't."

"You slept well. I think I heard a little snore."

"I don't snore. It was the wine."

"I thought it was the company."

"That too."

"I checked in on you, but Midnight was the only one who slept with you." My heart fluttered.

"And I appreciate it, Simon."

"I would have rubbed your back if you couldn't sleep."

"What a generous offer." I checked my empty mug, not knowing where to look.

"One sleepover down, and nine to go."

"Are you flirting with me?"

"I just want you to sleep well."

"You do? And how might that happen?"

"That's up to you." *Sixteen hours here and he's coming on to me.*

"I'm a new widow."

"You don't look like a widow, at least you didn't last night."

"It was the wine."

"The wine fanned the flame. The spark lit the fire I saw in your eyes. Very dreamy."

"The wine made my lids heavy." He smiled.

"That's not what Midnight told me."

"And what did he tell you?"

"That there were many hornymones flying around last night." I laughed out loud and felt my face flush.

"Hornymones? That's a new word."

"Not to kids your daughter's age. They think we're beyond making passionate love." Simon's eyes were bright blue, and drawing me in.

"Do you say that to all the ladies?"

"No. I'm very picky, but my radar zones in quickly when there's a clear signal coming my way. I can always pick it up."

"I didn't know I was sending signals."

"Those granny pajamas aren't fooling me."

"You're trying to seduce me." I couldn't stay calm.

"I'm only offering. You're safe here and I'll leave you alone, but I know that's not you want."

"I haven't played this game for decades."

"The rules haven't changed. It's still boy meets girl, and each plays out their cards."

"Our cards were played out long before Blair got sick."

"I know."

"How do you know? What did Blair say?" I was upset.

"Nothing. You did."

"I never mentioned our personal life."

"You didn't have to. You tired of him, but good wives rarely wander."

"I hope he kept our intimate life private." I felt betrayed. Again.

"He never said a word, but after working together for years you know who's happy in bed and who's not. We all know that things naturally fizzle out." Simon yawned and looked at me again, raising his eyebrows. And that's when women are ready for something new."

"Really? Is what men think?"

"It's not what they think. It's what they know. Why do you think people stray? Look at you. You're a beautiful woman. Sitting right here across from me. No passion in her life for at least..." he counted five fingers and put them up. "Five years?" I had no idea how or why he came up with that number, or to tell him if he was right. He played the seduction game well, and drawing me in. He played his card. "Here I am, ready, and willing to help."

"You said that wasn't going to happen. In fact, the expression you used was that you wouldn't 'jump me'."

"I did say that. And I said that for a reason."

"The reason being to make me feel safe here."

"You are safe. And I will never hurt you."

"I'm not ready." *I think.*

"Ready for what?'

"For what you're proposing."

"Proposing? Oh no, I am not proposing. I am offering. You are ready, and you don't need to convince yourself yet." I looked at Simon, smiling unabashedly about his intentions. "I will re-introduce you to the finer pleasures of life." He stretched his arms over his head, tilted his head and patted the spot next to him on the couch. I didn't move, but Midnight settled himself beside him. Simon chuckled, patted the cat, and lowered his voice.

"If you need time, you've got it, but I can see it in your eyes. Ease your burden. Enjoy some passion without having to go find it. I'm yours for the taking."

He smiled, discretely re-adjusting the growing arousal in his jeans. He then rested his folded hands over his zipper, content that I had noticed. He was definitely ready, and I felt curious.

"You're a very persuasive man, and…"

"And I know you won't wait until the end of the day. I don't think you'll last an hour, with us sitting here with nothing else on our minds." His magic was working, as I'm sure it had with many others. He took full advantage of his attributes. "You know, there are new tricks we've learned over the years. I have lotions that will float you to heaven and back. Nice and slow." His voice became deeper and more seductive. "And being with a woman who hasn't been satisfied for a long time is really my…" He let the unfinished sentence linger. *Such a smooth talker.*

Simon took his hands away from his zipper to reveal the large bulge in his jeans. My body tingled in response to feelings that had been suppressed for years. His mellow smile melted my resistance.

"Nothing to do, no where to go, and no one to interfere." I picked up my cup, forgetting it was empty.

"I need a shower." He smiled, leaning his head against the back of the couch, shifting his gaze between my eyes and the bathroom door.

"I think I should help you."

"I…I don't think so." He groaned softly. "The look on your face tells me you really do need help." He readjusted the package in his pants, and the tip of his penis now edged its way above the top of his loose jeans. He made no effort to conceal it, aware I had seen it.

"Simon, you are…" Simon got up off the couch, sauntered towards me and took my hand. I was on fire. His strong arms helped me out of the chair, and I couldn't resist.

"Making you happy? Come with me. You need a little help. Unfamiliar house…unfamiliar bathroom…not sure where the shampoo is. You might get lost." I couldn't resist as Simon led me quietly to the bathroom. He slowly turned me around to face him. I leaned weakly against the countertop, and he pressed his entire body against mine gently, swaying me from side to side. *I haven't even unpacked…*

"I haven't brushed my teeth…"

"Mmmm, coffee breath, my favorite. His hands rested lightly on my shoulders and his erection leaned into me, arousing a new surge of lust. His hands moved to my back, and up under my pajama shirt. They felt large and warm, moving gently up and down my back, and then below my belt line. He caressed my waist, then slowly eased my shirt up and moved his mouth to my right nipple, licking it, then blowing air against it. His mouth moved to my left nipple. My legs felt wobbly.

Clothes still on, he led me into the warm steamy water of the shower. He undid his zipper, and freed himself from the confinement of his clothes. He leaned my back against the tiled side wall, closing my eyes with his fingers. He kissed my forehead, the tip of my nose and then my mouth. He separated my lips with his, water streaming between us. His hands moved back to my nipples, clearly outlined under my shirt. He applied soap to his hands, then slowly applied the lather in circles to my breasts, starting with my nipples and circling around them lazily. He gently freed one of my sleeves, then the other, lazily lathering my breasts again more firmly before moving to my back. Slipping off my pajama top and camisole in one move, my hands rested limply on his shoulders before he guided them to his member. He lathered my hands, which in turn lathered him, now high and firm.

"Easy, Grace, nice and easy. Take your time." He repositioned my hands above my head and watched as the steamy water tingled against my breasts. His lips gently sucked each nipple, his tongue rolling each tip in a rhythmic motion. His soapy hands moved slowly down my back, then radiated to the front of my waist. While one hand played randomly with my breast, his other soapy hand slowly lowered my soaked pajama bottoms to the shower floor. His hands moved up and down my thighs in a circular motion, moving closer to the middle with each cycle. His hand followed my thighs up to where they met. He lathered his hands again and both of his hands found a place to play.

"I'm not sure I can stand much longer."

"I'll help you. I want you totally satisfied." Simon repositioned my foot on the shower seat and slowly continued his rhythmic movements. He knelt down and continued with his tongue. He leaned in to hold me, as if to share the orgasm pulsating through me. I felt his heart pounding strongly. His member found its way home and continued its steady rhythm until he climaxed. I was drained, and shivering. He brought me to a state of pleasure I could not last recall.

Simon turned the tap off and gently kissed my eyes, nose and lips. "Hope you don't mind washing these clothes in cold water."

"Why?" I whispered.

"We drained the hot water tank. And worth every drop."

"That was lovely."

"It's been a while since you had company in the shower."

"I can't remember when."

"I have more tricks to show you."

"I can just imagine."

"But later, because you're cold, and I'm starving. Leave the clothes and we'll wash them after." Simon passed me a towel and left to dress and make breakfast. Still weak, I dried off and went to my room, laughing in spite of myself for wanting to dress in privacy. If this was day one, it was going to be an interesting week.

Breakfast consisted of western style eggs with caramelized onions and fresh, toasted bread that Simon had picked up from the bakery earlier while I slept. We spent a lazy day on the couch, sharing intervals of silence with bits of each other's past. I don't ever remember doing that with Blair, who the conversation eventually shifted to. Because Simon spent more daylight hours with him than I did, he knew much about my life. It was Simon who convinced Blair I deserved a day at the spa for my fortieth birthday, which Blair would never plan on his own. He also persuaded Blair to stop complaining about my hair salon fees, and which nightclubs Tess should avoid. Simon and Blair had monthly lunches at a seedy strip club, using the excuse that the food was good and cheap.

"Free wings with pizza on Wednesdays." It would have been easier not to know.

"And what else?" I pressed on."What else was for sale there?"

"Lap dances were half price." I hadn't expected him to answer.

"And did Blair take advantage of that discount too?"

"Would it change anything if you knew?"

"So the answer is yes."

"The answer is very rarely, but yes."

"Anything else I should know?"

"Not really." I felt nervous.

"Did he ever have an affair?"

"Why would you ask that?"

"Because you would know."

"Someone was interested in him, but he never slept with her."

"Did she have a name?"

"You don't know her."

"Try me."

"I'm not sure. Maybe Nikki. Grace, that was at least ten years ago. She worked at the lumber yard where we got our supplies. She had a wandering husband who eventually left her. Blair gave her some good advice, and told her she was better off being poor and single than staying with him. They met for coffee a few times. Blair figured out soon enough that he would become just like her husband if he cheated on you, making that two broken marriages. So for the bad stuff you think he did, he still valued your marriage, perfect or not."

"Interesting." I wanted to believe him.

"Me, I leave before things get too complicated. Life is too short. If I have to spend more time working on a relationship than enjoying it, I end it."

"You've had a few."

"I won't deny that. Every relationship deserves a chance."

"What makes them work?"

"Beauty isn't everything, but it's a motivator. Intelligence helps, not only with earning capacity, but choosing which battles to fight, and which to leave alone. Needy is not good."

"There must be more."

"There's lots. Good sex keeps a partner coming home. I never screwed around, unless we mutually agreed our relationship was not exclusive."

"Anything else on your wish list?"

"Since you asked, I'll tell you. She earns bonus points if she cooks, cleans, and gets her own oil changed." I chuckled.

"So that's why Blair told me to schedule my own car maintenance."

"It freed him up to do more around the house."

"No, it freed him up to spend more time where he shouldn't." Simon ignored that.

"And there's nothing worse than fake," he rambled on.

"Fake like what? Like nails?"

"Boobs, nails, eyelashes. All that stuff. There's nothing worse than opening a gift expecting something natural, and getting plastic. I'm all for self preservation and looking pretty, but when the body parts don't match, it's as good as over." I gave up being angry, waiting for his next chauvinistic comment. With nine sleepovers left, it was unwise to argue.

"Breasts are beautiful. Over time, they are supposed to get softer, and line up or down their own way. Every woman wants a centerfold body, but we figured out that only one in a hundred has that body."

"Good of you to admit that. We don't hear that often. If we all accepted aging gracefully, everyone would be happier." Simon went on.

"You women beat yourselves up too much. You also compete with each other. So what if you have a few lumps and bumps in places you don't like. Accept them. Make the best of it."

"Point taken."

"You are naturally beautiful, Grace." It was an unexpected, genuine compliment.

"No one's said that for years."

"You are." I had difficulty acknowledging it.

"You know what made me horny last night, which incidentally was a long time to wait until this morning?"

61

"I haven't got a clue. Should I take notes, for future reference?" Simon picked my foot off the couch, inched closer to me, and took my sock off. He held my foot in his hand, and lightly kissed the tip of my toe.

"These toes are beautiful. They're clean and soft. These pretty toes don't need to have fancy polish on them. If you care for your feet, it tells me you take care of yourself. That makes me want to be near you. Simple as that."

"Anything else?"

"Well, if you're asking, it's also sexy cleavage. You leave a little to the imagination, like I see now, but not enough to see the presents underneath. I see your lacy bra strap, and the space between where it touches your shoulder and your skin. I like that." Simon undid another button of my shirt and with his finger fondled that space, my skin tingling in response. He was smooth. "When I saw you at your house yesterday with a bit of make up and that clean, white shirt, I was ready to take you, right there." I flushed. If Simon's intent was to repair my self esteem and my sexuality, he was quickly mending what Blair tore apart. And it felt nice.

I could not remember having a lazier, more satisfying weekend. It unfolded into a vacation from everything but work. Simon was courteous, giving me space yet luring me into his. On the second night, I accepted the invitation to share his bed. As promised, Simon was a very creative lover. We spent hours exploring and satisfying each other each night, oblivious to the world around us. The only tension between us was erotic.

April 29th

The last days at Simon's ended as they began, filled with easy dinners and lovemaking, which made my last days of work tolerable. I purchased new towels for Simon and linens for my bed at Livy's house. I met Sophie at a tiny bistro near Simon's for lunch to reassure her that I was alive and well. Soft Italian music blended with the aroma of fresh oregano and garlic. I wondered how many of Simon's other lovers had dined here. Blair would have fidgeted and balked at tasting something new. Sophie's interrogation began soon as we sat down.

"Looks like you're enjoying your stay with the cabana man."

"No stress, and no commitments."

"So.... when did you get naked with him? My guess is the second night." Sophie laughed out loud when I blushed. "I'll take that as a yes. Have you got a picture of him?"

"No."

"You should, and put it on your phone screen so that what's-her-name will see."

"Her name is Livy."

"And you move tomorrow?"

"The day after tomorrow."

"Maybe Cabana man can visit and spread his testosterone around. I'd like to come for dinner when they're both around. Should make for some interesting conversation" Sophie snickered, devouring the antipasto.

"That won't happen. I'm keeping a low profile. Nobody but you knows I'm there. I need to start job-hunting, and I want Tess to visit me. I need to know that she's okay. I've barely talked to her in a week." I felt like I had abandoned her. Sophie noticed, put her utensils down, and took my hands in hers. Her expression became serious.

"Look at me. Stop those useless thoughts. Listen to me. You quietly ran the show at home for at least twenty years. Tess is a smart cookie, and you know she'll follow your stable footsteps. You're doing a great job, and I'm jealous when I see how well she's doing. Now take a break, enjoy the moment, and quit worrying about everything else. You deserve a little heaven, and the only person who is going to judge you is you." *She's right.*

We shared dessert, split the bill, and I gave Sophie my new address. I picked up enough red geraniums to fill the clay pots in Simon's backyard and splurged on a new white shirt and jeans to wear tomorrow.

April 30th

The stark reality of my new world hit on Monday, my last day at work. Simon left his house before me. A packed lunch, labeled with a 'G' made into a happy face, leaned against my coffee mug on the kitchen counter.

I drove to work with the radio off. Other drivers were courteous, as if they knew to give me more space. The plant parking lot was dotted with a few vehicles, some familiar, and others I didn't recognize. Walking into the plant, I opened the glass door that led to the manufacturing floor to take a final look. It was damp, and morbidly quiet. Most of the machines had been disassembled and shipped out. Pools of oil on the floor were the only reminder of a once productive and noisy workplace. I felt like an outsider looking in.

The HR department was also uncomfortably quiet. I overheard Paul arranging an interview for himself and giving references for other employees. While packing up the final boxes of beneficiary files, I realized I was now a "friend with benefits."

The final four employees, myself included, met with a recruitment agency. Paul gathered us together like a protective parent, and directed us to a local eatery for an extended lunch where we exchanged lofty goals and emotional farewells. As no one was permitted to return to work, the various old potted plants other office staff left behind would whither away with the memories of Bernard Steel Works. Paul was the most emotional, promising good references and coming to terms with his own future. We didn't say good bye as our conversations would continue over Livy's back fence.

Effective today, I was no longer a Bernard Steel Works employee, and officially unemployed. It was a sick feeling. Not wanting to return to Simon's house, I drove to a large park nearby. I went for a long walk through winding brick paths. A handful of pigeons watched me from their perch on the shoulders of a bronze statue of an unknown soldier, splattered with bird droppings on his helmet, shoulders, and combat boots. The sun was bright, but the day was chilly. I returned to my car, took a few deep breaths, and tried to picture what tomorrow would bring. The lunch Simon packed lay on the passenger seat. The "G" was a small comfort as I unfolded the brown paper bag. A chicken and veggie wrap, red apple, and four small Toblerone bars rested in a dinner serviette. Each chocolate melted slowly in my mouth as I leaned against my seat and closed my eyes. The air cleared my head as the chocolate soothed my spirit, if only for a little while.

Simon had the table set, complete with candles and flowers when I arrived. The kitchen was warm, and the wine was cold. He kissed me lightly on the cheek and asked about my day. Dinner was a feast of roast pork, grilled vegetables and baked potatoes. I was grateful for his company. He reassured me that I was not the lost cause I had labelled myself to be. Simon turned the music on softly, transferring our drinks to the living room.

"Simon?"

"Yes?"

"I know we have no commitment to each beyond today, but you are welcome to visit my new place. You can meet Livy and Wilson, my new boss." Simon was distracted, watching my lips.

"I'd like that. Maybe you'll need a carpenter," he said softly, taking the wine glass from my hand and moving closer to me. Simon ran his finger in the space between my bra strap and skin and slid it off my shoulder. He undid my shirt button, enough to reveal the lace of my bra. I melted, again.

"You are such a perfect picture," he whispered as his strong hands massaged my thighs and slowly worked down my legs. He picked up my feet, one at a time, lightly kissing each of my toes and licking the bones of my ankles. He unbuttoned the rest of my shirt, slowly from the waist up, drawing a moist line with his tongue up to my bra, then blowing on the wetness he created. Straddling me, he unzipped his jeans. He slipped my shirt off, lightly outlining the edges of my bra with his fingers, then reaching under it to softly fondle my breasts. Simon removed my bra and dipped his fingers in his glass. He wet my skin with his fingers. He closed my eyelids. I heard the ice clinking in his glass, and felt his wet lips on my body. Simon eased himself out of his jeans, then mine. He continued his exploratory journey until we arrived in paradise one more time.

Simon lay quietly beside me. Although he said he'd like to visit me at Livy's, I wondered if he would. Simon's relationships were not about love, but about autonomy and sexual gratification. While we finished our drinks, he said I needed time to get settled before he'd visit. I wasn't convinced he was sincere. For ten days, I was pampered and refreshed. I hoped Simon would remember me, unsure if the feeling was mutual. I slept in my room, preparing for quiet nights alone again.

May 1st

Simon woke me, nuzzling his unshaven chin into my neck, and laid down beside me. The belt buckle of his jeans was cold against my back. He brushed my hair away from my face, laying next to me and supporting his head with his hand. His voice was just above a whisper.

"Mornin', Gracie."

"Mornin'."

"Restful night?"

"I barely moved."

"The perfect guest."

"A generous host."

"Enjoyed your week?" He kissed my forehead, then each cheek. *Maybe the last.*

"Yes."

"You're so beautiful. You deserve only the best."

"Thank you." He rolled out of bed, stretching his arms high enough so that his shirt became untucked from his jeans.

"Sorry to kiss and run, but I'm already late for work." I watched his face. "Are you okay?"

"I will be." I felt sad, and he knew it.

"Will you call me when you're settled at Livy's?"

"I will." The expression on his face became business-like.

"Keep the key for the day, in case you need to come back. It will be an exciting day."

"It will."

"Grace?"

"Yes?"

"Remember to take care of yourself first." His final moist kiss landed on my shoulder, the cool air sending tingles down my spine as he left the room. I rolled over, looking out the window into the back yard, wondering how many similar goodbyes were said in this bed, or his, and how many purses held duplicates of his key.

It started to rain again. Simon's scent lingered on my skin from the night before. I heard him whistling as he shut the back door, content and ready to move on. The rumble of his truck leaving was replaced with Midnight's meows. The huge feline jumped on the bed and stared at me, telling that me it was time to get up. Kneading his front paws on the mound of my hip bone, still warm under the covers, he checked the activity in the back yard, then meowed again. I scratched the fur behind his ears and he purred loudly. I sat up, cross-legged in bed, wrapping the covers around my shoulders. We both stared at the rain. He meowed and went to wait patiently by his empty bowl in the kitchen. *It was time to leave. I'd paid my rent.*

I showered and dressed, tucking a 'Thank You' card in the new stack of towels on the counter that said:

Simon:

Thank you for your hospitality.
Don't let your heart retire.

Grace

I wrote my new address and my phone number in the card. I made coffee, stripped my bed and washed the sheets. They would be ready for the next guest before I left. Midnight devoured his breakfast, likely his second serving. I sipped my coffee, leaning against the counter in the small kitchen. Simon left a defrosting bagel on a plate beside the toaster. I returned it to the freezer, not in the mood for breakfast. Midnight inspected my plants, which Simon assembled near the back door. I showered, dressed and wedged them between suitcases and other packages, determined to pack my car and not have to return to the house. I left Simon's key beside the towels, gave Midnight a scratch behind the ears and locked the door behind me. I backed out of Simon's driveway, not noticing that the outdoor planters, which I had filled yesterday with geraniums, had toppled over in the rain.

I drove to the bank and settled the final bills from my old house. Returning to my car, with clothes wet from the rain, I pulled Livy's contract from my glove compartment to review the details of the move. My house key would be available at the law firm after two o'clock. The car dashboard read eleven o'clock. With no desire to shop, no errands to run, and no job to go to, loneliness wrapped around me like a dark cloud. I watched the streams of rain separate around the bug spatters on my windshield until the condensation made a curtain. I didn't want to call Sophie, who was working. I had distanced myself from my old friends when Blair became ill, and ignored their calls after he died. At that time, I couldn't be bothered. Maybe I was depressed, and didn't realize it. No, it was grief. I'd never had three hours, with only my stomach and gas tank to fill. Sophie's advice, which was not to talk about my stay at Simon's, was good. I wouldn't have to explain why a new widow spent ten days sleeping with her husband's best friend.

Out of habit, or mindlessly, I drove to Bernard Steel Works. There was no traffic on this once busy street. Two rain-drenched men had just erected a flashy 'FOR SALE' sign on the front lawn, giving listing details for a North American commercial realtor. Eddy, the kind old security guard recognized my car and flagged me over with a wave of his baseball cap which was embroidered with the name of a new security agency. He was grateful to be employed, but at half his Bernard Steel Works salary. He fetched a parcel from his office, explaining that a man who wouldn't identify himself delivered it. It had no return address. Eddy wanted to mail it, but heard I had moved. I took the small but heavy square parcel, wrapped in plain paper, and scribbled my new address for Eddy on the back of a grocery receipt. He inspected it, his bifocals hovering unevenly at the end of his nose.

"Mmmm, Chestnut Boulevard. That's a pretty fancy street, young lady. You must have a better severance package than me."

"Not likely, Eddie. I'm renting until I find a job. Maybe three months." Eddy noted that on the back of the receipt.

"Maybe July?"

I nodded. "Or maybe longer." Fingering the package in my hand, I hugged Eddy tightly and left. My growling stomach missed breakfast, and it was almost noon. I drove to the coffee shop, where I had picked up my morning coffee for years. The parking lot overlooked the deserted factory. The rain continued, and my hunger trumped my curiosity about the package. Hoping to avoid being recognized, I purchased lunch via the drive through, and parked in the lot facing the factory.

I devoured my sandwich and coffee, while I looked at the neatly wrapped parcel. My first and last name was printed in thick black ink on a blank shipping label similar to the ones from the factory. The wrapping was secured with wide clear tape, which I peeled it off to expose a plain, black cardboard box. I wiggled the lid off to see Toblerone miniatures in the box. I fished my hand through the chocolates, then emptied them onto my lap. A parchment envelope was wedged tightly into the bottom, with my first name printed on the front. Inside was a parchment card with dried flower petals on the front. I popped a chocolate into my mouth and read the small, neatly printed words which filled the inside and back page.

May 1st.

Dear Grace,

The real heroes of the world are people who take the time to make a difference in some one else's life. (I'm not that creative - that came from another card). Two years ago my wife (44 and too young) died, and you helped me with the paperwork. You listened to me talk about her. I loved her, and still miss her. You were patient, and always had a kind word to say when I needed help. You always had time for me, and I really respected you for that.

I heard you also lost your husband, and I am sorry to hear that. He must have been a nice man to have such a wonderful wife. Now that we are both single, would you have dinner with me? I asked my friend to go to the security gate and get your address so I could send this to you, but the guard told me your address was private. He said you moved, but he would try to forward it to you.

I know it is very soon after your husband's death, and if the plant was still open, I would have given you more time. But now that we are no longer there, I am afraid I would lose you, or my courage, if I didn't write this now.

If you are interested, we could meet at The Lobster Shack by the plant on the Thursday before the long weekend in May. I am hoping you get this letter in time to decide. I hope seven o'clock would be a good time, and I will wait in the lobby for you. If you decide not to meet me, please leave a note with the hostess and I will understand. If there is no note, I will look for you.

Hope to see you soon,

Jim (from the Tool Room)

I tucked the card in my purse. Jim was a nice man who I never expected to meet again. I had a quick image of how much smaller his behind was than mine, assuming he'd also made that comparison. I remember how devastated he was when his wife died, and how differently I felt about Blair. A pang of guilt poked at me.

I was touched by his letter, and surprised by the invite. He had two children, close to Tess's age. Having just left the sizzle of Simon, I tucked the letter in the box. I was not playing that game again for a long, long time.

I stopped at the bank, a grocery store in Livy's neighbourhood, and a quaint flower shop. A chalkboard sign on the front door advertised hand-tied bouquets 'while we gossip'. The scent of gardenias filled the shop. I picked a generous assortment of white flowers from buckets lining the floor. I wished my stylist could duplicate the blonde highlights of the florist's thick, shoulder length hair. His fingers quickly manipulated the stems into a spiral twist. He secured the arrangement with rope twine and clear cellophane with his lime green shop label. "Mmmm...must be someone really special, or you've been very bad..." he whispered as he rang in the purchase.

I turned onto Chestnut Boulevard, and saw Livy's white Volvo in her driveway. I parked behind her, choosing the front door. The oversized bouquet was almost as wide as her front door. Wilson barked inside in response to the door bell. Livy opened the door, her face lighting up when I handed her the flowers. She was comfortably dressed in jeans and a light blue, long-sleeved sweater. Her skin was clear and free of makeup. Wilson competed for attention by dropping a toy on her bright pink toenails.

"Welcome, Grace! Welcome," Livy chimed, burying her face in the flowers. She recognized the florist's label. "Thank you! I love flowers from this shop. Isn't he a doll, and don't you love his hair?" I laughed.

"Every woman must love his hair."

"Come on in! We've been looking forward to you coming, weren't we, Wilson?" Wilson shook his head vigorously in unison to her comment, picking up his toy. A leather suitcase was parked near the leaded glass doors, which led to an office beside the staircase. An open laptop sat on a large glass-topped desk in the pristine, celery green and white room.

"Thank you, Livy. It's good to be here. How was your trip?" I asked nervously, parking my purse on the stairs near her suitcase and feeling like we were starting all over again. Wilson approached it cautiously and dropped his toy beside it, sniffing it apprehensively.

"Wilson, don't even think about it," Livy warned, gradually raising her voice until he retrieved his toy, and slumped down beside her. "Busy! I came home late and was too lazy to unpack." She looked at her watch, and took it off. "I'm still on Indonesian time. Wilson gets antsy every time he sees my suitcase. Sometimes he hides my purse, knowing I can't leave without it. Intelligent, but very emotional," she laughed, rolling her eyes and petting him affectionately. He rolled onto his back, unsuccessful in getting a belly rub. Livy peeked out the window. "Let's get your stuff inside before it starts raining again and have some tea before we both unpack." That sounded wonderful, and I unloaded the plants first.

"If you don't want to worry about these, we'll put them in the solarium, and the gardener will mind them. Most of the ones there were my great aunt's and if I had to look after them, they'd be dead," she laughed.

Livy transferred the plants as I unpacked the car. She also brought tea and fresh pastries on a large tray to the solarium while I settled nervously into a chair. The clouds were visible through the glass ceiling of this storybook setting; ribbons of blue sky now weaved between them. I peaked under my tea cup saucer.

"This looks familiar. The Spode pattern was the same as my grandmother's."

"Really? Aunt Maddy had these dishes forever," Livy chirped away, calming me quickly. Minutes turned into hours as we became re-acquainted. Livy was exhausted from jumping through time zones.

She worked for a company in Toronto which imported carved wooden furniture and home accessories for upscale interior designers. I recognized some classic Stickley pieces of furniture in this house. Livy mentioned the ornate mirror in the living room came from China, but not the similar piece that framed the nude picture in her room.

"If I'm not on the road, I'm deep in some airport room matching shipping labels to the container contents. They arrive on different flights so I spend hours there. Most of the Toronto airport customs and security people know me by my first name."

"All these exotic places."

"Indonesia is a neat place to visit, but not to live. Initially I was blown away by the culture. Imagine a family of four weaving through traffic on a moped. It's as scary as it is skillful." She yawned deeply and continued.

"I love the work, and it keeps me so busy that I don't have time to get lonely. My phone is my lifeline. And Wilson, he's as close to a husband as I'm going to get with this schedule." *Husband? That's unexpected, but calming.* I was immediately curious about the portrait in her room.

"You mentioned someone named Taylor the first time we met," I said, feigning ignorance. "Was he an ex?"

"Ahh, Taylor. You must not have seen my room." I lied, shaking my head. Livy took a deep breath and passed the dessert tray.

"Taylor is, ah, actually a female." I did my best to act surprised, not sure if I was ready to digest what Livy would say.

"Taylor is also a buyer who lives in San Francisco. At the time we worked the with the same distributers. We met at a trade show in San Francisco about four years ago. Taylor was going through a bitter divorce with her husband, and my husband had just checked out. It was my first of many visits to San Francisco and she took me around the sights and shops. We struck up a friendship, strictly platonic, and I stayed at her place whenever I was in town. Our common bond was really shopping, and avoiding dating men. That went on for about six months. After one very sleep deprived night, and too much wine, Taylor came on to me. I was too drunk to resist, and assumed she would be too drunk to remember the next day. One thing led to another, and we began this clandestine relationship, which lasted a year. We met once a month, and I'm convinced it continued because we were both lonely. She's bisexual, but I had no interest in women, before or after Taylor. Quite simply, one night became a year." I worded my next question carefully.

"We've all had messy relationships. But why did you mention your room?" Livy wiggled her nose, hesitated, then continued.

"Because there's a portrait of Taylor, beautifully naked, above my bed." Livy watched my reaction. I stayed calm.

"There must be an interesting story behind it." Livy nodded slowly, concentrating on her third choice of pastry.

"Oh, there is. Taylor imported many oversized, gilded frames, and the one in my room was on display at the exhibit where we first met. Her boss gave it to her in lieu of commission, and it stood propped up against a wall in her house, with no picture in it. I said that she needed to fill that frame with something really dramatic. She also knew I liked it. Months later, the framed portrait arrived on my fortieth birthday. My prim and proper English cleaning lady, who also worked for my great aunt, was here when it came and helped me open it. It was a very awkward moment, to say the least, because she recognized Taylor. She left that day, never to return. I wasn't sure what to do with it at first, because I was ending our relationship. No one was spending time in my bedroom but me. I couldn't put it anywhere else in the house, or hurt Taylor by hiding it, and she didn't want it back. So up it went above my bed. Taylor moved on with her life, and I with mine, and it just stayed up there. The frame is huge and valuable, and almost impossible to find a picture to fit in it. The bedroom walls have faded, so it looks worse with nothing above the bed. And, let's face it, it made for some pretty interesting conversations with the few guys who spent the night. One guy thought it was me, because Taylor and I look alike. And now that I've said more than you were interested in hearing, feel free to have a look at it." Although I had no prejudice towards same sex relationships, I appreciated knowing the portrait's history.

The sun had set by the time Livy oriented me to the nooks and crannies of the house, and the assembly of agencies that maintained it. The house deserved respect, and had been lovingly preserved. Livy hoped to live here indefinitely, but had no idea what the ultimate plan for the house was. To me, it was paradise.

I wasn't bringing any furniture into this house, but my clothes would be delivered in a few days. We delayed unpacking until the morning, as we were both exhausted, albeit for different reasons. We were settled in our respective bedrooms by nine o'clock, with Wilson guarding us closely. My new sheets were luxurious and crisp, and the street lights soft and calming. The Chestnut estate was old, but to me, a new place to heal, rest, and plan my future.

May 8th

My first week living on Chestnut Boulevard was like being on holidays for three. I hadn't heard from Simon, and made no effort to call him. I struggled with the true cost of consensual sex for a week, in exchange for accommodation. Was I stupid, vulnerable, or just naive? The sex was great, but careless. It was also humiliating to divulge my risky activities to the curious stare of my doctor, but a great relief to find out that Simon hadn't left me any lasting, unwanted gifts.

Livy proved immediately to be a delightful housemate. She was witty, intelligent, and intrigued me with her worldly knowledge. I understood her love of travel and meeting new people. What grief she experienced as a child sparked her desire to find, and see, the best in people. Compassionate and dedicated to her job, she worked countless hours in exchange for rare long weekends at home.

Wilson and I bonded quickly, and he saw much more of me than Livy. He slept at the top of the stairs, assuming the new responsibility of guarding two masters. It took me a few days to remember to step over his big frame on my way to the bathroom at night. I took great pleasure in walking and feeding him. He gave me a purpose. I drafted a new resume, feeling old because I started my job at Bernard Steel Works the day after a ten minute interview. I submitted my resume to a company within walking distance of my new home, hoping I could walk Wilson at lunch if Livy was away.

The neighbours on Chestnut Boulevard were significant contributors to the economy. Wilson had many canine friends, whose owners welcomed me warmly. The couple across the street had twin sons, who only surfaced in daylight to get in or out of their minivan. Senior couples lived on either side of Livy. Her house was second from the corner, and Jack and Ina Adams lived at the corner. In their early nineties, they celebrated seventy wedding anniversaries at this address. Their back yard faced Paul's side yard. The same lawn service maintained these homes. Ina still curled her hair with bobby pins, and never left the house without wearing wrist length gloves, and a netted felt hat to match her suit. She looked like an older version of Jackie Kennedy Onassis, and took her role as keeper of their house very seriously. Jack was still making good use of the sports blazers he wore to work decades ago. They rarely participated in conversations riskier than weather predictions. The aroma of Ina's baking was heavenly if my windows were open. Occasionally, we were gifted warm goodies on Royal Albert china. She reminded me of my grandmother, keeping us occupied on rainy Saturdays, baking sugar cookies from recipes she inherited from her mother.

The couple living to the right of Livy were a stark contrast to the Adams. Lenny and Jenny Russell were eccentric and unpredictable. Their free-form gardens were a mixture of weeds and perennials, which Jenny sporadically maintained. Her standard wardrobe was worn jeans and an oversized tee shirt left over from some film production Lenny had worked on in his glory days. Bras were not a staple of her wardrobe. Jenny regularly entertained me with animated stories, her winged arms flapping and setting off a chain reaction to her pendulous breasts.

One rainy afternoon, I was enjoyng Mrs. Adam's cookies with tea. The light was on in the Russell's kitchen the kitchen and the blinds were open. Jenny working at the kitchen counter, wearing a grey shirt I recognizing as part of her gardening ensemble earlier that day. She had discarded her jeans, wet from the dewy grass, but kept her oversized white socks on. As she opened an upper cupboard door and reached up, her shirt rode up to expose her substantial, nude bottom. Sinking into the couch, I was relieved the room was dark. Jenny sported a tattoo on her right buttock, which disappeared when her arms came down. In walked a barefoot Lenny, also with only a T-shirt on. His shirt covered his backside, from which his skinny legs with wasting muscles protruded like walking sticks. He walked in and out of my view a few times, periodically reaching under Jenny's shirt, to fondle various parts of her anatomy. Livy's prim and proper cleaning lady would have horrified.

Livy left for business on the second week, and I was alone in the house for the first time. Still learning which floor boards creaked and when the mailman came, I felt very comfortable. Tess visited, content, and happy with the break in her routine. We had breakfast in the solarium, and pizza in the upstairs study while watching movies. Being around a dog was a novelty to Tess, and Wilson took full advantage of the attention. It felt good to have her with me. I was honest in explaining that my financial losses were significant. Where we would eventually settle would depend on the new job I got.

I had left Jim, the Toblerone man's note on my night table, and Tess read it when she crawled in my bed in the morning.

"Mom, who's Jim?"

"An employee I used to work with."

"Why is he hitting on you?"

"He's not. He lost his wife a few years back. He's lonely."

"He asked you to dinner."

"He wants company. It's nice to feel appreciated."

"You're not going out with him, are you?"

"Probably not. Angel, the Lobster Shack is not a romantic place. People meet there for a cheap meal."

"I don't want you to go out with anybody else."

"I'll keep that in mind."

"I'm serious, Mom. I can't deal with you seeing someone else." Her lower lip pouted.

"This guy feels connected because we both lost our spouses. When his wife died, he was devastated. He loved her very much. Tess, I promise no one will ever replace Dad, or ever separate us." Silent and lost in her own thoughts, she clung to my arm for a long time.

When Tess left, I had a good cry. Wilson stayed close to my side, sensing my grief. At sundown, we went for a second walk. Returning to a silent house made me lonely. I read Jim's letter again. He sounded the opposite of Simon. Livy would be back in a few days, and would give me some good advice.

I tried to be productive. A nearby college offered interesting courses if I remained unemployed in September. With my salary continuing until December 31st, I had time to find work before dipping into my savings.

Livy insisted we keep the housekeeper, and I felt uncomfortable when she came. Never having had this luxury before, I ran errands when she came. I switched to the same brands of groceries Livy did, and kept the kitchen stocked with her favourite foods. I credited Wilson with helping me lower my numbers on the bathroom scale.

When Livy came home, this time from Thailand, I was as happy to see her as Wilson was. She gave me a big hug and a silk scarf with symbols that meant success, which I promised to wear for job interviews. She was exhausted after thirty hours of flying and layovers. Wilson and I watched her devour leftover spaghetti. I showed her Jim's letter.

"Good for you. Are you going?"

"I'm not sure."

"The Lobster Shack, eh? Not what I would consider a risky place for a date. He probably picked it because many people eat there alone, and he won't stand out if you don't show up."

"Ahh, you're right. Any advice?" She held the card in one hand, swinging her empty fork in the air.

"Well, consider the logistics. Dinner at the Shack takes about an hour, including appetizers. So if it's a bomb, you've wasted an hour and twenty dollars, assuming you skip dessert and split the bill." She squinted at the card. "I'd invest the hour in him. It took him at least that long to write this card." She had a valid point. Livy rubbed her hands across her full but lean stomach, inflating her cheeks.

"Call it a cheap meal, or a practice date." She laughed loudly.

"Perfect."

"That spaghetti was the best, Gracie. It's so nice to have these surprises, and I'm glad you're here. Wilson's not clinging to me, and I feel safer with you in the house. I hope you feel the same."

"I do," I said contently. Exhausted and full, Livy gave me a another warm hug, and headed for bed. Wilson followed her protectively as she dragged her suitcase up the stairs.

May 17th

Dinner with Jim happened on a warm evening. Dressed in a white cotton shirt, black jeans and sandals, I arrived five minutes late, and Jim was already seated and drinking beer. I recognized him, craning above a booth to watch for me. He was overdressed in an outdated navy suit, blue shirt and wide floral tie. He was clean shaven, and had a new hair style. He rose quickly and shook my hand with his sweaty one. I felt anxious, and told him so.

"I'm nervous too, Grace," he stammered.

"It's been a few months..."

"Six months to be exact. Eddy in Security said you got my card. I'm really glad that you came."

"Thank you. It was a fluke that I stopped by there."

"I came early to get a good booth. Far enough away from the bathrooms so you can't smell them or hear them." *Yuck.*

"That's very thoughtful."

"And more private, in case someone from the plant comes in." I hadn't considered this.

"Good thinking. You're all dressed up."

"Yup. The last time I asked a girl out was before I met Audrey. My daughter told me to wear a suit, but she didn't know I was coming to the Lobster Shack." he chattered.

"You look fine," I reassured him. "So, what's interesting on the menu?"

Jim ordered deep-fried shrimp, followed by deep-fried fish and chips. I opted for the lobster salad. He also ordered another beer and wine for me.

"Sorry to hear about your husband. He must have been a great guy."

"Thank you. He was a good dad, and a great carpenter."

"So he was a tradesman?"

"Yes. Mostly new homes."

"He's not been gone long."

"Ten weeks today." I cleared my throat.

"Geez, Grace. I didn't realize it was so soon."

"It's okay. Time helps the healing." Jim hung his head.

"I miss my Audrey. I still visit her grave every week." *Wow.*

"I'm sure it keeps you connected. Did you plant some flowers?" I didn't know what else to say.

"Yup, but the cemetery has strict rules, and if you plant something they don't like, they make you remove them. The water spout near her grave is broken."

"I see."

"The supervisor says it's in the budget to be fixed next year."

"That kind of sounds like Bernard Steel," I said, trying to change the subject. When the appetizer arrived, Jim ordered yet another beer.

"Yup. I can't say I miss the place, but I miss my friends."

"Hmmm. Are you working now, Jim?"

"Yup. I got a job right away. I can't sit still. I'm lucky because I got my full pension, and benefits." I knew that because I processed his paperwork.

Jim dipped each greasy, battered shrimp into the sauce, spilled some on the table, and unknowingly smeared it around with his sleeve. *Forty minutes left.*

"That's great. You're too young to retire."

"I worked six days a week. I couldn't just stop. I'd go nuts. How about you?" he mumbled, mouth full and food visible.

"I was there for twenty years, so I have a small pension."

When dinner arrived, Jim ordered more beer. He was such a contrast to Simon.

"I hear you were one of the last to leave."

"I was, and it was pretty depressing."

"I just saw the 'For Sale' sign. They'll never sell that old place. Too much crap in the soil."

"I didn't hear anything about the soil." I picked though my salad as Jim stuffed his mouth full. French fries slid off his plate as he tore at his food. Sauce accumulated around his mouth, which he cleaned off with his tongue. I lost my appetite, and put my utensils in the unfinished salad.

"You're not eating that?"

"I'm done."

"Mind if I finish it?" He pulled my plate over, not waiting for a reply. He continued eating, using my fork. I excused myself and went to the bathroom, checked my phone and my teeth, combed my hair and reapplied my lipstick, h*oping the bill was there when I returned to the table.*

There were two pieces of cherry cheesecake and coffee on the table when I returned. *A ten minute penalty for loitering in the bathroom.*

I ate half of my dessert and slid the rest to Jim, who finished it.

"You know, Bernard was polluted. I'm surprised more guys didn't get cancer. It seemed like everybody's husbands and wives did."

"The air and soil toxicology reports were within normal range." I said, actually remembering seeing the original reports.

"That's what they wanted us to hear. You know, propaganda. I didn't believe a word of it. I'm sure my wife got sick from washing my clothes, and you know, from my, ah, secretions," Jim said, between loud gulps of coffee. "Your husband died. You think that's just a coincidence? I don't."

"His doctor confirmed it was lung cancer, from smoking." Jim had no defense.

"Too bad. Where's Barry buried?" A guttural burp surfaced from his beer- laced breath.

"His name was Blair, and he was cremated."

"Then where do you visit him?"

"I don't. His urn is in storage, with some other things." His jaw dropped. "I respected his last wish." Jim straightened up.

"He scratched his head long enough to make a dent in his gelled hair. "His wish to be cremated, or you not to visit him again?"

"Both. Could we not to talk about this anymore?" He got the message.

It was a welcome sight when the waitress presented the bill, which Jim paid. I left the tip. As we left, he asked me out again and I politely declined, saying I was not ready. I wouldn't give him my number, lying that I might move away to find work. As I shook his hand, he planted a greasy kiss on my lips before I could turn away. Our cars were parked beside each other. I got in my car, repulsed when he unloaded a mouthful of spit before entering his. Not wanting to be followed, I talked to myself on my phone. I waved goodbye twice, and kept talking until he eventually drove away. I needed to coast, for a long, long time.

June 1st

That feeling of floating through my day replaced a previous life that was so focused on deadlines and details. I puttered around in the gardens, leaving the lawn for the yard maintenance crew. This was another luxury I never had. I replaced the icicle pansies in the urns on the front steps with short burgundy ornamental grass, vibrant flowers and lime green potato plants, which a nursery delivered for the gardeners. I imagined replicating this someday in the front yard of my own house. My home.

I sent some resumes to nearby places, based on their proximity to Livy's house. I received an email about scheduling an interview at a small insurance company, a thirty-minute walk from Livy's house. *Perfect.*

Livy helped me with my image. I'd lost a more few pounds, thanks to Wilson, and a healthy kitchen. I upgraded my wardrobe, convinced by Livy to invest more in quality than quantity. My outdated clothes went to charity. Livy arranged hair appointments for both of us, a referral from the florist with the gorgeous hair. He transformed my brown shoulder length mop to auburn layers, infused with copper highlights. I was lectured about investing in good hair products. A petite, Polish esthetician reshaped my eyebrows, threatening to send my picture to the tabloids if I ever neglected them again.

For my interview, I wore a suit. Feeling confident, I arrived fifteen minutes early to face Candy, whose outfit violated every office dress code policy. As I followed her down a narrow hall, oversized arm holes in her red sleeveless shirt revealed bulging saddles of skin. A barbed-wire wreath tattoo was partially visible on the small of her back. The overworked seam of her white pants created a chasm, dividing her dimpled bottom far deeper than could possibly be comfortable. Candy led me to a messy office to wait for a Mr. Vaughn.

Mr. Vaughn was no improvement over his receptionist. Poured into a dumpy suit in desperate need of pressing, he described the job as an entry level clerical position, but I was not under any circumstances to touch his African violets, which had long outgrown their pots. He'd call soon if I qualified for a second interview, shook my hand, and winked at me. His hand remained on the curve of my lower back as he led me back down the stained carpet of the hallway. I left him to use the bathroom to wash off the stench of his nicotine-stained hands. A toilet flushed, and Candy reappeared. Skipping the hand-washing, she applied another clumpy layer of mascara. She whispered that she was resigning next week to get married. I congratulated her as she waved a cluster of diamond chips under my nose.

The streetcar occupants on my ride home all looked tired and bored. Mr. Vaughn called within the hour with a job offer, which I declined with as much courtesy as I could muster. My mother's advice rose from my conscience, reminding me to never burn my bridges.

When I walked Wilson that evening, I saw a 'For Sale' sign on Paul's front lawn. I knocked on his door. Paul was happy to see me.

"Gracie! How's the dog walking business?" he asked, appearing tanned and relaxed. He was relocating soon to new job, shared his contact information, a quick hug, and some encouraging words.

July 1st

June coasted lazily into July and life on Chestnut Boulevard remained comfortable. The gardens were breathtaking and time spent with Livy and Wilson was not only enjoyable, but therapeutic. We became very close friends. My old life seemed very distant. Tess visited us often, and was thriving. Paul moved to Cleveland and his house remained vacant. Occasionally, a flashback of Simon's electricity stirred my senses, but overall I was quite content being alone.

Livy's hectic schedule took her to places I'd never heard of. I'd worry like a mother when she was away, and she was genuinely touched by my concern for her well-being. She often brought me a small gift with a story about its origin. She constantly reassured me she was safe. On her long weekends home, we would vegetate, laughing over hair-raising stories about her bartering adventures, and the hand gestures she used to overcome language barriers. She described in detail the Indonesian culture she was now so familiar with. Furniture manufactures utilized dozens of people living in remote villages to craft pieces from wood right in their homes. Workers chain-smoked in decrepit factories, petrified of reporting any safety violations for fear of losing precious income that supported multiple family generations.

The villagers swooned over Livy's blonde hair, blue eyes and fair skin as if she were a goddess. Men made shy advances, with the glimmer of hope that Livy would be their gateway to new lives in America.

If there was an especially unique piece of art or furniture that arrived, I'd be summoned, with lunch, to her company's warehouse to see it. Her co-workers admired her enthusiasm and creativity. Livy carried multiple shopping lists for clients who trusted her good taste. Her boss occasionally rewarded her with extended layovers in exotic resorts. Bali was her favourite, and when she offered me a flight using her travel points to join her in the fall, I was ecstatic. She was such an amazing woman, but I often wondered how she could squeeze anything more into her life, such as a partner.

Contrary to my first impression, Livy was not wealthy. She shopped wisely, and her only real treasure was her aunt's platinum and diamond eternity ring, which was always on her right ring finger.

One evening over pizza, we dissected our marriages. Livy was divorced from a wealthy real estate broker, twelve years her senior. She married him for what she thought was love, despite signing a pre-nuptial agreement. He was more interested in sex and an escort to social functions, then cultivating a marriage. A true trophy wife, she left after three years of the same abuse and neglect she recognized in her adopted parents' marriage. She fled with a few suitcases, less than she brought to the marriage. Her only matrimonial ring, which she first saw at her wedding, was a gaudy reconfiguration of mismatched gems inherited from his family. Livy laughed bitterly, describing how she printed 'Y_U REPULSE ME' with a permanent marker on the white marble kitchen counter, placing the ring between the 'Y' and the 'U'. Years of counselling helped her recover, and these fees were the only financial settlement she was awarded. Livy never missed a session, determined she would never be hurt again.

What Livy lacked in family, she compensated for with a large and diverse circle of friends. Many lived in cities she frequented often, and also called on her when she was home. Other than the elusive Uncle Norman, she never mentioned having relatives. She avoided serious relationships with men, but occasionally had an overnight guest. She never mentioned

Taylor or their history. Other than warm and welcoming embraces when greeting or leaving for a trip, she had no romantic interest in me.

I sold my car, with Livy's encouragement, because it needed work and I rarely used it. I had some savings, which was a novelty to me. When Livy traveled, I chauffeured her to the airport, and at her insistence, used her vehicle to run errands.

Our friendship meshed tightly together. I felt closer to her than any other friend, and was somewhat protective of her when others called for her. After all, Livy trusted me in every way; with confidential secrets, Wilson, and of course, her home. I knew every rattling pipe, squeaky door, and character flaw. I knew each finicky botanical in the solarium and outdoor gardens, and appreciated the painstaking care they required. I admired the dedicated employees who had maintained the property for years. Wilson now occupied my room when Livy was away, but returned to his guard post at the top of the stairs when she came home.

July 14th

Livy left on her next buying excursion, this time to China. I found a scribbled note on the kitchen counter after she left, pleading for me to accept a six-month lease extension. I was thrilled. Kristen Castle, the same lawyer I had initially met with, witnessed my signature on the lease renewal at her office. Less suspicious, her narrow eyes still scrutinized me before I was dismissed again. She asked about my job search, and I responded in my sweetest voice that the job market had been soft this summer.

July 17th

I submitted my resume to the local hospital, hoping for something administrative but willing to volunteer, and I did get a call from the volunteer coordinator. The hospital was an easy ten-minute walk, and after a short interview, I was asked to help in the flower shop. I accepted, with the hope that this may lead to a paying job.

Livy and I communicated often when she had time. She was enjoying her trip, landed a few new contracts and was excited to show me some unique pieces of art when she got home. She even visited a Volvo dealership to see the new models. Already gone a few weeks, she expected to be away longer than usual, and as always, would forward me her flight itinerary.

My first day at the hospital was great. I felt confident socializing with all sorts of people. Fitted with a loose pink smock and sensible shoes, I used kind words for worried visitors, and congratulated new fathers. The florist with the great hair, a very personable guy, delivered buckets of reasonably priced bouquet arrangements which always sold out.

July 31st

I hadn't heard from Livy in more than a week, which was unusual for her. After a second prompt, she texted me back.

'So sorry, my friend. Very busy. Back Aug 3rd, with a new surprise! Met a great guy, and am bringing him home for a few days before he flies to New York. Will send details when I arrive. We're on different flights. His hotel is near the airport, so I might spend the night there. No need to pick me up - will call when I arrive. Take care. Miss you big time!
Luv, Liv.'

August 3rd

Whoever Livy brought home would be wonderful, yet I felt awkward sharing what was also my home. Yes, my home, but not my house. I missed her like a sister. My florist friend created a masterpiece of flowers for the kitchen, and delivered it to me at the hospital flower shop. I could have sold it twice in the three hours I was there. I washed Livy's car and bathed Wilson, regardless of his need for one. I checked Livy's flight itinerary, which was on time. I took Wilson for an extended walk and fed him. We were ready for our Livy to come home.

Livy's arrival was on schedule for 11:50 PM. I flipped between the news channel and the late shows. Wilson began pacing at 10:00 PM, wondering why we weren't down for the night. I rubbed his neck and back. His ears perked up and he tilted his head when I told him Livy was bringing company home. When I stopped talking, he resumed pacing, periodically groaning about the change in his routine. Livy called me at 11:40 PM. Her flight arrived early, but she had a lot to clear through customs. She couldn't wait to come home. When I switched the phone to speaker mode, Wilson barked, wagging his tail and pawing my knee. Livy was excited, chatty and anxious for me to meet Nigel, her new man. His flight was due to arrive soon. She said not to wait up, and that she would call tomorrow morning. Relieved she was back on Canadian soil, I lumbered off to bed, with Wilson shuffling behind me.

August 4th

I bolted upright in bed to the unexpected sound of the old house phone ringing beside me. My bedside clock flashed 7:35 AM. Fumbling with the receiver and swallowing dryly before saying hello, a male with strong South African accent spoke.

"Would Olivia Bless be home?" Not recognizing his voice, I asked his identity.

"My name is Nigel." My heart skipped a beat.

"Oh, yes. Hello. This is Grace, Livy's housemate." I said hoarsely. "Are you the Nigel that she was meeting last night?"

"Yes, that's correct. She was to meet me when my flight landed, but she must have come home instead." I attempted to organize my thoughts. Wilson groaned lazily beside my bed, not in his usual spot in the hallway when Livy was home.

"Could you hold for just a minute? I'll check if she's here." My heart pounded as I rushed barefoot down the hall and around the stair railing. Livy's door was ajar, and her bed lay untouched. I hurried downstairs, Wilson in pursuit, our steps pounding the risers in unison. No suitcases in the hall. No purse or shoes scattered in the front vestibule. Her vehicle was in the driveway where I left it. I called her name loudly. I ran upstairs, a strange fear grasping at my throat. I sat on the bed, catching a few breaths before picking up the receiver.

"Nigel?" My hands were trembling.

"Yes."

"She must have been delayed at the airport."

"Then I misunderstood her."

"When did you speak to her last?" Nigel asked, his accent and speech accelerating. I couldn't understand him, and asked him again.

"Olivia texted me at 11:44 PM, Canadian time. She was held up in customs, then was to meet me after. I waited until 3:00 AM but couldn't locate her. I assumed she went to the wrong terminal or gate, and she wasn't at my hotel. I texted her when I checked in, and fell asleep." It didn't make sense to me. Livy knew the airport well, and wouldn't make mistakes about terminals or gates.

"That's odd. Livy called me at 11:40 PM and told me she might spend the night at your hotel."

"Then she must still be at the airport."

"I'm going to the airport, Nigel." I checked the time. "I'll be there by 9:00 AM."

"Where can I meet you?" he asked. I imagined Livy's elbow poking my side, telling me to be nice to him. I had no idea where to meet him. *This man should call a cab, assuming he works. Of course he works. Livy would not bring home a stray. I hope. Be nice, Grace.*

"I'll pick you up."

"If that's not an inconvenience."

"I'll be there in an hour. Which hotel?" I wanted reassurance he was at the same hotel Livy told me.

"Outside the main entrance. I'm in Suite 901, if you wish to ring me back to confirm." I wrote his hotel and cell phone number quickly, repeating them back correctly. "You'll be driving the Volvo?"

"Yes." *He knows the car. That's good.*

"Nigel, when did you last see her?"

"In Shanghai." He paused. "Two days ago."

"It doesn't matter right now. I'll meet you in an hour."

I showered, dressed and took Wilson for quick walk. I checked my cell phone. Nothing from Livy. I checked the house phone again. Nothing. Maybe she was sick, and went to the hospital. Maybe the customs office was detaining her phone because an item she brought raised suspicions. It had happened before. I imagined her, exhausted, but still looking like a Vogue magazine cover.

I drove too fast to the hotel, missed the driveway, turned around and maneuvered through traffic back to the entrance. A tall and very handsome man dressed in a pressed cream linen suit confidently approached the car, and gave it a once over. He bent forward to look through the passenger window, a lock of dark wavy hair falling over his eyebrow. His eyes were coal, blending with his deeply tanned complexion. I cautiously opened the window and he nodded politely.

"You must be Grace."

"I am." *Livy has chosen well.* Nigel tossed a worn, tan leather laptop bag on the back seat, but had no suitcase. He crammed his lanky frame into the seat beside me, adjusting it to accommodate his long legs. I smelled clean skin and faint cologne, the scent of tangerines. I shook his powerful, tanned hand.

"Nigel Anderson. Pleasure to meet you, Grace. You look like your photo."

"My picture?"

"You and Wilson are on her laptop screensaver." I didn't know that. "She's excited to see you both."

"She's not usually gone this long." I eased into traffic, and headed for the airport. Nigel ran his manicured fingers across the dash and centre instrument panels.

"Nice car. So she does drive a Volvo."

"Why would you say that?"

"Because I own a Volvo dealership in China."

"That is ironic." *Now I know where he's returning to.* "How long have you been in China?"

"About three years."

"And that's where you met Livy?"

"Precisely. At the dealership. She popped in to look at the new models. My Chinese salesman couldn't manage the language barrier, so I stepped in."

"China's not your original home."

"Correct. My father is South African, and my mother is a true New Yorker. They live in Manhattan now, but I grew up in South Africa."

"That's a lot of air miles," I kept the conversation light.

"I'm on my way to visit them, after a few days here with Livy."

"When did you meet?" Nigel glanced at his phone.

"Exactly seven days ago," he beamed.

"Ah, a new romance. Have you been here before?"

"A few times. It's very cosmopolitan."

"Yes it is." There was a gap in our conversation because of the roar of air traffic. We entered the airport parking garage, circled a number of levels to find a spot. Nigel retrieved his bag, and we walked to the terminal. He was at least six-and-a-half feet tall. We kept checking our phones. No word from Livy.

"Should we could try her office?"

"Good idea. Do you know the number?"

"I do." I dialed her office number, and a receptionist I recognized answered. "Hi, Abby. This is Grace Sheehan."

"Hey, Gracie. I was just about to call Livy."

"That's actually why I called. Has she checked in with you this morning?"

"No. She messaged me last night when she arrived and said she had stuff to process at the customs desk."

"That's the same message she left me and her friend."

"Her friend from China?"

"Yes," I replied, looking at Nigel.

"Where is that girl, anyway?" Nigel checked his phone again, shrugging his shoulders.

"That's why we're calling. We haven't heard from her since last night. We just arrived at the airport, and are assuming she's stuck at customs. I'll have her call you when we find her."

"Ditto here." Abby took my cell number. We found a customer service desk, and a young man in uniform smiled politely. Explaining our dilemma and giving him Livy's name, his synthetic smile evaporated.

"Could you spell the name, please?" When Nigel passed Livy's business card over, he immediately picked up the phone.

"It's Angus from customer service. I have two people here looking for Olivia Bless." Her name rolled off his tongue as if he knew it well. He wore a grave expression. Nigel shook his head and whispered, "Something is wrong." Angus said a few quiet words over the phone and hung up. He cleared his throat.

"Someone will be here shortly to assist you." He kept Livy's business card in his hand. Avoiding eye contact, he waited silently, shifting his focus between the monitor and the expansive terminal. He fidgeted with his name plate and straightened his tie. Within minutes, two men arrived, one behind the other. A paunchy, grey-haired security guard positioned himself beside a tired police officer in a protective vest. The officer approached us, leaving the security guard behind. Angus handed Livy's business card to the officer who inspected it, flipped it over and without looking up asked, "You're looking for Olivia Bless?"

"Yes." My throat was parched. "What's wrong?"

"And you are?" he asked, watching both of us.

I introduced myself, then turned to a distraught Nigel, who started to fidget, which unsettled me more. Suddenly and repeatedly, he put his hands over each set of pockets in his suit. The officer put his hand closer to his gun.

"No, no," Nigel hissed, exasperated, tossing his passport and wallet on the counter. The officer snatched the passport.

"Nigel Anderson. I live and work in Shanghai. I arrived in Canada last night. I was scheduled to meet Olivia..." The officer blinked his eyes repeatedly, shook his head, and raised his index finger to interrupt Nigel.

"Relax," he said cautiously, eyeing him carefully. "We'd like a few moments of your time."

"Look, let's..." Nigel was interrupted.

"We need to speak with both of you in private."

"Why?" I asked.

"There has been an incident involving Ms. Bless."

"What kind of an incident?" I interrupted.

"I can assure you we'll give you all the details you need to know."

"What happened?"

"We would appreciate your assistance by asking you both a few questions first."

"I don't understand."

"You will soon. Our station is onsite. We'll go there to discuss your concerns."

"But where's Livy?" I insisted.

"Ma'am, we'll answer all your questions as soon as we clear up some of ours," he replied clearly and slowly, watching Nigel intently. Nigel picked up his bag and gestured for me to go ahead of him.

We were escorted through the enormous glass terminal, our footsteps silent on the shiny terrazzo floor. I struggled to keep pace with Nigel and the constable. The portly security guard fell silently into step behind us. Nigel secured his bag strap over his shoulder and anchored the bag tightly between his arm and chest. We weaved through travelers, some balancing unstable mounds of baggage on luggage carts, while others rushed wheeling carry-ons behind them. The officer took us through a long, sterile and inconspicuous hallway. He abruptly stopped and swiped a security card, which opened a set of frosted glass doors. We were led to a small, empty room where a middle-aged female in civilian clothes sat. Limp handshakes were exchanged. He introduced us to a detective who asked that we call her Kathleen. She was in dire need of good night's sleep and a major overhaul with the florist's hair stylist. Her coarse blonde hair made its own statement, with the left side noticeably more untamed than the right. She repeatedly tapped a pen from tip to end on yellow lined paper, watching us choose our seating. She commanded the conversation.

"Thank you for consenting to help us with this case." *I didn't consent to anything, nor did I know Livy was part of a case.*

"Before we can offer any details to you, we need to ask you a few questions. Sir, I'm going to ask you to step into another room - we need to speak with Mrs. Sheehan alone." My heart skipped a lot of beats as my brain tried to process what was happening. I watched Nigel leave, suddenly feeling I was watching a crime show and he was the accomplice in something horrific. The constable escorted him out of the same door we came in. Nigel clutched his bag, not looking back. *Am I going to see this guy again, or read about him in the news?*

The constable returned. Detective Kathleen passed the paper and pen to the constable, then initiated a slow and methodical layering of questions. She remained expressionless.

"I'm not sure what you know, but there has been an incident concerning your friend." *Calm down, shut up, and try to listen, Grace.* "Please tell us your relationship to Ms. Bless. The more details you give us, the better. Please take your time and speak slowly. We are recording this information." *Just like a TV show. Should I be asking for my lawyer?*

I took a deep breath and began by explaining, in disorder, my dilemma of losing Blair, then my job and selling the house. Detective Kathleen seemed exasperated. She circled her hand and motioned to me to speed up my story. *Very rude.* The constable interjected, politely asking for my driver's license to confirm my name and address. He took photos of it with his phone. She shot an annoying stare at him. Kathleen wouldn't win any hospitality votes.

"So how long have you known Ms. Bless?"

"Since early April. I think April 9th."

"Can you describe your living arrangements?"

"I moved in with her on May 1st. She's a very nice person."

"Do you pay rent?" It seemed to be an irrelevant question.

"Sort of. Because an estate owns the house, I split the utility bills with her, which is $500.00 per month."

"Mmmm. I know that area. That's a very inexpensive arrangement for that neighbourhood."

"My former boss, who was her neighbour, introduced us. I look after the dog when Livy's away."

"What's his name?"

"Wilson. He's a golden retriever."

"Not the dog. The neighbour." She was not impressed with me.

"Oh. Paul. Paul Maxwell."

"Are you, or did you ever have a romantic relationship with Ms. Bless or Mr. Maxwell?" I was insulted by the inquiry.

"What? No! Absolutely not." I glanced helplessly at the constable. His expression was flat. Her thick eyebrows became one when she leaned forward to continue her interrogation.

"When is the last time you saw Ms Bless, Mrs. Sheehan?"

"I think it was July 18th, almost three weeks ago."

"And how do you know Mr. Anderson?'

"I don't. I met him this morning."

"What can you tell us about him?'

102

"Very little. He's Livy's new boyfriend. She met him a week ago in China and invited him to stay for a few days in Toronto. He recognized me when I picked him up because Livy showed him a picture of me." The constable wrote quickly.

"Yes, we have her laptop." *Her laptop? What's going on?* "And other than Mr. Anderson, did she mention any new friends or acquaintances?"

"No. She has friends all over the world. Please tell me where Livy is," I asked softly, now certain that something was drastically wrong. The detective looked at the constable, who put his pen down while she folded her hands as if to pray. Her voice lost some of its edge as she looked directly at me.

"We appreciate this important information." She took a drink of water and exhaled a slow and deliberate breath. There was a knock on the door, and an exchange of nods. I opened my mouth to speak, and she held up her hand to silence me. The constable returned with Nigel, looking haggard and angry. He slumped in the seat he occupied earlier. The detective looked at both of us. "There has been an incident in this terminal involving a female, which we feel certain is Ms. Bless." I gasped. Nigel stood up.

"Look, just get on with it," he snorted. She ignored him and continued.

"Last night, or rather early this morning, at approximately half past midnight, there was a shooting in a public access area."

My lungs stopped breathing. I couldn't inhale or exhale. Nigel's tanned face paled. "Despite our tight security measures, it appears that someone fired two shots, one of which struck Ms. Bless. Although we are still interviewing witnesses and reviewing security videos, many people saw her fall and we were very quick to get her help. She was rushed by ambulance to hospital. Despite the efforts of the emergency medical services here and at the hospital, I regret to inform you the doctors were unable to save her. I am sorry to give you this unfortunate news."

The room spun. I felt nauseated. Nigel's head dropped to his hands, his long fingers clenching his tousled hair. The room became very cold. Nigel spoke first.

"Where is she?"

"With the coroner." Nigel sank into his chair, exasperated.

"What? Why?" Kathleen remained professional. She provided a perfunctory explanation in a slower octave.

"In Ontario, by law, the coroner is tasked with finding the circumstances surrounding any unusual, or unexplained death. To do so, he or she needs to answer five questions – who, what, where, how and by what means. The last question, specifically 'by what means' is broken down by natural causes, accident, suicide, homicide, or unknown." I watched her mouth continue to move, unable to grasp what she was saying. She ignored me, directing her attention to Nigel.

"So far we only know where she died and based on a very preliminary investigation, how she died. With the coroner's findings, we need to decide whether Ms. Bless was the victim of a homicide." The word homicide echoed in my head. Exhaling heavily, she wrapped up her explanation.

"We are the lead investigators, and will update you as the case progresses." Nigel was not satisfied, and pumped her for more details.

"So you have no idea who did this?"

"It's too early to tell. This airport is an enormous, heavily guarded facility, however thousands of people pass through here at a relatively fast pace." Nigel looked hard at his watch, and counted his fingers for emphasis.

"So after nine hours you know nothing else yet?"

"The one piece of concrete evidence is in Ms. Bless."

"What does that mean?"

"The bullet penetrated her chest and is still lodged in her heart." This statement I heard clearly. I was going to vomit. "The coroner will forward that evidence to us shortly." My stomach heaved and I gagged.

"I need to use the washroom." Noting my distress, the constable took my elbow and led me quickly to the bathroom. In the stall I lost whatever liquid was in my gut, the taste of bile repeating in my throat. My legs felt rubbery. I sat on the toilet, feeling faint and chilled to the bone. Instinct took over and my head fell deeply to the gap between my knees. I was freezing, tasting sourness on my wet lips. The toilet paper wouldn't unravel off the roll. I picked impatiently at the edge, ripping a tuft of layers off to wipe my mouth. I attacked the jagged layers again, using the next wad to absorb whatever I could spit out. I couldn't believe what was happening. The little cubicle spun in front of me. *Don't faint,*

Grace. Please don't faint. The door from the hallway to the bathroom squeaked opened.

"Hello?" The constable's voice echoed through the cold room. "Are you okay in there, ma'am? Would you like me to call for help?" The constable asked quietly, attempting to maintain both my privacy and my safety.

"I'll be all right," I responded, and heard the door squeak shut. I stood up. Hovering over the toilet and unable to restore my balance, I sat back down on the cold porcelain, forgetting I had lifted the toilet seat up. Angry visions of Blair's neglect to replace the toilet seat mixed with more bile accumulating in my throat. Revolted by what human waste or germs touched my clothes, I stood up quickly. The coat hook on the cubicle door blurred, multiplied to two hooks, then back to one. There was gum in my purse to kill the taste in my mouth. *Where was my purse?* My brain programmed my feet to stand, and turn around to flush the toilet. *No flush handle.* A small black circle on the tiled wall above the toilet looked like a sensor. I waved my arm across it. No response. I repeated the effort vigorously. No change. Two women entered the stalls on either side of me. Undaunted by their environment, they made dinner plans.

As I opened the cubicle door, the whoosh of the toilet water flushed behind me. Shaky, and attempting to regain my composure at the sink, I washed my face and hands. The paper towel dispenser was empty. *Shit.* Weighing the option of drying my face and hands on my white shirt or returning to the cubicle, I chose the latter. The two women exited their cubicles to see me return to the stall. I tore the last shred of toilet paper away from the roll. I dried my face and hands, catching my ghostly image in the mirror. I wiped the black smudges away from my eyes, and recounted what the constable said. The bullet was still lodged in her heart. A heart, recently fluttering with new found happiness, was silenced.

Murder. *Murdered. Please...not Livy.* Shock abruptly shifted to grief. Opening the bathroom door, I was unable to stifle my loud, throaty sobs. The police officer put his hand on my shoulder.

"I'm very sorry, Mrs. Sheehan. She must have been a nice person."

"You have no idea," I bawled. He kept his arm on my shoulder, guiding me slowly back to the office. Nigel, looking dejected and exhausted, squeezed my hands and offered me tissues. Livy would have loved this gesture. The detective's facial expression softened, but continued with her questions.

"I realize this is difficult for you both. Did she have an ex-husband, or boyfriend, other than you, Mr. Anderson?" Kathleen shifted to face me, but Nigel took the lead.

"She divorced a man twelve years her senior after three years of marital abuse. He's a commercial real estate developer here in Toronto. She hasn't seen or spoken to him in years." I confirmed Nigel's statement, and gave his name to the constable.

"Any kids?" We shook our heads in unison.

"Family?"

"She has one living relative, an Uncle Norman," I sniffled.

"Who lives where?"

"A little village called New Pelham."

"Full name? For notification purposes. Next of kin." The surname spelled into the mosaic tiles on the front entrance floor of Livy's house was a constant reminder.

"Chestnut. Norman Percy Chestnut. I've never met him. Will you notify him?"

"Yes. Normally the local police does, however, in this case we will because of the circumstances. After we question him, the coroner's office will arrange to release Ms. Bless. We'll contact both of you tomorrow to sort out a few more details. Mr. Anderson, I assume you'll remain at the same hotel?" Nigel paused, and looked at me.

"Yes, I think it's best. I'm booked for two more nights." Kathleen turned to me.

"Mrs. Sheehan and Mr. Anderson, can our officers drive you home?" I declined, and offered Nigel a ride back to his hotel. Kathleen attempted to tame her unruly hair, checked her phone, and faced me.

"There's an unmarked cruiser stationed outside your home, and will be somewhere nearby for the next few days. A couple of detectives will also stop by the house. They're reviewing Ms. Bless's laptop and phone interactions, and may need to gather more evidence. Also, there will be a media release soon, so I'll warn you that reporters will attempt to contact you."

"That's all we need."

"We'll get you to your car to minimize any exposure here, but I would advise you to avoid them completely. Finally, if either of you believe someone would harm Ms. Bless, if she had enemies, or there was unusual behaviour she was involved in, please call right away. Even something trivial, or out of the ordinary for her. We're always available." Nigel and I nodded numbly. We were provided with business cards, and dismissed.

The constable led us through a barren hallway in the opposite direction to a fenced compound holding both marked and unmarked cruisers. He opened the front door of an unmarked car for me. Nigel crammed his long legs in the back seat, behind a mesh barrier. We were driven to Livy's Volvo and cautioned again about the media. Nigel offered to drive, but in the same breath confessing he rarely drove. We sat quietly in the car for a few minutes, absorbing the last few hours. He broke the silence as I drove out of the airport parking maze.

"What a nightmare."

"Ditto." Nigel hesitated, then spoke softly, looking out his window.

"We owe each other nothing. I've known Livy a week, but it felt like a year. If you believe in love at first sight, this was it. We kissed within minutes of meeting. She took my breath away, and the rest of the world didn't matter." Nigel's chin trembled, his voice distant. It was hard to drive through my tears. "The first time we parted was when she flew home. We had heaven on earth, and I would have sensed if something was wrong, or if someone was trying to...hurt her...." Nigel's voice wavered. I pulled into the hotel entrance and stopped. I believed him.

"Would you prefer to come to the house? Maybe you shouldn't be alone."

"No. No thank you, but that's very comforting." Nigel wiped his face. "Grace?"

"Yes?"

"Would you be kind enough to let me know what happened?" Nigel pulled out a thin silver pen and wrote on the back of his business card. "I'll be in New York City until August 20th". His name was embossed in gold on the matte black card. His coal eyes lost their luster.

"I promise I will. I'm glad I met you." I attempted a weak smile. Nigel gathered his things.

"And I too. I think we need each other more than we realize. Will you be all right?" He was genuinely concerned.

"I hope so. I've got Wilson at home." Crushed by this tragedy, I patted his shoulder. "We're in this mess together. We both adored her."

"She inspired me... and now..." he faltered.

"Call if you need company, and I'll do the same."

"Thank you. Thank..." the sobbing resumed.

"Take care, Nigel." He shook my hand, unfolded his long frame uncomfortably and hoisted his leather bag over his shoulder. He shut the door, and I watched him walk to the hotel foyer, where a couple of middle aged men approached him, armed with camera equipment. How would they know who Nigel was already, and where he was staying? I did not want to linger, and sped away, anticipating the security of the police presence when I arrived home.

I drove down Chestnut Boulevard, anxiously piloting Livy's car as if it was the first time. The car Livy would never drive again down the street she would never see. And the dog who would slowly realize he'd lost his master. A car was parked in the driveway when I arrived. The unmarked cruiser backed out, allowing me to park, then pulled in behind me. I heard Wilson barking in the house. Two young, male officers casually approached me, their badges as shiny as their boots.

"Mrs. Sheehan?'

"Yes." The officers identified themselves as Morgan and Ryan.

"The detective told you to expect us?"

"Yes."

"You've had an upsetting morning."

"That's an understatement." I fought back tears.

"Mind if we check inside first? Everything around the outside of the house looks fine." Relieved by their presence, Wilson was not, when I unlocked the back door. He barked loudly while the officers checked the house.

I fumbled through the simple task of making coffee for them. The phone rang, and I jumped when one of the officers yelled, "Don't answer that!" The call display showed the Adams number next door, which I advised the officers, but as directed, I let it ring. There were three additional messages, from numbers I didn't recognize. I heard the officers' heavy shoes rumble down the stairs as the last bit of coffee gurgled through the filter. The taller officer radioed in the 'all clear' message.

"You're safe, Mrs. Sheehan. Beautiful home." Morgan, a tall, very muscular officer, smiled with a boyish grin and white teeth. Ryan was his lean, clean cut, bespectacled partner. His last name sounded French.

"Thanks. I moved here in May." Ryan asked a few more questions, some of which I couldn't answer. He then asked which room was Livy's.

"Is, ahh...the woman in the portrait Ms. Bless?"

"No, it isn't." It was a gift from a friend, and it turned the guys on." The officers glanced at each other, camouflaging smiles behind their coffee mugs.

"And were a lot of guys up there?"

"None since May 1st. And not many, from what I heard, before I moved in."

"Any women?" Ryan's left eye twitched. *Did he just wink at me?*

"None." I answered their next questions before they asked them. "My husband died four months ago. I lost my job in April. I sold my house, and am staying here until I find work. I house and dog-sit when Livy goes, uh, was away on business. We're house mates, and nothing more." That satisfied them. Morgan scrolled through his notepad.

"And the owner of this property is, ah, the estate of Madeleine Chestnut?"

"That's correct. A law firm in the city manages the estate, and their lawyer is Kristen Castle. I was going there on Tuesday to extend my lease." I suddenly realized she may want to terminate the lease. Morgan saw my panic.

"We'll talk to them. Because Ms. Bless's death is still unexplained, they should keep business as usual."

"Why?"

"Because since we're not sure what we're dealing with, anyone watching the house shouldn't notice anything different."

"Gee, that's reassuring."

"We'll keep the house under surveillance for as long as necessary. I know this is difficult, but try to be aware, and follow your normal routine."

The officers also listened as I checked the phone messages. Livy's girlfriend called about a lunch date. The hospital also called, asking me to volunteer the next day. The officers suggested I take a short leave of absence. *Not so good for my reliability.* Two reporters called, vying for stories. The officers confirmed their numbers by checking their own data bank, and reminded me again to avoid them. The Adams next door left no message, but I suggested they were just nosy seniors. Both officers put their empty mugs in the sink, and headed for the door.

"Mrs. Sheehan, an unmarked car will keep watch in the interim. You are safe here, but please call if anything feels different or seems unusual."

They left, and Wilson was happy to monopolize my attention. I appreciated his company now more that ever. He followed me to the fridge. Grabbing a bowl of cereal, a glass and a bottle of wine, I double-checked the doors and trudged upstairs. I crawled into bed in my clothes, flipping through TV stations until an old comedy appeared. I put the half-finished bowl on yesterday's newspaper strewn across the carpet and watched Wilson finish it. My hand ran through his soft, warm fur. TV characters cackled in the background as I attempted to make sense of the last twelve hours. I sipped the wine, shifting blankly between the TV and the window. Who would ever want to hurt Livy? Did she have a secret life? Was this Nigel guy really who he said he was? Was Livy's traveling for business a front for something illegal? *How long can I stay here? Do I still want to stay here? Who'll look after Wilson? They better let me keep him. How will I explain this to Tess? Who is this Uncle Norman? Will he move into this house? What will the lawyers tell me....* The uncertainty of my future took me back six months, but the questions were all different...

The doorbell rang. *Leave me alone.* The radio said 5:45 PM. The wine bottle was empty. The bell rang again. I got out of bed, stiff and unsteady. The wine numbed me, if only for a few hours. I came down the stairs, expecting the police again. Mr. and Mrs. Adams were at the back door. I wished they would leave, but sure enough their be-speckled stares persisted, with Mrs. Adams' frail arms straining against the weight of a casserole dish. I opened the door.

110

"Oh, my. You poor dear," Mrs. Adams stared, shaking her head. She edged past me and unloaded her burden on the kitchen counter. It smelled wonderful. I'd eaten only cereal since yesterday. Ignoring me, Mr. Adams grabbed Wilson's leash as he thumped his tail against his thin legs.

"Back in ten minutes," he yelled as Mrs. Adams poked through the kitchen cupboards, oblivious to him. I set the island counter with place mats and cutlery. "Now find some nice wine and we'll watch the news when Jack comes back." *Oh shit, Livy's murder will be on the news.* "Can you put the TV on, dear? It's almost six o'clock." I adjusted the screen to face the island. Mrs. Adams pulled the casserole foil off to reveal a heavenly concoction just as Mr. Adams returned and the hall clock chimes rang. As if on cue.

"Is it on yet?" He flashed me the same protective look as my father used to, his eyebrows wrinkled and overgrown. "The police were at our house already. We told them you were very good neighbours. Young lady, if you're afraid, you can stay with us tonight," he offered. The 'old people' smell of their house was not inviting at any time, let alone tonight.

"Sit down," he said, patting the seat of the middle stool.

Straddled like a child between grandparents, Mrs. Adams filled my plate while Mr. Adams rationed my wine glass to half; more than enough for now. Mrs. Adams coached her husband on the adjusting the TV remote until the volume was blaring. Wilson disappeared when news anchor's voice exploded.

"Another homicide occurred yesterday evening in Toronto, this time at the airport. This is the third murder in three days, raising the level of concern for both police and the public..." A video panned the inside of the airport, zooming in on a small area of the terminal where police were cleaning up yellow and black caution tape. The scene switched to a grainy photograph I recognized as Livy's wedding picture. The reporter linked the unexplained slaying to 'the report of a missing woman, believed to be Olivia Bless.' He described Livy as a wealthy and attractive business woman, known to many, who traveled extensively. Confirmation of the murder victim's identity by police was being withheld until her next of kin was notified. When the scene switched to an open front door of a sprawling mansion, the caption on the screen identified the overweight, balding man as Livy's ex-husband. With a pathetic frown, he professed his eternal love for her and claimed to maintain regular contact. That was news to me; the police would figure that out soon. The next clip, of Nigel entering the hotel lobby, identified him as an acquaintance of 'the missing woman'. I saw myself driving Livy's Volvo away in the background, as two reporters pushed microphones into Nigel's face. He ignored the smattering of questions connecting him to Livy. Other than the reference to her ex-husband, I learned nothing new.

The phone rang. Mrs. Adams picked up the receiver, hesitated, then passed it to me. It was Sophie.

"You're home! I'm coming over. Have you spoken with Tess?"

"Not yet."

"Then you better call her before she sees it on the news. See you in half an hour." She hung up before I could object. I stared blankly at Mr. and Mrs. Adams. They stared back, like parents waiting for an explanation.

"It's my sister. She's coming over." Mrs. Adams clasped her hands, as if to pray.

"Oh good. Now we won't worry about you being alone. I'll just put these leftovers in the fridge. Come on, Jack, we're leaving. Call if you're afraid, honey, and Jack will run right over." Sweet as he was, the only thing Mr. Adams could protect were the secrets he could no longer remember. And he couldn't run.

Appearing from somewhere were Mrs. Adam's home-made brownies, followed by fragile hugs from both of them. I let them out the back door, then checked the lock on the front door. A modified van with a TV station logo was parked across the street. Two men stood nearby, one videotaping the house. The other, holding a microphone, was the same man that was at Livy's ex-husband's mansion. They came up the stairs and rang the doorbell, while my heart pounded as if their were thieves. Actually they were, of my privacy. I'd seen similar scenarios many times on the news. After three unanswered rings, they retreated to the van.

Sophie arrived within minutes, and the media reporters charged at her. Armed with an overnight bag and enough groceries to keep us quarantined for a week, she was clearly surprised, but remained silent. I let her in, and then texted Tess to brief her, reassure her that I was fine, and promised to keep her updated.

Sophie listened as I updated her, and passed on the detective's warning about not discussing anything about the case. As much of a nuisance as Sophie could be, having her with me was better than being alone. We walked Wilson under the shield of darkness, and cut through Paul's back yard to avoid exposure. Out of courtesy, I called Nigel. His voice mail picked up. I asked if he was alright, and invited him to stop by the house. I thanked him for being supportive, and gave him the option to call back, which he didn't.

August 5th

The call came from Detective Kathleen early in the day. The compassionate tone of her voice was much different than the previous day. Livy's identity was confirmed, and she died from a gunshot wound to her heart, fired from a distance of twenty feet. With the help of video surveillance and multiple, distinct tattoos, the shooter was tagged as a gang leader. A rival gang member, dubbed 'Hector,' was in hospital following surgery to extract bullets from the same gun that killed Livy.

Hector and Livy landed within minutes in Toronto, on different flights. Livy and another innocent traveller were caught in the crossfire of bullets aimed at Hector. The other victim's injuries were minor. The shooter was apprehended at his girlfriend's house in a midnight raid, and charged with murder. At this point, the detective explained, the police had no reason to believe this was anything more than an act of retaliation in a gang war, and there was no connection to Livy. She was very innocently in the wrong place, at the wrong time.

Kathleen again offered her condolences, and acknowledged our help in the investigation. After she spoke with Nigel to clear up a few inconsistencies, his passport was returned and he flew to New York as scheduled. There were, however, a few issues to resolve with the police, who would contact me shortly.

A black, unmarked cruiser arrived at the house just before noon. Sophie was with me, and greeted officers Morgan and Ryan at the back door. Wilson was as displeased with them today as he was yesterday. Sophie swooned over them with coffee and Mrs. Adam's brownies. Morgan complimented Sophie on her baking, who gave no credit to Mrs Adams. The officers confirmed that Livy's ex-husband last saw her two years ago in divorce court. The officers asked to speak with me privately, and I sent a reluctant Sophie out to walk Wilson.

The living room was chilly, even with the sunlight streaming into this normally comfortable part of the house. Morgan sat on the leather sofa beside me, while Ryan led the conversation. He explained that when a suspicious death occurs, the coroner's office releases the pathology report to the police who are following the case. He asked about Norman Chestnut. I knew he was Livy's uncle. Kristen Castle, the lawyer, confirmed that Norman was Livy's next of kin. They hoped I knew something more, however I'd never met Uncle Norman, nor was I aware if Livy had been in touch with him. Morgan left three unanswered phone messages at Mr. Chestnut's home. Before they could publicly release Livy's name, they needed to make a sincere effort to notify him. Livy died two days ago. I didn't know how I could help.

Ryan said that since Mr. Chestnut lived within reasonable commuting distance, they planned to drive to New Pelham tomorrow. Impulsively, I asked if I could go with them. Having had more contact with Livy than anyone, I wanted to be there for him when he heard the news. Because this was unusual, Ryan needed pre-approval from Detective Kathleen, and if she agreed, we could meet at her office tomorrow morning.

Wilson and Sophie were sitting on the front step chatting with a reporter when the police left. I called her in, shielding my face from the camera with the front door. She took her time coming in. Scolding her was pointless, but I reminded her that for our safety, the police told us to avoid the media. Sophie argued that because the case was solved, there was no danger. After a heated argument inside about my privacy, she agreed to not talk to anyone else, at least not until after until Uncle Norman was notified.

We spent the rest of the evening watching whatever news Sophie could find about Livy, which was no longer the local lead story. To my chagrin, we watched a reporter and photographer following a silent Sophie walking with Wilson. She frowned when she saw her image on the screen.

"Gee, I didn't think my hips were that big," was her only comment. Another interview with Livy's ex was aired, still contradicting the information the police gave me earlier. A sign on the front door of Livy's office stated the company would be closed for three days. When nightfall came, Sophie slept in Tess's room. Wilson circled quietly though Livy's still and pristine room, then assumed his post at the top of the stairs.

August 7th

Tuesday was unusually cool and windy. I dressed in a straight black skirt and crisp white shirt. The law office receptionist offered her condolences when I arrived at 10:00 AM as directed. Ryan and Morgan had already updated Kristen Castle, who sat stoically behind her massive desk. Her gaze shifted slowly to the bank of windows, not focusing on anything in particular, then back to us. As if reciting a eulogy, she said the end of an era was coming to the Chestnut estate. Her firm had represented the Chestnut family for over fifty years. Kristen's father, a retired partner, knew the family well.

"Livy was a restless soul who had trouble finding her niche in life, and we were so happy and relieved that Livy settled into a life she enjoyed and a job she prospered in. And then this happened. Her loss is also ours." We sat quietly as the words sunk in.

Kristen offered some background information. Livy and Uncle Norman were encouraged to maintain contact with each other, and hopefully restore some harmony within the fragmented Chestnut family. It was helpful to know their whereabouts in the event of such an unfortunate situation such as this. When Kristen finished, she asked me to wait in the reception room while the remaining trio met. I paced until the receptionist returned me to my seat between the officers. Barely nesting my bottom in the chair, I was advised that I could continue living on Chestnut Boulevard providing I continue to care of Wilson. There would be no change in my rent, and the car would remain available to me for reasonable purposes, whatever that meant. This arrangement was subject to change, contingent on future discussions and approval from Uncle Norman, who was actually more involved than just an annual Christmas visit. The officers were provided Uncle Norman's current address and I could accompany them. Once he was notified, the notice of death would be released and the estate would arrange the funeral.

Kristen reminded me how fortunate I was to live in this house. The firm would monitor the property, inside and out, and a new inventory was needed to update the status of the house and its contents. She requested that I leave a key to the house, which I obediently slid across the desk. An adjuster would inspect the house within forty-eight hours, which irritated me that someone needed to confirm that I hadn't tampered with or destroyed anything. It was really the least of my worries. I still had a very affordable place to live. As we left Kristen's office, I was happy that I could accompany the officers to New Pelham, however I was responsible for my own transportation, which was fine with me.

I let Sophie know that I was tied up with with legal issues, and would join her for dinner. She would walk Wilson. As the officers and I rode down the mahogany-paneled elevator, we talked about Uncle Norman. I knew nothing about him, or where he lived in New Pelham. The road trip would surely be an adventure.

I followed the police car out of the parking garage, then through a drive thru for tea and lunch. Traffic on the highway was light and cars responded to the presence of the cruiser by braking and shifting lanes, creating the same havoc I often contributed to. We drove down the Queen Elizabeth Way towards Niagara Falls. I rarely drove in this direction. Prosperous industries with well-maintained properties flanked one side of the highway, while Lake Ontario, to my left, was dotted with sailboats and cargo ships. At noon, while passing the exit signs to Hamilton, I listened to the news. Livy's death was history. She gave me shelter, confidence and the comfort of a solid friendship. Short as my time was with her, she was my newest, and closest friend, and I would share this with her Uncle Norman, who I was about to meet soon.

As we entered the Niagara region, splashy billboards welcomed us to wine country. The cruiser exited the highway and headed away from the lake through a small town. The road cut through vast farmers' fields and tidy rows of grapes. A sign in front of a church warned that 'He who throws dirt loses ground.' New, large homes nested spaciously between neatly preserved farms when we turned onto Old Chestnut Lane. It was ironic that Uncle Normal lived on Chestnut Lane.

The August drought painted lawns an even colour of dry wheat, contrasting with the luscious green of corn fields, grape vines and nursery stock. We climbed a very gradual slope. At the first stop sign, a weathered sign read 'Old Chestnut Farm and Country'. Chicken wire and fence posts were this week's special, and judging by the worn lettering, could also have been last season's special. I passed an old garage with an antique car parked in an open bay. Old metal signs decorated the barn board exterior. A small man with a sleeveless white T-shirt tucked loosely into oil-stained jeans came out of the garage and put his hands on his hips to catch the novelty of a cruiser driving through. I doubted that residents locked their doors here. A small sign on a big post pointed to a tiny lane that said 'The Old Chestnut Tree'. No wonder Uncle Norman lived here.

A quaint old church at the top of a hill was a stark contrast to a new 'Welcome to New Pelham" sign across the street. We passed four large custom built homes, then turned into a long gravel driveway that cut through a wooded acre. A rusty, overstuffed mail box balanced precariously on a wooden post at the entrance. The driveway, littered with dozens of neglected newspapers, was furrowed with deep ruts. Tall, evenly spaced black walnut trees formed a canopy of emerald green. The driveway ended two hundred feet later in a clearing.

Nestled in the woods was a large, stately two-story home, somewhat similar to the Chestnut home in Toronto. The landscaping, abandoned long ago, contrasted with a path of neatly mowed grass which cut through the woods to the only nieghbour. The stucco house was painted a dark chocolate, with the foundation covered in rounded quarry stones. Large white casings framed the doors and paned windows. An oversized porch was supported by four large pillars, and curved roof lines replicated three sets of curved upstairs windows. Patches of green moss dotted the cedar roof, and overgrown ivy crept across the stairs. However tired and neglected, the house remained an architectural gem.

The windows were all closed on this breezy August day. The officers opened their doors simultaneously, and one confirmed their location via the radio attached to his bulletproof vest. As I turned off the car, Morgan approached me first.

"Nice drive."

"Beautiful."

"Are you still okay with all this?"

"Of course," I said bravely.

"So, just to recap, your friend Livy was this man's niece, but hadn't seen him since Christmas?"

"I think so.""

"Now, please stay outside until we come for you," Ryan said.

"That's fine by me." I leaned gingerly against the Volvo, rehearsing what to say to this mysterious man.

The officers stepped between the weeds bordering the sidewalk. Each wooden stair groaned with the officers' weight. Morgan clacked the dusty metal door knocker, moulded into a large "C". I felt anxious for them, like a parent. No answer. Morgan knocked louder and longer. Still no answer. He tried the door. It was unlocked. Morgan yelled into the house and cautiously pushed against the squeaking hinges. Ryan moved his hand to his revolver and raised his hand to remind me to stay outside. Clutching my purse, I calculated how long it would take to escape back over those ruts. *Maybe I shouldn't be here. I should have backed my car in. What if someone hurt him too?*

From the front entrance, I heard the officer yell.

"Hello! Norman Chestnut – are you in there? This is the police." No answer. They merged forward in single file, leaving the front door open.

Ryan called Norman's name again, his voice deeper in the house. Silence, but for the distant summons of the officers.

I breathed deeply and looked around. An old, steel blue Mercedes, in dire need of care, was parked to the right side of the house, facing white garage doors. Stray leaves and twigs accumulated in the windshield well. I peeked into the driver's window. More newspapers cluttered the passenger seat. Crumpled fast food bags lay on the floor.

Morgan's towering frame appeared at the front door with a phone to his ear, reciting Uncle Norman's address. He made eye contact with me, and disappeared back in the house. I waited, and waited some more.

Impatient and now curious, I walked cautiously up each groaning stair and peered through the open door. The front lobby was eerily familiar, with the same black and white mosaic tiles as the house on Chestnut Boulevard. The name 'CHESTNUT,' laid into the tiles just like in Livy's house, was partially visible. Dirt, shoes and more newspapers were strewn across the floor. A wooden hall table held a large oriental bowl, overflowing with mail and flyers. The house had other, additional similar features to Livy's, but smelled like some old people's houses. The hallway ended at the kitchen, which I imagined was a replica of the original kitchen on Chestnut Boulevard before the fire. The stench of dirty dishes stopped me. Livy would have been appalled.

The stairs to the second floor were also the same. Quietly, I climbed the dusty wooden steps to the bedroom where the officers were conversing. In the distance, I heard the unmistakable siren of an ambulance. I gagged from the smell of old urine that infiltrated the stale air.

A loud squeak from my weight on the wooden floor distracted the officers from the crumpled heap of a man, lying precariously on the carpet by the bed. Ryan chirped, "Grace, meet Uncle Norman. Uncle Norman, this is Grace". His salutation was a week groan. "Stay put, old fellow, they're almost here," Morgan said, kneeling beside him and lightly keeping his hand on the man's shoulder to minimize his efforts to move. The ambulance siren was getting louder.

Uncle Norman was partially wrapped in a tangled mess of dirty maroon sheets which followed him onto the carpet. A pillow, neatly positioned underneath his head, was the only semblance of order in this room. A plaid, flannel shirt and stained jeans hung on the bedpost. They could have stood up on their own from the dirt.

Uncle Norman looked like a homeless transient, plucked from the street and dropped where he didn't belong. His face told a long story of hard living. His long, unkempt mop of grey hair and beard matched the colour of his skin. His bloodshot eyes, the same vibrant blue as Livy's, looked at me. He mumbled something inaudible. The expression on his face saddened as he picked weakly at the soiled sheet in an attempt to cover his exposed thighs. He suddenly moaned, wincing in pain.

"Easy, fellow, they're here now," Morgan comforted Norman. The ambulance silenced its siren and approached the house. I opened the front door. Two paramedics sauntered in. The older male, weighted down with an assortment of equipment bags, walked heavily as I led them up the stairs. The spacious bedroom became smaller and much hotter with the newcomers.

"What happened here?" the tall, lean female paramedic asked Norman directly, her gloved hands unzipping an equipment bag. As he mumbled inaudibly, the officers filled her in.

"This house is registered to a Mr. Norman Chestnut, and we assume this is Mr. Chestnut," Morgan said, lowering his voice and turning away so Norman couldn't hear him. "We arrived to notify Mr. Chestnut of the death of his niece in Toronto, and found him in this position, minus the pillow," Morgan said.

"Hmmm," she smirked and knelt beside her patient. "Are you Norman Chestnut?" Uncle Norman nodded feebly. The other medic, his abdominal girth stressing his shirt buttons, took notes on a tablet as she fitted an oxygen mask over her victim's face. He didn't resist.

"Mr. Chestnut, this oxygen will help you breathe. Can you hear me?" Uncle Norman nodded once.

"Did you fall out of bed?" He nodded again.

"When did you fall? Did you spend the night here?" He stared at her blankly, his eyes glassy with tears.

"That's okay, Norman." He nodded again, a tear following the path of a wrinkle across his face.

"I'll start an IV to get some fluids into you. You should feel a little better after we get you to the hospital, and doctor puts some pain medication in here." She successfully inserted the intravenous needle into Uncle Norman's vein. Her partner complimented her skill, while pecking on his tablet and murmuring about Norman's dehydration. As she carefully cut away the sheet to expose more flesh, I moved out of Uncle Norman's line of sight to spare us both embarrassment.

"Still got your Christmas boxers on, Norman....you need to get the summer ones out. Now, can you point to what hurts most?" She methodically assessed every inch of his tall, nearly naked frame. He pointed to his right hip. The paramedic gently moved Uncle Norman's right knee – he yelled loudly, throwing his head back in pain.

"Yep, might be broken." She continued her assessment, dictating as her partner documented. "He's got more bruises than he should for a three-foot fall. Norman, are you on any medications, maybe a blood thinner?" The patient pointed a bony finger towards the bathroom. I walked to the en-suite. On the counter were a couple of prescription bottles and a bottle of Aspirin which I passed to the female medic.

"I see you take something for your blood pressure and this is for your cholesterol, right? Any other medication or supplements that you take?" He shook his head. "Do you have allergies?" He shook his head again, more tears spilling down his cheeks. "We'll take this medication with you to the hospital. You might be out of commission for a while." She looked at the other paramedic.

"I'll get the stretcher," he responded, and returned with Ryan, and a wheeled stretcher. Ryan took pictures of the scene. Both the officers and the paramedics rolled Norman cautiously onto a back board, who roared in agony with every move. The smell of feces and urine was overwhelming to everyone but Norman. Morgan and the male paramedic carried Uncle Norman, secured with three seat belt straps over a sheet and orange blanket downstairs. Ryan kicked a heap of mismatched towels at the top of the stairs out of their path.

"We'll follow you," Ryan told the medics. He looked at me. "I can't force you to come, but it would help if you answered any questions we can't." He fished through the jeans on the bedpost. Not finding what he was looking for, he searched the bedroom dresser tops and drawers, retrieving an old brown wallet. He dumped it in a plastic bag the paramedic gave him, and was the last one out the front door.

I returned to the Volvo and followed the procession through winding country roads until we approached a more urban area. The hospital was a new, modern structure surrounded by farmer's fields. I followed the officers through the ambulance entrance, feeling conspicuous and again questioning the value of my presence. I was ushered to a waiting room by a nurse who documented my name and a bit of history. The officers joined me shortly after. The nurse said Norman was going for X-rays, and the officers asked if the doctor could assess Uncle Norman's ability to understand the news they still hadn't delivered. She nodded, and asked us to be patient, as the wait would be a few hours. My phone rang.

It was Sophie. I didn't answer, and instead walked over to the coffee shop, and returned with three coffees and muffins. We sat in the packed waiting room, and two hours dragged into three. A new nurse asked us to follow her. We were introduced to a very young, attractive, female doctor in green scrubs that hung loosely over her curvy frame. Identifying herself as Dr. Mel, she spoke quickly and softly in a French accent in the hallway outside Uncle Norman's cubicle.

"So, we've assessed Mr. Chestnut. He indeed has a broken hip and understands he will need surgery to fix it. We anticipate this will happen in the next day or two. After surgery, he'll be discharged to a rehab facility until he can learn to manage himself independently. He lives alone, yes?" We all nodded. She took a quick breath and faced the officers. "So, to answer your question, he is cognitively able to understand what you need to tell him. We can arrange for a social worker to offer him some grief counselling." She looked directly at me, took my hands in her tiny ones and said sincerely, "My condolences for your loss. Now if there are no further questions, business is booming here."

I followed the men into the crammed cubicle and remained behind them. Somewhat cleaned up and dressed in a patterned hospital gown, Norman's facial expression was calmer than a few hours ago. The oxygen mask was gone, and his skin was pale pink. Morgan introduced himself and Ryan again, and told Norman again who I was. Ryan asked him if he could hear what they were saying. In a raspy garbled voice, Norman whispered, "I know why you're here."

"You do? Why?" Ryan gently probed him.

"Saw the news," he mumbled, looking away. "You can go now." The officers confirmed quietly what Norman already knew, who turned away from them. They would inform the law firm what happened and how to reach him. They said nice things about me, I'm sure only to make him feel more comfortable around me. I felt out of place.

"Any questions before we leave?" Norman shook his head. I walked them to the exit door, wanting to bolt rather than face the old man. A few deep breaths later, I re-entered the cubicle to tell Norman I was leaving and would see him at Livy's memorial service. He had pulled his bed sheet up to his nose and was shivering. Looking thin, frail and abandoned, I felt terrible for wanting a quick exit. I found some blankets and covered him, tucking them in under his feet. He looked like a mummy. Norman shrank deeper under the blankets and whispered something inaudible. I leaned cautiously towards him.

"My teef."

"I beg your pardon?"

A crooked index finger surfaced and pointed to his mouth. "My teef."

"Your teeth?"

"And my gwasses," he nodded as the same finger moved to his eyes.

"Where are they?"

"Home." I looked at my watch. Almost 5:00 PM. Sophie would be worried, or fuming, probably both since I hadn't called back.

"Why don't I bring them tomorrow?" I said, instantly regretting the offer. He eyed me suspiciously. I faked a smile. "I promise. Remember Livy's dog? Wilson? I need to go to Livy's house and let Wilson out." My explanation worked. The crooked finger was replaced by two thumbs, facing up. I deliberately checked my watch, reassured him again that I would return late tomorrow morning, and fled.

There was nothing else on my agenda, other than moping and mourning. Livy would have helped her uncle, so it was the least I could do.

I left the hospital and called Sophie. After answering a third of her questions, she agreed to stay until I returned. I decided that finding the glasses and teeth today would be better than disappointing Norman if I was late tomorrow.

My route back to New Pelham was different, and took longer this time to find the house. My heart thumped as I inched up the driveway again. The potholes seemed bigger and closer together. I parked the Volvo facing the road, ready for a quick getaway. *Get away from who?* The door remained unlocked, as the police had left it. Perfect. In and out. Entering the front door, the smell brought me back to earlier today. Even in its state of disarray, the house did not match Uncle Norman, but definitely matched Livy. I took another short tour of the main floor, my shoes leaving prints on the dusty floors. A number of furniture pieces matched those on Chestnut Boulevard. The fireplace mantle, a simple but thick beam of walnut, was lined with postcards. I recognized Livy's writing on all of them, the most recent one dated the first day of her final trip. The inscription was bittersweet:

> Hi Uncle Norman! Here I am again in Jakarta.
> This picture is this view from my hotel room.
> It's 41 degrees in the shade. I'm having something special made
> for you – can't wait to show you when I visit in September.
> Stay well! Love ya lots!
> Livy

Under her signature was a drawing of two thumbs pointing up. I considered taking the postcard to the hospital, but thought otherwise as it would bring more grief to an already miserable man. My watch said 6:00 PM. I looked in the kitchen and a rundown recliner in the living room, but saw no eyeglasses. Walking up the stairs, I headed first for the bathroom, which I should have used before I left the hospital, but wouldn't here. The stench of dried urine made me gag. I forced open the bathroom window, every crank of the window casing requiring effort. A denture cup sat on the counter. I unscrewed the lid, retching at the smell and lumpy appearance of the rancid solution. I emptied it into the sink and ran the water. No teeth in the cup. I rinsed the receptacle a few times, poured some mouthwash into the cup, recapped it and shook it vigorously. I emptied the solution again, took a toothbrush from the counter that should have been replaced months ago. Resisting the urge to vomit, I brushed the cup, inside and out, until it would pass inspection at the hospital.

The bedroom smelled worse than the bathroom. I rolled up the small carpet where Norman had soiled himself, and put it outside the front door. I opened both bedroom windows – the outdoor air was fresh and breezy. I caught the faint smell of a campfire. Each corner of the room was filled with piles of laundry or stacks of dust-laden books and magazines. A vibrant Persian rug covered the dusty hardwood floors, faded from sunlight and neglect. There were no dentures or glasses on the bedside tables, dressers, or on the table which held the TV. I dreaded sorting through the sheets of the queen-sized bed, panning the room again more carefully. Nothing caught my eye. I gingerly lifted the sheet off the floor. Nothing. I took the pillows off the bed and floor. Nothing. Two mismatched socks hid in the blankets. The bottom sheet partially uncovered a mattress pad which was no cleaner than the sheets. No bumps worth investigating under the sheet. I refitted the bottom sheet over the mattress cover and threw the rest of the linen back on the bed. The last spot Uncle Norman laid was on the carpet. Nothing near the vicinity where the discarded carpet laid. *Maybe under the bed?*

I knelt down, picking grape stems and seeds from under my knees. The pungent odour of stinky socks forced me to hold my breath as I put my face under the bed. Success. A bent pair of bifocal glasses lay just under the edge of the bed accompanied by more filthy socks and boxer shorts. My focus narrowed in on the grand prize. Uncle Norman's dentures, at least one half of them were squarely nestled under the middle of the bed. How they landed there was a mystery. Holding my breath, I slid under the bed. Clusters of dust balls had multiplied over many seasons. Treasures in hand, I resurfaced as a filthy mess. The grime on the front bodice of my white shirt permeated the fabric, and I only spread it by trying to wipe it off. The same for my black skirt. I laughed, in spite of myself in the bathroom mirror, picking dust out of my hair and rubbing dirt off my legs. *Smart move, coming today instead of tomorrow.*

A very loud and deep "HELLO!" from the first floor scared me. I knocked Uncle Norman's glasses from the counter to the floor, responding in a high pitched squeal.

"Hello! I'm coming down!" My hands shook as I opened the denture cup over the sink and deposited the dentures, caked with food residue. I struggled to screw the lid back on. I picked up the rimless wire glasses, and entered the upstairs hallway. I froze at the top of the stairs. A tall male silhouette filled the frame of the open front door. I held the glasses and denture cup in one hand, steadying my shaky descent on the stair banister. My knees shook at the same rate as my teeth. The stranger remained silent and still until I reached the bottom step.

"Can I help you?" he said sternly.

"I, I found what I was looking for," I spit out nervously, offering up the glasses and dentures as evidence. They meant nothing to him.

"Did you, now? I live next door. And you are?" The shirtless man stood well over six feet. His firm abdomen and chest meant business.

"I, I, I'm Grace Sheehan." I stuttered, hoping he would clear the door and let me run. He kept hovering, a successful intimidation tactic.

"Where's Norman?" His hands moved slowly to his hips.

"At the hospital."

"The hospital? What happened?"

I explained, in no particular order, what happened, forgetting to include the tragedy that brought me to New Pelham. His deep voice softened as he stepped out of the sunny doorway. He looked at the dirt on my shirt and skirt, one eyebrow raised curiously.

"A broken hip. That's too bad."

"Yes, it's terrible," I stammered.

"When did it happen?"

"The paramedic predicted he was on the floor for days."

"Hmm. At most two days, because I was here on Saturday. I usually check in on him every few days." My breathing settled, and I displayed the items in my hands. My full bladder sent another strong signal. I sped up the conversation.

"He'll be there for a while. He asked me to bring his dentures and glasses. I found them under his bed."

"That would explain your shirt."

"I doubt anyone's been under there lately."

"Or in the rest of the house."

"He wasn't expecting company."

"He never has company. He's a recluse. Your white car looks familiar, though."

"It's his niece's. I'm heading back to Toronto now, but taking these to him late tomorrow morning."

"If you were a thief, these wouldn't be your first pick. Even if you had a dental plan," he chuckled. "So you're not the niece?"

"No." *If I don't pee very soon, I'm going to have a big problem.* I squirmed, looking at him a little desperately. "Look, is there a coffee shop nearby?" He looked puzzled. *He doesn't get it.* Humiliated, I explained my desperation to use a bathroom, anywhere rather than here.

"There's no coffee shop, but you can come next door to my house. It's cleaner than Norman's, if that's your concern." *It's either his house, or in the woods.* I accepted, and tried to lock the door, but had no key.

"He never locks it, but I will after you leave."

I left Norman's things by the front door and followed his quick pace through the narrow clearing of grass between the two houses, which ended at the side yard of his house. His property, like Norman's was also about an acre. He opened the front door of his impeccably clean home, but remained outside. "Walk straight through to the kitchen, then turn right twice." I kicked my shoes off and ran, the porcelain tiles cool on my feet. The house was simply decorated. I returned the hand towel back to its orderly fold and retraced my steps. The neighbour seated on his front steps, his back muscles defined and tanned. His hair was thick and wavy, with more brown than grey.

"Better?"

"Much better." I walked past him down the steps and turned around to face him. He formed a visor with his tanned left hand to block the sun from his eyes. He wore no jewelry.

"When nature calls, you have to listen. And speaking of listening, I forgot your name."

"Grace. Grace Sheehan."

"Fred. Just like my father. And his father. He gave my dirty shirt an amusing glance, and looked amused. "You look thirsty, Miss Grace Sheehan. There's not much in the fridge, but I have lots of water." I didn't correct him on the 'Miss' part.

"I've inconvenienced you enough." I was thirsty, and hungry, and prepared for a long lecture from Sophie. I apologized again for the intrusion.

"No worries. I'll get you some water." He stood up, dusting off the backside of his shorts, and within a minute was back with a filled, reusable water bottle with the name of a school on it. I thanked him and took a refreshing swig of the cold liquid.

Fred followed me back to Norman's house. I retrieved the denture cup and glasses. He asked if there was anything Norman needed. "Does the hospital have his niece's number?" I gasped. I had omitted the most crucial piece of news. I lowered my head, but kept my sight line on his eyes.

"That's the reason I came. She died."

"What?" I gave him a brief summary of the last week, hiding my emotions as best as I could. He was visibly upset. "Norman will be crushed. I never met her but I know he adored her."

"I know. She was my friend, too. The police came with me to tell him the bad news, but he already knew." Fred's sandaled foot stepped on a small twig in the grass, snapping it into pieces.

"So now he has no one."

"I think you're right."

"Who's making the funeral arrangements?"

"No one yet. He'd had enough bad news today. Someone from the law firm representing Livy's estate will probably contact him."

"He's in no shape now to manage his own affairs, let alone his niece's."

"You're right again. I feel terrible about it. He didn't know I existed six hours ago. As of now, all he wants from me is his teeth and his glasses, and he wasn't convinced I'd keep my promise."

"Well, you must have a conscience, not to mention messing up your nice clothes shimmying under a bed in a stranger's house to find a stranger's teeth." Fred's teeth were much nicer than the half set in my hand. "I'll even clean them before I deliver them." I gulped at the thought of it.

"Yuck. He'll never tell you, but he will appreciate it." I shook his extended hand, his palm double the size of mine. He opened the driver's door of the Volvo.

"Say hi to the old guy for me, Miss Grace Sheehan."

"It's Grace, but most people call me Gracie."

I gave my clothes a few good swipes before getting in the car. He closed the door behind me, his hands retreating to his hips. I drove slowly away from the house watching his shoulders rise and his face cringe when the bottom of the Volvo scraped against a rut in the driveway.

August 8th

My day began early with a refreshing walk though fog with Wilson. We were both having breakfast when Kristen Castle's office called. She knew that Norman was aware of Livy's passing and her wishes to be cremated, which the firm had arranged. My heart sunk. She was planning the memorial service. I told her of my plans to deliver Norman's teeth and glasses. She praised my generosity, and reminded me that she handled Norman's legal matters. She asked how I got into his house. It was easier to explain that his neighbour had a key, then to say that no one locked it. She asked me for his name and address, and I only knew 'Fred from next door.' She reminded me that someone was coming to Livy's house to take inventory. I told her Wilson was home, and that the dog walker walked him mid-afternoon.

My second ride back to the hospital was almost as stressful. Norman was transferred to a surgical ward. When I entered his room, two beds were rolled up high, with fresh sheets folded back and ready for new occupants. Norman's name tag was taped to the bed closest to the window. There was nothing on his side or over-bed table and I debated where to leave his glasses and dentures. A nurse walked in and I identified myself as a friend of the family. Norman was in surgery, and was expected back within the hour. I decided to wait and was directed to the waiting room. It was 11:00 AM. I held up my end of the bargain, and wanted Norman to know.

In the waiting room sat an elderly, very round visitor in a floral dress, wearing flesh-coloured support stockings and hair too black to call her own. She smiled nervously at me but said nothing. I reciprocated, choosing the couch that faced the door and out of her line of sight. She pulled a glass canning jar from a shopping bag, opened the metal lid and drank some of the clear liquid. With some degree of effort, she hoisted herself from the chair, put the shopping bag under it and waddled out of the room. Today's edition of the local paper was the only thing in the room worth reading. I used the bathroom, which was part of the waiting room and opened the door to find Fred facing me in the doorway.

"I thought you might be here. Well, not exactly here in the bathroom," he grinned and I blushed. Two take out cups were tucked in his hands. "Coffee's on the left. Tea is on your right. Milk in both, sugar on the side. I'll drink either." I thanked him for the tea, and resumed my original spot on the couch. Fred settled in the chair, unaware it was the elderly lady's seat until his foot kicked her bag. He moved to the chair beside me. Looking much less intimidating then yesterday, his ordinary features would blend easily in a crowd. He could be a little younger than me. An old watch was strapped to his left wrist, and he wore a black golf shirt and yesterday's shorts. His clean feet were tucked into worn sandals.

He looked around. "Looks the same as the last time I was here." I took the bait.

"When you were here?"

"Many times over the last five years."

"For the same person?" He shook his head.

"Both of my parents. They're gone now."

"I'm sorry."

"Me too. It was a long and drawn out agony for both of them, and a relief for us when they passed." He was quiet for a few minutes, and it seemed inappropriate to speak. He stared into his cup.

"My mom was eighty-eight and my dad was eighty-six." I searched for a neutral question.

"And who did you look like?"

"Definitely Fred number two, who looked like Fred number one."

"And is there a Fred number four?"

"Nope. But my daughter's middle name is Frederica. It was the honourable thing to do."

"What's her first name?"

"Claire."

"My daughter's name is Tess."

"Nice name."

"Thanks." Another long pause, and a glance at the ceiling.

"It's also honourable that you came today. A nice gesture."

"Thanks. I feel sorry for him. It's been a nasty week." Fred pulled out his wallet and produced a piece of yellow lined paper. He unfolded it and passed it to me.

BLESS, Olivia (Livy) Jane, passed away suddenly on August 4th as a result of an accident in Toronto, Ontario, in her 44th year. Livy was predeceased by her parents Fraser and Trixie Bless, and is survived by her loving uncle, Norman Percy Chestnut of New Pelham, Ontario. A memorial service will be announced at a later date.

My dearest Livy:
You were born on Christmas Day,
A gift of life, a shining ray,
Into a world that gave you grief,
Where you fought to find relief
I will watch your shining star
In the night sky, dark and far
Be brave, my child, I'll see you soon
When my soul crosses the moon.

Goosebumps covered my skin. I passed it back to Fred.

"It was on the dining room table, beside an empty liquor bottle."

"He must have finished it much sooner than the bottle because it's beautiful."

"He stole it." Fred passed over a torn newspaper clipping of someone's obituary announcement with the same paragraph.

"There you go. Smart thinking."

"I'm not sure what to do with it."

"I told him about the call from the lawyer this morning, and her request for his contact information.

"You can give her my number. I've been watching out for him for a few years, so she should be grateful for that." He wrote his name and number on the back of the stolen obituary and handed it and the yellow paper to me. "Norman will be out of commission for a while. Let them take the burden off him." We settled in to wait for Norman. I put the papers in my purse, then offered him a section of newspaper. Predictably, he took the sports. The lady in the flowered dress waddled back in, shuffled her feet backwards into the chair until her calves made contact, and fell into it. She smiled and nodded her head gently, observing us for a few minutes. She took a big swig of liquid from her glass jar, leaned her head against the seat, and was snoring within minutes.

We sat in silence for another thirty minutes, rotating through sections of the paper.

"Is this your day off?" I asked.

"I'm off in the summers."

"Teacher?"

"Yes."

"High school?"

"In a sense. I run a program called Second Chance through the school system. It's for kids with behavioural issues who've run out of mainstream options to graduate from high school. It's their final chance, which would be a better name for the program."

"I'm impressed."

"Don't be. Some days it's not."

Our other visitor woke up suddenly with a snort, looking at us and then her watch. She fished into her bag and uncorked an amber prescription bottle of pills. She took two with another swig from the jar, planted her swollen feet solidly on the floor, and with a heave out of her chair, ambled over to the washroom. A varied assortment of bowel sounds were audible over the next few minutes. The sink water splashed, followed by the repeated pulling on the paper towel dispenser. I thought back to Fred walking into the room earlier this morning. With her bathroom mission accomplished, she re-positioned herself back in her chair and produced a tin box from her shopping bag. She opened the waxed paper wrapping to display some perfectly shaped biscotti. The smell of vanilla and butter blended with the putrid air emanating from the bathroom. She set the box onto the coffee table and pushed it our way. Her accent was strong and Italian. "Eat! I'm a mayka myself! Fresh yesterday!" I smiled and declined. Fred reached over and took one.

"Mmm...delicious," he said. It was crunchy, with lots of almonds. She pointed the hand holding her half eaten biscotti to Fred, and then to me.

"Your husband have some, so you have some too!" I chuckled. The bathroom odor killed my appetite.

"Elvira?" a nurse dressed in scrubs approached the lady. "He's back, but he's very sleepy. Two minutes, Elvira, and then you must go home. He needs to sleep."

"Nursa, everything okay?"

"Yes, everything is okay. But nothing to eat yet. Big operation again." She hugged the nurse, picked up a biscotti, put it in a napkin and hid it deep in her pocket. "I'll have it on my break, honey." She looked at us. "Elvira is the best baker we have." A second hug exchange. "Now how many minutes, Elvira, before you have to go home?"

"Three, nursa, only three." They laughed heartily and the nurse disappeared. Elvira scooped the biscotti and waxed paper out of the box and placed it onto the newspaper, dropping the empty box back in her bag. She targeted me again with her finger. "You too skinny. Eat." She laughed and hustled off with her bags. *Too skinny...I've never been skinny.*

Another thirty minutes rolled by before the same nurse walked by our room. She stopped and returned, eyeing the biscotti.

"Who are you waiting for?"

"Norman Chestnut," Fred answered.

"Oh, he's been back for a while. I didn't realize anyone was waiting for him. He's still really groggy. Only one visitor at a time. And please limit your visit to a few minutes."

"Two minutes?" I asked. The nurse smiled.

"To Elvira, two minutes is two hours. How about five minutes for each of you?" Fred nodded. "Five minutes it is." He passed the biscotti to the nurse who gladly accepted. I encouraged Fred to visit first and he was back in seven minutes.

"He's as peaceful as a lamb. Sound asleep, like he should be. Your turn. Shall I stick around until you come back?" It was a nice offer but I sensed it wasn't his top priority. I declined, and thanked him for the tea, not sure what else to say.

"I'm sure he'll appreciate your help when he gets home."

"I'll swing by and cut his grass. I'm not around tomorrow but I'll come back the next day. Nice meeting you again, Grace." He walked me to Norman's room, leaving me with a warm handshake.

I hesitated before entering the room, feeling awkward. Norman was a healthy pink colour, and looked much better. His hair was a clean and messy mop of grey. I noticed a faint resemblance to Livy. How I missed her, and pictured her fussing over him. His chest rose up and down in slow, rhythmic breaths. I set his denture cup and glasses on his overbed table, then searched my purse for paper to write him a note. The only thing I found was the yellow lined paper obituary. I looked for the other newspaper clipping with Fred's name and number and couldn't find it. I regretted cleaning out my purse because there wasn't even a receipt, let alone a pen to write a note.

Another nurse entered the room, hinting I leave and let Norman recover. She said he needed non-skid slippers because the hospital didn't supply them. And that maybe I could help him with his meals because they were short staffed and that it wasn't her job. My jaw tightened. For the encore, she produced a paper bag and suggested I do his laundry. The dirty Christmas motif boxer shorts were in the bag. I asked for a pen to write him a short note. She told me to get it from the desk clerk.

"That mustn't be your job either," I mumbled. She scowled and left, taking her attitude with her.

I walked back to the waiting room, hoping Fred's number was with the newspaper. The room had been tidied up and the papers were gone. Fred's last name was Smith. I could pass that much on to the lawyer. I went back to the nurse's station and asked the clerk for a pen. She kindly obliged and asked if there was anything else I needed. I explained the obituary notice, which she kindly made a copy of and faxed to the law firm. She said a discharge planner would meet Norman in the next day or two, and encouraged me to return. I explained that I was not related, but I would see what I could do. I thanked her just as Nurse Nasty came into the nursing station for more of Elvira's biscotti. I walked back to Norman's room. He was sound asleep. I took a quick peek at his feet under the blanket to estimate his slipper size. His foot was about an inch smaller than the long side of the paper with the obituary notice. I could remember that. I tore the blank bottom of the paper off and wrote the note:

Hello Mr. Chestnut.
Sorry that I missed you.
I hope your surgery went well. Here are your glasses.
But I could only find half of your teeth. I will bring you
some slippers when I come back in 2 days.
Take care, and hope you feel better.

Grace Sheehan
(Livy's friend from Toronto)
August 8 (12:30 PM)

I wrapped the note around Norman's teeth and glasses and left it on the over-bed table within his reach. Nurse Nasty brought me a list of toiletries he needed and left without saying a word. I kept the list, returned the pen to the desk clerk and drove back to Toronto.

Wilson was as happy to see me as I was to see him. I sorted the mail, all addressed to Livy. Not sure what to do with them, I asked the lawyer, who wanted everything. She received the fax the hospital sent of the obituary

Norman wrote. I gave her Fred Smith's name, and would forward his phone number when I found it. I changed quickly while Wilson squirmed impatiently by the front door, until we walked. With the police cars and TV reporters gone, we were edging back to a new normal.

Lunch was a walk around the house with a peanut butter sandwich in one hand and tea in the other. Livy's presence lingered in every corner of the house. I really missed her. Her coats hung in the back hall, with shoes discarded in the order that she flung them off her feet. Her bedroom carried the scent of her perfume. Such a waste of life.

I thought passively about Fred and wondered if he saw Norman today. He seemed genuinely interested in Norman's well-being. I pulled out the list the nurse at the hospital gave me, and left it on the kitchen counter.

August 9th

The morning newspaper published Livy's obituary exactly as Norman had written it, with the exception of the memorial service announcement. Details of the service were entrusted to a nearby funeral home. The service would be announced at a later date. Information about the law firm was also printed, which I found unusual until I saw the legal notice in the same paper, which directed those with inquiries or claims against Livy's estate to contact the firm.

Kristen called to remind me that a couple of insurance adjusters were coming to inventory the house. I was instructed to keep my possessions separate, remain available to answer questions. Within the hour, a man and woman arrived, and produced business cards representing an insurance company. They expected to remain at the house all day, armed with a camera and a tablet. The first picture the man took, which upset me greatly, was of Wilson. He then continued photographing items as the woman pecked at the tablet. I was given permission to walk him, which upset me even more.

When we returned, the adjusters were cataloguing the artwork. As I predicted, there were questions about the nude portrait above Livy's bed. I confirmed it was not Livy, unsure why it was relevant, but wondered what would happen to it. Livy was right; it was a conversation piece, regardless whose wall it would occupy next.

The couple left for two hours. I drove to a department store, but only after the Volvo was photographed inside and out, including the odometer. From Norman's hospital list, I purchased a toiletries, non-skid slippers and a summer bathrobe. I added a large print book of crossword puzzles, a small bag of scotch mints and a deck of cards for good measure. A generic get well card and a small journal with lined note pages completed my shopping.

The adjusters were busy in the back yard when I returned. I unlocked the garage and the tool shed for them. They uncovered an old baby pram, protected with a dusty white sheet. A few toys were in the basket under the carriage, and I imagined Livy's small arms around and old doll. I was asked if what I purchased today should be catalogued. Offended, I dumped the contents of both bags and showed them the list the hospital gave me. They told me to submit the receipts, and took photographs of everything, including the receipts. Back in the house, they rummaged through the closets and kitchen cupboards. They left at dinnertime, not soon enough for me.

The Adams shuffled over within minutes of the adjusters' departure. Shepherd's pie and green beans from their garden were on the kitchen counter before I could object. Ina uncovered a plate of warm butter tarts.
"Good old fashioned food," Jack said, hoisting himself onto a bar stool. Ina slapped his hand as he stole a green bean. I took my middle seat between them. They inquired about the pair that just left as I set place mats and cutlery in front of them. This would be embellished and gossiped to the other curious, and equally opinionated senior neighbours.

Supper was delicious and the butter tarts were divine, heated and topped with maple walnut ice cream. Ina lectured me about Jack's cholesterol as I scooped a mound into the centre of the tart on his plate. His argument was consistent; he'd been eating ice cream for eighty-nine years and had no intention of stopping now. We watched the news together, and they were back home within an hour with full bellies, new stories and clean dishes. I wondered if Norman liked butter tarts and set the last one aside for him. The pastry was so flaky that he could easily manage it with half a set of dentures.

August 10th

11:00 AM seemed like a good time for the next delivery to Norman, which avoided the traffic rush hours. The dog walker was on standby. I drove to the hospital and parked. I balanced yesterday's butter tart, Norman's things, and my purse. I felt like Elvira, but better dressed. I checked the waiting room first, hoping that someone returned the obituary notice with Fred's phone number on it. No such luck. I walked by the nursing station to Norman's room. He was in his bed, with his sheets arranged neatly around him. His hair was combed, and his glasses were on the table. He looked content, or well-medicated.

"Allo, nice lady." Elvira greeted me softly. She sat beside the man in the other bed in Norman's room. Norman lay still, his linens tucked tightly around his withered frame. His mouth was wide open and his breathing was shallow. Two intravenous lines dripped into a main line, taped to his right arm. A catheter bag hung on the bed railing. His complexion blended with the pale pink of the top sheet. Elvira's demeanour was solemn. I emptied my load on the chair next to Norman and put the butter tart near to his glasses. I chose another chair in the room and sat near Elvira. She had a different floral dress on, and her black hair was arranged in a makeshift beehive. Her water jar sat on her husband's table next to his full glasses of juice. I shook her moist hand, and she held mine.

"No time to make biscotti today, Elvira."

"Only time to pray and worry," she said quietly, shaking her head.

"Have you been here long?" She put both hands over mine and nodded. "Your father was up this morning. Firsta time. He is sad too."

"He's not my father. I'm a friend of his niece. She died a week ago." She clutched her hands and put them to her heart.

"He crya lots. He not your father?" I shook my head.

"No. Not my father." She pointed to the bags on the chair beside Norman. "You bring him things?"

"He has no family. He needed slippers." Elvira reached into the side table and offered up her husband's navy slippers. "Thank you, but I bought some already."

You take them backa to store. My Antonio no need them."

"I'm sorry he's not well." She shook her head slowly.

"Where your husband? Not come with today?"

"He's not my husband. He lives next door to Mr. Chestnut."

"Too bad. He nice man."

"He liked your baking."

"He like you, too." I wasn't sure how or why she came to that conclusion. "You have husband?"

"I did. He passed away."

"Oh. So sorry. Where you live? Near hospital?"

"Toronto."

"Toronto! You come alla da way from Toronto?"

"Yes." She shook her head again and took my face in her hands.

"Too far. You nice lady, you needa nice husband."

"Too soon, Elvira. It's too soon."

Norman and Antonio were still sleeping when a woman, introducing herself as the discharge planner, walked in. Shuffling through papers as she spoke, she was there to determine when Norman could return home. I told her that I was not related, nor his caregiver, but might be able to answer some of her questions. Because his multi-level house was a barrier, Norman would be transferred to a rehab facility until he could safely function at home alone. I took her outside his room and told her about Livy, and asked when he would be well enough to travel to a memorial service. She said it was up to the doctor, but she estimated it would be four to six weeks. She jotted the rehab centre name he would convalesce in on her business card, and handed it to me before she left.

It was 11:45 AM when lunches arrived. Elvira beckoned me to follow her down the hall. She picked up Norman's tray and passed it to me. She found Antonio's tray and set it on his table. Elvira re-arranged the plastic dishes and cutlery to her liking, peeling the lid off his soup. She prayed and made a sign of a cross over the food. Norman stopped snoring, but his eyes remained closed. I looked at the menu sheet tucked under his soup. His full name and birth date were listed. He was eighty-three years old. His low sodium lunch consisted of beef vegetable soup, a tuna salad sandwich, and sliced peaches. I made as much noise as I could with the plastic cutlery, and laid his glasses within his reach. The lenses were opaque with grime, likely last cleaned by me. I washed and dried them in the bathroom sink, and as I came out, I saw Norman's open eyes shut instantly.

"Norman, wake up. Lunch is served," I said cheerfully. His eyes remained shut tight. Elvira snapped her fingers at him. He opened his eyes slightly to see her wagging her finger at him in shame. "You no foola da nice lady. I see you! Be nice!" He shifted his blue eyes slowly back to me, then scanned his tray.

"Your soup's getting cold." I offered him the plastic spoon. His hands remained under the covers. I handed him his glasses. One hand slithered out, and put them on the bed sheets. *Maybe he's too weak to hold them?* I put them back on the tray and handed him a spoon, which he put it down on the table.

I sat in the chair, confused and a little frustrated. He said nothing. Elvira spoke up.

"Tsk, tsk, tsk. You hurta da nice lady. If you hurta her, she no come back. She go home to Toronto and you be stuck witha'nobody!" By the end of the sentence her accent had risen a pitch higher, and both hands were in the air. Norman obeyed her. He put his glasses on and ate the soup in silence. Feeling unwelcome, I set the get well card under the butter tart and pointed to it. I used my sweetest voice.

"It's homemade by my neighbour who's six years older than you are. I hope you enjoy it." I left the bag of toiletries on his bed near his knees.

"I have to leave soon." I picked up my purse and pulled the funeral home information out. I said I hoped to see him at the funeral service, extending my hand to shake his. He parked both his arms back under the covers. Elvira was livid. I stood up slowly and walked quietly out the door. Without realizing that she was following me, Elvira was out of breath by the time she caught up to me halfway down the crowded hall.

"Lady, he very mean, but he very afraid." Upset, I didn't want to get involved more than I already was.

"His neighbour will help him."

"You come back. He need you."

"I'm not so sure." She pulled me towards her and hugged me tightly, which saddened me. Her skin was a sweaty combination of vanilla and salami. "You're a good wife, Elvira. I hope Antonio gets better soon." She shook her head.

"No, nice lady. He no get better. But I stay til God takes him." I felt pain in my heart for her. I left her and walked to the end of the hallway. A chair sat outside the last patient room. I sat down, and took a few deep breaths. From my purse, I pulled out the journal I had bought with Norman's slippers. It was black, and wallet-sized, embossed with a pearly Japanese scroll design on the cover. I found a pen and wrote in it:

August 10th, 12 noon

Regarding Norman Chestnut, to whoever reads this:

I just saw Norman and delivered some toiletries to him. Today his discharge planner said he would be moved to the rehab centre once he leaves the hospital. Tucked in these pages are some details about the memorial service for his niece Olivia (Livy) Bless. Would you be kind enough to remind him of this information? The number of the law firm handling Livy's estate is included.
Thank you.

Grace Sheehan (friend of Livy)

P.S. Fred, if you read this, I lost the paper you left your phone number on – I'll leave my number at the nursing station. Nice to have met you. Good luck with Uncle Norman. G.

I left my phone number at the desk but wasn't sure where to leave the journal. I walked by Norman's room. Elvira saw me and hobbled out. I asked her to put the book in his side table drawer after he fell asleep, preferably where he couldn't reach it. She re-assured me that she would, took the book and shook my hand firmly with her sweaty hands.

My return drive home was long to construction delays and vacationers hauling trailers and boats. My mind kept wandering back to Norman. I pictured myself, alone, incapacitated and in an unfamiliar place. I hoped that if he had no family, he might at least have a few friends. My parents were gone, but Tess and Sophie would be there if I needed them. Fred seemed committed to mowing Norman's lawn and checking in on him. *But how sincere would he be in three months, or when he returned to school in September?*

Norman had the same interest in me as he did in Elvira's comments about his behaviour. It was not my problem. I turned the radio up and inched back to Toronto on the highway.

August 14th

The law firm called me early in the morning, essentially to confirm what I already knew. I was not a thief, nor a potential suspect to steal, alter or tamper with anything at the house on Chestnut Boulevard. I also must have passed whatever inspection the auditors felt necessary to allow me to stay at the house and get on with my business. The problem was that there was no business to get on with. I kept ruminating about Livy's death. Simon was history. And with Norman's situation mixed into the equation, I was not productive at doing anything other than eating more than I should. Thank goodness for Wilson, who I worried about more than myself. I took him for his morning jaunt, and gave him lots of leverage on his leash. I always felt better both mentally and physically after our walks. If something happened to him, I would fall apart.

I picked up the morning newspaper from the front veranda step. The day was sunny with no humidity, unusual for mid-August. I ate breakfast outside, parked in a rattan chair that Livy brought back from Indonesia. The slate floor was cool on my bare feet. Wilson curled up in the other chair, occasionally opening one eye to inventory my plate. I scanned through the paper, but couldn't absorb much more than the headlines. There were many jobs listed in the careers section, and online, but little that

I was remotely qualified to do. The obituary notices published two pages of announcements. Every deceased person left family members to grieve their loss. If Norman died, would his obituary list only dead relatives? Who would write his obituary notice, and why was I even thinking that? Maybe Fred? If Norman recovered, would the legal people offer Wilson to him? Fred probably read the little black journal and discussed the notice with Norman. I hope. Fred hadn't called, not that I really expected him to, but it would be nice to know that Norman was okay.

Staying away from Norman was hard because I knew what it felt like to be alone. I called the funeral home to get an update on Livy's memorial service. There were no new details, but no calls from Norman or Fred. I had a second cup of tea on the veranda and stared at the lawn. It was nine o'clock and I had no plans for the day. *Nothing.* If I drove to Niagara, I could be back by dinner. I argued with myself again that he was not my problem. I looked at Wilson. He was snoring, and not too happy to be herded back into the house. I showered and dressed quickly, and was out of the house by 9:30. I thought about bringing something of Livy's to Norman, but reconsidered it when I realized then the insurance adjusters would have to amend the Chestnut Boulevard inventory list.

Driving to Niagara was always easier than returning to Toronto, even in construction. I parked on a side street near the hospital and beside a bakery, which reminded me of Livy bragging that her grandmother made the best Empire cookies. Round shortbreads with jam in the middle and white icing topped with a maraschino cherry. I walked in to find none in the glass display, but two on the counter, marked half price. I bought them, and walked up the stairs to Norman's floor, arguing with myself for coming. Approaching Norman's room, I smelled disinfectant, mixed with powder and urine. He was in the same room, sound asleep. Antonio's bed was vacant and ready for a new patient. I took the chair from Antonio's side and parked it about four feet from the foot of Norman's bed. I sat quietly in the chair, and watched him snore softly. An IV bag with an antibiotic hung on a pole and was infusing into his vein. This was new. I sat for about twenty minutes before a young nurse came in. She smiled at me, checked the IV and the little gadget clipped around his finger. She watched him briefly and smiled again.

"How's he doing?" I asked.

"He had a rough night, so we should let him sleep." I pointed to the IV bag.

"That's new."

"Yes. If he wakes up or starts coughing again, could you let us know?"

"Sure."

I watched the lunch trays arrive, and went to find Norman's. Elvira beat me to it. She looked twice at me before she recognized me.

"Nice lady, you come back."

"Please call me Grace. How's Antonio?"

She picked up his tray and shrugged her shoulders. "No difference. I talk to God. He say Antonio no ready yet."

"Hopefully he will get better."

"He won't," she said confidently. "You see Normano?"

"He's sleeping."

"He very sick. Ammonia. Maybe even superbug." *Ammonia? Oh, pneumonia.*

"That's too bad. How many days has he been sick?"

"Yesterday they move Antonio, so maybe yesterday. It make a no difference to Antonio, but it make a difference to me." She pointed to the room across the hall from Norman's room. "They say he need to move. Yesterday I look outside da window at da street, at da beautiful trees. Today I looka at parking lot." She reached for Antonio's tray, and I took Norman's. I deposited it quietly on his over-bed table and sat down again. His lunch was identical to the last meal I saw, except his soup was green pea.

I heard Elvira across the hall praying out loud in her pre-meal ritual of blessing his food. Ten minutes later, as she put Antonio's empty tray out on the trolley, our eyes met. She stood outside Norman's door and whispered, "Antonio no eat, so I eat. Somebody gotta eat it. If not, they trow it out. Bigga waste, so I eat." She poked her head in Norman's room, ignoring the sign to put a mask on.

"He sick, he sleep, so you eat too! You too skinny." *Nice. You too chubby.* "You finda da book, Gracia?" *What book?* I had forgotten about the journal. She pointed to Norman's night stand. "I go see Antonio. Ciao, nice a lady." She disappeared into Antonio's bathroom, ignoring the sign that designated it for patients only, and shut the door.

Norman was still snoring when I walked silently to his night stand, littered with medical supplies. The top drawer would open only a few inches. The journal lay between Norman's teeth and glasses. I slipped it out of the narrow wedge. No one had torn out my note. I turned the page. The writing on the next page looked like chicken scratch. I could barely make out the words. I read it a few times before it made sense.

Nice man, nice lady comma here to see Normano.
She bring him cooky.
She not marry. You marry?
Maybe she bring you cooky.
I leave you cooky.

I turned the page.

Elvira,
Thanks for the delicious cookies – I ate them all.
I am happy the nice lady came – I'm sure she makes very nice cookies.
Maybe she will bring some cookies for all of us.
I hope she comes back too.
Thank you for praying for Norman – I think it is helping.
I think about you and Antonio often – it is a marriage made in heaven.
Make sure you take as good care of yourself as you do Antonio.

Fred
P.S I have a wife.

I turned the page again.

Grace:
Sorry I missed you. Norman had a few bad days.
He has a lung infection because he's not mobile.
He is on some painkillers, and antibiotics.
He's sleeping during the day, but up at night coughing.
Hopefully he will settle down and get better soon.
I didn't talk to him about the service because he was too
sick, but I'll be back to see him on Aug. 15.
Elvira said you came around 11:00 AM.
We can chat if you can make it down on the 15th.

Fred
P.S. Thanks for checking in on Norman – he asked about
you last time.
P.P.S. The journal is a good idea.

Norman was still motionless, and I doubted he would wake to have lunch.
I found a pen and added a note.

Aug. 14
I was here to visit from 11:00 – 12:30. Norman slept
the whole time. I will come tomorrow. He didn't eat his
lunch, but I left some cookies if he gets hungry later.
Grace (Sheehan)

I left Norman's lunch tray, and put the Empire cookies on his over
bed table. I removed my mask, and sanitized my hands outside Norman's
room. I crossed the hall to say good bye to Elvira, but she was slouched in
Antonio's wheelchair, with her mouth ajar and snoring like a freight train.

August 15th

Wilson and I had a good walk in the morning. I spoke with Tess, who was content doing her own thing. She was looking forward to going back to school and needed help with tuition. I called Sophie, and regretted it after two sentences. She wanted to know every detail of my recent days, lectured me about getting involved in some one else's affairs, then fished for details about Fred. When I said he was married, she switched to Norman, until she learned he was eighty-three years old. After warning me about spending time with older men, she hung up.

On my fifth trip to the hospital, I learned more about Elvira and Fred, but nothing new about Norman. He was under isolation precautions because of his pneumonia and possibly other infections, so I donned the required face mask before entering his room. He was asleep again, and looked like he hadn't moved since yesterday. I sat down quietly in the chair at the foot of his bed. The bag of cookies I brought yesterday was still on the table. I glanced across the hall. Elvira sat in Antonio's wheelchair beside Fred, who sat close to her in another chair. Her head was buried in his shirt, with his arm around her shoulders. A pile of crumpled tissues littered the floor. He glanced in my direction and made a sad face. I silently mouthed the word 'Antonio?' and he nodded. He looked up at the ceiling, then at me. I pointed up and mouthed 'Gone to heaven?' and he nodded again. I teared up, struck with sorrow at the loss of a marriage where two people remained devoted to each other until death. Sadly, I had never felt that in mine. I sat for a few quiet minutes, composed myself, threw the mask in the isolation bag outside Norman's door, and ventured across the hall.

Antonio's bed lay barren, sheets arranged as if he might return. When Elvira became aware of my presence, she folded her hands in prayer and said, "It was time. His time here finished. Now he wait for me," she wiped her weary eyes and mouth. I could only say 'I'm sorry.' Fred eased his arm from around her shoulders. My eyes welled up and Elvira took my hands in hers. "Don't cry, Gracia. Izza good day today. He izza in heaven. God have a nice place for him... witta bigga garden. We hadda sixty good years together, well maybe 59 and a half." She then put her hands on Fred's face. "He such a good man, my Antonio. Like you, but small." She kissed Fred on both cheeks. "Tanka you, tanka you for your caring, Freddy. You so, so nice." She looked at me and took my hand. "You so nice, lady. Don't cry." I cried harder. *Why was I so upset over this man's death?*

"Elvira, when are your children coming?" Fred asked quietly. She brought the big dial on her watch close to her face.

"Two o'clock." Fred looked at me. "And how's our other patient?" I spoke softly.

"Sleeping very soundly." Fred rolled his shoulders a couple of times to loosen the stiffness. The front of his golf shirt was wet in small patches, some from Elvira and the rest from sweat. He looked at the clock on the wall. It was almost noon.

"We're going to take you for lunch, and then we'll drive you home."

"No, no, no. I take bus home."

"Absolutely not. You've been here the whole night. The nurse told me so. You're hungry and exhausted."

"I take taxi."

"You will not take taxi. We'll go across the street, get a bite to eat and then we'll stay with you until your family comes." She looked at me.

"She coming too?"

"I hope she's coming. We all need to eat." Our eyes met. "Grace, can you join us?"

"I just got here."

"Elvira needs us more than Norman does right now."

"You so nice," Elvira said again, as Fred helped her ease her stiff, round body out of her chair. She didn't let him go, but when he turned to see a small, worn suitcase on the floor, she looked purposefully at me. I took the cue, picked it up and followed them. I debated briefly whether to stay with Norman or talk about death. My options seemed equally dismal. Fred was patient with his partner as she leaned on him heavily, stopping every few minutes to catch her breath. She grabbed onto the back of his belt for support as she stepped off the curb and onto the street pavement. I tagged behind with the suitcase.

In the restaurant, we were surrounded by hospital staff and visitors escorting other patients. When lunch arrived, Elvira prayed loudly in Italian and blessed us, and our food. She ate heartily and answered Fred's gentle questions, regardless of whether her mouth was full or empty.

Elvira and Antonio supported their children through university on Antonio's salary as a janitor. She was proud to have 'chosen' Antonio at her sister's wedding. Her proudest accomplishments in life were her marriage and family. She attended church daily. "I pray for everybody. I even pray for you. Now, Freddy. You aska me lotsa question. My turn." Elvira polished off her meal, and stifled a burp. She lifted her chubby hand up, and pointed to Fred. "Freddy, where your wife? She never come. She no like Normano?" Her question unsettled him.

"It's complicated, Elvira." That didn't satisfy her.

"Whatsa so complicated?" Fred pointed to his watch.

"Not enough time to talk about it today." She weaved in a few more questions about his wife, and the more Fred diverted the topic, the more curious I became. Fred paid for our meals. I left the tip, and boxed the rest of my lunch to send home with Elvira.

I waited with Elvira while Fred retrieved his vehicle, pulling up in a silver SUV. I paid my respects, hugged her, and handed her the suitcase. Fred drove her home, and I returned to Norman, still asleep. Fred was a secure buffer.

Norman's floor had the waiting room where Elvira and I first met, and also a small outdoor patio. I left a note on the white board outside Norman's door to let Fred know I was on the patio.

Four chairs were lined up, facing the sun. A single chair sat under an umbrella. I pulled a second chair out of the sun and sat down. The view was a parking lot. Nothing to distract me, other than questioning why I was here in the first place. *I need a real job...*

Fred joined me thirty minutes later. Neither of us spoke for a while. Ambulance sirens periodically interrupted the awkward silence. "How did you make out?" I asked.

"Pretty good. Her kids were already there, so that was a relief. Well, they're not kids. They're in their sixties and look like younger versions of her."

"You're back sooner than I thought."

"She lives close by and could walk here if she was well. She's got tomatoes growing in her flower beds. She wouldn't let me leave without giving some for me and 'for da nice lady.' I don't think I'd be picking tomatoes the day my spouse died."

"She's a nice lady."

He turned to me and smiled. "And you are a nice lady, too."

"Thanks. Elvira's a pretty resilient soul." A long pause again. "Was Norman sleeping?"

"No, he was awake."

"Shouldn't we go see him?"

"He's on the bedpan."

"Wonderful. The fibre must be working." Fred smiled again.

"The nurse said it takes him a while."

"Okay, then. That's always good to know." That lightened the silence. He scanned the vineyard.

"There's a game I play with my students when they first come to my class."

"What's it called?"

"Five Questions."

"Hmm. What are the rules?"

"There's only two." I watched as cars circled the parking lot for vacant spaces.

"What's rule number one?"

"You have to be honest."

"That's a good rule. So, how do you play this game?"

"It's very simple. We ask each other five questions. One question per turn."

"Who starts?"

"We flip a coin." Fred opened his hand. A quarter was already centered in his palm. "Ready to play?"

"That depends on rule number two."

"You can opt out of answering one of the five questions. Which means you have to answer all the rest."

"So if I skip one question, you can also skip one?"

"Right. Here's a hint. Plan your questions in sequence, expecting not to get an answer to one. And, of course, you can't ask the same question twice."

"Now it's not so simple."

"Trust me, it is. Are you ready?"

"Sure."

"Heads or tails?"

"Tails." My stomach tightened.

Fred flipped the coin high in the air. It spun repeatedly and landed near our feet on the concrete. As we both leaned forward to look, our heads bumped lightly. It was tails. Fred smiled. "You go first."

"How old is Claire?" An uncomplicated start. I estimated his daughter would be close to Tess's age.

"Thirty." *Older than I expected.* His first question was the same.

"How old is Tess?"

"Twenty." *Maybe my next question would answer two.*

"How old were you when she was born?" He smiled.

"I figured that would be your next question. I was eighteen." That made him forty eight now, and three years my junior. His second question was easy.

Where were you born?"

"Toronto." I felt gutsy, and asked his wife's name.

"Holly. Actually Holly Anne." *So she really exists.*

"How old were you when you had Tess?"

"I'll pass, but I had her in my twenties."

"Ah hah, third question, and she gives a range but doesn't answer my question." Fred shook his head and smiled. "You realize that's the only question now you can opt out of answering." I regretted it, but didn't want to change. At my turn, I hoped for multiple answers.

"Where does Holly live?" He rubbed his right eyebrow a few times before he answered.

"I'll pass." His question was reciprocal.

"Elvira told me you weren't married. Was there ever a husband?" I raised the ante, and gave him three bits of information.

"Yes. He died of lung cancer almost six months ago." Fred's expression changed.

"I'm sorry."

"That's okay. I'm over it." His eyebrows arched in curiosity. I pushed the topic more subtly with my final question.

"Does anyone else live at your house?"

"No." So he was married, but neither Holly nor Claire lived with him. And he wouldn't disclose her location. At least for now. I had more questions, but he wasn't offering more than one answer. His last question caught me off guard.

"Can I make you dinner tonight?" *What?*

I swallowed hard. Five minutes ago I would have said no, but there was something interesting about this man that he was not willing to share at this moment. I stalled.

"Can I give you an answer after we see Norman?"

"To see if you trust me?" He was hurt, which confused me.

"Trust you? It has nothing to do with trust. I'm just not sure how to answer."

"I do. It's usually one of two choices. But you can think about it." Fred stood up and looked at his watch. "I think Norman's probably ready for us." I followed Fred back into Norman's room. I defended myself as he passed me a mask.

"I trusted you enough to use the bathroom at your house."

"Your bladder was trusting that I had a bathroom." Saying no now to dinner would make the visit with Norman very uncomfortable, so I didn't say anything more about it.

Norman wasn't very social, but at least he spoke. Fred introduced me again as Livy's housemate, and told him I was taking good care of Wilson. Norman eyed me with the same demeanour he would give a skunk. I sat down in my usual spot with Elvira's basket of tomatoes under my chair. Fred sat closer to Norman. He inventoried the items on the bed side table. Some dressing supplies, hand sanitizer, the brown bag of cookies and my card. There were no other cards in the room. Fred opened my card and read the caption and my writing aloud. He handed it to Norman who looked at it with disinterest.

"See, I told you she was a good person, Norman," who forced a mumbled thank you.

"So, what's the doctor telling you?" Norman looked directly at Fred.

"Pneumonia."

"Yeah, we heard that too. Are you feeling any better?"

"Coughing less."

"That's good news. Any idea when they'll let you out of here?"

"About a week."

"A week? Let's see, if today's the 15th, that means they'll discharge you around the 22nd. You know you can't come straight home yet, right?"

"They're fools."

"No they're not. Did they say where you're going after here?"

"The rehab centre."

"Good - so you know. When your hip heals and you can get up and down the stairs at home, we'll all be much happier."

"Yep."

"I think the doctor said about six weeks."

"He's crazy."

"Old bones don't heal overnight, Norman. Let's figure this out. Six weeks takes us to the end of September. And when you get home, somebody will come to help you until you're a hundred percent."

"I don't need help."

"Yes you do."

"No I don't."

"Why don't we cross that bridge when we come to it."

"The physio is coming."

"To see you?"

159

"Yep."

"That's good. That means they haven't given up on an old dog like you."

Fred picked up the little brown bag that on the night stand and eyed it curiously. "What's in here?" Norman looked at the bag as if he'd not seen it before.

"Don't know."

"Want to have a look?" Norman shook his head, ignoring me.

"You open it." Fred looked in the bag. "Looks like some broken cookies. Who brought these?"

"Don't know." I'm sure he knew. Fred winked at me.

"Not only is she nice, but she bakes." He pointed to the bakery logo stamped on the outside of the bag and smiled. "Why, I think it says Grace's Bakery on it. Elvira might have some competition here." Norman didn't find it funny.

"You want one?" Norman shook his head and mumbled, "All yours."

Fred looked carefully into the bag, took a piece of broken cookie and popped it under the mask and into his mouth. "Mmm, Empire cookies. My grandma used to make these." He offered the bag to me. I shook my head.

"You know what, Norman?" An irritating silence from the patient. "Grace was a friend of Livy's and you should appreciate that. I'm sure she can tell you some recent things about Livy you don't know. You might not feel up to it now, but maybe when you feel better. She's driven here from Toronto already a few times just to make sure you were okay. She didn't have to do that." Norman looked at me indifferently. "There will be days where I can't help you. So if Grace is willing, she might come visit when I'm back at school. I trust her." *There's that word trust again.*

"I know."

"Good. Now I we've overstayed our visit, so we're heading out. Is there anything you need before we go?" Norman shook his head. Fred put his hand on Norman's shoulder and patted it a few times. Norman looked up at him and nodded. I got up and extended my hand to Norman. This time he took it, but the hand shake didn't convince me I was worthy. Fred retrieved a tomato from the basket under my chair and handed it to Norman and said goodbye. Norman watched me leave without even a nod. I almost expected the tomato to land against the back of my head.

It was a relief to get the face mask off and use the hand sanitizer. We walked down the busy hall, then silently took the stairs down. I stewed over the dinner invite. *Fred was married. Period.* We got to the front foyer of the hospital. The sun had disappeared and although the clouds were light, a few drops of rain started to fall. Fred looked at me, then at the basket of tomatoes in his hand. "So, here we are."

"Here we are."

"You haven't said yes, so I guess the answer is no," he said. I stalled again.

"What are you going to do with those tomatoes?"

"Give you half, and make chicken cacciatore with the rest."

"Can I take two, and a raincheck on the dinner?"

"I suppose that's fair. Any particular reason?"

"Yes. He has four legs. And a bladder." *A perfect excuse.*

"Good reason. Does he like Italian?"

"He likes anything, except cats."

"All right, then. The raincheck has an expiry date."

"Oh. And when is that?" I asked.

"The date is negotiable, but the offer ends today."

"Which means we set a date today?"

"That would be nice. I would prefer if we set a date, but not call it a date."

"I'm fine with that."

"Were you planning on seeing Norman again?"

"Yes, in about a week," I picked the time frame at random. "Livy wrote Norman a card that said she had a gift for him, but I'm not sure what it is. I saw the card on his mantle. I don't think he has seen it yet, so I was hoping to find it and bring it to him." Fred picked three plump tomatoes carefully from the basket.

"So one week from today, you'll come for dinner?"

"Which is August 22nd, if that suits you."

"It does. And hopefully Norman will be at the rehab centre."

"All the better."

"Maybe see Norman first, and then come over? No pressure."

"Sure."

"I really do appreciate it. He's a pain, but it's no fun for him either."
I softened.

"I know. He's lonely."

"May I call or text you in the morning on the 22nd to let you know where he'll be?"

"Sure." I wrote my number on the back of the bakery receipt, but didn't ask for his, and he didn't offer.

It rained all the way back to Toronto, and for two days after that.

August 19th

I called the volunteer coordinator at the Toronto hospital, who scheduled me for three shifts. I looked forward to wearing the pink smock. My first shift back involved another orientation with a 'senior' volunteer who was closer to Tess's age and hoped to work in Human Resources. She showed me the job posting board and career websites. Short shifts as they were, I was tired when they ended.

I got home from my third shift to find two messages on the house phone. Kristen Castle called first, and Fred's soft and pleasant voice was the second message, which I rewound and played back a few times.

I called Kristen, who was pleased that Norman was on the mend after speaking with 'a Mr. Fred Smith.' I was curious as to why they had spoken. Mr. Smith said my visits cheered Mr. Chestnut up, which would help his recovery. She also appreciated my concern for his well-being, and if I was mindful of driving the Volvo, the estate would reimburse my gas mileage if I chose to visit him weekly. If I let her know when Norman was transferred home from the rehab centre, she would finalize Livy's memorial service. She thanked me again, and left me wondering if I should buy my own car.

When I called Fred's number, the greeting was a female's voice, which said after four rings:

'You've reached the Smith residence. We're not here right now,
so please leave a message and we'll get back to you shortly.'

I cringed and hung up without leaving a message. If he lived alone, as he said he did, why did the message say "we're not home" and, who's voice was on the greeting? *So what's with the dinner invite?*

I walked Wilson in a foggy drizzle, and one trip around the block was enough to get him wet and sloppy. The house phone rang as I toweled down Wilson and quarantined him in his room to dry. I let the answering machine pick it up. It was Fred.

"Hi Grace. Someone called and didn't leave a message. It said private name and number, so I was hoping it was you. I'm home now, so give me a call."

I wasn't sure what to say to him, but would appreciate a few more answers before having dinner, which wasn't 'a date'. I poured a glass of wine and changed, sat down in the solarium and called back. The voice message clicked. The sound of the female voice bothered me more the second time, and I hung up again. The house phone rang. It was Nigel Anderson. He was returning to China tomorrow and I had no new information for him. He probably wouldn't return for the service, but asked me to let him know the date. My cell phone rang as I said goodbye to Nigel. As predicted, it was Fred.

"Hello."

"Hi Grace." He paused for a few seconds. "How have you been?"

"Fine."

"Were you busy over the last few days?"

"Yes. Very busy."

"Busy is good. Keeps you out of trouble."

"Yes it does. How's Norman?"

"Much better. I saw him this morning. He's using a wheelchair, and I can see grumpy old Norman coming back."

"That's good to hear."

"Grace?"

"Yes?"

"Is something wrong?"

"I'm not sure."

"You're not sure?"

"Fred, remember that game we played?"

"What game?"

"The Five Questions game."

"Oh, right."

"Can we play it now?"

"Oh, oh."

"Do you need a minute for your questions?"

"No. And we'll skip the coin toss. You go first."

"Fine. Why is there a female voice on your phone greeting?"

"Ah. Easy answer. The kids I teach have creative minds, but not always with good intentions. My number's unlisted, but somehow it was leaked to some of the kids. The female voice acts as a deterrent for prank calls. It's an old message that I never erased." It made sense. *Kind of.*

"Who's voice is on the greeting?"

"My daughter Claire. I'm sure you love to hear Tess's voice." *Of course.* "If Norman is transferred tomorrow, will you see him at the rehab centre?"

"Yes." I still regretted asking the last question.

"Does your daughter live nearby?"

"Toronto." *Surprised again.*

"Can you come around eleven when he's discharged?"

"Yes. Where does your wife live?"

"At a different address than mine." His turn.

"Are you going to change your mind about dinner?"

"I'll pass."

"You'll pass on dinner, or you'll pass on the answer?"

"I'll pass on the answer."

"Very well then, I'll take that as a maybe." He gave me the rehab centre address, the same as what the discharge planner gave me, and said a quiet goodbye.

August 20th

The facility where Norman was transferred to was a stark contrast to the modern, state of the art hospital he left. It was almost the same distance from Old Chestnut Lane, and nestled among lush maple trees that had matured with the facility. A historical plaque described the refurbished building as a sanatorium for patients recovering from tuberculosis in the days when the disease was an epidemic. Large covered patios, and a pretty gazebo hosted clusters of patients and their visitors. A middle aged woman in a wheelchair sat behind the information desk in the front lobby, shuffling papers until she found what she was looking for. Zebra-printed bifocals balanced precariously on the end of her tiny nose.

"Let's see, Norman Chestnut. Wing C," she chirped. Finding his room on the third floor was easy. Large windows overlooked the courtyard I had just walked though. The view was picturesque, whether Norman was in bed or his wheelchair. I found him in one of three beds in a room meant to accommodate four residents. Beside each bed was a wheelchair. Clean and soiled linen carts, walkers and other supplies filled the space where the fourth bed should be. Norman was wide awake, his expression more anxious than angry. He looked relieved to see me.

"Hello, Norman."

"I just got here."

"Good. You're lucky to have this view."

"When's Fred coming?"

'Pretty soon, I think."

"I need my clothes.'

"Clothes?"

"They said you would bring my clothes. I have no pants. I need my pants."

"Okay. Let's make a list."

"Don't need a list. I need pants, a shirt, and the other things." I grabbed a receipt out of my purse and started writing on the back.

"What other things?"

"Fred knows."

"Then why don't we wait for Fred?"

"I need shoes."

"Where are your slippers?"

"Can't have slippers."

"Why not?"

"So I don't fall. I need rubber on the bottom." He looked desperate.

"Okay. Don't worry. We'll talk to Fred when he gets here."

I was relieved when a nurse in hot pink scrubs walked into the room. The colour was a lovely contrast to her flawless dark skin.

"Hello there, Mr. Chestnut. Welcome." She came closer to Norman. "Can you hear me all right, Norman?"

"Of course I can hear you," he snapped. She stayed close to him, but remained in control.

"Oh Norman, you want to stay on my good side, because I'm the one who gets you special privileges. Now, can you see my name tag? What is my name?"

"I need my glasses." She rummaged through a white plastic bag with a red drawstring. The clothes in the bag were still the same ones he wore when he was admitted to the hospital. I could smell their ripeness from where I stood. The nurse's expression never changed, until she found the glasses.

"Bingo!" She passed them to Norman. He held them in his hand.

"Put them on, Norman. I need you to read some things." He obeyed. They were crooked, but at least they were on. "Now what's my name?"

167

"Sandra."

"Can you see what it says under my name?" he squinted and adjusted his glasses.

"Nurse manager."

"That's right. That means I'm the big cheese here, and if you have any problems, you need to talk to me. If your family has any problems, they should talk to me too." Sandra reviewed some admission papers, and asked him if he understood them. He nodded, and she asked him to sign them. He scribbled a signature. She was about to hand a copy to me, but stopped.

"Is this your daughter?" Norman and I shook our heads with equal vigor. "Relative?"

"I don't have no family." She didn't miss a beat.

"Then you're very lucky to have this lady visit on your first day. She looked to me for an introduction.

"Grace. Friend of a relative." I thought that would suffice, but Norman shot me a seedy look.

"I have no relatives." She looked at me.

"He's right," I corrected myself. "She was his only relative, and very recently passed away."

"I saw that in the chart. I'm sorry for your loss," she continued. "We have a wonderful bereavement support group here, and a really good social worker we can set you up with, Norman."

"I don't need that horse crap. I just need my clothes."

"No foul language here, Norman. We enforce our Code of Conduct policy. Let's be clear about that." Norman mumbled an apology.

"Accepted. Now don't worry about clothes. We've got a whole wardrobe of extra clothes until we get yours laundered." Norman looked at me.

"She'll clean them." Sandra passed me the plastic bag before he finished the sentence. His grin was huge with victory over me. For the first time, I noticed he had both top and bottom teeth.

I made a note to ask the lawyer about getting him some new clothes and running shoes. Sandra asked who to call in case of an emergency. We both said Fred, who was coming soon.

Sandra gave us a short verbal orientation of the facility, pushing Norman in his wheelchair. She told us that Norman would start an aggressive physio and occupational therapy program shortly. Norman waved his hands in the air.

"I don't need no occu-therapy. I'm eighty-three friggin' years old, for crying out loud." Sandra kept her pace.

"Norman, an occupational therapist is like an architect, but for your body. She's going to figure out how to get you home safely, and keep you there. We want you as independent as you were before you broke your hip. The physio will help you re-build your strength. You don't want to stay here any longer than you have to, do you?"

"I want to go home now."

"Going home is the perfect goal. Most residents say the food is pretty good, but it's not like home. So that's another reason for you to work with the rehab team. We want to get you home too."

Fred walked in and Norman perked up. Sandra said, "Wow, not one but two visitors. What a lucky guy you are. She shook Fred's hand firmly. "I'm Sandra, the nurse manager, and you must be Fred."

"I am." He was dressed in vibrant, plaid shorts and a bright polo shirt. He also wore cologne. A fresh hair cut exposed untanned skin around his neck. He wiped small beads of sweat off his forehead with his shirt sleeve. He smiled at me, and I felt calmer with him present, even though our last phone call left more questions than answers. Fred looked at the other residents in the room. One was sleeping and the other was eyeing us suspiciously. Fred looked at Norman. "How you doing there, neighbour?"

"Just got here." Sandra handed the admission papers and an orientation folder to Norman and excused herself. He threw them on the overbed table.

"I need clothes."

"What kind of clothes?"

"Pants. I need pants."

"Okay, big guy. We'll get you pants. They're not gonna kick you out if you don't have them today." Fred leafed through the orientation pages in the folder, and pulled out a sheet. "Here the list of clothes you need." Norman looked at the sheet like it was more important than the admission papers. Fred offered the lone chair to me. I moved it a little farther away from Norman and Fred, and sat down. We exchanged polite smiles.

He walked over to the resident who was sleeping across from Norman's bed and quietly picked up a second chair, then sat down on the other side of Norman's bed. He faced me, and browsed through the folder. Norman started nattering again.

"I need money." Fred's eyes stayed on the folder.

"What do you need money for?"

"The paper."

"What paper?"

"The newspaper."

"You never read the paper."

"I do now." Fred pulled some change out of his pocket. "Do you need it right now?" This agitated Norman even more.

"I want my own money." The change went back in Fred's pocket.

"Settle down, old chum. We'll get you organized here, and then we'll get the paper delivered, or I'll bring it to you." That made Norman angrier. He crossed his arms over his chest, and his face turned scarlet. Fred stood up and left the room. Dead silence. Again. *What am I doing here?*

Fred stood outside the door for a few seconds, and then knocked on it. Instead of Norman, a female voice in Norman's room called out in a high pitched voice, "Come in!" Fred walked back in the room and looked at Norman.

"I'm gonna start again. Hello Norman. How are you?" Norman ignored Fred, distracted by the female patient.

"What the hell! No one told me there was going to be a woman in the room!" Norman was not referring to me. "Where's that black woman? Get her in here!"

"Settle down!" Fred was embarrassed and impatient.

"I'm not settling down. Get that god-damn nurse in here now!" I left to find Sandra, the nurse manager, while Fred scolded Norman. It would be much easier to walk out of the building. Sandra was in her office beside the nursing station. In a diplomatic voice, I explained the drama. Her chair scraped the floor as she got up and I followed her brisk footsteps back to Norman's room.

I could see the frustration on both men's faces. Sandra came within inches of Norman's face, and set her hand on Norman's shoulder. The tone of her voice never wavered from a low pitched boot camp bellow. "Now look, Mr Chestnut. You just got here. You were assigned this room because it was the only one available. You are a guest here, and just like everyone else, we will treat you like our guest. As in any place where guests stay, those who break the rules are evicted, or as we call it here, discharged. If we discharge you, you will be going to a place that's a lot worse than this one. So, Mr. Chestnut, I suggest you be as patient with our staff, and the other residents, as we have been with you. When a bed becomes available in a female room for Mrs. Steinbeck, we will move her. But right now, she has as much right to be in this room as you do. Is that clear, Mr Chestnut?"

Norman sunk deep into his pillow. His eyes remained wild with anger. She didn't let up.

"You will follow the rules. And your first rule is to attend all our programs. The first program we will send you to is mindfulness, and that class starts tomorrow. Now if you will excuse me, have a good day, everyone." She winked at Fred as she left the room. Norman, stung by defeat, hissed to Fred that Steinbeck sounded Jewish.

"Shut up, Norm." Fred shot back and walked out. *Oh, great.* Norman glared at me and mumbled.

"This is all your fault." I couldn't help but laugh.

Fred returned shortly, calmer than when he left. He read excepts from the admission brochure, as if he was reviewing a homework assignment with a student. Mrs Steinbeck was in her bed, babbling away about following rules which I soon realized gathered were rules in her own mind, which was somewhere far away from the rest of us in the room. Norman grumbled under his breath.

Fred sighed. "Here we go again." He looked at me sadly and shook his head. He motioned me out of the room, leaned back against the hallway wall, and apologized.

"Why are you apologizing? It's not your fault."

"I pressured you into coming to help me. I'm sorry. I should have been more up front about his behaviour before I asked you."

"He's a cranky old man. You said he was a recluse. Now he's a recluse who's out of his element."

"Grace, if you want to leave, I won't blame you." *I don't want to leave, but why? Who am I helping? Livy's gone. Myself? Is this void in my life so big that I need to fill it with these strangers? They've probably figured me out. Always there to help everyone else, except myself. Is this what loneliness is about?*

I had drifted away, just like Mrs. Steinbeck.

"Grace?"

"Oh. Sorry." I flushed. Fred ushered me back into Norman's room, leaning his hand lightly on my shoulder. His cologne smelled like grapefruit and spices.

"Do I have to worry about you too?"

"I'll be fine," I smiled. Sandra's scolding, along with our time in the hall was effective in settling Norman down. A new nurse entered the room to take Norman's vital signs and complete the admission's physical exam. Fred announced our exit. Norman looked helplessly at Fred.

"I want to go home."

"And you will. Now mind your manners." I said a polite goodbye. Fred reassured Norman that one of us would visit in the next few days.

"When?"

"Not sure, Norm. But I promise you soon." Fred took Norman's list, returned his chair next to the sleeping resident, and took Norman's dirty laundry.

Sandra waved goodbye from her office as we passed. Fred kept a polite distance from me, but opened each door. The day was beautiful, and the breeze was warm. He gestured toward a gazebo nearby.

"Can we sit for a few minutes before you go?"

"Sure." We sat on chairs with bright floral cushions under the gazebo. I sat down first and he chose a chair across from me. He leaned back, watched me silently, his hands folded across him. He had a dimple in his chin. His eyes were bright, but his expression apprehensive. The wind sent more of his cologne my way.

"What a morning. Now you know Norman."

"He's quite a handful."

"More like a tyrant." I laughed, and nodded.

"How did he earn his living before he retired?"

"He was an arborist. He pruned and looked after trees."

"I wouldn't have thought that by the looks of his property."

"He gave up on that, and almost everything else."

"That's sad. Like him, the shrubs need a little love."

"He squawks at me if I try to trim them."

"He must have had some wealthy clients to afford his property."

"The real estate here is much cheaper than Toronto. Norman worked for NPC. New Pelham Chestnuts."

"What's that?"

"It's a long established, world-renowned research farm in Niagara. It was originally a big farm surrounded by chestnut trees that grew different types of fruit, which Niagara is well known for. The property owner was a university professor, and a hobby farmer. He retired early to research nut trees, then started growing species that bore edible nuts, including chestnuts."

"Interesting."

"The farm, unique to this area, became known for it's research, and was named New Pelham Chestnuts. Horticulture scientists from all over still conduct research here. Not only does the farm sell delicious nuts, it has many generous supporters. There's even a little museum of artifacts from the original farm."

"I've never heard of it."

"Many people haven't. Many chestnut trees were lost years ago to a fungal disease. Thanks to NPC, the species was re-populated to produce nuts again."

"Nuts in Niagara. Hmmm."

"Yup. Norman said he worked there because of the name. NPC. Same initials as Norman Percy Chestnut. He still wears old clothes with the NPC logo on them.

As for his money, I'm sure some of it is old family money. But then again, he never spends it."

"So is he connected to the Old Chestnut Tree I drove by on the way here?"

"No, but again it's the reason why he built his house there. NPC also stands for the New Pelham Cemetery, which you may have noticed is across the street."

"Too many NPC coincidences. How long has he lived there?"

"Maybe ten or fifteen years. And alone for at least nine."

"It's a gorgeous house, if you can see beyond the neglect. Such a big house for one person."

"His niece talked him into building it as an investment."

"Livy?" He nodded.

"Yes. I moved next door after his house was built."

"Did he tell you that his house has the same layout as Livy's?"

"Really? No, he didn't."

"The tiles in the front entrance are identical. Both houses have the word CHESTNUT written in black and white tiles. It was strange walking into Norman's house. It even has some of the same furniture."

"She apparently was there often during construction, which brought them closer together."

"I'm sure you know that Norman's lawyers are managing Livy's estate, and will arrange her funeral when Norman has the stamina to attend. That old Chestnut money is carefully monitored, and spent cautiously."

"That explains why some landscape company measured his lawn yesterday, or what used to be lawn. Maybe someone will look after the house."

"If they think the outside needs maintenance, wait until they see the inside."

"It's been like that for at least nine years. It was perfect before his wife checked out."

"Checked out?"

"I think she left him because he was such a miserable bastard."

"So if he's eighty-three now, he was seventy-four when she left him?"

"That sounds right. I'm surprised she stuck around that long."

"Livy never mentioned her."

"Neither did he. And she was a saint. She never did anything right, according to him. Apparently she left one day with only the clothes on her back, and no one saw her again."

"Is she still alive?"

"I'm not sure. I think so. I never saw an obituary. She was a local lady, so I assumed she moved to get away from him. And he wouldn't go chasing after her. He refuses to talk about her."

"What was her name?"

"Nancy. And she called him Normy when she wasn't mad at him."

"Another happy couple."

"He was absolutely miserable before, and even more so after she left. He wouldn't spend a nickel unless he had to. Other than what Livy talked him into buying. I have no idea how she persuaded him to purchase such high-end furniture, even if she bought it wholesale. Everything was the bare minimum."

"What about the old Mercedes in his driveway?"

"It was some old lady's car who died a few years ago. I think her name was Maddy."

"That was Livy's great Aunt Madeleine. She broke her ankle and died shortly after."

"That car was in pristine condition, until he got it. It's not been washed since he inherited it. On hot days, I wanted to hose both him and the car down."

"He was pretty ripe when we found him."

"And sick."

After a long pause, Fred slouched back in his chair. He stared directly at me with an odd expression.

"She's sick."

"Who's sick?"

"My wife." Caught by surprise, I tried to remember our last Five Questions game. Now it made sense, and I felt terrible.

"I'm sorry. That's not what I thought."

"What did you think?"

"That it was another bad marriage that fell apart. Two incompatible spouses that went their separate ways, and never bothered to divorce."

"And what else?"

"That your daughter was an unexpected gift, and you married for her sake."

"Not the case with us. Holly was my one true love."

"I met Blair when I was sixteen."

"Your husband?

"Yes."

"Your one and only?"

"There was only one other guy." *Simon. What a mistake.*

"While you were married?"

"No, no." Fred didn't ask more, and I didn't offer. He shifted in his chair.

"So now you know why I'm still married."

"When did your wife get sick?" He scanned the horizon.

"Many, many years ago."

"Before you moved to New Pelham?" He nodded silently. I was curious, but leery of prying. "That's a long time."

"She was ill long before I realized what was happening. When we moved to New Pelham, to a new environment, she got worse."

"Like, physically sick?" He watched me as he shook his head.

"Sick, like mentally ill." He closed his eyes and put his head back gently to rest against the chair. Neither of us spoke for a while. His voice became quiet. "This may sound cruel, but's sometimes it's easier when they die, Grace, than when they stay alive." I thought of Blair. Fred rose from his chair. His shoulders remained slouched and he looked older now than when he walked into Norman's room an hour ago. He took his car keys out of his pocket and asked me if I could find my way home. I wasn't in the mood to have dinner, nor was he in the mood to make it. We walked back to the parking lot together. His car was three parking spaces away from the Volvo. He opened my car door for me, and hesitated before he spoke.

"Grace?"

"Yes?"

"Do you trust me?" *Why is he bringing this up again?*

"I have no reason not to." I saw frustration in his eyes.

"You didn't answer my question." I knew that I'd offend him if I didn't answer, but his question begged for an explanation.

"Yes, Fred. I trust you," I answered, not certain if I was being completely truthful.

"Thank you. And that's all I'll ask of you." He didn't say another word. I wanted to touch his shoulder, but he stayed out of reach. He watched me as I drove away, standing with his hands stuffed deep in his pockets.

Driving to Toronto gave me lots of time to think. I knew the basics of marital law, in the event of divorce or death. But I had no idea what happened when a marriage failed because of illness. Fred was forty-eight, and I assumed Holly was around the same age. Maybe she had been institutionalized, which explained why she didn't live with him. I wondered how long she'd been there.

I wondered if Fred visited her, and what they might talk about, if she talked at all. Maybe she lived in a locked-down unit, far away. Or maybe she lived with their daughter. I had many questions, but at least I had a few answers.

I ate scrambled eggs on toast with Elvira's tomatoes when I arrived home, and watched the news in the kitchen. I wondered what Fred had for dinner. Maybe chicken cacciatore for two, or scrambled eggs on toast for one.

I also wondered if Fred thought my trips to Niagara would end. Or if Norman would mellow after Sandra had tuned him up. I would update the law office tomorrow that Norman was transferred. If she approved, I'd buy him some clothes and shoes. When I bought his slippers, I correctly estimated his size. Waist circumference was trickier, however, than slipper length. Maybe Fred could fill the inventory list from Norman's closet. *Or, maybe I should stay out of it.*

The day was ending with the same beautiful sky it had started with. The eggs curbed my hunger for a few hours, until I craved something cold and sweet. Wilson and I walked to the local ice cream stand. Families with kids in strollers lined up at the outdoor order window. Had Fred done this with his family? Despite his complicated life, we could be friends. There was something intriguing about him. We would have had dinner tonight, and it would have been just that; dinner and some good conversation. Through Norman, via Fred, I could have learned more about Livy. It would have been harmless.

I felt stuffed after finishing the ice cream, but craved more. I sensed it was my heart, not my mouth or stomach, that needed sustenance. I watched the people around me. The couple on the next bench fed a few spoons of ice cream to their toddler, then with my permission, fed the rest to a drooling Wilson, which delighted the toddler. A young couple shared their dessert, and kisses. Two boys sat behind me, one whining that his brother got a bigger scoop. Their frustrated mother tossed his cone in the garbage and snipped, "Now for sure your brother has more." Wilson saw the ice cream fly into the garbage, wondering why the woman didn't give it to him.

The walk home took more effort and the setting sun created long shadows on the sidewalks. A few sprinklers sent intermittent streams of water crystals across dry lawns. No one called me, so I phoned a girlfriend to chat, and the call went to her voice mail. Sophie wasn't answering, and I didn't leave a message. I called Tess who asked what was wrong, and why I was calling. She was going out with friends after work at the university. Wilson stayed close to me as if he knew my mood was low. I had nothing to do but search job postings, with Wilson crowding me on the couch. I finessed my resume again and applied for a few jobs that were similar to the one I had left at Bernard Steel. They weren't exciting, but ones I knew best. There was no excitement when I pressed the send button. My mother used to tell me that each day mattered, and served a purpose. Sometimes it was obvious, and sometimes I had to find it. I needed to start looking for that purpose again.

That night, Wilson was restless. He moved from the top of the stairs, then to the doorway, and finally to the foot of my bed. I woke up with him on my bed, and he gave me a look that said we both still needed more sleep. It was nice to have another warm body near. Four legs were less complicated than two and trust was never an issue.

August 23rd

I let a few days pass before my next trip to Niagara. I was bored. The housekeeper came to clean what she didn't need to, and tell the law firm that I wasn't trashing the house. So I left.

Arriving at the rehab centre, the gardeners were on a break, sitting in the gazebo when I parked my car. Their shirts were stained with sweat on this very warm day. A wheelbarrow full of weeds and shrub trimmings sat on the grass next to a hose and lawn tools. As I headed towards the sliding glass doors, they opened before I activated the sensors. I saw the wheelchair, with Norman in it, wearing a hospital gown and a worn tartan housecoat. His socks had been white, many washings ago. His new sneakers still held a plastic loop from the price tag. He was not expecting to see me. He wheeled his chair with laboured effort towards the parking lot. A pair of crutches were tucked in between him and the chair, the rubber feet sharing the foot rest with his shoes. He was on a mission, and ignored me. I turned back and followed him.

"Good morning, Norman. Looks like you're getting your strength back." He avoided me.

"Yep."

"Going out to get some sun?" I walked behind him along the sidewalk. He ignored me.

"Yep. Have you got a five?"

"Like dollars?"

"Yes, like dollars." I pulled my wallet out and withdrew a ten dollar bill that sat beside a lone twenty. I offered it to him and he flashed me a short lived, but broad smile. He gently slipped it out of my hand with two fingers, careful to avoid touching mine.

"Thanks."

"What do you need money for, Norman?" By his expression, I had no business asking.

"The paper." I pointed to the newspaper boxes by the front entrance. He shook his head. "Not those."

"Where are you getting the paper from?"

"It's being delivered." He knew I wasn't buying his story.

"Expensive paper. Who's delivering it?" I suspected the 'delivery' might be from the beer store which Norman might camouflage in newspaper and smuggle back to his room. I walked around the chair to face him. He turned the wheelchair to the edge of sidewalk, and with some maneuvering of his good foot, brought the chair to where the sidewalk met the parking lot. The delivery vehicle arrived. It was a taxi, and the driver got out and approached Norman. His hands were empty. He gave me a quick nod and asked Norman if he could get himself into the taxi. Norman rammed his wheelchair against the back door of the cab.

"I'll need a little help," he lied sweetly to the driver.

"Where are you going in your pajamas, Norman?" I didn't expect an answer, and didn't get one. The driver intervened.

"Old Chestnut Lane." I caught on.

"Norman, who discharged you? You're supposed to be here for six weeks." The driver looked at me, confused. "You're not coming with this guy?" I shook my head.

"Absolutely not. And he's not going to Old Chestnut Lane unless he's been discharged or has a day pass." The driver looked at Norman, who offered the ten dollar bill, which the driver took. The locks on the car doors clicked shut just as Norman struggled to open the back door. The driver leaned against the front passenger door, waving the bill at Norman like a handkerchief.

"How far did you think this was going to get you?"

"I get a senior's discount."

"Senior or not, this won't get you to where you thought you were going." Norman extended his hand to me for more bail money. The driver winked at me and then asked Norman where his suitcase was. Norman's reply was swift.

"I didn't bring one." I stood behind Norman, shaking my head. The driver played along.

"Then I need to see your discharge pass, buddy." Norman snorted and pointed at me.

"She threw it out. She said I didn't need it." The game was over, and after that comment, I was ready to leave. The driver handed Norman the ten dollar bill back. He stashed it in his pocket, and flipped me his middle finger.

Two rubenesque women, including Sandra, hustled out of the glass doors of the rehab centre towards us. Their loosely harnessed breasts swayed in unison under their uniforms as they hurried towards us. The cab sped away as her tirade began. Hands planted on her ample hips, Sandra scolded him as the other nurse wheeled him back. Sandra asked who would pay the two thousand dollars for the wheelchair he was stealing. Norman yelled that I would, and I laughed out loud. The nurse pushing him mouthed silently to me that this was his second escape attempt in two days. We rode up the elevator together as Sandra's rant continued. The nurse parked Norman outside the nursing station, passed his shoes to me, suggesting I hide them on his top cupboard shelf. She tied the wheelchair to the railing and then went about her business. Eventually Sandra ran out of breath and words. Fixing her hair with a few confident pats, she flashed a gracious smile, returned to her office and shut the door.

Mrs. Steinbeck was no longer Norman's roommate, when I returned the shoes to Norman's cupboard. There were two new track suits folded on the top shelf, labels still attached. His shoes went on the top shelf, and I closed the door. On his bed side table was an apple juice container, but no straw. I opened the drawer to find a few. Seeing the journal from the hospital, I opened it. The last entry was dated yesterday.

Aug. 22
Grace, if you read this, thank you for coming back. You are indeed generous and kind. I hope Norman behaves for you, as he did for me yesterday. He asked when you were coming again. I won't bother you if you decide not to further complicate your life with us. I'll be back on Aug. 24 and probably Aug. 26 (around 11). I'll be at school both days early in the morning. If you're not here, I will understand.
Fred
P.S My greatest fear is to have regrets at the end of my life. Not seeing you again is one of them.

I found a pen nestled in the drawer between the straws. Norman would wait, as I took a few minutes to prepare my reply.

Aug. 23
Hi Fred,
I saw Norman today. I'm volunteering tomorrow but will come back on the 26th. He has $10 hidden in his housecoat which he got from me. He tried to bribe a cab driver (twice) to take him home (I witnessed the 2nd escape attempt). If he rounds up another $10 from you, he may succeed.
Regards,
Grace
P.S. I too have fears and regrets. Yes, it would be nice to see you again.

I tucked the journal deep in the drawer, and out of Norman's reach. I returned to the hallway where he was watching the activities around him, and he was surprised that I was still there. He emptied the juice box, and stared at me. I offered to take him outside. He shook his head. I asked him if he wanted me to sit with him. Again, he shook his head. I asked him if he would mind if I came back in a few days, and bring some books from Livy's house. He hesitated, then nodded. When I asked him if he wanted anything else, he produced a loud belch. Thirty minutes with Norman, and I'd had enough. I extended my hand, only to see if he would shake it. He didn't.

Back in the car, with no reason to rush home, I headed in the general direction of New Pelham. The transformation from city into country was quick. I rounded a hilly curve where the road divided a cattle farm. Cows grazed near the fence, with young calves scattered around them, either napping or nursing. I passed by a nature conservation area, and a few parked cars with empty bicycle racks. I remembered some of the picturesque homes on my first trip to the hospital. When people dream about country living, this fit the description nicely.

Old Chestnut Lane and a sign pointing to 'The Old Chestnut Tree' came up before I thought about being lost, and I turned there. A dozen colourfully clad cyclists raced by me, barreling down a deep valley with enough momentum to ease them half-way up of a short, steep hill. I passed Norman and Fred's driveways before realizing it. I also hadn't noticed the quaint cemetery located across from Fred's house. I turned at a stop sign and drove into the back entrance of the cemetery. Historical brass plaques were mounted on a pair of stone pillars. I inched along a narrow gravel lane. There were rows of weathered limestone plaques, some leaning against each other or the huge trees. The lane divided rows of more recent tombstones from the rest of the cemetery and ended at Old Chestnut Lane, facing Fred and Norman's properties. I stopped at the curve of the lane, about fifty feet from the road. There was no car in Fred's driveway. I opened the windows and turned off the car to rest. The breeze was cool and smelled of hay.

I took a deep breath and exhaled slowly. I got out and shut the door quietly, distracted by mindless thoughts and the August breeze. No radio music to float me into another moment in time. The rows between tombstones were mowed recently. Old, stately maple trees framed the lane. Century-old stones were laden with lichen growing into their faded inscriptions. Perennials extended beyond the plots they were intended for. Wreaths rested against stones, faded like the memories of their occupants. Rust from a miniature toy train stained a monument ledge. A faded ceramic angel kneeled on another, praying to the heavens with one arm missing at the elbow. Lives summarized in a handful of words - some describing grief, others long and happy lives. A square, shiny black granite bench served as an open invitation to rest. I sat on the warm stone and inhaled, closing my eyes and fingering the inscription my fingers rested against.

An approaching vehicle brought me back. Fred's silver SUV turned into his driveway. He collected a few grocery bags from the back seat and glanced at the cemetery before unlocking his front door and disappearing inside. Feeling uncomfortable being here with no explanation, I got into to the Volvo, shut the door quietly, and debated whether I should back the car out to avoid being seen. I did nothing wrong, but I felt like I had. Something drew me here. I drove forward slowly. Small twigs from the massive maples crunched loudly beneath my tires. By the time I reached the road, Fred was standing on his front steps, hands on his hips, watching me. He pointed to his bare feet and motioned me over.

My heart thumped loudly as I drove down his driveway, feeling sheepish, yet pleased to see him. I left the car running. He approached me, then squatted down to eye level.

"Looking for a bathroom?" I flushed.

"I have no idea why I'm here." He glanced across the street.

"Nothing stimulates self-reflection quite like mortality."

"Well said. It's a quaint old cemetery."

"With a lot of visitors. Some permanent."

"And some like me, just passing through."

"Some cyclists rest there."

"It's very calming."

"Thirsty?"

"I could be."

"Then get out of that hot car."

"I'm invading your privacy."

"You're not. I invited you."

"I didn't think you'd be here."

"What difference would that make?"

"I wondered if you thought I abandoned Norman."

"You wouldn't be the first, or the last."

"He hates me." Fred opened my door. I got out, and we both leaned against the car facing his house, his bare feet splayed on the smooth concrete sidewalk.

"He doesn't hate you. He's afraid to lose the upper hand. And as long as you give him permission to control you, he will."

"He almost succeeded."

"You saw him today?"

"I did. He tried to escape." Fred laughed.

"A man on a mission. He hasn't left his house for more than a day at a time in years. He'll be more content when he gets home."

"I'm sure the staff will be just as happy to get him there."

"And he'll resist every offer of help when he's discharged." Fred walked up the sidewalk towards the house. "Something hot, or cold to drink? The kettle's already boiled."

"Tea would be great."

"Shall we stay outside or would you like to come in?"

"It's gorgeous out here."

"Milk and sugar?"

"I'm impressed you remembered." Fred went inside. I sat down on the warm concrete step, facing the sun. I kicked my sandals off, the right one bouncing down the stairs onto the sidewalk. As much as I loved the city, I knew what attracted people to the country.

Fred was at the screen door with two full mugs and an unopened box of animal crackers under his arm. I opened the door, taking a mug and the crackers. There was just enough room for both of us to sit on the front step. Fred opened the crackers, and passed them to me. "It's as close to home-baked as you're gonna get here." They were fresh, crunchy and full of good memories.

"I haven't eaten these since Tess was a kid."

"It's one of the few things Claire expects when she's home."

"It's Oreos at our house." Fred's leg muscles were defined, and his bare feet were long and narrow. I inhaled deeply. "Ever feel isolated living out here?" Fred chuckled.

"Some folks think this is the wilderness. To me, it's the best of both worlds. It's rare that I regret living here."

"The days must long when you're off school."

"The days aren't, but sometimes life is. I have too much time to think in the summer. You know that expression, sometimes you count the days, and sometimes you weigh them."

"That's what I was doing across the street."

"Were you bored? Or just restless?"

"Restless."

"Because you don't know why you're here? Alone, with nowhere else to go on this hot and sunny summer day?"

"Yes and yes again. I have that feeling more and more often now. My life needs more purpose." *Why am I telling him that?*

"That's an important stage of grieving. It's part of moving forward." *He's right.* "And, also going slowly so that you don't have regrets. Or make mistakes."

"What do you mean by that?"

"Well, let's start with the 'alone' part. I'm alone because I have to be. I don't want to be, but that's my choice, and it's a tough one. If and when I am ready to make different choices about my life, I must be smart about them."

"Are you saying you don't have a choice because you're still married?"

"It's one of many, but that's the primary reason."

"There are more?"

"Again, if and when I don't want to be alone, I'd need some really good advice. I don't want to be perceived as being the bad guy."

"By who? Your wife?"

"No, not Holly. She still wears her wedding ring, but she barely knows who I am. It's the rest of the world I'm worried about, and especially Claire."

"But Claire is an adult."

"Yes. An adult who has never had a solid relationship beyond her parents."

186

"So she'd have trouble accepting you moving forward?"

"It's not that simple. Claire has always been in both our lives."

"But that's a good thing. She should be."

"She was just a baby when Holly got sick." Fred glanced at his watch. "This story has a many chapters."

"Tell me a few."

"It all started with Holly becoming anxious. When Claire was born, Holly was afraid she'd die in her sleep. You know, the overprotective mother."

"I remember doing that."

"This 'Sudden Infant Death Syndrome' thing was in the news a lot and Holly could't get it out of her head. Every night it was the same thing. Holly wouldn't sleep. We saw the doctor a few times about it. Claire had regular check ups, but Holly was convinced that there was something wrong with her. The poor kid went through a battery of unnecessary tests, which settled Holly down until Claire was about a year old. Then she was slow to walk, but the doctor wasn't worried about it, because Holly carried her around all the time. Then she became fixated on that, day and night, until Claire finally started walking. When that issue resolved, Holly became neurotic that Claire wasn't eating right. I now know it's typical of many toddlers, but she refused to eat anything but cereal and bananas. Then Holly thought that all the other food was being poisoned, and became obsessed with researching genetically modified food. Claire's doctor settled her fears, for about a minute, before Holly went on to the next thing."

"Did she get better?" Fred shook his head.

"No. She got worse. With every new pre-occupation over Claire, she became more paranoid. She thought a little mole on Claire's back had bugs in it. That was about the time West Nile Virus became a pubic health concern. I was trying to finish my teaching degree and keep our little family together. We were living on handouts from our families and student loans. No doubt, we had a rough start, but I was so pre-occupied with my own responsibilities that I didn't realize what was really happening. I missed the big picture."

"And what was that?"

"That Holly was mentally ill. We were constantly seeing Claire's pediatrician, so Holly's own doctor didn't know what was going on until she had a major breakdown."

"What happened?"

"Again, she thought there was something infiltrating the house that was making her and Claire sick. First it was mould growing behind the walls, then the carpets were full of chemicals, and then the paint had lead in it, and we were all being poisoned. She decided one day that she couldn't stay in our house any more."

"Wow. So did you move?"

"Eventually, yes. Holly wouldn't believe me when I repeatedly said there was nothing wrong, but she was obsessed. It was endless. She wanted to move and that was it. She ended up living at her parents' house with Claire until we bought this house. By the time we sold our little house and moved here it was a year. I was lucky enough to get a temporary teaching job, so we bought this place on a prayer and the premise that my job would become permanent. I borrowed the down payment from my parents because the bank wouldn't lend us any more money. It was a rough few years."

"And once you moved here?"

"She got better for a while. Our house was half-built, which was actually an advantage, because I kept showing her that there was nothing growing in the walls. She inspected every single pipe and faucet before it was installed. Half the time she had no idea what she was looking for, but as long as she had input, she was less suspicious and things were calmer. She had many other fears, but the doctor gave her some new medication to quiet her mind, which worked for a while." Fred's voice was quieter and his words were heavy. He leaned forward, with his head hung down. I rubbed his shoulder gently. He didn't resist. Through the dampness of his skin against his shirt, he smelled like clean clothes.

"It must have been tough raising a little kid as well." He looked across the street to the cemetery.

"Far from easy. I tried my best to keep it together. Holly's parents were understanding to a point. They wanted to protect their own, but her mother kept trying to get her off the medication. And every time that happened, Holly would be normal for a while, then spin out of control again."

"How did she manage with Claire?"

"Between both sets of parents, there was always someone watching both of them. I was out of school at the same time Claire was, and for that reason alone, I am so grateful to be a teacher."

"I'm sorry. For all of you."

"It gets more bizarre, but that's for another day."

"That is a complicated opening chapter."

"Yes it is. And on that note, the rest of the groceries need unpacking."

"I'll be on my way." My bottom was numb and my brain was full. Fred stood up and offered his hand to help me up. He had a strong, firm grip.

"Please don't go. I know I owe you dinner, but would you settle for lunch?" I stood up in and slipped into my sandals.

"I interrupted you. Why don't we do it another day?" My stomach growled, as if on cue, and he heard it.

"Because I just did groceries. We both need to eat, and you have your 'let's have lunch in New Pelham outfit' on." I laughed.

"I'm inconveniencing you."

"You're the nicest inconvenience I've encountered, and more polite than that hungry lion in you stomach." I blushed, and relented.

Fred opened the door for me. I parked my sandals neatly beside his in the front lobby, but wanted to slide them inside his to see if they fit. His house was clean, with few accessories that were dated, but dusted. There was no evidence of a female presence, excluding his phone greeting. I followed Fred to the kitchen where some groceries were still in bags, and others were scattered on the counter. It was compact, with a small breakfast bar.

"Please." He pointed to the bar chairs. What laid on the counter would make a dietitian proud. From the fridge, he produced a large piece of fresh salmon. "Shall we have this?"

"Wow. How can I resist?" He dove both hands into the grocery bags, and held up a bunch of asparagus like a doctor holding a new baby. I giggled.

"Grilled?"

"I thought you said lunch."

"We'll have dinner at lunch." It was easy to watch Fred unpack his groceries. He washed and arranged fresh fruit in a bowl. He scrubbed the vegetables before wrapping them in paper towels and neatly arranging them in the fridge.

"Can I help?" Fred washed the asparagus and handed them to me with a white rectangular bowl and paper towel. His hands were damp but warm. The tiled surface of the breakfast bar sparkled. Fred wiped up a few water spots with a clean white dishcloth, unlike the one in my kitchen.

"Is rice okay?"

"Perfect. Did you plan to make this for dinner?"

"Yup, but it will taste better for lunch with good company."

"Thank you." I snapped off the tough ends of the asparagus and arranged them lengthwise in the bowl as Fred cooked. He took out a spotless, white cutting board and sliced the salmon in two pieces, wrapping and freezing the smaller piece. He mixed a concoction of spices and minced garlic in a bowl, adding olive oil and a thick amber solution from a bottle with a Chinese label. No recipe in front of him for reference. He basted the salmon on a sheet covered in foil. He stirred the basmati rice as I inhaled the delicate aroma. In a frying pan, he beat three eggs and spread them over the hot pan surface, flipping them once and sliding the cooked circle onto a plate. He winked at me, then chopped green onions and mixed them with frozen green peas. I watched this chef weave his way effortlessly through the meal preparation. *Savour this, Grace, if only for today.*

"It's not too early for wine, is it?" He pointed to a cupboard with a few bottles of local wine. The glasses were on racks below the wine. Fred noticed the film on the glasses before I did. "They don't get used a lot."

I washed and dried them with a fresh tea towel. "Is white okay with salmon?"

"Perfect." I poured the wine and passed it to Fred who raised it to me. "What shall we toast to? That the fish turns out?" I felt bold.

"Maybe to friendship?" He grinned, clinked my wine glass, then paused for longer than was comfortable for both of us.

"To a really nice person who...who..." He was flustered.

"Who doesn't know the difference between good and bad wine?"

"Sure. This feels awkward, having a chef cook for me." I looked around the kitchen. He pointed at the stove.

"I enjoy cooking, but I'm lousy at entertaining."

"Not to me."

"Trust me, very few people have sat in your chair."

"Any women?" He lifted his hand and counted on his fingers.

"Lets's see. In the last five years there was Claire, my insurance agent, and a neighbour who brings me preserves." He held up three fingers.

"Ah, a suitor."

"Mazie. She's a retired spinster teacher who needs a little favour every now and then."

"Any special favours?" I teased.

"If you call cleaning the gutters or shoveling snow from her driveway special. Her last year teaching was my first, at the same school. Every once in a while she brings preserves over, asking what Norman's up to."

"So it's Norman she's after."

"She's been trying to invite herself over there for years but Norman wants nothing to do with her. They're of the same vintage, and they'd make a fine pair."

Dinner was cooked to perfection, served with new cloth napkins from which Fred hastily removed labels. We ate at the breakfast bar facing the breeze coming from the large, open kitchen window, Fred's broad shoulders nudged occasionally and unapologetically against mine. As the trees in the back yard moved gently, so did our conversation. Fred relaxed more after a second glass of wine. I enjoyed every minute there, and it was close to four o'clock when we finished the dishes.

Fred walked me to to the car and opened the door for me. The last person to do that was the funeral director at Blair's service. Today's warm sun was such a contrast to the misery of that bitter, cold day.

"This is the nicest day I've had in a long time," he said.

"I'll second that. All because Norman broke his hip." Fred spoke quietly after a moment of thought.

"I'd prefer it if you left Norman out of this. I'm very private about my personal life, and want to keep it that way."

"I respect that."

"Grace?"

"Yes?"

"Remember when I asked you if you trusted me?" *Again?*

191

"I do."

"You said you had no reason not to trust me when I asked you the last time we talked about this. Now I am asking the same in return."

"Okay." I felt uncomfortable, and he knew it.

"I'm married. Even though I haven't been with my wife in years, in the eyes of the law, I am still very, very married. Please understand me when I tell you that you are the kindest woman that has been anywhere near me since Holly got sick. When I saw your car across the street, I was hoping it wasn't you, because I was afraid that a day like today would happen. And now that it has, it feels good, but not right."

"Fred, nothing happened."

"I know it didn't. I'm sorry."

"What are you apologizing for?"

"For leading you on."

"You didn't. We shared a meal, and talked openly and without guilt about your wife. I didn't feel you were doing anything wrong."

"I do."

"Then you need to deal with that."

"I'm not ready to."

"Only you can decide that. But I respect you. And yes, Fred, I do trust you. I wouldn't be here if I didn't."

"You have no idea what that means to me." I'm not sure what made him say that but it wasn't the time to ask.

Fred closed the door and squatted down again to my eye level. When our eyes met, he looked away. I touched the hand leaning on the car that was steadying his balance.

"I lost my husband because he died. It wasn't a good marriage, but it wasn't until after his death that I realized just how unhappy I was being married to him. No. Let me rephrase that. I used to enjoy being married, but I got in such a pattern of going through the motions of being married that I had forgotten what it was like to be happy. Today, Fred, I feel happy. And I haven't felt that way in a long time either. And...and... and I don't want to feel guilty about the fact that it was you that made me feel that way." Fred said nothing and I continued, feeling more confident with every sentence.

"You have an ill wife and based on what you've told me, that won't change. I took a vow when I got married and I can't remember the exact words, but it mentioned sickness and health, and something about parting at death. It may have been worded a little differently at your wedding but I'm sure the rules were the same." He kept looking away, but I felt compelled to finish my thoughts. "There are many things that end a marriage. Death physically ended mine, but emotionally, it was over long before Blair died. I didn't know it, but Blair did when he started breaking the rules. I think you need to look at why you're still married. Whatever keeps you married, I will absolutely respect that, whether it's today or a year from now. But you have to respect and trust yourself, and that is much harder to do." *There. I said it. Whew.*

Fred was silent. I started the car, not expecting a response. He looked deep in my eyes which fed my hungry heart. I ran out of words, as did he. I turned the car around and left him standing in the driveway. I was proud of what I said, and how I felt.

By the time I turned onto Chestnut Boulevard in Toronto, I didn't remember the better part of physically driving home. I was falling for Fred. I could touch him, sense his thoughts, feel his compassion, smell his skin, and felt sick on the third round of reminding myself that his married heart was out of bounds.

September 1st

The funeral home left a message on my phone. Livy's memorial service was scheduled for September 10th and the announcement was posted. Anyone who had contacted the funeral home was notified of the date. I had no obligation, but was invited to attend. Today was Friday, and the service was the following Saturday. I hadn't worn a dress since Blair's funeral and my closet had a few sparse choices. Nothing seemed appropriate. I went to the mall and shuffled though racks of dresses at the department store, none of which would meet Livy's standards. On my way home I passed by the dress shop Livy took me to after we purged my wardrobe. The perfect dress was right there, on a mannequin in the window. I pictured Livy putting her hands to her cheeks and saying, "Gracie, if you don't buy this dress, I won't speak to you until you do." It was navy with white trim, with simple classic lines. It was much too expensive, but Livy deserved a fine farewell. I also splurged on navy pumps with red soles. She would have squealed with delight.

September 10th

I arrived at the funeral parlour the following Saturday for the 11:00 AM service, early enough to pick an inconspicuous chair. The room was very large and the seats were arranged in U-shaped rows. An ornate wooden lectern graced the middle of the room, and five reserved seats with gold chair covers were positioned in the curve of the front row. There was a space between the reserved chairs and the rest of the seats. The room filled steadily to capacity. I recognized Lenny and Jenny, Livy's eccentric neighbours, who brought the Adams, dressed in their Sunday finest. Kristen Castle took one of the reserved seats, and her secretary positioned herself in the row directly behind her. Two well dressed females arrived, one accompanied by a middle-aged man, who was also nicely attired. A female in the second row looked familiar, and it took a few discrete glances to recognize Taylor from her nude portrait in Livy's bedroom. A few rows behind her sat Nigel Anderson, looking like he had stepped off a Milan runway. He nodded politely. I was touched that he came.

The last guest to arrive before the minister was Norman. Fred stooped behind him, directing the handles of Norman's wheelchair into the tight space next to Kristen. Norman wore a navy suit, white shirt and dark tie. Whoever put him together, and I guessed it was Fred, got the sizes right. My heart pumped loudly. I faced the left side of the lectern, six rows behind

Norman and Fred. Norman sat slumped in his chair, looking no farther than his new shoes. Fred faced forward. I'm sure they'd both rather be in New Pelham.

A large portrait of Livy rested against a carved wooden easel at the front of the room. I'd never seen this picture before, but recognized the familiar, ornate frame as something she would have brought from Indonesia. Very similar, if not identical to the one of Taylor in her bedroom. My gaze shifted from the portrait to Taylor, who was watching me. She slowly raised her eyebrows, and gently nodded her head. She ran her fingers through her blonde hair and smiled slightly. I felt uneasy from the message I hoped she wasn't sending me.

The minister approached the lectern and began his eulogy with such a loud voice that it was offensive. I wondered if he intended to keep the audience awake, or if that was the natural projection of his voice. His words were predictable, and he double checked Livy's name each time he plucked it into his script. It seemed like it was just another service to him. He hovered over the lectern to create a more dramatic effect, and I was relieved when he finished. The short presentations by other participants were kind and softly spoken. Their message was resoundingly clear. Livy sculpted her life into something many dreamed of creating, but few took the risk. A beautiful woman who was 'well loved, and loved well'. Norman was acknowledged as Livy's only living relative. The minister read an unexpected statement near the end, asking if anyone who may be aware of any other relative of Livy's, to please see Kristen Clarke after the service, or contact her. As she raised her hand, a rustle of people shifted in their seats and panned the room to locate perhaps her biological mother, or a mysterious relative. The minister asked for a minute of silence, and all was still again. He sped through his closing remarks before inviting the group to an adjacent room for lunch.

Fred and Norman were the first to leave, and the room was eerily quiet considering the amount of people present. I felt a hand on my elbow as I entered the reception. It was Nigel, as polite and kind to me as when we initially met. He was back in New York on business when he received the notice, and flew in for the day. We exchanged small talk at a table for four, facing the wall. Nigel regretted coming, feeling more grief than calm. I felt more like an observer.

Lunch consisted of some of Livy's favourite foods, and she would have approved of this send off. Nigel arrived by taxi, with his luggage stored in an office at the funeral home. I offered to drive him to the airport. As Nigel retrieved his belongings, I overheard Norman speaking to one of the funeral directors. The conversation was unusual. Norman was asking peculiar questions about cremation, such as where missing dead people were buried once they were found. He also asked if the funeral home ever received ashes anonymously, and what was done with them. Fred was cordial, but obviously uncomfortable with these peculiar questions. The director responded politely, and shut the conversation down gently. When Nigel reappeared, I introduced him to Fred and Norman as Livy's close friend, and the exchange of words ended there. Fred's handshake was warm and prolonged. Stepping away from the others, he said he missed me, and I said the feeling was mutual.

I drove Nigel to the airport. At Nigel's request, we recounted the days before and after Livy's death. I told him I was happy that Livy had met someone special, but initially was leary of him.

"Why?" he asked.

"Because she had some less than perfect relationships, and I was wondering if you were one of them." We chuckled together.

"That's reassuring."

"And when we drove to the airport together, before we met the police, you were holding that laptop bag much too tightly. I was afraid of what you were hiding in there." He grinned.

"What did you think was in there?"

"I don't know. Espionage papers....or maybe stolen artifacts...."

"My dear lady, what a vivid imagination you have." I didn't stop there.

"And then when they separated us to interrogate us, I thought they put you in jail." Nigel rolled his head back with amusement.

"And I never thought more of you than her dear, sweet friend, word for word as she described you."

"I'm sorry if I offended you," I said sheepishly.

"For the record, my family owns many blocks of real estate in New York City. I do quite well in China, but your impression is very entertaining."

"Well, my second impression is that of a very respectable man. Had the circumstances been different, the story would be too."

"So true, so true." We were two people who knew Livy for a very short period of time, but cared deeply about her. He said the most precious gift to a man is a woman's heart. He dreamed of growing old with her, and I hoped some day to feel the same about someone. Like old friends, we exchanged a long and comfortable hug at the airport and he left carrying the same leather luggage and laptop bag. We agreed to stay in touch, but I doubted that either of us would.

I drove back to Chestnut Boulevard, and was surprised to see Fred's car parked in the driveway. Norman was in the front seat of the car with the door open. Fred was leaning against the same side of the car, minus his his suit jacket and tie. I parked on the street. He smiled.

"Didn't expect to see us so soon?"

"No, but it's a nice surprise." Remaining in his seat, Norman got right down to business. He pulled a postcard from his lapel pocket and passed it to me. It was the card from the fireplace mantle at his house, and the last card she wrote. I could hear her voice as I read it again:

Hi Uncle Norman! Here I am again in Jakarta.
This picture is the view from my hotel room.
It's 41 degrees in the shade. I'm having something special made
for you, and I can't wait to show you when I visit in September.
Stay well! Love ya lots!
Livy

Fred spoke for Norman, inquiring about the gift Livy was sending him.

"We weren't sure when we would see you again so Norman asked me to show you this card." I had searched, but had no idea what the 'something special' was or where it had been sent. Norman's stare was interrogating. Fred was checking Norman's mail and there were no packages from Livy. It had been five weeks since her death, and the same date as the post mark, however her card was undated. I knew Livy had stayed at the same hotel from her itinerary.

I invited the men inside, but Norman balked. Fred raised his hands in surrender. I offered to contact Livy's employer, but admitted that I had no idea what I was looking for. I also said that his gift may still have not arrived, as shipment deliveries from Indonesia could take months.

I asked Norman if he'd like to see Livy's house again, but he shook his head and stared ahead, repeatedly checking the latch on his seatbelt. I gave him the postcard back. Fred suggested that they return when Norman was more mobile. I asked Norman directly if he would like me to come back to visit him. I interpreted his half nod as a yes. His frail hand reached out to close the car door.

"End of that conversation," Fred said and shut the door. "Today is his first day out. He called four times in the last two days to remind me about today, and never said a word all the way up or at the service until just before we left the funeral home. He's pooped, and his pain meds are wearing off."

"I heard bits of his questions to the funeral home attendant about the ashes. What was that all about?"

"He was trying to make her squirm."

"It worked. She was wringing her hands behind her back." He laughed softly. Fred looked more handsome today than I had ever seen him before. His eyes were bright and clear. Norman started tapping the window for Fred to get back in the car. "If he sits in there any longer, he'll accuse me of trying to suffocate him."

"When will he be discharged?"

"The target date is still September 29th."

"What day of the week is that?"

"Thursday. The head nurse knows I can bring him home, but not until I finish school."

"Why don't I visit next week and see if he would let me bring him home?"

"He won't admit it, but I know he would. We've been his only visitors."

"That's so sad. And what about you? Are you okay with that?"

"I'm very okay with that. Every little bit helps, and of course, it would be nice to see you again." My heart skipped a few beats.

"I'll check my schedule. Can I call or text you?" *What an excuse. My calendar has nothing but empty spaces.*

There was an awkward moment, and I extended my hand instead. He took it and held it, putting both of his warm hands around mine. He stumbled over his words.

"Thanks, Grace, for understanding." Norman knocked on the window again. "Lecture time," Fred chirped, getting into the car. He rolled the window down and I met Norman's disapproving stare.

"I hope you'll come back for a visit. You can see Wilson again." His eyes lit up with excitement, then back to misery. *Wilson!*

"Can't waste time. Summer's over and Fred's back at work," Norm barked. "It's stuffy in here, and my throat's dry. Let's get home, boy."

"Don't go! You need water." Before either could object, I scooted around to the back of the house, careful not to roll an ankle in my new pumps. I let myself in, and Wilson out of his crate. I changed to flat shoes, grabbed two of bottles of water, hooked Wilson's collar to his leash and brought my offerings outside. Norman's face lit up with the broadest smile I'd seen yet. I passed the water to Fred as Norman came to life. He opened the car door himself. Either Wilson recognized him, or was starving for affection, but he eagerly relished the attention and slobbered all over Norman's new suit.

"Wilson!" I turned around to see who had yelled his name. It was Taylor, with her window open, pulling up in a rented black minivan. Wilson abandoned Norman and ran out the length of his leash towards her. Norman shut the door quickly and ordered Fred out of the driveway, and he obeyed. Fred waved at me as Taylor's van pulled in. She got out of her vehicle and Wilson's nose went right for her crotch. I yanked on his leash with no success.

"Hello to you too, fella!" The woman gave him a tight squeeze and he jumped on her. I pulled him down, but he remained close to her, his tail wagging furiously.

"I know buddy, I miss you too! Now sit!" Wilson obeyed immediately, which felt odd. She wiped her hands against her firm backside and extended her hand.

"You must be Grace. I'm Taylor." She was indeed the girl from the portrait, skin as flawless as the picture. Just like Livy, she had perfect hair, teeth and clothes. She won the aesthetic lottery.

"Pleased to meet you, although unfortunately under these circumstances."

"And I'm assuming that was Uncle Norman leaving."

"Yes, and my boyfriend was driving him home," I lied.

"The place looks great." She looked around, pausing at Livy's bedroom window.

"Her lawyer's office just appraised the house and its contents. I'm not supposed to be letting anyone in."

"Oh, I know. They were barracudas when she moved in here, and I'm sure things haven't changed. I heard the announcement at the service about any mysterious relatives coming forward. I'm sure it's about claiming estate money."

"Perhaps. I know you and Livy were very close."

"Oh, we were more than close."

"Livy told me."

"She did?" Taylor squeaked. "I loved that girl so much. She had a rough life. Shitty childhood. A lousy marriage. Creepy boyfriends. And then, she morphed into this beautiful butterfly. Forgave all, well, maybe most of those losers from her past, and learned for the first time to love herself. I just feel so lucky to have been a part of her life." She became teary. "I'm not after anything. I just wanted to pay my respects." Taylor opened the rear doors of her rented van. "And you can tell those lawyers they can add this to their inventory." It was the portrait of Livy from the funeral home, smiling stoically. It filled the whole back of the van. Taylor whimpered, and I cried. Wilson looked at the both of us, realized he wasn't going anywhere, and sat down to watch us.

Livy's picture was so real. Taylor dabbed at her smudged makeup. "I couldn't keep this. She just keeps looking at me and looking at me. When I heard about the memorial service, I brought this along so that maybe... maybe it could go to her uncle..." A spark was lit when she mentioned Norman. I pulled a box of tissues out of the Volvo and handed her some. I hugged her and whatever message I may, or may not have interpreted that she was sending earlier was gone.

"I'm sure Norman would be pleased to have it." I explained Livy's mystery gift dilemma.

"Not surprising. Sometimes it takes months, and sometimes it never comes... regardless of who you bribe and what goes on the customs papers," she sniffled. With great effort, we managed to carry the heavy picture inside and rested it against a wall in Livy's office. "Livy would have watched herself work in this office. Good-bye, my love," Taylor sobbed into her wad of tissues.

"Why don't you stay for a cup of coffee, or a glass of wine until you calm down. We'll sit on the porch." She checked her watch.

"I feel like a hooker after a rough night." I couldn't help but laugh.

"A hooker doesn't wear a linen suit like that."

"She might in California, and she'd be just as happy to get out of it... and these stilettos." Taylor kicked her shoes off to show red pressure marks across her bare toes. She carried them gingerly to the chairs on the porch, where we had a glass of wine. "I'm sorry about the intrusion. I hope your boyfriend didn't mind, but I just had to give that picture away."

"It will make Norman very happy."

"And, mmmm, if you're ever in San Francisco, I'd be happy to show you around. It's a beautiful city."

"I'm sure it is."

We exchanged a cordial hug, and Taylor left. I was exhausted, and it was only the middle of the day. I gravitated back to Livy's office for a quiet moment and sat at her desk. Her eyes in the portrait were magnetic, pulling you close and keeping you there. I hoped Uncle Norman would like the picture. It was still Livy's gift.

I scooped up my red-soled pumps before Wilson did, and put them away. My feet were tired, but happier than Taylor's. I propped them up on the front porch, and calmed my heart with more wine.

September 18th

I landed not one, but two job interviews the following week. When I bought the dress for Livy's memorial service, there was a 'Help Wanted' sign in the boutique window. I chatted briefly with the owner, who was not aware that Livy, who shopped there, was gone. She wasn't sure if I was serious about the job and waited until after Livy's service to call. The second job was at a bank. The boutique job paid less than the bank, but offered a generous staff discount, and the women employed there were around my age.

I was offered the boutique job, which catered to career women with classical tastes. A huge one-time discount allowed me to purchase clothes at the store to wear at work. Knowing little about the fashion industry, I was trained to compliment clients, but never encourage them to buy something I would regret seeing them wear in public. It was not about selling, but making a woman look good, which gave this boutique its sterling reputation.

On my first day off, I made my next trip to Niagara and arrived at my usual 11:00 AM. Norman was walking down the hall away from me, using a walker. His gait was steady and purposeful. At the end of the hall, he turned around, and was halfway back when he saw me. No nod to greet me, and no hello. He kept walking toward me, then stopped. I spoke first.

"Good morning."

"You're late," he barked.

"For what?"

"To help me."

"Help you what?"

"Walk."

"You're doing a pretty good job without me."

"That's because you never showed up." He continued down the hall. I watched him until he turned around and came back towards me. I remained pleasant. "How many laps do you have to do?"

"As many as I want."

"How many laps until they let you go home?"

"I can go home any time."

"Then why aren't you there yet?" He looked at me like I was stupid.

"Because I live by myself!"

"So if you lived with someone, you could come home?" He nodded and shuffled by me. I walked with him, resisting the temptation to swat the baggy back side of his sweat pants with my purse. He ignored me. I tempted fate. "So if you lived with me, you could be discharged?" He focused on his steps and growled.

"I ain't living with you." *Heaven forbid if he agreed.*

"Then if I stayed with you, you could come home?" He stared at me, his voice loud and gruff. "Nobody lives with me, ya hear me, nobody!"

"Norman, what did I do wrong now?"

"You should have been here all week. And you never came."

"I didn't know that. You said I could visit, and here I am. I'd like to help, but I don't know how, unless you tell me." On his next lap, I saw him tiring. "Can you come outside and sit for a little while?"

"Lunch is coming."

"What time?"

"Twelve."

"We've got lots of time. The fresh air will be good for you." His hesitation lingered.

"I gotta let the desk know."

"So go and tell them, and I'll meet you at the elevator." He shuffled over to the desk and exchanged a couple of sentences with a staff member behind the desk. She poked her head over the counter and spoke loud enough for both of us to hear. "Just make sure you stay around the gazebo area. Shall I run your lunch down?" I looked at Norman, who responded politely. "No, thank you." After all those negative encounters, it was a stark contrast. He walked as quickly as he could to the elevator, and pushed the button. The elevator opened immediately and I followed him in. He sat down on the seat rest of the walker, with beads of sweat forming on his forehead. He ignored me and walked out of the elevator first. By the time he got to the gazebo, he was out of breath and energy. After what seemed like five long, silent minutes, I mentioned the weather forecast. He snapped at me, testing me again.

"Look at me, Norman." He shot a glance my way, then looked across the street. "Not good enough, Norman. Look at me." I waited until he eventually looked at me.

"Now listen carefully. I won't come back after today, if that's what you want. It's your choice. I offered to help you, maybe once a week, and you accepted. I'd like to enjoy visiting you, but every time I drive the two hours here from Toronto, I instantly regret it, especially when you're so miserable. Every time I arrive, I feel like you're going to spit in my face."

"I won't spit in your face."

"Then why do you hate me?"

"I don't hate you."

"Then why are you so nasty to me?" He was silent for another uncomfortable minute.

"I'm not nasty."

"You're worse than nasty. You're disrespectful and if you don't change your attitude, I won't come back." *There. I've said it.* More silence. I persevered. "Do you really want help?"

I heard a faint 'Yes'.

"I don't want to be your friend. I don't want your money, and I don't want to stay with you."

"Me neither."

"At least we agree on that." If you're stewing over the gift that Livy was sending you, I don't know what, or where it is. I'm trying to find it, but can't guarantee I will. I committed to helping you, and if you are serious, the tradeoff is that you treat me with respect." His voice became a whisper. I felt the same way I did after scolding Tess as a child.

"I will respect you." I negotiated for more.

"From now on?" He nodded his head. "And we'll put our differences behind us, and work together to get you home, by yourself?" Surprisingly, his lower lip quivered. Another nod. I extended my hand, and he shook it. "Now, can I get your lunch?" He nodded again, and I headed for the glass doors, glancing back to see Norman wiping his eyes with his shirt.

When I brought Norman's lunch down, he was seated in a chair at a table under the gazebo. I set his tray down, and he thanked me. I brought two coffees, took mine off the tray, and sat a comfortable distance from him. I found the granola bar and apple in my purse that I'd packed earlier. We both faced away from the parking lot, overlooking the rose gardens. Norman smelled his soup in the melamine bowl, pleased with whatever it was. He crushed crackers into it.

"You must be hungry. You finished a marathon this morning," I said.

"That's the most I've walked yet."

"Good for you." I switched topics. "Would you like to know a little bit about me?"

"Sure." As Norman ate, I told him a little about Blair's recent death, and the series of events that led me to Livy. For the first time, we had a civil conversation, and I was surprised that Fred had told Norman a few nice things about me. I inquired about his neighbourhood, hoping to learn more about Fred without asking. He started by complaining about the taxes and snow removal, then said he was glad to have Fred next door. He knew that we each had one daughter, and about how Fred raised Claire.

"It's a crying shame. Holly was a real nice girl," Norman shook his head.

"So I've heard."

"You know she's crazier than a cuckoo bird."

"Really? It must be hard for Fred to see her."

"He used to go every Sunday, but then he stopped."

"Is she far away?"

"About an hour away. In the looney hospital. He took me once, three or four years ago. It was a sad sight. Pathetic. Now he only goes once in a while. She doesn't even recognize him." I felt terrible.

"You had a wife too?" Norman sat upright.

"We're not goin' there. She was good for nothin'. Thought we needed all this fancy junk. Cookin' stuff no human bein' should be eatin'. That woman was trying to kill me!" I laughed.

"I doubt it. What did she cook?" I asked, thinking that topic would be safe because he brought it up.

"Stuff I never heard of. What's wrong with peas and carrots and maybe corn on Sunday?"

"They say variety is the spice of life."

"I didn't want no spice in my life."

"She was trying to expose you to wonderful new tastes."

"Nothin' wrong with the old tastes."

"What happened to her?"

"She ran away." He was clearly agitated. I softened my tone.

"Did you try to find her?"

"What for? No reason to."

"Did the police help you?" He shot me a stern look.

"Bah! The only good thing they did was call a tow truck to get me outta the ditch in a snowstorm."

"They helped you when you broke your hip."

"They should've let me die."

"You don't really mean that, do you?" He looked far away. "You're almost back in one piece again. You have a beautiful place to go home to, and wonderful neighbours who care about you."

"There's just Fred."

"What about Mazie around the corner?" He rolled his eyes.

"She's more useless than..." He remembered his manners, or lost his train of thought.

"More useless that what?" Fred's voice came from behind us.

"Well, hello, there. Norman was just describing Mazie."

"Ah, Norman's favourite neighbour," Fred teased, putting his hand on the back of Norman's shoulder. I checked the time; we'd been outside for almost an hour. Fred settled himself beside Norman, dressed in jeans and a long-sleeved T-shirt. After a few more minutes of conversation, Norman was nodding off. Fred nudged him gently. He bounced back, asking who would take him home when he was discharged. Fred told Norman not to worry. Satisfied, Norman carefully stood up, and aligned his legs with his walker. He excused himself, and headed back to his room for a nap.

"Wow. What happened to Norman the tyrant?"

"I whined, he apologized, and then we moved forward."

"I'm impressed, Grace."

The conversation marinated with small talk. I told him there was no progress in finding Norman's gift. Fred congratulated me on getting a job, and getting the day off that Norman was scheduled to be discharged. We sat quietly for a while. It felt good just to be near him. I casually mentioned that Norman told me it was difficult for Fred to visit Holly.

"He's right. I used to go weekly, but now it's monthly, and sometimes less. I know, but she doesn't." He said Holly's lucid moments rarely existed. When she no longer knew what day it was and eventually who he was, his visits became more sporadic. He breathed deeply, gathered his thoughts and carried on.

"Because of the scenic hills around here, this area attracts a lot of local and international cyclists. It's pretty, and physically challenging. We have people who stop to fix their bikes in our driveway, or just sit on our grass to rest. Most cyclists are amazing people, and it's not unusual for them to stop and ask questions or take a break. One day, I came home from school and Holly was trying to cook a meal for half a dozen shady guys she thought were cyclists, and had invited over when they stopped to check one of their bikes. At that stage of her illness, the only meal I ever came home to was either burnt, frozen or hidden. She was running around the house trying to decide how to seat these people at the table. She had put a pot of unpeeled potatoes on the stove to cook. Potatoes, and nothing else. None of them knew her or me, and right away, I suspected they had bad intentions. They were drinking our beer and sitting under our tree, so I told those guys to leave because she wasn't well, and they did so peacefully. I knew it was too simple."

"It could have turned out much worse."

"It did. When Holly realized I ordered them off our property, she was furious. Then, we had another situation. She invited a carload of religious

208

people into the house, who waited for hours for me to come home because Holly told them I would give them money which we didn't have." Fred put his hands through his hair and looked into the sky, his face pained with heartbreak. I offered him Norman's untouched coffee, and he drank it.

"The breaking point was when I came home and found a strange guy in the house, who I think was one of the guys she was trying to cook potatoes for a few weeks before. He and Holly were upstairs in our bedroom, but didn't hear me come up. He was naked, and she was almost there, obeying every order he gave her, and willingly. Who knows what would have happened. The thought of it still makes me sick. He was stoned, or drunk, or something; easy enough for me to hold down until the police came, but Holly became uncontrollable, jumping on me, scratching me, and trying to free him. It was unbelievable. She wouldn't put her clothes back on when the police finally came. And to make matters worse, she threw herself down the stairs, hitting her head on the floor. She got up, and kept screaming. It was a terrible, terrible day. I'm so glad the police witnessed it, because I'm sure they all would have accused me, and that would have been an even bigger mess."

"How awful."

"The police found our stuff in his pockets and knapsack. Some he stole, and some Holly said she gave him to rid her of bad spirits. At one point, she even told the police I wasn't her husband. Grace, I was so shocked I could barely function. That was my wife! Thank God Claire wasn't home."

"So, what happened to Holly?"

"The police took her to the hospital, which she agreed to, as long as it wasn't by ambulance. If I suggested it, she would have fought me."

"Did they admit her?"

"Oh yes. She was, as the medical people say, admitted under 'Form 1' which is an involuntary hospitalization. She was diagnosed as a schizophrenic, with an acute psychotic episode. She was both suicidal and homicidal. An MRI of her head and a neurologist confirmed she also suffered a brain injury from the fall. From that time on, it was never the same. She lacked judgment, and was not capable of being left alone."

"How did Claire manage?"

"Well, by that time she had enough insight to know her mom was sick, but didn't understand why I couldn't, or wouldn't, stay home and look after her. I tried to protect Claire by keeping the serious stuff simple, until she figured it out on her own."

"That's horrible."

"I wouldn't wish this on my worst enemy. With mental illness, not everyone responds to treatment. Which happened in Holly's case."

"But aren't there any new medications or treatments for that?" He leaned forward in his chair.

"They tried all kinds of different combinations, and the best combination is what she's been on for the last four years. She can function enough to shower and get dressed and go to the washroom by herself. She knows enough to eat, but not when or what to feed herself. She can't manage her medications. And of course, she thinks I'm someone else, although sometimes she recognizes Claire."

"No wonder it's so tough to see her."

"I've tried to go more often, but I just can't."

"It must be hard for you to let go."

"I have strong moral values, and I've purposely avoided any opportunity to test them. When Holly was transferred to long term care, I shut down too. The only season I acknowledged was winter. I never appreciated spring or summer because I knew winter was coming again. Thank goodness Claire was well on her way in life. For years I did nothing. I went to school, came home, checked on Norman, got up the next day, and did it all over again. It wasn't until my principal suggested I teach troubled students, that I started to, well, maybe not accept my future, but acknowledge it. The more sad stories I heard about their lives, the more I was grateful that even though Holly was ill, Claire turned out just fine."

"They're lucky to have you."

"And some days, I'm lucky to have them. If I can say anything positive about Holly's illness, it's that as a result of it that I'll never give up on those kids." Fred sat back in his chair. "I often compare my situation to theirs. I'll never get over it, but I will eventually deal with it better." He rubbed his temples with his fingers. I looked at my watch. For an hour I had forgotten about my life, and was totally absorbed in his. A good man, who had been dealt more than his fair share of grief. Somewhat like Livy, but in a very different way.

"What does Holly look like?" He looked at me. *Why did I ask that?*

"Would you like to see her?" *What?*

"If you don't mind." From his wallet, he produced a faded picture with a torn corner. A young girl beamed at a birthday cake, with a female standing behind her. The photo had an imprint from his wallet seam and most of the woman's face was worn away. The cake had twelve candles on it.

"That was eighteen years ago, when life wasn't perfect, but Holly could still bake a cake."

"Sorry. I shouldn't have asked."

"Don't be. A lot of people ask." He looked at the picture. "I didn't realize the picture was so worn. I should go see her."

"Would it help if you weren't alone?" *Grace, what are you thinking?*

"You mean, bring Claire?" His eyebrows arched. "Oh, you mean bring you?" He was silent. "I don't know. No. I don't think so."

"You're right. It's a bad idea. I spoke before I thought." There was a long, quiet pause.

"Are you hungry? I am starving..."

I drove, with Fred beside me in the Volvo, following his directions to a nearby bistro. We ate lunch on the noisy patio. Our conversation was much lighter, with no mention of Holly. We decided to both meet Norman when he was discharged. After lunch, we returned to the rehab centre parking lot. Fred lingered in the car, then covered my hand with his, and squeezed it gently.

"I'd like to kiss you, but I won't. Not without your permission," I whispered. He didn't respond. "Please let me know when it's okay." His hand didn't move. After a moment, he reached over, avoiding my mouth, and kissed my cheek.

"Goodbye, my friend." He smiled, and left.

September 24th

I accepted Fred's invite to a Saturday morning rehab meeting for Norman. Fred met me at the front entrance, with a smile and hot tea, grateful that I came, although I wasn't sure why I was invited. Norman and his rehab team were already gathered in a small room, with Norman looking like he was facing a firing squad. Fred introduced me as a friend of Norman's family.

The meeting was held to plan his safe transition home. Before discharge, a therapist needed to complete a home safety assessment, with someone present. Norman refused this twice, before realizing this was his gateway home. Because of his fragile mobility, he needed someone to check on him daily, for the first week. He balked at this too, until Fred reminded him of the alternative. Norman barked, "I don't know what the big deal is." Fred answered.

"The big deal, Norman, is that none of us want you back in the same mess that got you here in the first place." Norman grunted and sulked, as the therapist took over.

"We'll leave a completed checklist, and everything should be done before you come home." The meeting ended and Norman watched us disperse. He sulked from the window in his room as Fred, the therapist and I, followed each other to Norman's house. The therapist gave suggestions, which she wrote on the checklist, from the minute she arrived. She outlined the main reasons seniors get into trouble on discharge. She walked carefully through the house; touching, checking and measuring. Every potential barrier was validated with a written suggestion to address it. She gave Fred the list to complete, and ideally in the next five days. The house was filthy, and that solution was self-explanatory. Norman needed grab bars in the bathroom. The stair railing was needed some screws tightened to make it sturdy and safe again. Some nutritious, easy to prepare meals would be helpful. She suggested we throw out all the floor mats. If Norman wore a housecoat, his belt should be sewn to his belt loops to prevent him from tripping over it.

When she left, Fred and I reviewed the list. We decided to tidy up what we could today, and pick away at some of the items.

"Not as bad as I thought," he said.

"I agree. Except the cleaning part."

"Livy forced him to get a housekeeper, but he fired a few of them, because he said they were getting into his personal stuff."

When I opened the fridge, the stench filled the room quicker than I could shut it. "Why don't I tackle this? I just need soap and water."

"I threw some stuff out, but quite frankly, forgot about the rest." Fred opened the fridge again, filled a vegetable crisper with rotting food, and put it outside the front door. I opened the kitchen window. Fred looked at my white shirt and walking shorts.

"Those don't look like cleaning clothes."

"They have to be washed eventually."

"Are you still okay with doing this?"

"I am, and if we're dividing this list, I'm sure you'd rather be installing the grab bars."

Fred went to his house to get tools, while I surveyed the main floor. The rich wood baseboards and fireplace trim were coated with dust. The plaster walls and high ceilings had never been painted. Multiple levels of coving were covered in spider webs. Norman matched the neglect, but not the stature of house. I wondered how Livy and his wife had coerced him into building this beautiful place.

As Fred walked through the front door, I had a flashback of the first time he stood in the doorway. It was fearful the first time, and comforting this time. He held a banged-up tool box in one hand, and three articles of clothing in the other.

"You might consider changing. That's too nice a shirt to be ruining." He passed me two women's tops, which I assumed were Holly's. Regardless of whose they were, I was not putting them on. The third choice was a man's striped shirt. I went to the bathroom and put the striped shirt on. The third button from the top was missing. The knit tops were too tight. I came out with the shirt buttoned to the top, keeping the gap closed with my hand.

"Did you pick this one for a reason?" I pointed to the missing button. An embarrassed grin followed a sheepish smile. "Now I remember why I stopped wearing that."

"You don't suppose Norman has a sewing basket?"

"Highly unlikely". Fred opened his tool box, sorted noisily through it, and produced a roll of duct tape. He tore off two large strips, and passed them to me. The tape stuck well. We both laughed heartily.

"Perfect. Another good use for duct tape."

"Livy wouldn't have let me leave the bathroom."

"You look lovely."

"Let's hope the tape holds up." He raised his eyebrows and tilted his head. He opened his mouth to speak, then thought otherwise.

"There's lots more if you need it," he chuckled.

We sat down at a dining room table that hadn't been used in years. High piles of unopened mail covered most of the table. Fred read aloud from the therapist's list again and we brainstormed. Kristen was working at the law firm when I called and I updated her on the therapist's recommendations. We estimated the house needed three people and three days to clean it. Kristen asked why I was in the house, and I let Fred take over. He gave her a cost estimate of the grab bars and a few other items. He emphasized I was cleaning the fridge before passing the phone back to me. She apologized, but wanted the complete story before releasing funds. I told her I would prepare and freeze some meals until he could manage on his own. She was happy when I agreed to send her the recommendations, including 'before and after' pictures. The cleaners would invoice her directly. When I hung up, we all felt better.

"The worst jobs just became the easiest." Fred left to purchase the grab bars so I could bring the receipts back with me to Toronto.

It took hours to clean the fridge. The stove, caked with years of neglect, would be delegated to the cleaning service, which Fred would arrange. I committed to make a few meals and bring them on Thursday, and when Fred returned, and he offered to contribute a few.

"Kristen wants the grocery receipts."

"Then wouldn't it make sense for us to get them together today?"

"Okay, but not today. Cleaning that fridge repulsed me."

"Maybe tomorrow?"

"Wilson won't be happy being alone again, unless you come to Toronto." Fred was initially hesitant, but then agreed. He found a pencil and an old receipt, which he flipped to the blank side.

"We need a grocery list."

"What are we making? What does Norman like?"

"Everything. Anything. I can't remember bringing leftovers to him that he didn't finish, and he probably licked the plate dry. That's when he was well."

"He said he didn't like spices."

"Maybe something really spicy. He probably complained just to complain. I'm sure he'll eat what ever you make."

Between us, we created a shopping list of ingredients for shepherd's pie, a chicken casserole, chili, and beef stew and agreed we would purchase the groceries together.

"Would you rather come up tonight and do the shopping? We could get an early start tomorrow."

"Not a good idea, Grace."

"There is a spare bedroom."

"I'm sure there is."

"I promise I'll keep my distance." *Simon said something similar...*

"I know you will." It was time to head home.

"Thanks again for your help. You made today very pleasant."

I pointed to the fridge and frowned. "Well, most of mine was pleasant."

Fred leaned towards me at the front door, planting a kiss on my cheek, followed by a warm embrace. His breath was hot on my neck. I didn't want to let go.

We agreed on a mid-morning arrival time tomorrow. Both my heart and my mouth sang all the way back to Toronto.

September 25th

Although I slept poorly, I felt energized and ambitious when I woke up. Wilson and I worked a few extra blocks into our morning walk. Fred arrived at ten o'clock, laden with bags of groceries as I was pulling homemade blueberry muffins out of the oven. He passed the bags up to me across the veranda railing and I brought them in the house. He also presented me with a white ceramic pot full of lush green herbs. Points for punctuality, and more points for nice surprises. Goose bumps sprouted all over me.

"Good morning, Ms. Sheehan!"

"It's a fine morning, Mr. Smith!"

"I knew we we were supposed to buy these together, but I woke up early and was restless." I set the coffee and warm muffins out on the veranda by the time he got up the front steps. He looked at the little table I had set.

"And I see you were restless, too."

It was a lovely fall day. A day that heaven had sent to earth. The odd tree leaf fluttered its way gently down to the lawn. Fred seemed as happy to be at the house as I was to have him near. Small chatter took us through two coffees before we came inside. He stopped abruptly in the front entrance when he saw the black and white floor tiles with the inlaid CHESTNUT name. He looked into the living room and shook his head at the replications from Norman's house.

"Wow! I know you talked about it, but I didn't realize the two houses were that similar."

"I know. It felt just as weird walking into Norman's house."

"As it does here." We toured the main floor.

"No wonder the lawyer asks so many questions. It's a valuable house to preserve."

"As is Norman's. I hope he can look after it."

"I do too. It's a great house, in a nice setting. I'd love to buy it someday, and he knows that."

We admired many of the same details, and I showed Fred upstairs. As with the male insurance appraiser and police officers, the picture of Taylor above Livy's bed caught his attention.

"Do you recognize her?" I asked him as his face flushed.

"Is that a trick question?"

I laughed, and briefed him on the backstory as we returned to Livy's office downstairs where her portrait was.

"Fred, I want to bring this portrait to Norman's house. He's got many bare walls and this house will be sold sooner that his."

"That's a great idea. He didn't know it existed until the service."

"Did he know Taylor?"

"Not that I'm aware of."

"Remember the missing gift that Livy mentioned in her post card?" He nodded. "Taylor suggested Livy's picture should be the gift."

"That's brilliant. The real gift may never surface. I'll bring it back today."

"Perfect."

Of all the rooms in Livy's house, the kitchen was Fred's favourite, and we spent the day there. He was in his glory with all the culinary gadgets. He played chef and I played gopher. We worked well together, weaving in and out of each other's space. He brushed against me a few times and I bumped into him, sending electric waves through me. I measured ingredients, cleaned and chopped veggies, staying close, yet out of his way.

We chatted quietly, avoiding any serious conversation. The kitchen saw more activity today then it had in months.

The moment came mid-afternoon. Fred asked me to hold the lid on the pot of potatoes I boiled for shepherd's pie so he could save the water for another recipe. It was impossible to clamp the lid without standing very close to him. The steam activated the smell of his cologne and drew me to him like a magnet. Both his hands were on the pot when I kissed his cheek. He put the pot down in the sink and took the lid from my hand. He took my hands in his and put them around his neck. He leaned against the counter and pulled me to him. I melted in his embrace. Kissing me longingly and lustfully, his hands were shaking as he held me in his arms. Burying his face in my hair, he inhaled deeply and moaned softly. He held me close, in silence. His skin was hot and beads of sweat formed on his face. The combination of his scent and the food cooking around us was a recipe for utopia. We held our long, silent, and tight embrace.

Fred separated himself from me gently and without saying a word, continued with his cooking. I wondered where his thoughts were carrying him, and I sensed it wasn't all about me. I went back to slicing carrots when he came behind me and kissed my neck again. The carrots were abandoned for the chemistry of passion. Fred's breathing became more intense and his kisses became longer and more wanting. I felt my feet leave the floor and my bottom land softly on the kitchen island. My legs straddled his body as he leaned into me. His hands were on my back, under my shirt, and mine on his. The softness of the flesh around his waist drew me closer to him. I felt him fumble nervously with the knot on my apron. He made comforting noises as I unbuttoned his shirt and held him close with my legs wrapped around the back pockets of his jeans. His skin was wet and his kisses left my face and wandered down my neck and between my breasts. He buried his face in my skin and inhaled. The breaths became softer and quiet. He put his arms around my back and held me very tight. He stopped, then pulled away. He fumbled with shaky hands to button up my shirt back, then smoothed out the creases. His eyes were glassy.

"I can't do this. I'm very sorry, but I can't." I was crushed, but understood.

"I'm sorry you can't do this either." He fixed my apron and touched my hair softly to arrange it into place with his fingers. He eased me back on my feet. He kept his apron on, perhaps in an attempt to hide a very visible bulge. Fred walked through the mud room and out to the back yard. I remained in the kitchen, and watched him as he stood on the deck facing away from the house, running his hands through his hair repeatedly. It was painful to watch him remain outside for another fifteen minutes. Knowing not to interfere, I poured more wine and mashed the potatoes.

The rest of the afternoon was very quiet. Positive or negative, I didn't want him to alter my state of bliss. We finished the meals, keeping as much of a distance as the kitchen permitted. I portioned meals into labelled containers and froze them. There was enough left over for two meals for both of us. Fred politely declined to stay for dinner. I asked him if he wanted to take the herb garden back, and he looked offended. I apologized and he felt worse. I confirmed I'd meet Norman at his house when he was discharged on Thursday. He nodded in appreciation, and left quietly. Who knows what was going on in his mind as he drove away. I wanted a future with Fred, knowing full well that it was impossible.

September 29th

I worked every day until, and including Thursday morning. It was raining lightly when Norman came home. I arrived at his house before Fred and Norman, and sat on the front steps to wait. The grass had been cut recently. I longed to see Fred again. Restless, I circled around the house and found an old broom lying near the back door. I swept the leaves off the front porch and down the stairs, and I heard the car approach. Neither Fred nor Norman were smiling, and Norman was not happy to see me. I kept the broom in my hand. Fred and the walker came out first, then the cane, then Norman. Fred scooped up a half-full garbage bag out of the back seat. Resting the broom against the porch, I walked slowly towards them. We were all on edge, each for different reasons.

"Use the cane, Norman." Fred pleaded. Norman ignored him and inched himself along Fred's car for support. Like a child, he walked precariously to the Volvo. Fred and I held our breath as he repeated the process from the Volvo to his car. Fred shook his head, threw up his hands, slammed the car door and took the cane. I picked up the walker, unfolded it and set it within reach of Norman. It was surprisingly light. Norman ignored it, almost stumbling on the uneven grass.

I followed Fred quietly. Norman grabbed the concrete post of the railing. He tested the first wooden step, as if to check that it would hold his weight. It was wet and slippery. Fred looked at me and shook his head. We watched him inch his way to the top step. He turned to Fred.

"Where's my keys?" They were in Fred's hands. Norman shuffled his way to the door and opened his hand for the key. Fred passed it to Norman who fidgeted with the lock and then used what strength he had left to push open the door. I looked at Fred and we braced for the next moment of his homecoming.

"What the hell! Who's been in my house?" he roared. I safely followed Fred into the house. The transformation was amazing. The cleaners did a great job, and the house smelled as good as it looked. Norman left his wet shoes on, and inched along the walls until he stopped in the kitchen. The stove looked brand new. Someone had left a frozen meal out to defrost on the counter. I opened it up.

"What's in there?" Norman barked. Silently, I turned to Norman and opened the freezer door to display the well-stocked contents. Fred had lined up the containers neatly, labels clearly visible.

"Your dinners." I pointed to the defrosted meal.

"This is a chicken casserole. You can heat it up in the microwave." Fred opened the cupboard door to show him new boxes of cereal and snacks.

"Welcome home, you old fart." I smiled at Fred. There was fresh bread on the counter and fruit and milk in the fridge. Norman calmed down, humbled by our efforts to get him settled at home. He edged along the wall to the dining room. The piles of mail were in four boxes, minus the newspapers but including some junk mail. He shuffled to the living room, then stopped. I followed Fred silently to where Norman stood. Fred had hung the picture of Livy above the fireplace. It took up the entire space from the mantle to the high ceiling. The moisture in Norman's eyes made them sparkle.

Fred said, "This might be your missing gift from Livy." The old man looked again at the picture for a long time, shoulders slumped and hands shaking.

"Rest in peace, my angel. My beautiful child."

My jaw dropped when Norman said "child."

"Your child? My gosh, was she your daughter?" He ignored me. I persisted. "Is Livy your daughter? I thought her parents died in a car accident." He looked at me, his eyes as blue as hers, but there was no other resemblance. He mumbled something inaudible to us. Fred changed the subject.

"Can I heat up your dinner, Norm?"

"Nope. I'll do that later."

"Then let's get you settled. We'll stay with you until after dinner - when you're ready for bed."

"I'm ready for bed now." Fred looked at his watch.

"It's five-thirty. It's still light outside."

"I'm going to bed."

"At least eat something first, then you can go to bed." Norman growled as he stared at the floor.

"I haven't even been able to take a leak by myself for two months. I just want to be left alone."

"But…"

"But nothing. I want to be alone." Fred moved into negotiation mode.

"Look, I'll make you a deal. You eat your dinner, I'll help you upstairs, and then we'll leave you alone. Even though the therapist said someone should stay with you. At least tonight." No response. I took that as a yes and went to the kitchen to heat up his dinner. Norman sat down carefully in a worn, brown leather recliner, using the arms to ease himself in. I brought his heated dinner plate, insulated with a kitchen towel, along with utensils wrapped in a serviette.

Fred and I watched Norman eat the meal like game show contestants waiting to hear who had won the big prize. Norm started slowly, picking at the meal. After a few mouthfuls, he picked up the pace, smacking his lips loudly and eating with his mouth open. He finished half of it, stopped, and handed the plate back to me. I deemed dinner a success, and put the leftovers back in the labelled container and into the fridge. I washed his dish and fork, and brought him a glass of milk.

"Milk helps your bones heal." He shook his head. "I'll have it later." I returned it to the fridge. Fred spoke.

"Are you ready to go upstairs?"

"I'm staying right here."

"You're not sleeping in this chair." Norm stretched the recliner out.

"Yes I am. Now lock the door on your way out." Fred persisted.

"You never lock the door. Let's go, Norm."

"I told you, I'm not moving." Fred threw his hands up again. I brought the milk back from the fridge, and set it beside him. Fred turned the light on above the stove and in the bathroom, and placed Norman's phone within his reach.

"Look at me, Norman," Fred ordered, and he obliged. "Promise me you'll call if you need help."

"I promise. Now get going."

"And don't forget someone is coming tomorrow to..."

"I don't need any help!"

"I hope you enjoyed your meal," I said, and heard a feeble thank you. Fred reminded Norman he would stop by in the morning before school. I walked out first, and as Fred was closing the front door, Norman yelled, "Hey!" Fred went back in, while I waited outside. I heard Norman say "What's with you two?"

"Nothing. She's Livy's friend, who feels obligated to her to make sure you're okay." Norman mumbled something offensive to Fred.

"No, I'm not, Norman, and I resent that. Besides that, it's none of your business," Fred hissed. There was a lapse, followed by his calmer voice. "Look, you need her. And I need her to help me help you. If you don't see her again, it's because you've been such a miserable troll. Now is there anything else?"

"How about a scotch?"

"Forget it. And don't bother looking, because it's all gone. Even the stuff you had hidden," Fred came out, looking exasperated. He closed the door behind him and frowned. "So much for the homecoming."

"At least he's home."

It was raining softly as we stood quietly on the porch, out of Norman's sight. I was stuck on Fred's threat that Norman would probably not see me again. Fred stared out over the mowed lawn, then asked if I had plans on Sunday.

"Three days from today?"

"Yes."

"Not so far." His voice stayed low.

"Would you like to meet Holly?" My breath caught like an icy wind. "Oh. I'm... I'm not sure."

"I'm going at two o'clock, if you want to come along." He pulled a small paper out of his pocket with the hospital details. Handing it to me, he said, "You can change your mind. Which ever way you decide." There was no embrace, or kiss, before I left. Fred walked down the stairs, said "Take care, Grace."

He drove away, somewhere other than toward his home, and I left too.

The next move was up to me. Troubled and tormented, Fred offered me a window to peek into his past. Holly might help me understand his loyalty to a marriage that existed only on paper. Guilt wove through my soul, followed by overwhelming curiosity.

I was pre-occupied by three things over the same number of days. I tried to picture Livy as Norman's child, but could not make the connection. Livy never mentioned that possibility. Maybe Norman treated Livy like a daughter, because of her parents' physical and emotional distance. From what little she spoke of them, nothing was nice. The second issue kept me restless and confused. I tried to imagine myself in Holly's position, but couldn't. Fred said she didn't recognize him, but knew who Claire was. *If I came, would she remember? And tell Claire? Would Claire ask Fred who 'the woman' was?*

I left Fred a message that I did want to meet Holly, then wondered why he offered. Maybe if I saw him with Holly, I would realize that I was more selfish then curious, and would ultimately hurt everyone, including myself.

My final concern was about living in the estate's house. My contract was extended until November 3rd. Making poor choices would compromise what I currently was fortunate enough to have. Maybe it really was time to pack up and move on.

Three issues, all intertwined, and each decision would impact the other.

October 2nd

Sunday arrived, and I changed three times, settling again on jeans, a white shirt and denim jacket. I was jittery, and tried to imagine the setting I would meet Holly in. I had never been to a psychiatric institution before, and based on the movies, it wasn't a pretty picture.

Fred's car was in the parking lot when I arrived. The building was large, built in the middle of the last century with patches of lilies and ornamental grasses blending into mature evergreens. Years ago it was called a hospital for the insane, and even though the reasons were the same, the discreet sign now said 'CENTRE FOR MENTAL HEALTH DISORDERS'. The front entrance had surveillance equipment everywhere. Holly's small world began and ended at the security doors. Motion sensors and video cameras recorded everything around the building. Fred sat in the front foyer on the edge of his seat, staring at his hands. He got up slowly. He was edgy, sleep deprived, and kept his distance at arm's length.

"How was your drive?" we said almost simultaneously. Nervous laughs followed.

"Fred, are you still okay with this?" It would be easier for both of us if I left now.

"I think so."

"Maybe I'll stay here until you're done." I sat down. *I don't belong here...*

"No. I want you to see her. I need you to understand." He looked at me carefully.

I followed him cautiously though a series of short hallways into the bowels of the building, each door unsecured with a swipe card Fred was issued at the main entrance desk. In a dark corner of my mind, I compared myself to Holly. I imagined her dressed in a hospital gown, shuffling down the hall much like Norman. I knew her hair was dark from the picture in Fred's wallet. It must be greying now, probably cut short for easy care.

Holly's unit was built like a cross. The nursing station in the middle had a clear view of all four corridors, magnified by monitors. Holly's room consisted of a bed, a desk and two chairs, but not Holly. On the wall was a laminated picture of a young woman I recognized as Claire. She was stunning, and the only resemblance she bore to Fred was the curve in her eyebrows. I followed Fred to the nursing station, where two staff in street clothes were chatting. One recognized Fred. He asked if there were any updates or upcoming appointments, and was advised there was "no change" and "just the usual" meetings. We followed the music to the activity room. My feet moved slowly as my mind raced to create a vision of Holly, which couldn't have been more opposite.

In a large, sunny room, an older gentleman was playing classical music on a piano. His hands expertly fluttered across the keys, as residents and visitors gathered to listen. Fred motioned me to a petite woman tucked deep into an armchair by the window, facing outside. Her beauty was striking; her face and lean physique were frozen in time. She looked like Claire's sister, rather than her mother. Dressed in a fuschia yoga outfit, her shiny, dark hair covered her shoulders. She had long, dark eye lashes and big blue eyes, free of make up. She was very simply, a beautiful woman.

Fred bent over and kissed her cheek. I touched my own cheeks, recalling his lips on mine. She pulled away, zipping her hoodie up and shielding her breasts with her hands. Fred was visibly shaken. I wondered if a resident or staff member had touched her inappropriately. Fred glanced at me, then spoke.

"Holly is well cared for here. The staff watch her carefully because she is so...so...vulnerable." I'm not sure if either of us felt any more reassured.

Holly watched him as he spoke, still clutching her chest. She remained anxious, and uncomfortable with Fred's presence. She looked at me.

"You're new." Fred re-directed her.

"Holly, do you remember me?" he said softly. "It's Fred."

"Fred?" She stared blankly at him, then back at me. "Are you both new here?" Her stare shifted back to Fred. "No, you were here before." Fred smiled weakly.

I extended my hand, which she held with her tiny hands. A braided gold band circled her left ring finger. I said it was pretty. She looked at it intently, and said, "I think it's my mother's." Fred pointed discreetly to the matching ring on his left hand, which I'd not seen before. Looking dejected, he switched topics.

"What was for lunch, Holly?"

"A tuna sandwich, celery sticks and milk. Or maybe soup."

"It's a beautiful day. Let's go for a walk, Holly." She pointed to me.

"Will she come too?"

"That would be nice. Holly, this is Grace."

"Are you new here, Grace?" My named rolled slowly off her tongue.

"Yes. I'm just visiting." She looked again at Fred. Her stare was flat. Whether he was a stranger, or her husband, she didn't know. She got up slowly. "I have to tell Cathy." Cathy was a nurse at the desk, who directed Holly to her room to put on a hat and sweater. Holly obeyed, coming out with a crisp white baseball cap on and showing Cathy she had her sweater on. Cathy gave Fred a swipe card to access the outdoor walking path, and instructed us to return the same way. Holly was quite happy to go outside, and knew the path to follow. I heard a faint beep and Fred pointed discreetly to Holly's ankle monitor.

"We go this way in group." I carried the conversation.

"How often do you go for a walk?" She answered eagerly, with pressured speech.

"Every day."

"Walking's good for you."

"Yes, it's good for you."

"How many people go?" She repeated the question a couple of times, then Fred repeated it again.

"How many people go for a walk with you?' She stared at him as if he had no business talking to her. She rambled off five names, twice and in the same order, then turned to me for approval. The paved path was wide enough for two people. Holly directed Fred to walk ahead, and me beside her. Fred obliged, hands pocketed as he walked. Holly told Fred to walk farther ahead of us, and when he was a few strides away, she leaned closely into me. "I hope he doesn't work here long."

"Why Holly? He's a very nice person."

"He's so big. And scary." I couldn't help but smile.

"Don't be afraid. He's just tall. And he would never hurt you." She shook her head, saying she wanted nothing to do with him. Fred glanced at us, and I knew he heard us. I understood his burden. I told Holly that Fred came to visit her. Surprisingly, she asked if we came together, and I answered we didn't. She complained of thirst, and reluctantly agreed that Fred could join us at the coffee shop. He brought coffee, and she remained cautiously distant from him, and then more agitated when he attempted light conversation about Claire. Shortly after, we checked in at the nursing station and returned Holly to her chair in the activity room. Fred navigated us through the same maze of security barriers. It was as difficult to exit the building as it was to enter, both physically and emotionally.

Back at our vehicles, Fred looked despondent, but said Holly was more talkative today. I said it was hard when relationships end, but memories give us nice things to remember. Fred nodded, half listening, lost in his own thoughts before he spoke.

"When people die, or divorce, there are endings. There are dates. And milestones. Some of my friends gave up and moved on. I've been floating for the last ten years with Holly, and who knows for how much longer. I'm stuck." After another long pause, he continued. "Then along comes this wonderful person who offers me hope, at the expense of...and..." he abandoned his sentence, stared ahead and re-organizing his thoughts. "And...I don't know which road to take. I don't know if moving on is more difficult than staying..." I took his hand and held it, unable to comfort him without feeling selfish. He squeezed my hand gently, then dug his hands deep into his pockets, and turned to face me after another long lapse of silence.

"Grace, I need some time."

"Some time. Okay?"

"Yes, time. I need time to be by myself."

"Like time away from me...such as...to be alone for a while?"

"Yes."

"Okay. I can appreciate that." He was silent, but I needed more clarity. "Is there a time frame?"

"I don't know. I just need to sort out my thoughts."

"Shall I stay away from Norman too?" He looked away. Another very long pause.

"That might be best for a while. Not for Norman, but only because he lives next door. He's allowed a few more people in, so he's okay right now."

"That's good. That's all right."

"I'll tell him you're not ignoring him."

"I do understand." Fred said goodbye and kissed me on the cheek, the same side he had kissed Holly earlier. I searched his face for hope before we departed, prayed this wasn't the end. Holly was vulnerable and needed protection, which he couldn't give. But what was his intention, or ability to offer her? This man had nested in my heart, and I didn't want to let him go.

October 9th

The first week disconnected from Fred was painful. I asked for more hours at work and got them. I spent time with Tess, Sophie and Mallory, and made plans with a few friends for the following week. I was asked to a meeting with Kristen when she returned to the office in mid-October. Because my current lease ended November 3rd, I went the office instead. I did not want to be homeless.

Kristen's secretary produced a thick file and looked at the first few papers in the folder. There was no new lease, but she saw no reason why it wouldn't be renewed. I was miserable about that uncertainty, along with not seeing Fred again. I ached to hear from him and to return to Niagara, but knew in my heart the importance of giving him time. I sent Norman a nice card, wishing him well and hoping to visit soon; a vague time frame, just like Fred gave me.

October 12th

My appointment with Kristen was for five o'clock. She greeted me warmly, more like an old friend than a business associate. She was happy that the house was still occupied by a "reliable" person. I signed another three-month extension, with no changes, but was advised that the rent may increase minimally with the next renewal. She said Livy's house would be eventually listed, but I would be given ample notice. I updated her on Norman and submitted the gas receipts from my trips to Niagara, and we made arrangements so I could soon take over the lease on Livy's car. She mentioned that I hadn't seen Norman since he returned home. I reminded her that he had support workers coming in daily, and that I was working part time and volunteering, which appeased her.

When she asked how Mr. Smith was, my heart skipped a few beats. I lied, saying I hadn't seen him since Sept. 29. She said he had called, but didn't give the reason, and I knew better than to ask. I assumed it was about Norman, and she reassured me that he was fine.

After our meeting, I joined some girlfriends from Bernard Steel for pizza. My mother always said if you steer clear of gossip, it will steer clear of you. I hadn't seen most of them since the plant closed. I missed a few of them, but not the gossip. Two were happily enjoying new careers. Two were optimistic that something good would happen soon, and the chronic complainer left us after one drink.

The waiter brought me a glass of my favourite white wine, courtesy of a man at the bar. I turned to the bar to see Simon, raising his beer glass. My friends gushed over him and despite my objection, invited him over. Dressed in denim, he strutted over and filled the vacant chair beside me. He enamored the ladies with compliments. When he insisted on driving me home, my friends dispersed quickly, leaving Simon and I alone. I regretted accepting the ride home when his hand slid to my thigh before we left the parking lot. I felt nothing. No electricity, unlike six months ago. I wondered who would lose this time, because he certainly won the last time.

"You can't still be single?" he asked.

"I'm not." I slid his huge hand off my lap. His smile was broad, and within a few stop lights, his hand was edged back, hovering close to my legs. I put my purse between us. He persisted, resting his hand across my purse. I joined my hands, resting them on my legs.

"Who's the new guy?"

"A football player," I lied.

"Really! Like still playing pro, or retired?"

"Still involved." I'd have to be more creative if he asked for more details.

"Who is it?" *Yes, Grace who?* Simon rambled off some names. I knew as much about football as I did about baseball, which was nothing.

"I signed a confidentiality agreement. I can't discuss it." *Great lie, Grace.*

"I won't tell."

"Sorry, Simon." He picked up my left hand.

"No rock yet?"

"Can't wear it in public." I concentrated to keep a straight face.

"Really. Gracie, you deserve to be looked after." *Yes, I do.*

"Thanks." Simon lost interest in me when we arrived at Livy's house.

"Wow, did he buy you this house?" He'd obviously forgot I had given him the address.

"Be careful, Simon. There are surveillance cameras on you, so stay the truck."

"Sure, sure, okay. If you ever need a place to..." I was out of the truck before he finished his sentence. My sandals clicked up the steps and I was through the front door while Simon was still looking for security cameras. Handsome as he was, he had little more to offer than his benefits.

October 15th

Fred finally called, and it was not the call that I expected. We exchanged pleasantries before he unloaded his dilemma, that being Norman. Fred spent the last ten hours with him in the emergency department. Norman broke his big toe, which was a minor problem for a person with good balance, but for a senior recovering from a broken hip, he was considered a high risk for another fall. He had fired every caregiver, the last one quitting before he had the chance. Fred's predicament was that he was leaving on a school trip on the 17th. He would see Norman tomorrow, but would then be away for a week. Two agencies had not called back about providing Norman support, and he had fired what available employees they had left. For obvious reasons, he didn't want to involve me, but was out of options.

"I know it's totally inappropriate to ask you for some space, and then call you to ask for a favour. Grace, I'm very sorry to ask you on such short notice, but he still needs someone checking up on him. He can walk a bit if he takes his time and is careful."

"Just like vacationing parents letting all the neighbours know their teenagers are loose in the house."

"Exactly. What I'm really asking, is that if no one calls back, would you consider spending a few days in New Pelham?"

"At his house?"

"God, no. I would never ask that of you," he said hesitantly. I heard a big sigh. "Grace, I really am uncomfortable asking, but I just know if someone isn't watching out for him, he'll fall and be in a worse mess than he is now. He's a mean old goat, but he has no one. It's not fair for you to drive back and forth, so would you consider staying at my house? You have every right to say no." He heard the deep breath I took and exhaled. "I know that you and the dog, uh, I mean you and Wilson are a package deal." *Who's bed would I sleep in?*

"Hmmm. I'd have to call work."

"I'll cover your salary and mileage, if you have to miss work."

"That's a generous offer, but I..." *Of course I'll do it.*

"I'm so sorry to dump this on you. I won't leave him, but I can't abandon the kids either. If I cancel, then no one goes, and the fees are non-refundable. Can you tell that I'm desperate?"

"Those are tough choices."

"I feel terrible."

"It's not your fault."

"Can I give you the day to think about it?"

"Sure." *Grace, be smart. Think this through.*

"Again, if you say no, I understand completely. No questions asked. It's a major inconvenience, but what made me call was when Norman showed me the card you sent. The old fart appreciates you, and so do I. Very much so..." My mind was already made up. I just had to clear it with work. He gave me his number again, although there was no need to.

Getting time off work was easy, but I still waited an extra fifteen minutes before I called Fred back.

"Thank you. Thank you so much, Grace. I owe you big time. You have no idea how much." He was even happier when I agreed to stay at his house. "I'll give Norman a good tune up before you come."

We worked out some minor details. Fred was leaving Monday morning, and would check on Norman before he left. He gave me the option of arriving Sunday night, but by the tone of his voice, I knew he preferred if I came on Monday. Fred would tell Claire I was housesitting and helping Norman to avoid any surprises. Five days around Norman was well worth one day with Fred. I barely slept Sunday night.

October 17th

I drove to Niagara with Wilson on Monday. As usual, the traffic was lighter than the traffic heading away from the city. Wilson loved the ride, and as promised, Fred left a key in an outdoor light fixture. I reached high to find it, relieved to feel the leather tag with my fingers. I unloaded the car and walked Wilson. He sniffed around Fred's main floor, then retreated to his open crate facing the back yard, where squirrels and other small creatures would keep him amused. On the kitchen island stood a bouquet of fall flowers. A small card, tucked into the flowers, said *'Thinking of You'* on the front. The journal from Norman's hospital stays lay beside the card. I opened the hand-written card.

> *Hi Grace. By the time you read this card I will have given out*
> *two detentions, but I'll also be thinking of you.*
> *I'll try to call you or Norman every night, Thank you*
> *again for your generous help. It won't be forgotten.*
> *Dinner's in the fridge.*
> *Stay well. Fred*

I opened the journal, where Fred logged Norman's past and future medical appointments and a brief update about his care. He left names

237

of the agencies he called, and his medication schedule. Meals were taken care of, and someone committed at the last minute to help him with his personal care, so my only task was to check in on him. Fred told Norman that I would visit in the morning. There was a new cup, and a tin of Empire cookies from a local bakery on the counter. I peeked in the fridge. A bottle of local wine rested on its side, with a small tag attached:

Dose: Sip at least one glass per night for stress relief, and repeat as needed (there's more in the cupboard)

Dinner was curried chicken, rice and asian veggies in a casserole dish in the fridge. I found the kettle and made tea, touched to see a new box of my favourite brand in the cupboard. I brought my suitcase upstairs. The master bedroom was to the right of the stairs. The room was painted a dusky blue and the bed was made up with pewter-coloured linen. I could see by the creases in the bedspread and pillow cases that everything was new. Fred had rolled back a corner of the bedding, with a small card folded in two, and perched on a pillow. I opened it.

Hope the sleeping arrangements are satisfactory. Thanks again.

I sat on the side of the bed. An alarm clock and TV remote sat on the night table. The faint scent of Fred lingered in the room. I lay back on the bed and stared at the ceiling. Thoughts of Fred in this bed floated in my head. The window was partially open and a car drove by, shifting my thoughts back to Norman.

I walked downstairs. Wilson ignored me, pre-occupied with the view. I changed my shoes and walked the path to Norman's house. Norman's old Mercedes in his driveway was covered with oak leaves. The lawn was cut and someone had pruned the shrubs around the house. It no longer appeared abandoned. I made noise with my sandals, climbing the front steps. After a few loud knocks, Norman's familiar bark said it was open. I eased the squeaky door open, braced for conflict. I entered cautiously, closed the door, and crossed the entrance.

"Hello Norman, it's Grace," I said, using my best, cheerful voice.

"In here." He sat barefoot at the kitchen table eating cereal, in worn flannel pajamas. A new coffee maker and kettle sat on the counter. If I was nice, Norman might be congenial. I offered to make coffee and he accepted. His walker was near the kitchen table and I purposely avoided mentioning it. I suggested if he got dressed while I did the dishes, we could have coffee on his front porch. He muttered something about staying in his pajamas. I bumped up the incentive by offering to bring Wilson over. That worked, and Norman used the walker to hobble over to the stairs. I asked him if he needed help getting up the stairs. I couldn't understand him, but assumed by his negative tone, it was no. I remained in the kitchen, cringing while listening to him navigate each step. After a few painful groans, he reached the top, leaving the walker on the main floor. I busied myself in the kitchen with the dishes, picked up spilled potato chips, and tried to tune out the grunting sounds from the open upstairs bathroom door. I cranked opened the window, rinsed the coffee mugs out and breathed in fresh country air.

Norman was downstairs, dressed but unshaven, within thirty minutes. He ordered his coffee. I took the full cups outside, casually holding the door open with my elbow for him. I pounded the chair cushions against each other to fluff them and repositioned the porch chairs farther apart, facing the front yard.

"Where's the mutt?"

"Coming right over." I took one gulp of coffee, and returned with Wilson, off his leash. He explored his new environment, marking his territory houses, and approached Norman eagerly, sweeping his tail across the mugs on the table. Wilson leaned his chin on Norman's lap, drooling onto his pants. Norman complained he wasn't trained, and as if on cue, Wilson proved him wrong by extending his paw to him, and they were friends again.

A car turned into the driveway and Norman took pleasure in hearing the car bottoming out in the potholes as it approached the house. A chubby woman in her forties, dressed in a pink scrub uniform one size too small, got out of her car. Without closing the door, she bent over to check for damage. Her lumpy bottom faced us, creating significant resistance against the seams of her uniform. As Norman let out a shrill whistle, she lifted her head in his direction and snickered. With one hand on her car and the other on her knee for support, she eased her self upright. Retrieving a bag from her car, she approached her patient. Deep creases wrinkled her uniform. Her dental veneers and plastic nails were the same porcelain colour. She must have made a good first impression, because Norman was smiling, which staged my exit. I grabbed Wilson and promised to return.

The rest of the day transitioned smoothly into the evening. I brought a few books to read, but was still distracted by my thoughts of sleeping in Fred's bed. The day ended without a call or text, but I woke up imagining Fred's head on the pillow beside me.

October 18th

When I saw Norman on Tuesday morning, I knew Fred's priority was him, because he called. Norman was still in his night clothes, using the excuse that today was bath day. He was short tempered, but happy to see Wilson again. With some prodding, Norman said that Fred was camping in the wilderness with his students. We had coffee on the porch again, and when the same car as yesterday returned mid-morning, Norman sent us on our way.

When I returned late afternoon, Norman was clean and dressed, but tired. I stayed long enough to heat his dinner, and told him I would pop by in a few hours. When I returned, he looked pale, asleep in his recliner. I felt his forehead, startling him. He swiped a hand at me, then snarled an apology. He complained of an upset stomach and attempted to stand up. He never made it out of his chair, losing his dinner all over himself, the floor and me. He looked up at me, glassy eyed, and vomited again. He slumped back in his chair, waves of nausea visible on his face. I placed a garbage bin from the kitchen in front of him, but he pushed it away. We sat in silence for a little while, staring at each other like two old cats, until Norman's colour slowly returned.

I didn't know where to start cleaning up, but Norman did, pulling his dentures out and passing them to me. Gagging, I started with them. The quicker this mess was gone, the better both of us would feel.

It took some persuasion to convince Norman to shower again. I watched him unsteadily, and with great effort, climb the stairs. He argued unsuccessfully that he could safely shower, and as a compromise, I turned the shower on while he sat on his bath chair. He showered with his boxer shorts on as I paced and fretted until he yelled that he was finished. I turned the shower off and passed him a towel and clean pajamas. I waited again outside the door forever, relieved that he was complaining again. He shuffled out, looking like a drowned rat. He was weak and flushed, and did not resist going to his own bed. He took the outdated medicine I found for nausea with a few sips of water. Safely tucked in, I cleaned up the bathroom and as much of myself as I could.

The downstairs was a bigger challenge. The dinner I set out for him earlier was not the cause of his vomiting. It remained uneaten on the counter, in favour of another container which smelled like spoiled food. I cleaned the living room, washed his clothes and towels and two hours later, the job was done. Norman snored soundly upstairs. I sat on the front porch, calculating that the nausea medicine would wear off in about two hours, when he would either feel better or need another dose. I checked on Wilson at Fred's house, then decided to wait it out at Norman's.

I walked around the main floor, looking for something quiet, yet constructive to do. The junk mail in the dining room looked like a good project. There was lots. I sorted piles of outdated grocery specials, lottery offers and pamphlets and put them in a box to recycle. This left one box of legitimate mail, which included many identical envelopes addressed to Nancy Chestnut. I placed his real mail in one box, hoping to beg for forgiveness if Norman was upset about it. I made some noise and took more nausea medicine upstairs. I turned the bathroom light on, which let enough light into Norman's room to see his colour. His face was soft pink and he muttered that he felt a little better. He willingly took more medicine and fell back asleep. I reminded him I would return later.

Fred's call came just as I stepped out of his shower. Wrapped in a towel, I sat on Fred's bed, taking in his voice. He was cordial and mostly business-like. One student had a stomach bug while at camp, so we shared clean-up stories. I heard teenage voices nearby, which justified Fred keeping his conversation impersonal. I looked forward seeing to him on Friday, and he politely said the same. After I hung up, I wondered when Holly last had the capacity to miss him too.

I checked in again on Norman after dinner and refilled his glass with soda water. He had a slice of toast in bed and went right back to sleep. I fell asleep hoping tomorrow would be easier.

October 19th

When I arrived in the morning, Norman was on a belligerent rant because I purged his mail. He called me names I hadn't heard since my days at Bernard Steel. I defended myself, explaining I didn't want to leave because he was ill, and thought it would be helpful. We negotiated that I would leave his things alone if he used his walker. It worked. Wilson remained the buffer between us.

The remainder of the week was long and tedious. Norman repeatedly tested my patience. He tried to manipulate me to put on his shoes when he could do it himself. I drove him to the Legion in town, as a compromise to bringing beer home. He got out of the car as quickly as his brittle body would move him, then refused to use his walker. Snubbing me like an indignant teenager, he hobbled inside the building.

I refused to leave, and besides, I had nowhere to go. I was invited to sit outside with four senior veterans on the patio while Norman drank with his old cronies inside. The veterans were more than willing to talk about him, and between the four of them, shared his history.

After he retired, Norman was hired as a bartender at this Legion, until taking liberties with the liquor inventory got him fired. He avoided people or situations that would complicate his life. He abandoned friends before they ditched him. He shared little, but asked for a lot. It was well known that he would never do anything for someone else unless it benefited him. Perhaps he did it for attention, or an afternoon of companionship. He was cheap, rather than frugal. Nancy remained a mystery. They knew there was a wife, but her whereabouts were unknown. Most men came here to get away from their wives, or complain about them, and Norman did both.

By the time Norman surfaced, his alcohol consumption far exceeded what his frail body could handle. Being ill a few days earlier didn't help. I supported his arm to get him into the car, with a bit of muscle from an equally fragile drinking partner. He slumped into the front seat. He was quiet as I drove, until I mentioned Nancy again. The alcohol made him more willing to talk, and he said she abandoned him.

"You know what she left me?" he snarled.

"Why, or what?"

"I said what."

"What did she leave you?"

"Alone." He laughed. Exaggerated and sad, but not that funny.

"Does she still live around here?"

"Nope."

"Did she move far away?"

"Yup - and it's mighty hot where she is."

"Like Mexico?" He roared.

"Like hell! And I hope she rots there!"

"That's not nice, Norman. Did she die? Is that how Nancy left you?

"She just left..." he slurred. "She left me once, and then again...and... and...and then she finally left me for good."

"What do you mean?"

"I told you, and that's all..." he drooled and spit the words out. Norman rolled his head back against his seat and refused to say anything else the rest of the way home. I pulled into his driveway, hoping he wouldn't vomit from the bumps in the driveway. Not sure if he had passed out or fell asleep, I had to rouse him. He leaned heavily against me as I got him into the house, petrified he would fall again. I insisted he used the bathroom before I left. I parked him in his living room recliner to sober up and sleep off the afternoon. I left him snoring, mouth hanging open.

Wilson and I walked over to the cemetery across the road. I didn't notice the three elderly women hovering around a dilapidated garden shed until I was halfway down the entrance path. They eyed me suspiciously, like I had disrupted an important, confidential discussion. There were no cars in the lane way. I felt their eyes on my back as I walked by them, praying Wilson could wait to do his business until we crossed the laneway to the orchard beside the cemetery. We circled enough trees until I was sure Wilson's reservoirs were empty, then sauntered back into the cemetery, periodically pausing to read the stone inscriptions. A few stones were labelled 'Chestnut', but none bore Nancy's name. She must have been cremated, or buried somewhere else.

The three senior women shared the black marble headstone that doubled as a bench. Chirping to each other, they became quiet when I approached. Thin as pencils, they wore jogging pants and different coloured scarves. Wilson took full advantage of their attention, parking himself beside them. Ms. Red Scarf backed away from Wilson while her navy and black scarfed counterparts fussed over him.

"He's very friendly." I said, curious about them.

"And so handsome. Are you the nurse?" Ms. Red Scarf pointed to Norman's house and edged closer, balancing her discomfort around Wilson against her auditory deficit.

"Not really. Just visiting for a few days." I kept the conversation neutral.

"How's Norman doing? We heard he took a bad spill." Ms. Black Scarf adjusted her hearing aid.

"He's coming along." Maybe if I offered information, I'd earn some back. "You must live nearby. I don't see any cars." They surveyed each, and let Ms. Red Scarf answer. "We walk from three different directions, and rest here before we walk home."

"A little walking club. Good for you," I applauded their commitment to preserving their health.

"We call ourselves the cemetery girls." Ms. Black Scarf bellowed.

"Well, that's an unusual name," I mused. Ms. Red Scarf explained.

"We walk in the cemetery so we can stay out of it!" They laughed so hard that one almost lost her balance. "We also visit our husbands, and see if any new residents moved in," she continued, still chuckling.

"Your husbands are all buried here?" I asked.

"All five of them." Ms. Black Scarf confirmed.

"Five?" Ms. Black Scarf pointed to Ms. Red Scarf.

"We've each buried two here."

"Sad, but convenient."

"We all knew each other, and, our first husbands knew our second husbands." *Now that's really convenient.* Red Scarf pointed at Norman's house.

"I hope he recovers soon. We don't want him here any time soon."

"Me too." I wondered if he was 'husband material' to any of them.

"Maybe he needs company. Should we visit and bake him a pie?" Ms. Black Scarf offered.

"Perhaps, in a few weeks." I heard Ms. Navy Scarf mumble something about not baking anything for the old goat. I figured she was the one who barely survived one husband.

"Should we skip the pie and visit?" Ms. Black Scarf asked. I thought Fred should screen Norman's visitors, curious as it would be to watch them fuss over Norman.

"He's got a flu bug right now, so maybe in a week or two. You wouldn't want to catch anything." They all took one step back from me. Ms. Navy Scarf hissed something about Norman having 'cooties', impatient for me to leave. I encouraged them to keep walking, and left, sure that I had fueled the gossip line.

Norman was in fine form when I saw him at dinner time. He was miserable, still wobbly on his feet and only moved to use the bathroom. He didn't want dinner, so I left dry toast and apple juice within reach. He slumped back in the recliner, and I left him to his misery.

My phone rang as I opened Fred's front door. His voice on the other side was soft, and sweet, with minimal background noise. He was happy. I filled him in on our day.

"Mmmm...the Legion, home of short beers and tall stories. And you had the pleasure of meeting a few of our finest citizens."

"It was a nice drive there. Back, not so much." I loved his laugh.

"How are the accommodations?"

"Perfect. Nice sheets, and wonderful dinners."

"It's the least I could do. I hope you're sleeping all right, and the dog is behaving."

"We're doing fine. And your troop?"

"A few unruly moments, but otherwise fine." I kept the conversation going just to hear his voice. Fred confirmed he would be home Friday after the last student was handed off to his family. He suggested dinner together, which I very much looked forward to.

October 20th

Norman remained miserable, regardless of what I did. His food was too hot. The coffee was too strong. I returned to the solace of Fred's house within minutes of seeing Norman. He called back twice, begging me again to take him back the Legion. I refused, and buried myself in a novel, frequently distracted by thoughts of Fred. Shortly after I heard a car drive down Norman's driveway, I saw a taxi drive by. The driver was the lone occupant. Maybe Norman had company, which would be a good diversion for both of us.

The taxi had delivered beer to Norman, and he was into his fourth bottle when I returned two hours later. Something snapped in me and I exploded. For a change, he was the recipient. I ranted about caring about him, but not being appreciated. He had exhausted my patience, and I was done.

I heaved the case of beer up off the floor and stormed out the front door. Anger surpassed logic as I hurled the container over the front porch and an impressive distance. Norman hobbled outside, fast enough to watch the beer fly across the lawn, waving his hands and yelling tirades of obscenities as the bottles shattered. As one bottle exploded into the air, I felt his hand slap my back hard. I turned around, wanting nothing more than to slap him back across the face, certain that he would fall. We glared at each other in a silent stand off, then his swearing profanities continued, with him yelling something about "pixie dust". I moved closer to him, my hand itching to punch him. I was this angry only once before, when the insurance company denied Blair's $100,000 life insurance claim. I forced myself to breathe.

"What did you say?" I leered at him.

"You heard me."

"No I didn't."

"The dust."

"What dust?"

"The fairy dust."

"What fairy dust? You said pixie dust."

"Dust is all the same. The dust that's wearing off your crown."

"I beg your pardon," I hissed.

"You heard me. The fairy dust. It's worn off your sparkly crown. And the crown is falling off your head," he snickered. I needed to leave, and started walking down the stairs. I could feel his spit on the back of my neck as he yelled, "You're not interested in me. You're only interested in your reward!" I turned around sharply to face him.

"And what might that be?" I was livid.

"The money."

"The money? What money?"

"You know very well what money. The Chestnut money. That's why you're here, isn't it? You think you're gonna get a big pay off for babysitting an old man! I know your kind." As angry as I was, I also found it funny. In fact, it was a relief. I laughed hard, and out loud. "You're not fooling me, lady," he sneered.

"Norman, if I wanted your money, I wouldn't have thrown your beer out. I would have taken you to the Legion all day, every day, and if you fell down the stairs and broke your neck because your were so plastered, those boys at the Legion, not me, would have been your star witnesses. But I didn't, because I want you to get better so you can go back to being alone, and the same miserable old goat you were before I met you. I've had enough of you!"

"Good!"

"Good for both of us. And make your own dinner!" I yelled, as my shoes pounded loudly against the stairs and I stomped back to Fred's house. I avoided looking at the beer, leaving the clean up until later that day when I calmed down. This week couldn't end soon enough.

I poured a full glass of wine and drew a hot bath at Fred's house. The only thing to make bubbles in Fred's bathroom closet was a hotel sampler of body wash. I eased into the steamy water, my wine glass within reach on the window sill. I closed my eyes and took a few deep breaths. The wine and water combination was working until I heard Wilson bark at the front door. He ran upstairs to me, and barked again. There were no unusual noises. He barked again at the front door, whimpered, and came up the stairs. His brown eyes looked at mine and he rested his head on the bathtub ledge. A minute lapsed. He barked again.

"Five minutes. Wilson. Give me five minutes. Or maybe ten..."

I got out of the tub, using one towel for my wet hair and another for me. Drying off, I took inventory in the floor to ceiling mirror, increasingly more aware of my lumps and bumps.

Wilson paced around me. I heard the faint sound of an alarm. I scratched his ears and told him to relax, but neither of us did. It was not an alarm, but a siren approaching as I dressed. Through the window, I saw the flashing lights of a fire truck as it slowed down in front of my house. Dread took hold as I ran down the stairs. The fire truck siren stopped just as the faint sound of a different siren approached. I ran a comb quickly through my very wet hair, slipped sandals on and ran to Norman's house, just as the ambulance parked behind the fire truck. A trail of blood was splattered across the front stairs, starting at the broken beer bottles. Two firefighters met me at the stairs while a third man helped the paramedics with their equipment. I recognized the paramedics from their last trip here.

"I'm staying next door," I blurted out for no reason. We followed the blood across the porch, which was smeared across the walls, and tiled lobby floor, almost obliterating the CHESTNUT letters. There were huge blood stains on the living room carpet. We found Norman in his recliner, one socked foot, and the other wrapped in a bloody dishcloth, secured with his hands. His eyes were glassy, his colour ashen. He glared at me, the look of vindication masking any sign of discomfort. One paramedic, loaded with supplies, almost fell on the bloody lobby floor.

The pile of empty beer bottles beside Norman's chair had doubled in the forty minutes since I had left. He consumed eight beers in two hours, the last four within forty minutes, excluding the time it took him to retrieve them from the lawn. I was amazed that after eight beers that he could still speak. I flashed back to my first encounter with Norman, under similar, but more critical circumstances.

The tall, slender paramedic, armed in purple gloves, spoke to him. "Didn't we meet here before? You had your Christmas boxers on."

"Not, sure, honey," Norman slurred.

"Had a bit to drink today, young man?" Norman cackled. "What happened?"

Norman took one bloody hand off his covered foot and pointed a crooked finger at me.

"She did it. It's all her fault!" he blurted out, spraying the medic with spit. My colour drained. I shivered with fear, and shock. *You bastard!*

She put her hand up to silence me before I could speak, a very difficult command to follow. Norman drooled and stuttered simultaneously.

"She was trying to kill me." I felt light-headed, and she gave me a warning look again, to remain silent.

"Now, why would she want to do something like that?"

"Be...be...because she wants all my money!"

I gasped.

"Your money?" the paramedic said, unbelievably calm, keeping him preoccupied while she assessed him. More sirens approached. I sat down, feeling faint. I pictured my mug shot at the police station, wet hair and all. Worse than the tabloid shots of drunk celebrities. The paramedic gently unwrapped the towel from Norman's foot. An enormous, gaping gash opened the entire inside length of his right foot. It bled freely, and she applied pressure again. "Looks like you've done some damage here. You may have severed an artery, sir. Does anything else hurt?"

"He broke his left big toe last week." I offered, from the security of the sofa. The paramedic looked quickly at Norman's other grass and blood stained sock, then concentrated on the new injury.

"There's glass embedded in the wound, but we'll leave that for the doctor. Where did you cut yourself?"

"Here, you fool," he slurred, pointing to his foot.

"Now, be respectful, sir. I meant where did it happen?"

"Outside. I tried to clean up the mess she made and wouldn't clean up. Left it for an old man to clean up...and...and...and I was so weak, I fell into it. She wouldn't feed me." Norman rolled his head in my direction. I was amazed he was so creative with that much alcohol in him. His words were sloppy, but his intent to belittle me was clear.

"What was in the mess?"

"A case of beer she was stealing from me." I shook my head in disbelief and stared at Norman. He ignored me. "She's supposed to be looking after me, but she wants my money, and now she's stealing from me...and..." That was the final straw.

"That's the third lie, Norman. Blatant lies." Norman beamed with victory. The female paramedic interrupted us.

"Okay, that's enough. Let's get you to the hospital." The other paramedic looked in my direction. "It might be helpful if you met us there." I hadn't processed this new insult yet, let alone going to the hospital. Again. Norman yelled.

"No! She's useless! I want Fred!"

"He'll be back on Friday," I said.

"Hum-mph. Figures." I had no intention of going to the hospital. Let Norman find his own way out of this mess. Again.

The female paramedic wrapped Norman's foot tightly with a pressure dressing and elevated it. Norman was transferred onto the stretcher. Now, almost incoherent, he babbled about my plot to kill him. He was starting to pass out, about the same time as two police officers entered the house. My hands instinctively clutched my face, tears wetting my fingers. One officer approached me, and put a hand on my shoulder to console me. "It's okay, ma'am, lady," he said as another, middle aged officer pulled out his notepad. *Here we go again...*

The ambulance and firefighters left together. The officers remained behind and I spent the next hour explaining what happened, including

Norman's accusations. They seemed somewhat amused, stating that he needed to cool down and sober up. One officer went upstairs and retrieved Norman's wallet. They suggested I call or go to the hospital in a few hours to see if the hospital needed more details.

I showed the officers where I threw the case of beer, and found a bucket to clean up the glass. One officer asked if I had put any of the bottles back in the case, which I hadn't. They counted the bottles. There were a few pieces of glass outside the case. One was the broken top of a bottle with the cap still sealed, and the other was the round base of a bottle. It was the broken top of the bottle that had blood on it. We tried piecing together how Norman cut his foot on the glass.

"He could have picked up a broken bottle and accidentally cut his hand, but not his foot. Maybe he did it deliberately, and unfortunately his poor judgement backfired."

They looked to me for a reaction. I told them about our argument earlier in the day. Feeling even worse, I defended him.

"He's been complaining since he broke his hip about losing his privacy and wanting people to leave him alone." The older officer closed his note book.

"Many seniors do feel lonely and unwanted. They do or say things to get attention, and it's not always positive."

I also told them about the Chestnut estate and the tight controls the law firm had on its finances. The officers' suggested that I update the lawyer. They then gave me the accident report number, and suggested I look into some local recreational programs for seniors that didn't involve serving alcohol. I'd pass that on to Fred. I just wanted take Wilson and go home. Fred had baggage. Not Claire, but Norman. *And Holly.*

I updated Kristen Clark when I returned to Fred's house, including the police officer's comments that he deliberately harmed himself. Once discharged, again, Norman would need more care. Kristen was very sympathetic. I told her it was time for me to get on with my own life, to which she asked if I planned to move out. I said that I'd let her know as soon as I had made a decision.

I stewed in the misery that Norman had created for all of us. I went back to his property, hosed down his outside steps and porch, then surveyed the inside. Blood had saturated a large patch of his living room carpet, and would need cleaning or replacing immediately. I laid towels over the bloody areas, and watched as they absorbed the blood. Nauseated by the sight, I left. It was not my problem.

I debated returning to Toronto, but felt strongly that Fred should know my story before he heard Norman's version. I made scrambled eggs and toast, and watched mindless comedies for the rest of the night. I called the hospital, but was advised that because I wasn't family, I wasn't entitled to any information, other than Norman was admitted. No surprise there.

October 21ˢᵗ

The first emotion that flooded me when I woke up was guilt, and robbed me of calming thoughts about Fred. I fretted when I heard a faint police siren, convinced they were coming to arrest me for elder abuse. When the siren faded, I returned to Norman's unlocked house, overwhelmed by the metallic stench of old blood in Norman's living room. The towels had soaked up a significant amount of coagulated blood on the stain-resistant carpet. I made penance for throwing the beer case by using a stain remover and hard work to clean up the carpet. The end result looked much better than I felt. The house now smelled like detergent, rather than old beer and blood. Norman wouldn't remember the mess. I scanned the main level of the house, seeing the box of mail still in the dining room where I left it. The letters addressed to Nancy remained unopened.

Fred arrived at dinner time, in a downpour, getting drenched dashing from his car to the house. My belongings were already in the Volvo. I had tidied up and made dinner. Fred was tired but happy to be home. I was greeted with a peck on the cheek and a quick hug, like compliant spouses after the thrill was gone. Fred already knew about Norman, and saw him before coming home. The piece of glass in Norman's foot severed some muscles, tendons, and part of an artery, which made it life-threatening. He had emergency surgery, and would be hospitalized for a while. I felt totally at fault, regardless of whether Norman had deliberately hurt himself or not. I had failed at my job. Fred poured generous glasses of wine for both of us, concerned that I was so distraught. Frankly, so was I. Perhaps it was because Norman was connected to Livy, and an extension of Fred, who had enough to deal with.

Fred took his duffle bag upstairs and changed into dry clothes as I put dinner on the table. He came down, a welcome sight in a light grey, long sleeved T-shirt and jeans. His wet hair was combed back, a few loose curls straying over his forehead. I was stuck on the vision of Norman's bandaged leg in my head. Fred put a box of tissues on my side of the table. He put his strong hands on my shoulders; his scent was intoxicating. I needed a hug, but couldn't ask for one. He sat down within reach, and rubbed my hand.

"Grace. Listen to me. It's not your fault, so how is it helpful worrying about it? He's been manipulating people all his life, and you were his next victim. He's an old man who wanted, and now received even more attention."

"That's exactly what the cops said."

"They were right. And it didn't take them long to figure him out." The wine was not soothing me.

"If I hadn't thrown the case of beer, it wouldn't have happened."

"If it wasn't this, it could have been something else. Maybe even worse."

That helped. A little.

We ate dinner in the dining room, where a few remaining chrysanthemum blooms from the garden in the vase adorned the table.

"If Norman knows he's been successful in derailing you, he'll see this as a victory. I've been a victim to his manipulative tirades too, Grace. Unfortunately this time for him, it's more than just stitches. He was snoring when I stopped by. The surgeon said he's not coming home anytime soon. And on that note, let's give Norman the rest of the night off, and savour this feast."

Fred inhaled the steam from the roast as he served me the first slice.

The rest of our dinner conversation was dedicated to Fred calming me with kindness. He was so stable. Such a caring man, with a solid sense of logic. I understood why his students listened to him when the rest of their lives were in chaos. I was envious that they were able to spend so much time with him.

For the first time in my life, I knew, rather than felt, that I was truly falling in love. I also knew that considering the circumstances, nothing may change. Wilson rested his head against my feet as if he knew I needed comforting.

We cleared the dinner dishes, moved to the living room and finished the first bottle of wine. We were both mentally and physically drained. The rain was beating hard against the window and I was dreading the drive home. Fred was in no rush to send me off, and the longer he talked, the better I felt. He opened a second bottle of wine. I should have declined, but didn't. Being here, at this moment, felt safer then being anywhere else. Wilson snored, pretending to guard the front door. Fred talked about his favourite disadvantaged students. We compared parenting teenage daughters, and their fierce fight for independence. Fred avoided any discussion about Holly, along with the other unmentioned topic, which was us.

I yawned and Fred followed suit, and when he poured me a third glass, I knew I wasn't going anywhere. It was dark outside when Wilson moved from the front door to the carpet on the opposite side of the couch that Fred was sitting. After taking him out and toweling him down, I sat down on one side of the couch as Fred sat on the opposite side, checking his mail. I tucked one foot under me and Wilson put his head on my other foot. Fred remained content and silent, with his feet on the coffee table. He looked at the lamp beside him, reached over to turn it on, then changed his mind. The street light offered the same level of ambiance as a small candle. Fred closed his eyes for a minute. He didn't resist when I put my hand on his shoulder, moving to his neck and massaging it. Soft sounds came from his throat. He turned away from me but moved closer so I could rub both his shoulders and neck. He groaned quietly as I worked through the knots in his muscles. I tucked my second foot under me to give me leverage as I kneeled, and kneaded my fingers down his back. I moved up each bump in his spine and then back down again, hands in symmetrical circles up the sides of his back and again across his shoulders. His muscles were looser and relaxed, as was he was when I finished.

He took my right hand and held it with his left one. He placed his right hand over mine and rubbed it softly. He rubbed my arm, with his warm touch gentle and tender. He remained beside me with his eyes closed, holding my hand for a long time. I felt small tremors in his hands. It was very dark, and raining hard by the time he leaned over and kissed my cheek. I cherished the moment with my eyes closed. He repeated the soft, light kisses a few times before he moved to my neck. His kisses were moist, inhaling and exhaling more deeply by the time his lips moved back to mine. I felt one hand on my thigh and the other in my hair. The faint smell of a campfire lingered in his hair as he drew me nearer to him. My hand found his neck and I slid my hand under his shirt. Another soft moan came from deep within his chest. He leaned in and kissed me deeply, his hand moving around my shoulders and to my back. Fred laid down with his back against the sofa and I laid down beside him with my back against his stomach. His bed had more room, but I wasn't complaining. He breathed softly, his face tucked in my neck and his arm over my stomach. His right hand played gently with my hair while his left hand rubbed my hips. He slid his hand gently under my shirt and moaned quietly and he caressed my stomach. My hand enveloped his and I weaved my fingers one by one through his. The ring on his left ring finger was gone. He eventually lay still, and his breathing was even and deep. I thought he had fallen asleep. After a few minutes, he whispered in my ear.

"Grace?"

"Uhmm..."

"Can we just stay like this for a little while?"

"We can stay like this all night."

"I'd like that. Very much." He nuzzled his face back into my hair. I felt his breathing become more intense as he pulled my hips against his. I felt his erection grow against me as he rocked my body gently and slowly in unison with his. I lay quiet and moved against him. He kissed my neck and shoulders, murmuring soft sounds, then became still again. The back of my neck was moist. Whether it was sweat or tears, it didn't matter. What I hoped was that the storm inside this man lying beside me was ending. I would wait for him. As long as he needed, I would wait.

October 22nd

Despite the prediction for the rain to continue, the stars lined up and brought a crisp, sunny morning to New Pelham. We began a new day in the same position we ended the last one. The first bladder alert came from Wilson who had slept on the floor beside us. Despite stiff bones and sweaty skin, it was a beautiful night. I felt long, feathery eyelashes brush against my neck, then a soft, good morning kiss to start my day.

"Thank you, Grace." he whispered in my ear.

"For what?"

"For allowing me the pleasure of your company, with no strings attached."

"Well, there are strings, but they're not attached."

"Precisely." I wasn't sure what he meant. He held me close to him and nibbled my ear. I responded by kissing him. He kissed me back, then pulled away. I kissed him again. He responded lightly, then pulled away again, followed by a deep breath. A sigh from me. A whimper from Wilson, who won the draw for attention. Fred sat up first, and Wilson responded by dragging his leash and and dropping it on Fred's feet.

"For a dog who doesn't know me, you sure have faith in me," Fred leaned in, his nose inches from Wilson's. Wilson dragged his leash back to the front door and banged his wagging tail against the door. Fred groaned as he eased his tall frame into a standing position. He extended his hand to me and pulled me up to stand facing him.

"Good morning, Grace." My arms found their way around his neck and he kissed my forehead. "I have a suggestion."

"I do too, but you go first." He grinned, easing me out of his arms.

"I'll take your pooch for a pee if you put the coffee on."

"That's not what I had in mind, but it's a start." Fred stretched his arms high into the air, and yawned loudly. His wrinkled shirt lifted over his jeans to expose a large, faded scar just below his waistline. I saw his bare chest the first day we met, but never noticed the scar. Fred saw my alarm, and before I could ask, said, "I have a second suggestion."

"What's that?"

"I think we should play five questions when I come back."

"I'm game for that." He put his sneakers on and grabbed his jacket from the closet.

"Remember my clues the last time. Think them through carefully right to the last one, because you only get five." He yawned again loudly, opened the door and followed Wilson out.

I debated having a quick shower, but all my things were in my car. I made coffee and washed yesterday's makeup off. The toothbrushing would have to wait. Fred returned as last bit of coffee sputtered the through the filter. I felt at home in this kitchen, and imagined spending more mornings here...

Wilson pushed his empty bowl across the floor until I doled out his kibble. Fred poured our coffee and I followed him back to the couch. He took the middle seat and I sat beside him. We toasted the morning and he pulled a quarter out of his pocket. I won the coin toss. I had many, many questions. Fred was full of energy, ready for the first volley. I started with the obvious, the scar, ready for an alligator wrestling story. The answer dropped like a bomb. It was from a knife which Holly stabbed Fred with, during a psychotic episode when she was trying to 'protect' Claire from him. I lifted his shirt and ran my finger along the wide, raised, silvery rope of scar tissue. He pulled the waist of his jeans down to his hip bone to reveal a second scar. It was shorter, but much wider. I felt sick. These were remnants of significant injuries. "There's a third one, where the sun doesn't shine," he said in an effort to lighten the moment, but made no attempt to show me.

"Oh my." His tender kiss on my forehead did little to comfort me. My strategically prepared questions vanished.

"Okay, my turn," he chirped, switching topics like nothing happened. I was still stunned. "Are you ready?" I took a sip of coffee, and nodded. "What's your greatest loss?"

He caught me off guard. It was not Blair, nor any material possession, and definitely not my job. My greatest losses were my parents. I adored them for their simple wisdom, sound advice and want for nothing but each other. I lost them within months of each other.

My second question went back to Holly and the scars, picturing her attacking Fred in this house with a carving knife.

"What happened after you got hurt?"

"I got my insides and my outsides fixed up. I was off work for two months, fifty percent physical, and fifty percent trauma recovery. Holly went to jail for attempted murder, where she obviously didn't belong." I forgot the game.

"Wow. When did this happen?"

He paused for a while. His eyebrows furrowed, then relaxed. "Remember I told you about the guy that was in our house, trying to seduce her?" I nodded. "Well, he fed her some unknown drug, and combined with the head injury from her falling down the stairs, she lost touch with reality. She was hospitalized, had lots of therapy with different psychiatrists and counsellors. I didn't tell you because I wasn't ready to share it with anyone. Very few people, except our parents, her doctors, and the police know about it."

"That's so sad."

"You would never know by looking at her. When you asked about meeting her, I didn't want you to know about the stabbing. What you saw of her, which was calm, but suspicious, is what she was like for years. That is, until she snapped. With medication adjustments, she was more stable, so we tried a couple of day passes home. On her second visit home, I thought it would be harmless for her to make shortbread cookies with Claire. She combined the recipe ingredients correctly and put the cookies in the oven to bake. She wanted to clean up. It was a perfect Saturday afternoon until she came down the hall and attacked me with a butcher knife. It was like someone flipped a switch in her, that's how quickly her behaviour changed. I yanked it away from her and threw it across the room. She wouldn't calm down so I got her out of the house. I couldn't even go back in the house to get our shoes on."

"What did you do?"

"I should have called 911, but using very poor judgement, I called Norman over to watch Claire while I drove her back to the hospital.

"With all those injuries?"

"I didn't realize how deep they were. I was driving on adrenaline."

"You could have bled to death. Or passed out."

"Or had an accident and made Claire and orphan." I gasped.

"That's awful!"

"Stupid would be a better description." My mouth hung open.

"Go on," I swallowed hard.

"She was reassessed and transferred back to the forensic unit. A brilliant psychiatrist connected us to a mental health case worker, who advocated on Holly's behalf to have some of her charges dropped via a court diversion program."

"What's that?"

"It's a program for people who commit criminal offenses and can't be held fully accountable because of their mental illness. The court diversion case worker presented the psychiatric assessments to the judge, who ruled that she was severely mentally ill. She was ultimately institutionalized instead of incarcerated."

'Wow."

"Grace, what rattled me the most was what I didn't know."

"And what was that?"

"The biggest knife we owned had been lying between our mattress and box spring for months. And I had no idea."

"How did you find out?"

"Her psychiatrist called me one day at school after he re-assessed her again, and asked me to check our bed when I got home. He asked her if she was planning on hurting anyone, and her intention was to kill me. When he asked how, she told him about the knife. She never mentioned it to him before." Small beads of sweat formed across his forehead. "I hated her being so sedated, but I'm so glad now that I listened to him and didn't object."

"This sounds like a movie."

"I wish it was a movie. And we were not the characters."

"What happened after that?"

"She never came home again. The courts ordered some independent psychiatric evaluations."

"Is that the normal process?"

"I don't know, but they all came to the same conclusion; that she was paranoid and psychotic. When you mix that with a brain injury, her chances of recovery seemed very unlikely. She remained on the forensic unit until they cleared the charges, and was transfered to where she is now."

"I'm stunned."

"So was I. For months. I never worried about myself before then, but after I found the knife, it took me a long time to see her. Holly had no insight, and therefore behaved like nothing happened. She had no recollection of any of it."

"I am so sorry, Fred. I keep saying that, but I am." His shirt collar absorbed the rivets of sweat running down his neck. He put his head briefly in his hands, then looked defensively at me.

"There was nothing else I could do. The doctors tried to stabilize her with medication and therapy, but it didn't work." His whole body shivered. "Grace, the feeling of finding that knife under the mattress was indescribable. My life...no...our three lives changed that day. I give the doctor credit for asking her about homicidal intentions every time, because if he hadn't, Claire would have been an orphan for sure."

"Unbelievable."

"And it was no longer just about us, but the safety of everyone. He called it homicidal ideation, then intent, which meant she had a plan, and intended to carry it through." I flashed back to the trust questions Fred asked me a few times. Was it about this...this terrifying history haunting him? Was it more about him trusting others, versus me trusting him? He shifted topics. "Okay, who's turn is it? Must be yours, and make sure it's a good one." He forced a weak smile.

My next question was drawn from my last thought, and I was anxious to change topics. I already knew that there were very few women who had been in this house.

"Have you ever slept in the same room with another person, male or female?" Fred looked at me, and tilting his head curiously to one side.

"Now that's a loaded question. Let me think a bit. You said the same room, but not same bed. Hmmm..." He perked up, scratched the top of his head and wiped the sweat off his neck with his forearm. "Yes. Yes I did. Two guys and I went to the Caribbean during spring break a few years ago and shared a room. It was a cheap vacation, I didn't have a lot of money, and there were two beds to a room. I lost the draw and got the couch. No sleep for me that week."

"What about school trips? Or holidays?"

"I always have my own room now, even if it is extra. I feel safer." Our conversation shed more light. He feared for his own physical and emotional safety. I waited for his next question. There was a long pause.

"Where do you see yourself in five years?" Another surprise question, and a quick response from me.

"With you."

He drew in another deep breath. I sat quietly and let my words sink in. He took a few long, slow sips of his coffee. "My turn." I took his left hand and pointed to his fourth finger. "What made you take your ring off?" Another surprise answer.

"I went to see a lawyer." My breath stopped. I waited for the explanation and didn't get one. I was stuck for something meaningful to say.

"Okay, then. How many questions have I asked?" I counted my fingers.

"Five, and you're all done," he said. "But I have one left."

"Five? I thought I was on number four."

"You wasted number three asking me about holidays and school trips, and I've only asked you four." He stood up, looked out his living room window, then turned back to face me.

"How long are you willing to wait?" My answer was easy.

"As long it takes."

"I need time, Grace. I can't explain it, but I just need time."

"I understand," I said, even though I didn't. But now I had hope, and some hope was better than none.

October 25th

Back in Toronto, life moved slowly. I missed Fred deeply. He hadn't shared anything more about not wearing his wedding ring, or seeing a lawyer, but I assumed that it was related to Holly's mental capacity. Maybe he was creeping forward with his life. Slowly. He didn't commit to meeting again, only that he needed an indefinite period of time. Again. Before I left that Saturday morning, I asked if I could call him in a few weeks. He said he'd call me, and I reluctantly agreed to keep my distance. Again. My feelings for him grew stronger every time I connected with him, and leaving on Saturday was like losing him again. I was in love. I dreamed about him and would catch myself smiling when anything about him came to mind.

The first week, I checked my phones constantly. Knowing when he would call was easier than not knowing. A few coworkers at the dress shop knew about Norman, but when I told them about Fred, I realized that was a mistake. All of them were married, and said this was adultery, and that I was the "other woman". The store owner stopped scheduling me for shifts. I felt worse. I had fallen in love, and nothing would change that. It happened.

I met Sophie for lunch, who grilled me about Fred, decided he was emotionally unstable, and told me to move on. If there was no commitment and no time frame, I shouldn't be hanging on, in her words, like a groupie. She urged me to see a counsellor because she said I was obsessing about him. I didn't think so, but agreed to go.

The counsellor was female, personable and got to the point very quickly. She gave me some hard facts, and then some homework. Fred was very married. Period. And he had told me many times. The ladies at the dress shop were protecting the sanctity and principles of their own marriages. Any relationship I had with him beyond a platonic friendship constituted adultery. So even though we didn't consummate our relationship, it was still an affair. This could have serious legal repercussions for him and that, she presumed, was his stumbling block. She suggested I put myself in Holly's position. Through no fault of her own, Holly became ill. She had no control over that, and neither did Fred. How would I feel about my husband having a relationship with someone else while he was still married to me, and I was the ill spouse? I defended Fred. Holly had been ill for many years. I told her we visited Holly. She thought my judgement was poor for going, and his for agreeing to it, which served no purpose other than confirming that Holly existed and she was sick, both of which I already knew. Had he made any changes to his will, finances or legal status? Those were questions I had no right to ask him.

The counsellor said Fred was contemplating his future and she gave him credit for settling his affairs before seeing me again. She also said this might take years. Was I content not knowing how long this play would run? Was I willing to pursue a relationship that society, for the most part, viewed as morally wrong? If I felt comfortable with my conscience, then it was my decision. She suggested that I choose a realistic time frame, like six months, for Fred to get his affairs in order. She said six months may be a long time for me, but not for Fred, considering the years he dedicated to his wife, and his efforts to avoid a relationship. I said I was willing to wait forever. She said that was unrealistic. Anything more than six to twelve months was a clear indication that he wasn't ready, and perhaps not worth waiting for. The decision was mine. My homework was to write him a letter, wait a week, and then send it if I still felt the same way.

November 8th

A courier delivered a layoff notice from my job effective immediately, citing a decline in business. I knew this was untrue, but nevertheless, the letter was difficult to read. Heading back to job searching would be harder now.

I wrote the letter to Fred. And re-wrote it. Many times. By the end of the week, the content was very different than the initial draft. I hand-wrote a card which had two golden retriever puppies on the front. It was simple, impersonal and to the point, just as the counsellor suggested.

November 8th

Dear Fred,

I hope this letter finds you in good health, and that Norman is well on his way to a smooth recovery. I think about you every day and want you to know that I care deeply about you. You had asked for some time and it is important for me to respect your wish. Fred, if I haven't heard from you in six months (which is May 8th), I know *that it will be time for me to move on with my life. Please give my best to Norman.*

Loving you now, and forever,

Grace

I read the letter again and mailed it, which was more painful than writing it. I gave Fred my ultimatum, which was heartbreaking. Now Wilson needed to console me. The tide had shifted; where I was used to caring for others, now I needed someone to care for me.

I went back to the counsellor and complained about her bad advice. She took me seriously and listened carefully. People around me had carried on with their own lives, and had forgotten about me. She suggested that I may have forgotten to care about them. She reminded me that I had been grieving many losses in the last year; Blair, my job, my house, Livy, even the clothing store layoff. And of course, Fred. She touched my shoulder, and spoke slowly. She said I was layering my losses, and each recovery period to grieve that loss would take a bit longer and than the previous one. She reminded me that I had little control over these losses and stood by her original advice about sending the letter to Fred. I needed to work on being at peace with the choice I made, and doubted it would affect Fred's decision. She passed me a clipboard with a card-sized sheet of white paper decorated with black scrollwork and a fine marker. I wrote the sentence as she dictated it to me:

I have earned the right to be happy.

I looked at the words. "What's that got to do with losses?"

"It's about letting go and accepting your choice. You're a smart lady, Grace, and have experienced many losses, but no one can deny you you the right to be happy." I kept staring at the words, looking for a deeper meaning. "Grace, it's not about what happens in six months, because it could happen sooner or later, with or without Fred. If he's meant to be in your life, then it will happen. Right now, he's the perfect fantasy in your mind, because he hasn't hurt you, or forgot to pay the bills, or farted in front of you, or lost his job. Your vision of happiness is so focused and narrow that you're frustrated and miserable because you think you'll never find it. What you think will happen down the road sometimes never happens. You don't know it yet, but when you find what you're looking for, you'll reach it in the 'right now'." Her index fingers went up and down up to emphasize the italics. "And in the 'right now', you'll still be doing the same stuff, like washing dishes, walking the dog, and waking up beside someone who you think is Mr. Wonderful. And you might still be wondering if you're happy."

I left with more homework, and that was to tape the paper on my bathroom mirror and repeat it aloud when I woke up and before bed. And I also had to promise to look after only myself and Wilson for the next two full weeks.

November 22ⁿᵈ

Two weeks came and went. The counsellor's advice was sinking in and some of my fog was lifting. The biggest corner of my heart was still saved for Fred, but I lowered my expectations. I kept reminding myself that the counsellor said: "If it's meant to be, then it will happen." I started to re-connect with old friends and colleagues. I volunteered more hours at the hospital. I got a temporary job as a float clerk in a department store for the Christmas holidays. I worked every shift I was offered, and went to the staff Christmas party. I was still feeling sad, but more open-minded.

As instructed, every night before bed, I repeated the words stuck to my bathroom mirror. I stopped looking for perfection, even though I still believed it was synonymous with Fred. Somehow, at the end of those two weeks, I felt a little more appreciation for the simple things that I had taken for granted for so long.

December 18th

I worked all day Sunday in the maze of the Christmas rush. I was tired of wearing black slacks, white shirts, and the store-issued vest with festive decorations on it. Most of all, I'd had enough of holiday music. I came home Sunday night after the store closed to lots of snow on the driveway and sidewalk which I shoveled while Wilson played in it. There were two sets of footsteps leading up to the front door and back to the street, which I assumed belonged to the letter carrier. The mailbox was full of envelopes and flyers. Livy still received correspondence, which I added to the law firm's pile.

I took Wilson for a quick walk and we both retired to the warmth of the house. Tess was home for the holidays, but out with friends. Sophie was bringing Chinese food for dinner, and our plan was to organize Christmas. She arrived with arms full of food. As advised by the counsellor, I tried harder to appreciate my sister, even though we had so little in common. After dinner, we foraged in the attic for decorations long abandoned by the Chestnut family, and created some Christmas spirit in the main rooms. Sophie left much later than expected, so I planned to sleep in because I wasn't scheduled to work until noon. Changing into pajamas, I tidied the kitchen up before bed.

Among the things on the counter that Sophie brought was wine she bought for Christmas and empty dishes she returned. Behind the wine bottles was a parcel the size of a shoe box, lying face down. It was addressed in pencil to Livy but her last name was misspelled. It had the right house number, but an incorrectly spelled street name. It originated in Indonesia, and by the tattered condition of the plain brown paper, it had been unwrapped and re-wrapped many times. The first of four visible shipping labels was dated a month after Livy's death. Because it was wrapped in the same colour package as the Chinese food bags, I hadn't paid attention to it earlier.

I texted Sophie, who said she found the package between the screen and front doors. I examined it with more care. The most current shipping label was dated yesterday. The box weighed about two pounds, and when I shook it gently, nothing inside made noise. I decided to deliver it with the mail to the law firm tomorrow morning. When I finally when to bed, I had trouble sleeping, thinking about what the shoe box held, instead of thinking about Fred.

December 19th

I brought Livy's mail and the shoe box to Kristen on Monday morning. She greeted me cordially as I unloaded the envelopes, saving the package for last. I never questioned anything Livy received, but this was an exception. I asked Kristen if she would consider opening it before I left. She was as curious as I was, and called a security guard in to check it. The young, uniformed male picked it up, shook it, and smelled it. He looked at all the labels and picked gently at some edges of the clear packing tape from the last re-wrapping. He called for a second security guard, who replicated the same activities that the first guard did. Together they determined that there was minimal risk, but suggested they stay while the package was unwrapped. I'm sure they were more curious than concerned.

Kristen came around from her side of the desk, and put the package on the coffee table which sat between the two chairs facing her desk. We watched like children as she photographed the unwrapping, along with the shipping labels.

The first layer of clear tape and brown paper wrapping was the hardest to remove. Several layers of Asian newspapers came away next. Kristen kept the paper. She held up a crudely assembled wooden box and showed every angle to the security guards. They nodded in unison for her to proceed.

She pried away a few dozen industrial staples with a letter opener, dropping the extracted ones in my extended palm as they came out.

Once the staples were pried off of the top of the lid, she carefully removed it. Long, thin shavings of white wood protected something bubble-wrapped, and taped tightly together. She cut the wrap open. Within the plastic lay thin layers of grey tissue paper. All heads moved closer to the parcel as she gingerly peeled away the last layer.

The treasure inside was a polished mahogany replica of Norman's house. I was awestruck by its beauty. The detail was incredible, right down to the outside stairs and bannisters at the front of the house. The front door was identical to the actual one. Even the door knob was on the same side. Kristen passed it to me, unaware of it's significance until I reminded her it was Norman's house, and showed her a photo that I had on my phone. I reminded her about the postcard Livy sent to Norman just before she died. This was the gift that never came. Until now.

A Indonesian craftsman must have dedicated countless hours from photographs to re-create the miniature. I wondered if the front door opened, and gasped when it came off. I thought I broke it, until I saw a small hole burrowed into the wood. In that opening was a folded piece of parchment paper no larger than the label on a prescription medication bottle. Only my baby finger fit inside the hole. I wiggled the paper out. My eyes watered when I recognized Livy's hand writing, which said:

> To my one and only Uncle Norman:
> I will always love you!
> Livy

I became emotional as the others remained silent. Kristen knew about the last time I saw Norman, and the incident that sent him back to hospital. Kristen informed me that Norman was back at the rehab centre, and asked if I could deliver it. I hesitated, considering our last disastrous encounter. She re-worded her request, suggesting I consider bringing it as a goodwill gesture. Feeling obligated, I agreed, but couldn't commit when. She said it didn't matter, because it was about the gesture, and not the date.

December 21st

I picked today to deliver Norman's gift. I had considered couriering it, but didn't want to compromise my relationship with Kristen. I was still living in a beautiful house, and very grateful for the security and the neighbourhood. I didn't start work until five o'clock and the weather forecasted sunny skies. I wrapped the tiny house in festive paper, complete with a card and bows, and headed to Niagara after breakfast. Longing to see Fred, I knew he would be at school.

The drive was easy, and the roads were clear. At the rehab centre entrance, large urns were filled with evergreens and oversized Christmas bulbs. A nativity scene was arranged under the gazebo. A gust of warm air greeted me when the sliding glass doors opened. The clerk at the front desk wore a Rudolph pin with a flashing red nose, which drew attention to her substantial cleavage. I asked which room Norman was in, and she scrolled through her list multiple times before finding it on the second floor, where he had been before.

The same smell of lilac and urine hadn't changed. I found Norman's room, and marched in, ready for battle. I budgeted exactly thirty minutes from time of arrival to departure. I put my purse and the bag with his gift on the window ledge.

Norman, mouth gaping open and snoring ferociously, lay on his back. His was the only occupied bed in the room, and his wheelchair was beside him. He had lost weight. His hair needed cutting, as did his eyebrows, and the hairs in his ears and nose. Residue from his breakfast was crusted around the corners of his mouth. I followed the outline of his body from his head down. The blanket at the bottom of his bed was crumpled in a big heap. Already restless, I hummed a Christmas carol and picked up the blanket and folded it neatly, hoping to wake him up up. The quicker he opened the gift, the faster I'd be on my way.

I stood at the foot of his bed, facing him. As I straightened the sheets around his feet I noticed the asymmetry; he must have one foot tucked under the other. I peeked at his feet under the sheets and saw one barefooted leg. A stump, bandaged below the knee, lay where the other leg should have been. Sweat formed on my forehead, and I turned from hot to cold immediately. Seeing white clouds, then sparkles floating in front of me, I sat down in Norman's wheelchair, and put my head between my knees. It didn't help, because it was the the last thing I was aware of before falling to the floor.

I came to, with four concerned faces peering over me. Norman's catheter bag was attached to the bottom rung of his bed railing, about a foot from my head, which was now on a pillow. I recognized Sandra, the nurse manager. "Long time no see," she smiled warmly, placing a cold cloth on my forehead. She and two other nurses helped me sit up. Norman was awake, leaning as far over as his restraints allowed him. I was helped into Norman's wheelchair, lined with clean incontinence pads. Sandra winked at me. "Just in case..."

Humiliated, I completed an accident report, and once the staff were satisfied that I was alright, left me with Norman. I stayed in Norman's wheelchair once I remembered what had gotten me there in the first place. I avoided looking towards his feet. Norman ignored my questions, asking me what was for lunch. I asked him how long he'd been there, and he said too long. I said Wilson liked the snow, and he asked who Wilson was. When I reminded him, he didn't know why I had the dog. Puzzled, I asked him if he knew who I was.

"Sally."

"I'm not Sally. I'm Grace."

"Sally or Grace. Either way, I'm not going."

"Going where?" When Norman put his hand on his stump, I assumed he meant physiotherapy. When I repeated who I was, nothing sunk in, until I mentioned Livy.

"Where is she? She hasn't been here all week." My heart sunk. He had no recollection of the date, or any recent event. He didn't know his address. I asked him what happened to his leg, and he couldn't answer. I wanted to cry. Again.

I pointed to the Christmas decoration on the door, and placed the box on his over bed table. I raised the head of his bed, his hair remaining an untamed mop of grey. He was delighted with the wrapping, then frustrated because he couldn't open it quickly. A nurse brought his lunch tray and set it on the window ledge.

"Whatcha got there, Normie? Looks like a mighty fine present," she chirped, helping him tear the wrapping paper away. She opened the box with the scissors, and we watched him scatter wooden shavings across his bed sheets. He couldn't remove the tape that secured the bubble-wrapped gift. I helped, ready to catch the precious little house in case he dropped it. He whistled when it came into view. It was even prettier in the day's light than in Kristen's office, the colour variations in the rich wood shone. He beamed, holding it up in both hands.

"What a nice little house," the woman said.

"It's my house," Norman boasted, holding it close. I was thrilled he recognized it. She looked at the gift, eyebrows arched.

"He's right, I said. "His niece had it made in Indonesia and sent it to him." She looked oddly at me.

"The niece in Toronto?" I nodded and she motioned me to follow her out of the room. "Norman, put the house on the table. We'll be right back." An aide came in, set Norman's lunch tray in front of him, and despite his protests, put the house on the window ledge. Norman wanted it on the bed.

"It will break if it drops. Eat your lunch, and then you can have it back."

As Norman picked at his food, eyes remained fixated on his treasure, the nurse told me that Norman's foot was amputated because he had developed a life-threatening infection after his surgery. After two surgeries and two general anesthetics within three days, in addition to his extra medications, his memory was affected.

"At his age, we can't predict if, or when he'll get it back."

"One step forward, and two steps back."

"Unfortunately, yes."

"Will he be able to go home?'

"Unless there's a drastic improvement, probably not. His progress has been very slow."

"So he'll be here for a few weeks."

"More like months." We returned to Norman's room. I put his half-eaten lunch away and returned the little house back to his table. I watched the expression of his face turn to sadness as he fingered the intricate details of the windows and the roof lines. I didn't tell him that the front door to the little house was removable, fearful he would lose it.

Before I left Norman, I gave him two greeting cards; one from the law firm and one from me. Unopened, Norman set them aside. I asked him if he'd seen Fred.

"He's bringing me home tomorrow."

"That's good news." I knew that wasn't true. I had a third Christmas card, addressed to Fred. I had written 'I think of you daily' and signed my name. I also mentioned Livy's tiny note tucked inside the house's front door. Unsure where to put Fred's card, I opened the bedside table, surprised to find Norman's little journal. Fred had kept it current. It chronicled Norman's hospital admission, progress and setbacks. The last entry was December 18th, three days ago, when Fred noted that Norman was on a waiting list for long-term care. Tucked into the back of the journal was a small envelope. I got goose bumps when I saw my name printed neatly on the front of the sealed envelope. I tucked it in my purse, opened the next page of the journal, and wrote:

December 21st

Fred:
I saw Norman today to deliver the real gift from Livy, which finally arrived. I'm sorry he remains unwell, and still feel partly responsible. I didn't visit sooner, as I thought it would be best for all of us. The front door of

the little house comes off. Inside is a note to Norman from Livy. Can you open it with Norman, as I'm not sure he'll know. Hope you are well.

Regards,
Grace

P.S. I found the envelope with my name on it, and will read it when I get home.

I tucked the journal back in the drawer. Norman was oblivious to what I was doing, still pre-occupied with the house, when I said good-bye. He didn't ask if I'd come back, and I didn't offer. With Fred's envelope buried in my purse, I drove home.

I walked Wilson, ate lunch, put on my festive vest, which did not reflect how I felt, and went to work. I postponed opening Fred's envelope until I returned home, feeling certain it was a message I didn't want to read.

My shift flew by, but couldn't end soon enough. I was home by 10:00 PM, took Wilson out, urging him to walk faster. As always, he ignored me. Finally home, doors locked and armed with wine and Christmas chocolate, I headed for my bedroom. Secure under warm blankets, I looked carefully at the postcard-sized envelope, and braced for whatever was inked in it. I used a metal nail file to open it carefully. It was a card with a pretty bouquet of flowers on the front, but no words. I pictured him choosing it with care. I opened it slowly to see enough words to fill the whole inside. My heart thumped loudly. I ate a piece of chocolate, and held a second piece for comfort, trying to focus. The card was dated six weeks ago, the exact date I wrote my letter to Fred, and renewed my lease.

November 8th

My dearest Grace:
    It has been a very long time since I wrote a letter like this. You are an amazing woman and I am finding myself thinking about you every day. As you very well

know, my life is simple, yet so complicated. I need to plan my future carefully and make wise decisions, as they will affect not only me, but also my family.

By the time you read this (and hoping you do), it may be a few weeks. I was hoping, despite all the grief he has given you, that you might visit Norman before Christmas. If you are reading this, my heartfelt thank you for doing so. It means more to me than it does to him.

Grace, I am asking you to be even more patient with me than you already have been. If you decide to move on, I will certainly understand.

Fred

The letter said nothing new other than he thought of me daily, which was encouraging. He was asking for more time and that was very discouraging. I was stuck again. It was not good bye, and for that I was grateful. I'd eaten all the chocolate without realizing it. I wondered why Fred hadn't mailed the card, knowing he must have checked the back of Norman's journal each time he saw Norman, and knew I hadn't seen him. It didn't matter. Only six weeks of the six months had passed. If he needed more time then, I'd have a difficult decision to make.

December 24th

The store closed early on Christmas Eve, and by the time I arrived home, Tess, Sophie and Mallory had completed much of the evening's preparation. We planned to be together both days, as it was unlikely we would ever spend another Christmas in such a picturesque setting. We voted unanimously to graze on appetizers and desserts instead of sitting down for a formal dinner. A gift, addressed to me, sat on the kitchen island. Sophie arrived at the house early, had answered the house phone call from Eddie, the security guard calling from Bernard Steel Works. He assumed I was Sophie, and asked her to pick up a package, which she did.

"I saved you some steps," she rationalized, knowing she had overstepped her boundary. "Open it, I'm dying to know what it is."

"So am I." I picked the Christmas bag up and smelled the faint but familiar Bernard Steel factory smell, combined with the scent of chocolate. I cut the ribbon and pulled out the decorative tissue. Some Godiva chocolates were hidden under a card. They were Godiva, not Toblerone. I read the Christmas card aloud, satisfying everyone's curiosity. It said:

Merry Christmas, Gracie.
If you're still single and want to get

together for drinks, please call me.
 # 6636

"Who is number 6636?" three voices asked in unison. I scratched my head to connect the number to a name.

"It's a Bernard Steel employee number." Sophie asked me if I was going to call him. I told her I wasn't ready. Tess carefully picked through the chocolates, selected one, and bit into it.

"Mom, it's okay if you call him," she whispered in a tiny voice. It was the first admission from her after Blair died that she was more accepting of me dating another man. I hugged her, and probably too tightly.

"Thank you, angel. That means a lot to me." I hadn't finished my sentence before I felt her muffled sob. With my own eyes moist, I held her protectively in my arms. "It's okay, Tess. It's okay."

Switching subjects, I asked Tess and Mallory to choose which appetizer to bake first, then sent them off to select old Christmas movies. As soon as they left, Sophie brought up the nameless suitor, # 6636.

"You're not still holding out for what's-his-name, are you?"

"His name is Fred. And keep your voice down, I don't want Tess to know."

"Why not?"

"You just witnessed why not. Not until I'm ready to date openly."

"Well, at least call 6366 back," she waved the card at me. "He's single." I snatched it from her and read it again.

"It doesn't say he's single. It says if I'm still single. Besides why wouldn't he leave his name or phone number?"

"To keep you guessing, Gracie." She nattered on about Mr. 6366, and forgot about Fred. I assembled the first batch of appetizers on a Christmas plate, and sent her to the family room so I could have a quiet moment alone. I wouldn't be mentioning Fred any time soon.

December 25th

My phone rang three times before it woke me up. It was 8:00 AM on Christmas Day. The caller was unlisted. I answered it, mouth parched.

"Merry Christmas."

"Merry Christmas, Grace."

"Fred?"

"It is." His voice was quiet and hesitant. I sat up in bed and checked the clock. "Did I wake you?"

"In the best way, on Christmas Day."

"I hope you don't mind."

"I don't mind at all," I whispered, crawling back under the warm covers. "Are you at home?"

"Yes. It's a very white Christmas morning here in New Pelham."

"Then it must be here too. Is Claire with you?"

"Not yet. She's at her new boyfriend's house, but coming later. And Tess?"

"She's here, with my sister Sophie and my niece."

"So you'll have company for Christmas."

"It'll be quiet."

"Same as our house." A quiet pause.

"Will Claire bring her new beau?"

"Yes. Today's the big introduction."

"I bet you're a little nervous."

"Like an expectant father." I chuckled.

"How's Norman?"

"No change since you last saw him. I debated bringing him over this afternoon, but I don't think I could handle him and Claire's new boyfriend at the same time."

"Would he know that it's Christmas?"

"If he was reminded, and then for only a minute. There's a lunch at the nursing home today, so I'll join him for that, and be home before the kids arrive."

"So he's going to a nursing home."

"Yes. I wasn't sure if you wanted to know." I hesitated.

"He didn't recognize me."

"His memory is worse now, but he loves the little house." I found that touching.

"It is beautiful. Did you help him with the front door?"

"I did. He wanted Livy to visit him."

"Awww. That's so sad. What about his own big house?"

"It's still there. And just as messy the last day you were there."

"It's such a beautiful house."

"It is. There's more junk mail piling up, and his basement is a disaster because he never let anyone down there. That's my project over the holidays." I didn't understand.

"Your project?"

"Yes. His house will probably be listed in the spring, but first I'm getting rid of some of the junk."

"Why? And when did you inherit that job?"

"When he made me power of attorney."

"Really? I thought the law firm was."

"They aren't yet. I agreed to it years ago, in a moment of weakness, when he needed a power of attorney for some insurance forms. Other than when I originally helped him set up his bill withdrawals at the bank, I've tried hard to steer clear of his business. Most of the rest of the business and legal end of things are managed by the law firm." *Enough about Norman.*

"So, how have you been?"

"Managing. And you? What are you up to?" I told him about my new job. "What happened to the old job?"

"It's a long story. One day I'll tell you."

"Are you working a lot over the next week?" I said that I would be off in three days. "Have you got plans for that day?"

"Not yet. Did you have something in mind?"

"If you're available, I'd like to talk to you, but I was also wondering if you'd be interested in keeping me company while I cleaned some of Norman's stuff out of his place."

"The last time I was in his house was not a good day."

"It was a horrible day for you. This time I promise you it won't be as traumatic. Kristen told me she's sending some insurance adjusters over to inventory the important stuff, but asked if I would purge the worthless stuff."

"They inventoried Chestnut Boulevard."

"Then I should be impressed that she trusted me to clean out his junk." The thought of spending time with Fred again made me feel giddy. "So, would you be interested in making the trip down?" I tried to stay calm as I spoke.

"I could be talked into it."

"I was afraid to ask."

"I can understand why. I would love to help you."

"Grace, I'd really, really appreciate it. Would it be alright if I called you the night before the 28th to confirm?"

"Of course."

"Grace?"

'Yes?"

"It's nice to hear your voice again."

"And I'm very happy you called. It's the nicest gift I'll receive today."

"Merry Christmas again. I'll call you in a few days."

"You too. And good luck with Claire's new boyfriend."

The phone clicked on the other side, and I held it close. Deep in my soul, I felt new hope. I was still so drawn to him, even if others said that I was wasting my time. The only thing I wanted this Christmas was hope, and he gave it to me bright and early before anyone, including Wilson, had stirred.

Christmas day was perfect, and carefree. Our dinner was delicious and everyone contributed in the preparation and clean up. Tess, Sophie and Mallory enjoyed long afternoon naps. I snuggled contently in the living room under Livy's cashmere blankets, and imagined Fred beside me. The parlour floor was littered with wrapping paper and small piles of gifts.

Mr. & Mrs. Adams delivered homemade treats and stayed for an hour. Their family had come and gone, and I that pretended they were my parents just for today. My guests woke and mingled with them until they went home to their naps. We all fended for ourselves, grazing on leftovers, re-examining gifts and reminiscing about past holidays for the rest of the day. I was very happy, in my own little world. My second Christmas would arrive in three days. And not soon enough.

December 28th

Tess went skiing with friends, which made going to New Pelham easier. I set my alarm, but was up much earlier. I wore comfortable jeans, colourful socks that Tess gave me for Christmas, and a hooded sweatshirt. This time, I was prepared to get dirty, and brought a clean set of clothes for back up.

I worked at trying to remain calm and not set my expectations beyond enjoying a visit. I packed a tray of desserts, including some of # 6366's Godiva chocolates. Fred called and asked me to bring Wilson, so I packed supplies and toys to keep him out of trouble.

I arrived in New Pelham mid-morning. Fred's driveway was cleared of snow, as was the path to Norman's house. He was at the front door before I parked the car. I left my change of clothes in the car so as not to appear presumptuous, but took the tray of goodies and Wilson's things. The dog jumped from the car into the snowbank and rolled around, messing up the neat borders Fred had sculpted in the snow and marking his territory.

There was not a more handsome man on earth that day than Fred, dressed in a worn sweatshirt and jeans. He was clean shaven with shorter hair. He held the door open, and hugged me tightly when I crossed the threshold. The familiar scent of his skin, blended with clean clothes and coffee, was hypnotic. I felt his kiss on my cheek, which fueled my desires. I kissed him on the lips and he responded with a soft, luscious kiss and another long hug.

"Perfect timing. I just made coffee." My boots and coat came off quickly, as Fred dried Wilson off with his towel. The house was sparsely decorated with simple Christmas decorations. Two overstuffed Christmas stockings lay against the fireplace hearth, one with 'Claire Bear' embroidered on it, and the other with no name. Fred brought coffee and warm lemon scones into the living room, and we sat down on the sofa, a few feet between us.

After some small talk, our conversation shifted between my job and Fred's students at school, and then on to Norman's health. I didn't want to see Norman, or at least, not today. I wanted to spend the day with Fred. He filled travel mugs with coffee and packed some more scones as I grabbed Wilson's towel and a few toys. The crisp snow under our boots was the only sound around us as we crossed through the clearing to Norman's house.

Although the site of the beer bottle accident was covered in snow, I shivered walking by it. Fred had cleared the snow away from Norman's driveway, his sidewalk and the front steps leading to his house. It was a perfect scene for a Christmas card. I was elated to be here, with Fred beside me.

He unlocked and opened Norman's front door. As I walked in, the house smelled different.

"The carpet in the living room is new."

"We had to replace it. The smell was pretty rank." I shuddered.

"It looks great." *Like nothing happened.*

We shed our outerwear like kids, and left it in a heap at the front door. Fred scooped some mail from the big bowl in the foyer. I took in my surroundings again, which was easier without Norman here. Despite all the negative events that evicted him, I still loved this house. Someday, a family would call it their home. I dried Wilson off, his tail flapping happily against me. Coffee in hand, I followed Fred as we toured the house again.

"How did all this junk pile up again in such a short time?"

"His confusion. The geriatric specialist said he already had dementia before he hurt himself the first time. Because he lived alone, and the changes were subtle, it would be easy to miss until he was assessed at the rehab centre."

"Maybe that's why he ate the bad food and barfed."

"Yup. So, as far as our project today, Kristen said to get rid of the junk, and hire a junk removal company."

"She must trust you."

"I'd like to think so. Mmm... which room should we tackle first...." he mused as I followed him upstairs.

The three upstairs bedrooms had the same layout as Chestnut Boulevard in Toronto, but slightly smaller. Norman's room was the biggest and most cluttered. The smaller rooms were sparsely furnished and dusty. The closets were nearly empty. Wilson went exploring on his own, and I heard him heading down the basement stairs.

"Is there any trouble that he can get into down there?"

"I doubt it. He can't make a bigger mess than Norman did." Fred pulled his phone out and started noting things. "Kristen wants a rough idea of any repairs that need to be done before the house goes up for sale." I sighed at the thought.

We walked through the bathroom and into Norman's disorganized bedroom. The smell of urine and soiled clothes was nauseating.

"They should have replaced this carpet when they did the living room," Fred said as he typed into his phone. When I opened Norman's walk-in closet, the stench was worse. I held my nose, sizing up the heap of soiled clothes on the floor. "We'll toss these in the dumpster. He's been wearing them for decades, and I already bought him more clothes."

At Fred's suggestion, I sorted through Norman's dresser drawers, discarding more soiled clothes. A bottom drawer contained a new dress shirt, and new boxers shorts, still in packages, which partially covered some black boxes, each different from the other.

"Okay to look in these?" I asked, as Fred walked over to me.

"Sure. This might be exciting." I pulled out the first box, which held a gold watch, with 'NPC: 25 Years' engraved on the back.

"What does NPC stand for again?"

290

"New Pelham Chestnuts. It must a recognition gift for his years of service. Remember, NPC are also his initials."

"I should know that by now." The second box was smaller, and held a gold tie clip and cuff links. "These should go to the lawyers."

"I agree. Same as the watch." The third box was the biggest and heaviest. I passed it to Fred. The inside fabric of the old box tore away at the seam when he opened it. A tarnished, silver pistol with an ivory and wooden handle lay cradled in the case. "This looks like an antique." The silver pattern overlaying the ivory was impressive. I laid the three boxes on the top of the dresser, recalling a question Fred asked me the last time we played the five question game.

"So, what's your most treasured possession?" I asked Fred, closing the drawer.

"My possession?"

"Yes. Not something intrinsic, like Claire or your job."

"Hmm, I don't really know. Probably my house, because it's one of the few things I own that's worth anything. What about you?"

"My parents' wedding rings. They're very simple gold bands, and when they both passed away, I had them made into one ring." He looked at my unadorned hands. "They're in a drawer at home," I explained.

"When did you stop wearing your wedding rings?"

"This sounds like the five questions game."

"I think we've moved up to the next level."

"And what's that?"

"Ask freely, and I shall answer." I leaned forward, planting a kiss on Fred's cheek, and he responded, kissing my lips.

"This isn't a very romantic setting..."

Wilson barked from the basement, and came upstairs when I called him. He paced impatiently, cycling through the bedrooms, covered with cobwebs. He looked at me is if to reassure me he was being good, then headed back to the basement. Leaving Norman's room, I opened a linen closet in the upstairs hallway. The deeper half of each shelf held neatly folded towels, sheets and blankets. If there was any indication that a woman lived in this house, it was here. I assumed that it was Norman who threw a few clean, unfolded sheets and towels in a heap on the same shelves. The newer linens could be donated to charity. Fred poked his head into the two other rooms, and the dirty bathroom, stating these would be projects for a day when the dumpster was here.

The dining room housed a sparsely filled curio cabinet of souvenir trinkets from England, which I found odd that Nancy left behind. Mismatched glass stemware stood near a pair of Tiffany crystal candle holders, sparkling even through the dust that had settled on them. Their value likely exceeded the cabinet and its other contents, which the insurance adjusters would look after.

Wilson appeared briefly, then retreated to the basement, which I hadn't seen before. We followed him down the squeaky wooden steps. The basement was open and unfinished. Spacious windows in the side and back walls bathed the room with light. Steel posts supported the interior of the house. Piles of boxes lay strewn across the floor, many filled with empty alcohol bottles. An old work table, covered with oily rags, sat angled in a corner. Considering the amount of clutter in this house, I was puzzled by the sparseness of the basement. It seemed odd that a man whose life spanned more than eighty years had so few, and such meagre possessions. Almost everything here looked worthless.

Wilson hovered beside a three-tiered industrial shelving unit holding tools, and more boxes. Fred pushed aside a few small appliance boxes on the floor with his foot to clear a path to the shelves. The top level held a dented metal box, full of rusty fishing gear. The second shelf held very old garden tools, many with wooden handles stamped with the same 'NPC' initials as Norman's watch. Fred suggested these be donated back to the New Pelham Chestnuts museum.

The bottom shelf was more accessible to Wilson than us, who was sniffing a battered black briefcase. Judging by the cobwebs and thick layer of dust, it had been undisturbed for years. I dragged it off the shelf. Heavy and bulging, it held more than it was designed for.

Fred repositioned a work table near sliding glass doors that faced the back of the house as I lugged the case over to the table. Wilson followed us, jockeying for position by putting his paws on the table to stay near the case. I blew some dust off of it. Fred used the rags on the table to wipe away more residue. We examined the briefcase like it was an archeological discovery. Sealed with an old brass lock, the NPC symbol was inscribed on a small brass plaque above the lock. Three engraved initials were scratched away, and unreadable. Fred couldn't loosen the lock. The leather, once soft and supple, was now brittle and cracked.

Fred pulled out a pocket knife and gingerly cut the threads along the stitched rear flap. Our faces were as close to the case as Wilson's. Fred pulled the back of the case away from the top flap. There were many envelopes stuffed into the case, but the weight came from an old cardboard box. The tape that once sealed it had gradually peeled away. I held the briefcase as Fred gently withdrew the box carefully to keep it intact. I set the case on the floor. A yellowed label on the box had separated from its adhesive. Mould and water stains had discoloured the paper and cardboard. The typed ink was faded, so most of the label was illegible. Fred re-positioned the label to brighter light. The last word on the first line spelled 'Home' with a local address barely readable on the second line. Fred gingerly peeled the label off the box. His face paled and he swore when he opened the top. Stuck to a clear plastic bag was a tag identifying the cremated remains of Nancy Chestnut.

"That bastard!" Fred hissed as his spread his hands over his forehead. I shooed Wilson away from the box. "That cheap bastard!" He looked out the window and shook his head.

"Now we now where Nancy went," I whispered.

"What a scumbag. I can't believe it!" Fred said, shaking his head again and carefully examining the tag. "I can't see a date on this."

"How long has she been gone?"

Fred hesitated, shrugging his shoulders.

"Years. Nine. Maybe ten. Wow. He said nothing to me. Now I wonder how she died."

"So do I. When I saw him in September, he said she left him twice, then cut me off when I asked more questions. He was also drunk, so I didn't take him seriously. And with his memory loss, we may never know."

"I still can't believe he didn't have the decency to give her a funeral."

"But we can."

"I hope he didn't hurt her." His remark alarmed me.

"Do you really think that he would?"

"Probably not. But obviously he kept her death a secret for a long time."

"Could we call the funeral home for more more details?"

"We could, but the lawyers should to deal with this. This is way more than I signed up."

"Poor Nancy."

"Let's get out of here. We've tampered with these ashes, not that we knew what we would find. I've had enough of Norman, and all of this for today." Fred's hand touched my back, and we went to climb the stairs, but Wilson returned to the table and put his paws back near Nancy's remains.

"Do you think he knows something we don't?"

"They're smarter than we give them credit for," Fred replied. He returned to Wilson, taking his collar and the briefcase, and following me up the stairs. I was happy to leave this house.

Back at Fred's house, he called the local funeral home, which had a name change, but same address as the tag attached to Nancy's ashes. Fred told the funeral director what little he knew about Nancy, and asked him to follow up with the law firm. He ended the call, then paused.

"I need to go back."

"Why?"

"The mail. The envelopes on the dining room table that are addressed to Nancy."

"Oh my goodness!"

We ate lunch silently, deep in thought. Fred retrieved Norman's mail and dumped the briefcase contents on his living room coffee table. The smell of musty paper permeated the room.

"We might find some answers here," he said, sifting through envelopes from a private Toronto school. I spotted report cards and school pictures, dating from Livy's early years through to her high school graduation.

"Norman was definitely in her life since she was young. Isn't it odd that Norman had all of these things, rather then her parents?" I asked.

"Maybe Livy asked him to keep them safe for her. You said she floated around for a few years before finding her way," Fred offered, pre-occupied with other papers.

"I still wonder if Norman is her real father. And what will Kristen do with all this stuff?"

"I'm not sure. Probably catalogue and archive it, and post notices hoping that someone claims it. If no one does, after a certain timeframe, it'll be destroyed. Grace, look at this." Fred handed me a stained envelope containing an adoption certificate for Olivia Jane Chestnut.

"Wow. The birth date is Livy's. And her middle name was Jane." Her birth mother was listed as Jane Smith. I looked at Fred. "No relation to me," he chuckled, after I said the father's name was listed as unknown.

"Why is her mother's name Smith, but her surname listed as Chestnut? And Norman was not involved? I still don't understand why he had all this, and she didn't. Did he consciously keep it from her?"

"Maybe he made a pact with her real parents to keep it a secret. Unless the law firm is willing to disclose it, we'll never know."

"I wonder what Norman would remember if we asked him?"

"He might tell us lots of things about Livy and Nancy, but who would validate it?"

Fred passed me a newspaper article, yellow and frayed. I unfolded it carefully. It was the story detailing the accident that took the lives of Fraser and Trixie Bless, Livy's adoptive parents. The story was the same as Livy had told me; Fraser was driving with a blood alcohol level well over the legal limit. The reporter traced the luxury sports car to the dealership, where Fraser bought it just four days earlier. There was no mention of a daughter. I leaned back against the sofa, missing Livy.

Fred then passed me Norman's will, dated many years ago, and notarized by someone at Kristen's office.

"At least everything is handled by the same firm." Livy stood to inherit everything, including Norman's house. Fred frowned as he skimmed it.

"Nancy isn't mentioned in this will, even though she was alive when it was written."

"That's strange." I said.

"Let's hope there is a more current one. As miserable as he was, there is no question that he adored Livy." Fred was right. Knowing we were crossing boundaries when we found the deed to Norman's house, pension and insurance information, Fred stuffed it all back in the briefcase.

Fred emptied Norman's mail onto the coffee table next, curious about the series of envelopes addressed to Nancy Chestnut. Post marked from London, England, Fred peeked through the envelope in the sunlight.

"I'm guessing it's some sort of monthly cheque."

"It looks these have been coming for years. Not only did he hide Nancy's death, he didn't tell anyone in England either. Maybe she was receiving a survivor or war veteran's benefits, or maybe a government retirement pension."

"She often said that he never gave her money. This could be what she survived on. At least he didn't cash them."

"Maybe his memory was already failing."

"The lawyers will sort this out." Fred threw the mail back in the box, and closed it. "Enough for today."

I hoped to learn more today, but not about Norman.

Fred kept his distance as we prepared dinner, and kept the conversation light. We ate at the dining room, as the sun set early in the room full of windows. Fred brought a dessert wine and two glasses to the living room.

The street lights illuminated the sparsely falling snow flakes, calming the world around us. Trying to avoid talking about Norman was impossible, because of all the ways he was intertwined in our lives. "I still wonder why he hated Nancy so much."

"Because she was sick, and he resented her for it?"

"I still can't believe neither of them mentioned it."

"Blair shut down for weeks before he died, both physically and emotionally. Maybe it was a protectant factor. I read somewhere that ill women are more likely to be abandoned by male partners."

"Hmm...I wonder why."

"Some men are not as emotionally resilient as you are. I remember some men at Bernard Steel never getting over their grief."

"It's painful."

"We both know that well." We sipped our wine and watched the snow fall.

"Grace," he whispered. I stiffened.

"Uh huh?"

"I want this to happen." He put his hand in mine.

"Could you be a little more specific?" I squeaked.

"Us." My heart thumped louder, then faster. Fred took his hand away from mine, raised his arms, then dropped them in his lap.

"Me too."

"I need to tell you something important, but my brain is so exhausted that I hope this makes sense." I emptied the wine in our glasses, as Fred took some deep breaths. I braced myself.

"I'm still married." *I know that.* I nodded my head. He shifted his position to face me directly.

"When two mentally well people marry, the assumption is that they both understand their own, and each other's intentions. But when one partner becomes mentally ill, such as Holly, trying to 'un-marry' that person becomes very complicated. To be honest, I was not interested in separating from Holly for a long time. I wanted to remain married because I always had that glimmer of hope that she would improve. It kept me going. I was busy with school, Norman to watch over, and until the last few years, Claire still needed support. I would have continued like this indefinitely, but then you appeared, and shook me out of my secure little nest." The corners of his mouth turned slightly upward to form a tiny smile. I didn't move, and he continued. "So technically, or I should say legally, mental and/or physical cruelty is grounds for divorce, but mental illness isn't." I sat quietly, but my mind didn't.

"What about mental illness and annulment?" His eyebrows arched.

"That's even more complex in matrimonial law. I know mental disability may be grounds for annulment, but only if the disabled person didn't understand what they were doing when they got married. If, however, they became ill during the marriage, it's much harder to undo. Holly doesn't have the capacity to understand divorce. She can tell a lawyer what it means, but she doesn't have the insight to understand the intent, or outcome of divorce." He sounded like a lawyer. "I'm still her husband, as well as her legal guardian and her power of attorney. She also still owns half of this house and therefore is entitled to half of everything we own."

"As it should be."

"Oh, I absolutely agree."

"But don't the rules say something like if you live apart from each other for one year, you can file for divorce?"

"I've been told that, however a mentally disabled person must be able to plan, or as the lawyer said "form the intention to live apart" to proceed with divorce. Holly was committed. She didn't make that decision, someone else made it for her."

"You said mental or physical cruelty. So what about the physical cruelty part?" I lifted his sweatshirt and gently ran my fingers across the scars on his hip.

"Valid point, but again she didn't have the mental capacity to understand what she was doing when she attacked me."

"Right." I swallowed hard and tried another approach. "What about adultery?"

"Obviously that's grounds for divorce, but again, she never knowingly committed adultery. She was drugged. And paranoid." Fred then realized I wasn't referring to Holly. "That's a bad, bad way to end a marriage."

"I lost my best friend because he cheated on his wife. I don't want to be a hypocrite." The picture was becoming clearer.

"So being with me constitutes adultery," I said quietly, remembering my counsellor telling me the same thing. Fred had the expression of a young boy who had confessed something bad.

"Grace, I have to respect myself before I can respect anyone else. I've spent my whole adult life committed to Holly, until now. If I'm going to proceed with this, I must do it properly."

"I agree with you. I must also be honest with you. I didn't plan or expect this either, but it happened. I'm deeply in love with you, if for those reasons alone. I trust you and I respect you." I could see the emotion in his eyes. "If you want me to wait for you, I will."

"I have no idea how long, or when."

"It doesn't matter. You asked me where I saw myself in five years. My answer is still the same."

"And if it takes longer?"

"I will still understand." He took my hand and squeezed it.

"Thank you, Grace. Thank you so much." I wanted to kiss him more than anything else, but also knew it was the wrong thing to do. We sat quietly and watched the snow fall. As usual, Fred read my mind.

"Do you want the couch or the bed?"

"I think we should flip a coin."

I won the toss. "This is the third time I won. I'll take the couch."
"I would have offered you my bed."
"I know."

We remained on the couch for hours. The intervals between our sentences were getting longer. I slipped my hand out of Fred's to use the washroom, and heard his quiet snoring as I came back to the living room. I sat quietly in the chair opposite him and watched his peaceful expression as his body relaxed. The snow continued to cover the still earth as I laid a blanket over him. He never moved. Wilson manned his post by the front door. I shut the lights off and went to Fred's bed, falling asleep where I felt I belonged.

December 29th

Howling gusts of wind outside broke my sleep. Re-orienting myself, I sat up, wrapping my arms around my knees. It was 7:00 AM, and I was scheduled to work at noon. Wilson was snoring on the floor beside me, his head on my clothes. I listened for noise downstairs, but heard nothing. The other side of the bed was empty, as I knew it would be. I lay back under the covers, thinking about the indefinite commitment I had made to wait for Fred. Again. I took inventory of all the reasons I came to that conclusion. There was so much more of this situation to explore. I wondered what level of communication we would have until his divorce. Could we meet periodically like old friends, or possibly new lovers? Could I kiss him hello and goodbye? What about our daughters? Would they resent each other, and us?

A new day arrived with new questions. I took a deep breath, and headed for the shower. I closed the bathroom door, certain there was no need to lock it. The water was invigorating. Wrapped in an oversized towel, I went back to Fred's room to change. The aroma of coffee floated upstairs, even though the doors were closed. Wilson was gone, and Fred must have delivered my overnight bag beside the closed bedroom door and took Wilson out and while I showered.

I put fresh clothes on, and felt ready for the day. As I came down the stairs, I heard Fred talking in the kitchen. I rounded the corner to see him holding the phone. He smiled and held up a finger, mouthing the words "give me a minute." I remained quiet and tiptoed with my coffee into the living room. Wilson returned to the kitchen and banged his bowls on the tiled kitchen floor.

"It's nothing, Claire. I just dropped a pot," Fred said with a mock expression of horror on his face. I rescued Wilson and waited in the living room until Fred hung up and found us. He rubbed Wilson's ears and held the dog's face in his hands.

"You nearly gave away my secret, buddy. If Claire and I don't talk every few days, she worries. It's much easier if I call her."

The morning was peaceful. We spoke very little. There was no need. It took Fred almost an hour to clear out the driveway and remove the snow from my car. He moved my car to face the road and came inside, sweaty and flushed from the cold. I had my overnight bag by the front door. Fred checked his watch. There were so many things I wanted to tell him, but couldn't find the words. Fred removed his coat and mitts, and wiped the perspiration off his face with his sweat-soaked shirt.

"If I shower, you'll be late for work. So you can have a sweaty hug, or none at all." I picked the first option. Fred put his arms around me and I melted against him as he inhaled a deep breath. "Your hair smells so good. I couldn't get close to you sooner, because I knew I wouldn't let you go."

"I love you, Fred." He held my face in his hands. His eyes were glassy.

"I love you too, Grace. My amazing Grace." It was the first time we exchanged those precious words. His lips moved to mine and I knew that if he asked me to stay, there'd be no hesitation. He was worth the world to me, and my life had meaning once again. His kiss was passionate. He leaned me against the wall and pressed his body into mine. It was pure joy. Nothing else mattered; from now on, his life, even if just a warm thought about him, would uplift my every day.

February 14th

I was one of the few temporary staff who was lucky enough to remain employed when the holiday rush ended, and landed a maternity leave posting in the Human Resources department. Sophie lost interest in my personal life after she joined a dating website and became an expert in short-lived romances. She gifted me a three month introductory membership, which I declined.

Fred and I had settled into a routine of talking or texting most days. At Fred's request, we remained clandestine, and to keep our attraction burning on a low flame, we only had face to face contact in Norman's presence. About once a month, Wilson and I drove to Niagara, with the law firm's blessing. The nursing home knew Fred and I were connected to Norman, but not each other. Romance within the confines of a nursing home was limited to a welcoming embrace and a farewell peck on the cheek.

When a Valentine's Day bouquet of red roses arrived at my house in the morning, I was overjoyed, hoping that Fred had made some legal progress. He asked me to dinner at a Toronto bistro. I fretted over what to wear, and settled on a low-cut black dress, regretting my choice when Fred met me in the lobby wearing khakis and a casual shirt. We were seated at a secluded booth and while enjoying appetizers, when my eccentric neighbours Lenny and Jenny Russell emerged from the booth behind us. Fred sheepishly excused himself and escaped to the bathroom until they left. I lied that Fred was my cousin, who was in town for a conference. The evening fizzled out shortly after that. Fred went home with the leftovers, and I with an aching heart.

May 6th

Reluctant to have a repeat episode of our Valentine's Day dinner, we reverted back to monthly meetings at the nursing home. The relationship was floating, and as much as I hoped for new answers, I tried hard not to feel resentful.

Each time we met, Fred looked better and Norman looked worse. He became more withdrawn and frail. His skin was translucent and often bruised from the effects of taking blood thinners. Instead of being miserable, his progressing dementia made him appear frightened and vulnerable. Even with our volatile history, I felt nothing but sympathy for him. Kristen was pleased that I remained committed to the visits, and I had no intention of telling her otherwise.

My lease on Chestnut Boulevard was extended indefinitely, and I felt certain my visits to Niagara had influenced this. While I dreamed of a more intimate place to meet Fred, I respected his need to maintain a low profile. He rarely mentioned Holly, and said nothing about a divorce. I accepted this. I had no choice. Tess knew I visited Norman and I made a point of casually including positive comments about 'Norman's neighbour Fred'. She questioned why I traveled so far to do 'volunteer work', but said it must make me happy because I stopped complaining months ago.

August 7th

When the phone rang in the early hours of the day, I knew why Fred had called. Norman passed away in his sleep during the night, peacefully and in the company of no one but his moonlit shadow. A year and a few days after the death of his beloved Livy, the last Chestnut heir had passed. By the time I called Kristen, she had received the death certificate, and made funeral arrangements for August 21st. Losing Norman upset me more than I expected, and I wondered how Fred and my life would continue.

August 21st

I chose the same outfit for Norman's funeral as I wore to Livy's memorial service as a tribute to her. It was a beautiful day, and the graveside service was held at the New Pelham cemetery across the road from Fred's house. Although I hadn't been there since December, my memory of the drive was as vivid as yesterday. I entered from the side street, and parked behind a red sports car near the back entrance to the cemetery. I was the last to arrive. I remember Fred often saying that New Pelham was paradise, and on a summer day like today, he was right.

The service began as soon as I approached the small assembly. As if on cue, the bells from the nearby church chimed twelve times. We gathered around the casket, under the canopy of an enormous chestnut tree. The grass had recently been cut and stray leaves swirled gently around our feet. An occasional gravestone, no longer tended to, was hidden by overgrown shrubs.

There were less than a dozen people present, including the minister and funeral home staff who doubled as pall bearers. The name of the funeral home that handled Nancy's cremation was stenciled in silver on the hearse's back window. A limousine chauffeured Kristen, her secretary, the minister and a cardboard box holding Nancy Chestnut's ashes. From the box, Kristen removed an engraved silver urn. I also recognized the minister from Livy's service, but this time his speech was sincere. I'm sure Fred wrote most of the eulogy, as I heard his words through the voice of the speaker. The funeral home staff stood stoically, respectfully supporting the arms of a sobbing Mazie, the spinster teacher that Norman detested. She was one of four crying females in the group, the other three being the cemetery club ladies. Minus their coloured scarves, they took turns consoling each other and rationing out tissues. Even the one who wouldn't bake Norman an apple pie was genuinely distraught by his loss.

One person I hadn't met, who bore a remarkable resemblance to her mother, was Claire. Taller than Holly, she was dressed in a tailored grey business suit and starched white shirt. One hand clutched a small purse, while the other was tucked securely through her father's arm. I wondered if she would sense anything different about her father when she leaned her head against his shoulder.

Nancy's urn was placed on top of Norman's casket and the pair were lowered into the earth. Mazie and her neighbours whimpered. A final prayer was muttered by those who knew it, and the service ended as quickly as it began. The minister encouraged the handful of mourners to meet for lunch after the funeral home attendants left quietly. The cemetery club ladies declined, paid their final respects and drove off together. Kristen, her secretary and the minister were heading back to Toronto. This left a forlorn Mazie, Fred, Claire and I. Fred thanked Kristen for attending and agreed to stay in touch.

My face and neck flushed when Fred introduced me to Claire as Livy's friend, and said I was a wonderful human being for dedicating so much of my time to help him with Norman. We shook hands and Claire thanked me. She was genuine and sincere. Fred took inventory for lunch, and Claire declined because of an important meeting. She shook my hand warmly, hugged Fred tightly, and headed off in her little red car. Mazie squawked that she was all for a good meal if he was paying. Fred had delivered Mazie to the cemetery, but left his car in his driveway, so the only vehicle remaining in the cemetery lane was the Volvo. I offered to drive, and Mazie loaded herself into the front passenger seat. Fred closed her door, and slid into the back seat behind her. I exited slowly out of the cemetery lane way, which ended at the road, and facing Fred's property.

I stopped abruptly.

One strikingly change from my last visit to New Pelham was the 'For Sale' sign posted on, not Norman's, but Fred's front lawn. I could barely contain my emotion, as Fred's eyes fixed intently on mine when I looked in the rear view mirror. He put his index finger to his mouth and pointed at Mazie.

"I'll explain after lunch."

"What was that?" Mazie barked, cranking her wrinkled neck around to the back of the car.

"We'll have a nice lunch!" Fred replied loudly.

"Are you from this neighbourhood, honey?" Mazie asked, running her fingers across the woodgrain of the dashboard.

"I wish I was," I said, still stunned, trying to understand why during our almost daily chats, Fred had not mentioned his intention to sell his house.

"Where shall we go for lunch, Mazie?" Fred yelled to the back of Mazie's seat.

"Someplace fancy, Freddy." *Freddy?*

"What about the diner? It's noon and the pies should be out of the oven by now."

"Sounds good to me!" she bellowed, her voice directed at Fred but landing in my ear.

I followed Fred's directions through rural hills and valleys, along the same roads that I drove Norman to the Legion. The diner was at the town's main intersection, as homegrown as its menu and staff. I lost my appetite and ordered a salad. Other then when she was chewing, Mazie controlled the conversation, directed at no one in particular. Despite refusing dessert, Fred reserved three pieces of coconut cream pie as he ordered our lunches, as this was the diner's main attraction for the regulars. Halfway through lunch, Mazie wanted to go home because she was developing the 'stomach problems' she warned us about repeatedly since we arrived. We couldn't stay for coffee, so our desserts were individually boxed, including takeout coffee for Fred and I.

I couldn't drive Mazie home fast enough. We arrived at her small bungalow in New Pelham within minutes, and she flung the car door open without saying goodbye, and scooted up her front steps with her purse and dessert box faster than I imagined her arthritic feet could carry her. Fred said he hoped she could get her 'stomach problems' to the bathroom in time, chuckling as he closed her door and returned to the back, rather than the front seat.

"Good old Mazie," Fred chirped. "You can't help but love her." I didn't respond, which didn't seem to bother Fred. "Let's have dessert at the Old Chestnut Tree, he suggested. "We'll toast Norman, because he ate his fair share of these pies."

I drove back to the historic Old Chestnut Tree landmark, avoiding pot holes in the narrow gravel lane. Fred ignored me, dabbling in small talk while I pouted. I was still fixated on the 'For Sale' sign on Fred's front lawn when I parked the car in the parking spot in front of the tree.

"Norman was so happy when he bought that plot at the New Pelham Cemetery." Fred managed to keep both dessert boxes and the tray with our coffees upright as he got out and closed his car door. He also opened my door. Good manners or not, I wanted an explanation, and soon.

The enormous tree was located in a picturesque setting. Two wooden benches faced it at right angles to each other. I sat down and tried to mask my frustration by reading the weathered sign that outlined its history. Tight metal cables, cemented into crevices of the tree, supported its massive branches. I crossed my legs, and one black pump slid carelessly off my foot. I kicked the other one off, feeling the soft, thick grass cool my feet. Fred passed me a coffee and a styrofoam pie container, which had a 'G' etched into the lid. I took a sip of coffee and put the unopened pie down on the bench between us.

"You're not having dessert?" Fred looked surprised. "You must have a taste."

"Not now." Fred opened his container. The pie looked, and smelled divine. White meringue was piled as high as the lid and decorated with toasted coconut. He fished two plastic forks from his pocket, slid them out of their plastic casing and handed me one. He filled his fork and took a bite.

"Mmm, it's still the best pie in New Pelham. And still a little warm. I think you should try just one bite." I looked at him and then pointed at the pie.

"You're pre-occupied with pie, and I'm pre-occupied with that sign on your front lawn. I thought 'we' were doing really well and...and...'we' were supposed to be open and honest. I've been patient with you, respecting and trusting you for months. My life has been an open book to you. I know I have no right to tell you what to do, but I'm hurt that you never mentioned you were selling your house." He procrastinated.

"Grace, I promise you we'll discuss the house and whatever else worries you before we leave here. I missed you. Please, let's just relax. It's been emotional for all of us."

I leaned back stiffly. Fred raised his cup toward the tree and then up to the sky. "Here's to the legacy of this mighty chestnut, and to you, Norman. As much grief as you gave me, no...us...I owe you my gratitude. If it wasn't for you, I would never have met this incredible woman beside me." *Incredible?* He put his arm around my shoulder, and it took restraint for me not to shrug it off. I raised my cup reluctantly to touch his.

"Thank you. Here's to Norman." I tried to calm myself down by breathing deeply.

I picked the box up and held it to my nose. It smelled like warm vanilla and cream. I opened the lid carefully to avoid tipping it over, and gasped.

There was more than pie in the box. Wedged into the centre of the meringue was a ring. A familiar ring. It took me a second to make the connection. It was the eternity ring that Livy had worn on her right hand. A circle of brilliant square diamonds, nested in a white gold band. It took my breath away. Fred glancing at me curiously, his eyes sparkling as I plucked the band out of the meringue.

"I told you this was a special pie."

"Stop it." I stammered, setting the box down to avoid dropping it. It was a hot afternoon, but I was shaking. "Help me understand...you...I...I'm stunned."

"If I may correct you, you might think you're stunned, but to me you are stunning." His expression softened as he looked at the precious treasure in my hand.

"This is, was Livy's ring?"

"Yes, it was. And part of her family for generations."

"I remember how beautiful it was. How did you get it?"

"Oh, it took a little negotiating."

"With who?"

"Kristen."

"Wow. Did Norman know about this before he died?" Not sure why I needed to ask that question now, but I did, and was surprised when he nodded.

"Yes. But whether he remembered, we'll never know."

"What, I mean how, ah, when did you ask him?"

"I didn't. He offered."

"What? He offered?"

"When he was still thinking somewhat clearly, he wanted to thank me for helping him after he broke his hip by paying me."

"He did? Norman wanted to pay you?"

"Yes, he did. And of course, I refused."

"And?"

"And then he suggested I choose something from the Chestnut estate because he knew there were no other heirs. With his permission, I met with Kristen and picked this ring. I didn't know the connection to Livy until Kristen mentioned that it was her favourite."

"Incredible." I needed to ask the next question. "Did you choose it for a reason?" He put his container down and looked at me with a puzzled expression.

"Yes, Grace, I did." He smiled.

I kept staring at the ring. I ran my nail along the side of the band; there were letters stamped into the metal. I strained but was unable to read the engraving.

"It says Tiffany." Appreciating its value and sentiment even more, I held it tightly.

"I don't know which finger to put it on."

"Which finger would you like to put it on?" My hands were shaking. I closed my hand around the ring, afraid it would fall or somehow disappear. Fred took my left hand in his and held it, then gently opened one finger at a time. He took the ring and held it in the sun. "It sparkles more without the meringue." The electricity of his touch ran through me.

"Grace, I want to spend my life with you," he said, swallowing nervously. "And I hope you still feel the same way." I felt faint.

"I do."

"I am legally separated, and feel terrible that I can't be more specific. I wish things would proceed faster, but it's beyond my control."

"I do understand." And I did. Fred stood up, keeping his hand in mine and walked me under the umbrella of the tree. We both looked up, the bright blue sky contrasting the emerald green leaves. Fred presented the ring to me, and spoke.

"Grace, would you wear this ring as my commitment to you, and to our future together?"

"Yes. Yes!" Fred steadied my trembling hand as he slid the ring, sticky side down and sparkly side up, on my left ring finger. The feel of the metal against my skin felt familiar, yet strange.

"Even if you have to wait?"

"As long as it takes." I couldn't take my eyes off my hand, even when Fred covered it with his. He put his arms around me and kissed me deeply. His lips were sweet and warm.

The Old Chestnut Tree protected us in its shade for the rest of the afternoon. Fred explained the 'For Sale' sign on his lawn. The law firm had posted multiple notices for anyone seeking familial or legal claim against the Chestnut properties in Toronto and New Pelham. As expected, there was no response. Norman's house, and its contents, would be sold or auctioned off, but a provision in Norman's will offered Fred the first right of refusal to purchase Norman's house, and at half the cost of the current market value. Norman's will was updated since Livy passed away, and after he broke his hip.

"Wow! That was extremely generous of Norman."

"As crotchety and cheap as he was, I was humbled when Kristen told me how appreciative he was of our help when he made that decision."

"And Livy's ring?"

"Well, Kristen didn't link us until Norman told her he wanted me to have her ring."

"Norman said that?"

"Yup. A month before he died, she arranged for me to pick it up."

"I'm speechless. It's beautiful."

"As are you." We embraced each other tightly, followed by a tender kiss. "There's more, Grace. There's going to be an auction."

"When?"

"Soon."

"We're witnessing the end of generations of a family."

"We are. Everything will be auctioned off. In his house, that is."

"Mmmmm...which makes me wonder about Livy's house."

"I can't speak for that, but Kristen has been very reasonable, so I'm sure she'll keep you posted. She wanted Norman's estate to be settled first, and she also knew I was very interested in buying Norman's house.

"You were?"

"Absolutely. To confirm that I was serious, and could afford it, I listed my house. I also wanted your opinion, but unfortunately Norman died within days of that, and Kristen wanted to proceed quickly. I didn't want you to see the sign without an explanation, but I couldn't remove it from my front lawn because Kristen was attending Norman's service. I listed my house, and submitted my offer to buy Norman's house yesterday. I knew you loved the house, but I had no influence in the lawyers' decisions, or the day that Norman met his maker."

"Now I understand. Completely." It all made sense, but felt surreal.

"You said someone needed to turn this house into a home. And I wanted it to be us. I wanted you to see the whole house again, which is why I asked you to help me after Christmas. I watched you in the house with me, to reassure myself that I was doing the right thing. Unfortunately, we didn't expect to find Nancy, or all the other surprises that day..." It all came together, and I was touched.

"I'd love nothing more. But what about your house?"

"That's the next link. As you well know, Holly is entitled to, and deserves half of everything we own. So, now that we are separated, I'm selling our house, and Holly will be entrusted her fair share."

"Claire's not interested in the house?"

"No. Not at all. She's a city girl, and let's face it, we've had more bad memories than good ones in that house. She also knows I'm buying Norman's house, and is fine with that. She won't get lost finding her father," he chuckled.

"Does she know about me, I mean, about us?"

"Sort of. I didn't want to compromise the legal stuff surrounding her mom and I, so we had some long conversations about my decision to

313

separate from Holly. At first she was very bitter, but the person that nudged her along was her new boyfriend, who is a lawyer. We knew nothing was likely to change with Holly's mental health, which was confirmed recently when I asked for an updated psychiatric evaluation. Remember the letter I wrote you asking you for more time? I needed to see her diagnosis and prognosis again in writing, and I insisted Claire read it as well. I wanted a fresh slate, and I'm sure you can understand how many steps it took to get to where we are today."

"Absolutely. Yes, I do, and I love you even more for it." We held another long embrace, which Fred ended, anxious to continue.

"Also, just to make the separation more defined, the power of attorney and any decisions about Holly's care were recently transferred from me to Claire. She can easily take that responsibility on. I'm not going anywhere, and she has a supportive partner."

"It will lessen your responsibility."

"The lines will be clearer. So, Grace, assuming you don't mind living across the street from Norman, would you officially make New Pelham your home if you're ready to let go of Toronto?" I was more than ready.

August 31st

When I got the call to meet with Kristen, I wasn't surprised. She appeared genuinely pleased to see the ring on my finger, knowing the heirloom would be cherished and create new history. I asked her about Livy's school records and documents that we found in the old briefcase at Norman's house, and why they ended up in his possession. Disappointingly, she didn't know. I also asked if Norman was Livy's father, and not her uncle. Surprised by that question, she said that was very unlikely, because the firm had managed the Chestnut legal issues for decades. If Norman was Livy's biological father, it would have eventually surfaced somewhere within the many interconnected legal documents. So, because there was no legal reason for it, there was no benefit in investigating it further.

Kristen shared some history behind some of the contents of both houses. There were ensembles of high-quality furniture that were purchased together and in other Chestnut family homes, such as Livy's adoptive parents, but eventually were sold or found their way back to Norman or Livy's house. She offered us the opportunity to purchase the pieces before they were auctioned off. Kristen smiled warmly when she said they belonged in a Chestnut house, just like we did.

Feeling a little bold, I asked if Fred approached her for some matrimonial advice. She hesitated, only to offer that another partner in the building was working with him. She knew Fred's intentions long before Norman passed. Glancing at the ring on my finger, she was smiling again.

September 6th

I hadn't seen Fred since Norman's funeral and the date he proposed, sort of, and we laid Norman and Nancy to rest.

Fred had to prepare for school, and then spent a few days away at a cottage with Claire. On his way home from the cottage, and after dropping Claire off, I invited him to Chestnut Boulevard to see some furnishings before they were catalogued for auction.

He arrived early, skipping brunch with Claire and her boyfriend, so that we could enjoy it together. His knock on my door came earlier than expected. I was grateful that I had showered and dressed after an early walk with Wilson.

Fred was tanned, relaxed and refreshed. Holding a full bouquet of pink gerber daisies, he was beaming. I took the bouquet, and kissed him with the passion of a woman in love.

Coffees in hand, we toured the house before breakfast, starting on the main floor. He knew the kitchen well from the day we prepared meals for Norman.

"I now see all the same themes as Norman's house." He turned quickly and kissed me, disrupting my thoughts. I put our coffees down, and moved closer, and put my arms around him.

"I've been waiting for this all week and I need another one." He bent down and kissed me again, a long and tender kiss. I leaned back against the door frame and held him, inhaling the faint residue of sunscreen. I ran my fingers through his hair, which was shiny, and soft. Although his hair had become more grey over the last six months, no doubt from the many overlapping and complicated events, his eyes sparkled like diamonds.

"I have been dreaming of this too, on a lumpy cottage mattress." He kissed me again, embracing me tightly. "I have some news to share with you," he whispered in my ear.

"Good news?"

"Is selling my house good news?"

"Fred! That's wonderful news." I kissed him again, my arms under his and holding our embrace. "Closing date?" He buried his face in my hair, inhaling deeply.

"Mmmm. Six weeks."

"That's great! And soon!"

"Have you got lots of stuff in this house?"

"Just the opposite. What little of mine that is left is in storage, because Tess took most of it for her new apartment." Another sweet kiss, the taste of coffee, with a hint of mint.

"So would you be interested in spending, say, Thanksgiving in New Pelham?"

"What about the day after Thanksgiving?"

"You could also spend it at the same address." He leaned into me against the door frame. I melted in his arms.

"And the day after that?"

"That's up to you. I'd hope it's with me."

"That would be just lovely." I took his hand and led him up the stairs.

"I've been thinking of what we need, versus what we each have."

"I've been doing the same. I'd like a fresh start."

"Any room in particular you want to focus on?"

"The same room you're leading me to."

"Not the bathroom?"

"Guess again."

"Grace, for obvious reasons, I am not interested in keeping my bedroom furniture," Fred said.

"And for obvious reasons, I don't want to sleep in Norman's bed." I led him down the hall to Livy's room. The room was immaculate, yet untouched, and only dusted since her death. Her furniture was exquisite, and expensive. He glanced at it, but was quickly distracted by the nude of Taylor. He turned away to face me. "I didn't expect to see that again." He was blushing.

"Remember, she's not Livy. I wanted to show you the bedroom set, and tell you this was the nicest set in the house, but..."

"But?" He was still facing away from the portrait.

"But she was my friend, and she was the last one to sleep here."

"Then we don't belong here." He followed me from Livy's bedroom into mine. The varying shades of cream and robin's egg blue maintained the serene atmosphere. The king-sized walnut four-poster bed faced the fireplace. I'm glad I had time to make the bed.

"Another master bedroom?" Fred asked, his hand following the smooth wood of the footboard.

"This is my room. For now. The set is an antique, and I think the original owner commissioned it."

"Were they nice people?"

"Very nice. They looked after Livy when she was younger."

"Do you like this furniture?"

"I love this furniture."

"Well, that's our room furnished." He sat on the bed, testing the resistance of the mattress. I sat beside him, doing the same. "Tell me there are no lumps like the cottage mattress I spent the last 3 days on?"

"Not even one. And there's been no one in it but me and Wilson, if he can get away with it."

"Hmm-mm." I inched over closer to Fred. We sat quietly, facing the window overlooking the street. A garbage truck was making its rounds. "The New Pelham garbage truck comes on Tuesdays," he said nervously. I edged closer, kissing him on his cheek.

"Tuesdays work for me." He kissed me on the mouth, and I put my arm across his back, rubbing it gently.

"The birds are a lot noisier in New Pelham..." He turned toward me, kissing me deeply, his arms coming around my shoulders.

"I love birds..." I lay back on the bed, and he did the same, both of us looking at the ceiling fixture.

"Isn't that the same light as in Norman's room?" He turned to face me, kissing my neck. I drew my feet onto the bed and wedged my knees between his.

"Maybe." He drew me closer and laid his head against my heart. We lay in silence, and as before, I felt the tremble in his hands. I put my hand against his chest - his heart pounded hard against his shirt. He lay still. Very, very still.

"It's been a long, time, Grace."

"I know." I unbuttoned his shirt, and eased him out of it. He watched me quietly. Slowly, I unbuttoned my shirt, and slipped out of my clothes, one piece at a time. As I stood before him, his eyes became moist.

"I have never seen a more beautiful woman." I smiled, and unzipped his jeans. The two scars on Fred's hip crossed where his torso met his leg, and a third scar, as broad as the other two, crossed the crease at the top of his leg. I kissed the top of the first scar, easing his clothes off. Fred moaned, his body reacting to my touch. He leaned over me, kissing my neck, shoulders and then my breasts. His hands were shaking as they explored my body. Slowly, he eased closer to me, overcome with emotion and passion. Our bodies joined, in slow rhythm and he took the time to be sure I was satisfied before he was. He held me as he cried, softly, and I didn't ask why. We lay together, my head against his chest, listening to his heart grow calm. He was soaked in tears, sweat, and love.

"You okay?"

"I think so."

"How's the mattress?" He smiled, and kissed my forehead.

"Very comfortable."

We didn't leave the bed for hours, holding each other quietly and listening to the sounds of the street below.

I got up first, and went to Livy's room to find the white, hooded terrycloth robe she kept for male house guests. I held it up to Fred so he could slide into the arms. I tied the belt securely and patted him on the belly.

"I think I need to feed you."

"You have fed me."

One Year Later

I believe the definition of living 'happily ever after' is what one makes of it. Many people dream of the perfect relationship and don't realize they had it, or didn't have it, until it ends. I'm still waiting for Fred to settle his legal affairs, but at least we are together. I found my dream job at the New Pelham library.

I cherish the time I share with my own daughter, and without him. Tess and Claire are very different people. We are not one big happy family, like we had hoped or expected. I learned the principle rule of blended relationships the hard way, which is to respect the bond between biological parent and child, even if you don't agree, and avoid offering opinions unless asked.

Fred has characteristics I adore, and an equal share that aggravate me. He organizes his sock drawer the same way he arranges the produce in the vegetable crisper of his fridge; by colour. He's pre-occupied with cleanliness and still does his laundry the way his mother taught him, even though there are better ways. I stopped trying to replicate her meals. They will never be as good. And after spilling vanilla on her recipe card, I've learned that while his treasures may have little value to me, they are priceless to him. Fred is Fred, and I will never try to 'fix' him, like I hoped to fix Blair. I've learned the hard way to give Fred the generous space that he needs.

Some nights, when he sleeps beside me after we've had a "discussion", I wonder if he is really Mr. Right, unlike Simon who was Mr. Right Now. Or Blair, who after just a few years I knew was not the right one, but yet I stayed.

I'm now content with wanting less versus more, whether it is intrinsic, or material. There is a theory that couples need only seven minutes of quality time each day to make their relationship work. I believe whoever came to that conclusion is right. Often when fewer words are spoken, the silence to appreciate them is like gold.

I don't need to look after Fred, but if I nurture myself, looking after 'us' comes easier. Fred taught me to appreciate who I am, and care for myself before minding others. That, above all, is what I am most grateful for.

I am happy, I think, but in different ways. I hope our road will always follow the same path, but only time will tell if our legacy together will live on.

~ THE END ~